EVERY DARK
DESIRE

Books by Fiona Zedde

BLISS

A TASTE OF SIN

EVERY DARK DESIRE

Published by Kensington Publishing Corporation

EVERY DARK DESIRE

Fiona Zedde

KENSINGTON BOOKS
http://www.kensingtonbooks.com

KENSINGTON BOOKS are published by

Kensington Publishing Corp.
850 Third Avenue
New York, NY 10022

All Kensington titles, imprints and distributed lines are available at special quantity discounts for bulk purchases for sales promotion, premiums, fund-raising, educational or institutional use.

Special book excerpts or customized printings can also be created to fit specific needs. For details, write or phone the office of the Kensington Special Sales Manager: Kensington Publishing Corp., 850 Third Avenue, New York, NY 10022. Attn. Special Sales Department. Phone: 1-800-221-2647.

Kensington and the K logo Reg. U.S. Pat. & TM Off.

ISBN-13: 978-0-7582-1738-7
ISBN-10: 0-7582-1738-2

First Kensington Trade Paperback Printing: July 2007
10 9 8 7 6 5 4 3 2 1

Printed in the United States of America

For my Nugget

Acknowledgments

Large-scale thanks to Angela for all those long-distance phone calls, especially the ones that lasted until well after ten. And, as requested, no thongs.

Chapter 1

Negril, Jamaica
January 24, 1994

In the darkness, something soft and wet slid across Naomi's mouth. Her eyes flickered closed and her mouth opened to receive the sacrament of a stranger's desire. Darkness nuzzled against her body in the canopied bed and skated across the sensitive surface of her skin. A sensation of pain floated down her throat. The pain was slight, but its hidden layer of pleasure made Naomi arch up in the bed in surprise, her lips parted and eager.

She couldn't see the woman's face, only felt bare skin pressed against hers, the fullness of soft breasts, and the rasp of lush pubic hairs against her skin. Fingers swirled closer to her clit, and Naomi moaned. The slow torture made her hips dance across the sheets, undulating against the smooth cotton that was softer than any she'd ever felt before.

"You are so beautiful," the woman, Julia, said against her belly.

Her cool breath sent ripples of desire eddying through Naomi's body. This was what she'd always wanted. The sure caress of another woman, hands settling on her hips with authority and intent, mouth falling on her nipples like cool rain. Naomi moaned and touched the back of Julia's head.

She smelled like jasmine. The scent curled inside Naomi, slipping into her nose, her head, and her body until all of her awareness was focused on this woman making love to her in a strange bed.

Julia's thighs fell between hers, widening them, spreading Naomi for the breeze from the open windows to caress her. Then it was Julia's fingers, cool and light, against her aching clit. The fingers strummed over Naomi, played her, until her hips made a bow in the bed and her own fingers clenched in the sheets. Naomi's body was drenched in sweat, swimming in its desire.

Julia smiled down at her, a sweet spreading of lips that was at odds with the wicked things her fingers did to Naomi's pussy. Naomi gasped with surprise at the wave of desire and aching need that lanced through her with each movement of Julia's fingers. Her eyelashes fluttered, the muscles in her belly clenched, and her chest rose and fell with each gasping breath that Julia pulled from her.

Julia stopped smiling. The benevolence peeled abruptly from her face, leaving a visage tight with hunger. Her fingers still moved sweetly inside Naomi, moving with ease in liquid heat, her thumb licked at Naomi's clit until all she wanted was the completion that the waves of sensation promised.

The volcano in her pussy erupted. Molten light danced behind Naomi's tightly clenched eyes as her body jerked on the bed, plucked into ecstasy by Julia's expert hand.

"Now it's my turn."

She barely heard the low whisper, only felt the cool breath on her neck again, then a fire at her throat that was swooning delight and unexpected pain. Naomi gasped. Julia crouched above her, the jasmine scent that was more than her perfume suffocatingly sweet as her bald head nuzzled at Naomi's throat and her mouth settled more firmly on vulnerable flesh. Naomi pushed at Julia's arms, but the woman was an immovable weight above her.

"No!" The lassitude from her orgasm abruptly fell away

and she pushed harder. Julia hooked her teeth more firmly in Naomi's throat. Pain ripped through her. "No!" She screamed her denial again, but Julia only moaned, a soft, singing sound of pleasure that raised the hairs on the back of her lover's neck. She grasped Naomi's arms, lifting her up and off the bed as she knelt in the soft mattress, devouring. Blood dripped down Naomi's neck, snaking down her shoulder before falling drop by precious drop to the white sheets. She felt as if she was being drained of everything—life, blood, consciousness. Her head flopped weakly back and still Julia continued to drink her.

"Stop. Please. I don't want this." At least that's what she tried to say, but all she managed was a strangled groan.

Naomi tried to make her arms work, but they were worse than useless. They dangled from her shoulders, dragging against the sheets as Julia suckled from her neck. The sound of her feeding, wet sucking sounds that moments before Naomi had associated with sex, attacked her ears.

This wasn't something that she could stop. This was no longer an act she could say no to. The moment she had walked into this hotel room she had said yes. Her body had screamed it, her breasts whispered it, and her pussy, eagerly salivating for Julia's hand, had given the ultimate permission. Naomi blinked frantically at the ceiling, her eyes already clouding with approaching death . . .

Chapter 2

Naomi was dead. She didn't know where the knowledge
came from, it was just there. Nothing in the alley moved,
nothing inside her moved. She forced herself to take a deep
breath. Nothing. A trembling hand rose, then fell with a wet
slap against her chest. The cool flesh felt torn and sticky with
blood. Her mind flickered back to her last few moments of
memory. The laughing yawn of teeth, blood-flecked and merciless. Clawed fingers hooked into the vulnerable skin of her
arms. Her rising screams. Then blood trickling over her lips,
setting her senses aflame.

The last place she remembered being, the palatial Negril
Hotel where her sister worked, with its shimmering blue pool
and equally sparkling tourists, was nowhere in sight. Instead,
she lay propped up in a stinking alley, made filthier with stag-
nant gray water, garbage, and the smell of stale piss. The
smells overwhelmed her, stinging her nose with their pun-
gency. Only two things were the same. It was dark. And she
was naked. Her back shifted against the damp concrete wall,
setting off a chain reaction of pain through her entire body.
Another set of smells stirred up. Fear. Vomit. Gunpowder.
Death. Naomi retched into a pothole until her stomach seized
up and cramped. Her limp hands twitched and slapped at her
thighs. It was so quiet inside her, so quiet. Even with the agony
of her body purging itself, the silence frightened her. No

heartbeat. No breath. No pulse to reassure her that she was scared.

Naomi sagged against the wall, whimpering like a beaten dog while her vision swam as she became aware of yet another layer of pain, a scraping rawness that crawled up her throat, settling into her mouth and teeth. Her back jerked away from the wall.

"You all right, girl?"

A hand touched her shoulder and, through her pain-filled haze Naomi grabbed it. And kept grabbing until the person's—a man's—screams joined hers. She buried her pain in his, tore at him until his blood splashed over her in a scarlet wave. The first incidental spill of blood across her lips and tongue lanced fire through her. Suddenly the pain in her body seemed for a purpose. She grasped more tightly at the man and began to bite and suck at his body—his wrists, face, and neck—until he was covered in teeth marks and the only blood left was on his clothes.

The pain disappeared. She pushed the vessel away and it fell in the street like an empty wine gourd. Her body shuddered with its new strength. Naomi wiped her mouth on the back of her hand and stood up. Despite her throat's soreness and the uncertainty of her balance, she felt vital and strong. Her mind didn't bother to grapple with the contradiction.

It was late. She was certain about that. The quarter moon burned against a sky strong with stars, but daylight was close. Something inside her flinched at the knowledge. Beyond her little alley, the street was teeming with traffic. People on foot, in cars, on motorcycles and bicycles. She could smell them. Their scent was so different from her own, like soft-fleshed fruit whose juice made her tongue swell and water. She made herself turn away from the contemplation of her next meal.

The odor of the city and its thick traffic so late at night told her that she was inland and miles away from Julia's Negril Hotel. So her mother had been right. That was a sin. That's why she was here now, miles away from her mother and her baby. She hoped they were safe in bed at her sister's. Her skin suddenly yearned to touch them, to feel them close. She held on to that desire, needing it to feel connected, to feel human.

Naomi needed clothes. The man's uniform was out of the question. She couldn't very well walk around town wearing a bloody and torn police corporal's uniform. But she couldn't parade around naked either. Naomi compromised by putting on the long undershirt and little briefs that fit her like a bathing suit.

The night was balmy, with winds that teased her new skin like breath. Her hunger was far away now so she was free to feel. Voices reached out at her from the street, raised in greeting, in quarrel, in affection. She wanted that again. She wanted to live again. But right now she wanted clothes more. Naomi stepped out of the alley. A young woman walked toward her, switching her small skirted hips while her breasts moved in a seductive rhythm under her sparkling blouse. Her gaze appraised Naomi's improvised outfit, and apparently found it lacking. The girl cut her eyes at Naomi and brushed past her. Or at least tried to.

"Good evening, sistren," Naomi greeted in a new purring voice.

The woman inhaled deeply as if smelling something particularly sweet; then she smiled. People moved in, ebbing around them, some looking at Naomi with interest, others with sneers. But she wasn't concerned about them. Naomi used the buffeting crowd as an excuse to pull the woman aside and away. The mouth of the alley opened up to receive them.

She had tried to use some patchouli heavy perfume to mask her true womanly scent, but Naomi found it and greedily inhaled it. She was a nice-looking woman. One of those types Naomi had always seen in the streets of town—whether Negril or Ochi—and longed to be. She imagined that women like this didn't obsess about the things that she did, didn't long to touch other women the way that Naomi wanted.

This woman's life must be so simple, uncomplicated by forbidden desires and the pain of wanting more than she had.

"Can I have your clothes?" Naomi asked.

"What?"

"I said," Naomi said, moving even closer, "your clothes are pretty." She touched the woman's blouse, incidentally caressing the swell of breast beneath the cloth. "Can I have them?"

The woman drew a quick breath. Naomi didn't give her a chance to do anything more. She grabbed the woman and swung her abruptly into the wall. Her head connected sharply with the filthy, graffiti-scrawled brick before she could scream. The woman's fear rose up hot and ripe in the alley before she abruptly lost consciousness. She smelled so good. So intoxicating. Naomi tugged off the woman's blouse, and her unbound breasts, brown and soft in the sickly yellow streetlight, had Naomi on her knees with her mouth open before she could stop herself. The unconscious woman's blood smell made her hungry, though she shouldn't have been, and the sight of her nakedness made her wet even though that shouldn't have been either. Naomi abruptly pulled back. No. She would not be like that beast who took advantage of her and made her into this.

She tugged off the woman's skirt, then covered her with the long shirt she discarded. Naomi also left her with the shoes. The boots she had taken from the policeman were better than those fragile stilettos. Even lying in the street, in the shadow of a garbage bin, the woman was still beautiful. Her breasts, the curve of her belly, the thickly pumping blood just beneath her skin made it hard for Naomi to turn away. But she did. She was nothing like the bitch who lured her to death. This was proof of that.

With the stolen woman's clothes on her back and an indefinable need gnawing at her belly, Naomi fled downtown Negril. She moved quickly through the self-herding crowd toward a place, any place, that could quiet her raging mind.

Minutes or hours later, she was on an unfamiliar beach. Naomi wandered down to the sand, past empty stalls with signs advertising FRESH STEAMED FISH and past bits of debris abandoned by the past day's fishermen—an old swimming fin half submerged in the water along with pieces of string and a broken knife handle adrift on the sand. The waves lapped over her toes, foamed and gentle. Her senses swallowed the sea's salt tang and the scent of something else on the breeze.

"You are beautiful."

Her body quieted. But not in surprise. Its surrender to stillness was like a kind of relief. She felt a coolness at her back, then the press of lips against the top of her spine.

"I knew you would make it."

Her body relaxed into the presence, sagged against it. Julia. Her mouth sighed the name. Then anger rose up. She growled and spun to face her killer. In the silvered moonlight, the woman was smaller than Naomi remembered, with velvet midnight skin and a slightly paler mouth, molten brown eyes, and a bald head. Julia looked blameless and completely absent of sin as she lay under Naomi's snarling ferocity.

Then she smiled. "Come on, do it. You need to."

Her jasmine scent reached up to wrap itself around Naomi, enfolding her in its sweet embrace. She wanted to taste her skin, to break it and slip inside her until this unsettled feeling was gone. Naomi growled again. She needed to drink more of the fervid blood Julia had fed her in their shared bed. The new vampire slammed the woman into the sand and mounted her unresisting body.

Julia bared her throat. "This is what you want."

Her blood was ambrosia. Spicy. And hot. It flooded into Naomi's body in a rush, washing her with power and joy. Under her, Julia chuckled, encouraging her to take more, to suck until she was full. "I fed well tonight, just for you."

Naomi intended to feed well too. She pulled deeply at the soft flesh under her mouth, her body unconsciously undulating over Julia, until the pleasure from her feeding and the tingles of arousal tripping across her flesh were one and the same. Julia's hand clenched in her hair, alternately pulling and pushing at Naomi. Soft gasps tumbled from the vampire's open mouth. Because she could be nothing else, a leech who fed on blood and secret desires. Naomi had seen enough American television to know.

Julia's legs widened and Naomi's thigh easily fell between them and curled up until it slid against the slippery slit under the dress. Her own body burned brushfire hot. Still sucking, she pulled at her own blouse, ripping away the stolen clothes in her haste to be naked, to find a relief from the heat building inside her. A cooling breeze rippled over her naked skin, but still she burned. Julia's gasps grew louder with each pull of Naomi's mouth and press of her thigh. The new vampire's hands tightened. Julia's orgasm jetted more blood into Naomi's open mouth, but still she couldn't stop. The smaller woman began to fight her, to push at her shoulders, pull her heavy hair, and even buck under Naomi's heavier body. She started to make desperate mewling noises.

"Stop—!"

Naomi ignored her and sucked harder. Then something plucked her from her feast and sent her sailing through the air. She landed in the sea with a massive splash, and a different salty wetness filled her open mouth. Naomi choked and tried to catch her breath before she remembered that she didn't need to breathe anymore.

"Stop means stop, puppy. You don't want to kill her, do you?"

Naomi looked up from her sprawl in the water and flipped her heavy wet hair out of her face.

"She's dead already anyway," she said.

The vampire who'd spoken looked down at her with contempt, then shook her head, turning back to the slight woman still whimpering in the sand. This beast was even taller than Naomi, quite an accomplishment since at almost six feet she'd always been considered ridiculously tall by most.

"And you," she said, reaching down to help Julia stand up. "Why did you give this thing your blood? You should have drained it and left it to die."

"But, Silvija, she—"

Julia's head snapped back from the force of the giant's sudden slap. She rocked back on her heels with a blossom of blood appearing abruptly at the corner of her mouth, but she did not fall. Silvija's grip on her collar saw to that. Naomi watched them for a moment before dropping back into the water with a splash. She felt divine.

Up above, the moon was an incandescent sliver in a sky that was layer upon layer of dark. Dark clouds, dark corona of the moon, dark universe. Darkness slid inside her, burrowing under her skin to settle into her hollow spaces, filling them. Changing them. She didn't even feel like Naomi anymore. Her pupils widened. The stars above her were tiny daggers of light, piercing her with their beauty and distant burn. Water lapped against her bare skin, cooling, cleansing. She lazily swam backward, aware of the two, no, five women on the beach and their talk, but was uninterested in it. The giant, Silvija, still towered over Julia with her wide hands straddling her own hips.

Three others stood slightly behind her, rather like lackeys or lieutenants, watching the giant and her slight companion. No one paid any attention to Naomi. She laughed softly. Then was struck by the musicality of her own voice, rather like a siren's with its high breathy quality. It had never been like that before. She laughed again, just to hear the sound, and then turned to dive to deeper water. A large hand dropped to her shoulder and held her back. Naomi growled and lashed her fingers across the face looming over her shoulder. Silvija. Scarlet trails of shredded flesh and blood opened on the broad face. Then the cuts healed.

"Let that be the first and last time you raise your hand to me, child."

Naomi glanced at her in disdain. So what if Julia let this

woman toss her around like a crocus bag full of breadfruit? Naomi sure as hell was not that cowardly to let that happen to her. She and Silvija were almost the same height, only the giant's body was broader, more solid and muscular than Naomi's, rather like a brute's, crude and roughly made.

"Fuck off."

Silvija laughed. Then threw her farther out in the water. "You first."

Naomi's legs scissored under her in the deep water. Ground was very far away and the giant was advancing on her again. The large hand grabbed her by the back of the neck and drew her under the water and up until they were eye to eye. Naomi coughed and sputtered, then realized again that she didn't need to breathe. Silvija wore an infuriatingly superior grin that was ghostly and wavering under the water. She held Naomi up until the slighter woman quieted in her grasp.

"That stupid girl may have made you, puppy. But I can break you if I choose. Remember that. I am law here."

Silvija mouthed the words, but Naomi understood them all clearly as if she was speaking aloud.

In her old life, the living life, Naomi would have cowered before Silvija, perhaps even begging to save her from whatever torments her extraordinarily large hands could bring. But that life seemed so far away, like a dream she had just woken from. Her eyes narrowed. Silvija must have taken that for some sort of acquiescence because she let her go, left her to float away on the gentle night tides of the Caribbean like so much flotsam. Even with her new arrogance—but could proper self-confidence really be called that?—Naomi knew that she had to be careful of this beast. Silvija swam away in smooth, powerful strokes whose wake buffeted her even more, pushing her away from the shore and the woman who had changed her life by killing her. Naomi made a noise of dismissal before following after the behemoth who thought she could rule her.

On the shore, they seemed more purposeful, all five pairs

of eyes looking at her with varying degrees of distrust. Naomi supposed that should have made her feel like an unwanted puppy. Still Julia's eyes were at once desiring and dismayed. Silvija must have cowed her well.

"Come, puppy," the giant said. "We can't stay here all night because of you."

Naomi made a clucking noise. "Perhaps I should tell you this now before our relationship goes any further." She walked to Silvija on feet that felt as light and hollow as birds' wings. "I am no one's puppy. No youngling, and certainly not a child. Especially not yours. *You* remember that."

Silvija had the audacity to laugh. Which, of course, Naomi thought that she would. Consequence was suddenly not a word in her vocabulary. She shot across the sand, feeling the power in her revitalized body, and smashed the giant across the face with her elbow. When she rebounded and jabbed for the giant's throat, a large hand grabbed her arms in a painful viselike grip. Before Silvija could speak, Naomi hissed, "You respect me, and I'll do the same for you."

"Fair enough. Puppy."

Then she threw Naomi down on the sand and woke her dead body up. With her taloned fingers, she slashed the skin over Naomi's belly, breasts, face, and thighs, and it stung with saltwater and sand even as it healed. Naomi had never felt such pain in her entire life. Her skin, her insides, her pride writhed with agony. Hurt seared through her senses, burning, bringing up low animal noises from the pit of her. Her body tried to curl up from the sand, but harder flesh prevented her completion of the movement. Anger burned from the giant's eyes. Did it hurt her to feel such rage?

"You may be Julia's little fuck toy, but Julia is mine. That means you are mine." Silvija's mouth was hard in fury. "And even if I have to beat you every day until you understand that, you *will* understand. You will earn your respect with us. Or you will have none."

Naomi gasped with pain. "Does that make you the head bitch, then?"

Talons ripped into her skin again. The pain this time was different, deeper, with an edge of arousal that Naomi tried to ignore. She didn't want to experience something like this with this creature. When she could focus her eyes again, the creature was laughing.

"Where did you find this thing, Julia?"

"In a garden," came the petulant answer. "She was sweet. Don't sour her, Silvija."

"Never." She stood up. "Come. Let's go. The boat leaves in just a few hours."

Julia helped Naomi to her feet, then snuggled against her. "Don't fight her. She only does what's best."

Naomi was too weak to give the response she really wanted to.

"Where are we going?" she asked.

"Home. Back to Alaska." Julia sounded very pleased.

"Excuse me." Naomi stopped. Even in her weakened state, Julia couldn't move her forward. "I'm not leaving here. This is my home. My family is here. This is where I was born."

"We are your family now. Wherever we are, that is your home."

"Stop reasoning with the puppy and come, Julia. We haven't got all night."

Naomi stiffened. "But I'm not—"

"We don't have time for this."

Someone snatched Naomi away from the smaller woman and threw her over a muscled shoulder. After a quick rustling of air and clothes, her back met soft leather. They were in a car, a limousine. Someone gave orders to the driver in a low voice and the car began to move. The smell of the sea was fading. So was Naomi. A hand draped over her bare stomach and pulled her close. Soft laughter followed her into a reluctant sleep.

Chapter 3

Naomi dreamed that she was alive. The sun touched her with its soft golden fingers, filtering through her hair left loose and heavy against her shoulders. Its heat snuggled into her bare throat and along her arms like an old friend. She leaned against the iron railing of the terrace, looking down on a gold and green Negril. The breeze was light. Laughter hovered in the air like music and she turned, smiling, to find the source of it. Her baby, Kylie, stood on the terrace, laughing and spinning in a circle, while the sun sparkled on her wheat biscuit skin. Naomi's mama stood nearby, watching. Her look was wistful.

"You'll miss us, Mimi," Roslyn said to her. "I hope this is worth it."

Naomi looked away from her mother when Kylie started to sing. It was a bright little song, a five-year-old's interpretation of a poem that Naomi knew well. She had learned the original Keats poem in school and had been so captivated by it that she turned it into a song and crooned it to Kylie in the womb and later in her crib. The idea of a powerful woman who seduced with her sweet roots and wild honey seemed both exotic and enticing at once. Kylie's giggles poured through the words as she sang:

> *I see a lily on your brow*
> *You're dying*

with anguish moist and fever dew.
You're dying
and on your cheeks a fading rose.
You're dying
withers fast there too.
You're dead.

Naomi met her mother's eyes over Kylie's head.

"Take care of her for me," she said. "I'm sorry."

Something hit Naomi hard in the back and she fell over the railing, tumbling head over foot past the many windows of the hotel. The ground, the pool, coconut trees, all rushed up to meet her. Naomi screamed, clawing frantically at the air. The sound of her own crying woke her up.

"Poor baby. She's not taking it well."

She heard Julia's voice from far off, a lisping mockery of sympathy that grated on Naomi's sensitized nerves. Sheets shifted under her naked body. A shadow moved over her, leaving her cold and sharply awake. Her body lurched up from the bed. Julia and one of the lackeys from the beach stood nearby. Her eyes caught them in midmotion. They froze as she stood up.

"Where am I?"

The lackey turned and walked out of the room, leaving Julia with her stricken yet still mocking expression. Naomi heard his softly whispered "Call if you need me." And grew angry. Did these creatures think that she had no self-control? Then she had to laugh at herself.

"On board ship, my love," Julia said, answering her question.

"Don't call me that."

"But you are. We made love. I saw you. I wanted you. I loved you. I thought you loved me too." Her voice was sing-song and childlike.

What kind of shit was this creature smoking that she thought

Naomi would love her because of one night? One night that had been as much agony as ecstasy, as much terror as pleasure.

"Where are we going?" But she already knew the answer, could feel it in her bones that shook with the unfamiliarity of being in this part of the sea.

"Don't play stupid, puppy. You know—"

Naomi shoved Julia against the wall and pressed her arm against Julia's windpipe, knowing that it hurt although the vampire obviously didn't need to breathe. "The head bitch can get away with that bullshit for now, but you . . . never. Do you hear me?"

Julia choked, grasping at Naomi's arm and fighting for words that would get the new beast off her. "No . . . I'm the one who made . . . don't . . ."

"Whatever you're trying to say it's never going to be okay to call me anything but my name. Do you understand?"

"Yes." The word was a rasp of agony. It choked off completely as Naomi pressed harder, barely restraining the urge to destroy the fickle creature under her. Naomi's body flushed hot, readying itself for something truly awful and ecstatic. She shuddered with the beginnings of pleasure.

Julia's hands clutched at her back, frantically raking the skin until pain and blood snaked over it. Her breasts pushed into Julia and against her will she felt herself grow wet and ready. Naomi shifted to grip Julia's throat and head and bring the gasping mouth closer. For a dead thing, her lips were so red. The smaller beast felt the change and the frenetic clawing at her back became a vise grip. Her leg fell between Naomi's and moved against the undeniably wet pussy and swelling clit.

It galled Naomi that she wanted Julia, but she couldn't help herself. Death or not, right now all she wanted to do was open up her pussy for Julia. Against the wall, Julia squirmed and gasped. Naomi liked the feel of the slim throat under her hands. Julia's helplessness made her clit swell even more. She wriggled against the smaller beast's thigh and growled low in her throat.

Then Julia was free and Naomi felt the wall slam into her back. Pain lanced through her as her tailbone hit the floor.

"Why do we always find ourselves in this position, puppy?"

Silvija stood over her, disapproval in every line of her body. She glanced quickly at Julia and made a dismissive motion with her head. The small fiend slid out the door clutching at her throat, her eyes wide with surprised delight.

"You need to be tamed, don't you?" A cool smile lifted a corner of Silvija's mouth.

That wasn't what you thought. The words rose up inside Naomi, but she kept them behind her teeth. "Try it," she murmured, tensing her body in anticipation.

"Maybe later." Silvija turned and left the room, locking the door behind her.

"Bitch."

Naomi stood up. Despite the inferiority of her strength compared to Silvija's, her body felt vibrant and powerful. Each pain she'd felt since death had come, then quickly gone, leaving her body feeling more robust and invigorated. She stretched her neck and felt the muscles elongate and vertebrae pop all the way down to the bottom of her spine. She was still naked. The new fiend looked down at her body with admiration and awe. Although the stretch marks from her childbirth were still there, the skin seemed firmer. Her sturdy thighs and hips, narrow waist, and lush breasts glowed with vitality and seemed even more pleasing than before her death. Fingertips skimmed her shape, relearning its curves and weight. In the mirror she seemed the same, perhaps with a bit more harshness in the eyes, a more feral quality to her that had not been there before. She smiled. Yes, definitely more feral.

In the shower, she washed her body with an unscented soap. Her skin now gave off its own scent, something faint that she couldn't readily identify, and it glowed with a deceptive softness in the light. Suddenly she remembered the words to Kylie's song that she dreamed, the dream that she woke from crying. It was a John Keats poem that she taught her daughter years ago, sung to her in the womb because it had appealed to her when she'd read it in school. "La Belle Dame Sans Merci." A poem about a vampire with wild eyes and a legion of dead and dying lovers behind her. Naomi met her own eyes in the mirror.

"When you're finished admiring yourself, come into the sitting room." Silvija's voice reached her through the bathroom door. "We need to talk."

Naomi almost growled back at the giant, but thought better of it. The time to make childish gestures of defiance was over. She pulled a robe over her body and went to see what the bitch wanted.

"Have a seat."

The oversized woman inclined her head toward a nearby chair. For spite, Naomi chose a farther one. Okay, so maybe the time for childishness wasn't quite past. After Naomi sat, the woman stared at her with a thoughtful expression.

"Julia said you were sweet before the change. That you were a woman of sacrifice and principle and softness."

How did the bitch know this? "And you want to know what happened to me?"

"I already know what happened. People like you, the ones who seem so good on the outside, are usually the ones with the soul of a devil just waiting to be set free. That is what this disease does. It strips away the masks, lays bare the creature beneath them all. You had been sacrificing yourself too long in your life, and now you are without mercy, without a thought for anyone but yourself and your own appetite."

"How poetic," Naomi sneered. But she was thinking about her dream and Kylie's song and what it all meant.

Silvija didn't take the bait. "No, just true." She sighed. "Which brings me to my point."

Her long legs stretched out in front of her and Naomi couldn't help but notice the long thigh muscles that moved like liquid under the white cotton pants.

"Julia shouldn't have made you. But since that is already done, we have to make the most of the situation." Silvija waited until she was sure she had Naomi's full attention. "Julia should have told you certain things, and perhaps she might have if you hadn't scared the piss out of her."

Really? "It's not my fault she's a damn mouse who's afraid of every shadow."

Silvija chuckled. "Since the shadows turn out to be noisome little you, I can understand why."

Naomi made a rude noise. Not even under the pain of torture would she admit that she had no idea what "noisome" meant. But it obviously wasn't good. Silvija continued.

"It goes like this: throw out everything you've ever heard about vampires. Almost none of it applies to us. Garlic doesn't do a thing to you. Same thing for holy water, tears, or any other bodily fluids from virgins. Stakes through the heart are useless too. You must, however, stay out of the sun—or you'll get a nasty burn that will ruin that pretty face of yours for a while. A single bullet can't really kill you, but a hundred or so of them at close range will do the trick so that you bleed to death as surely as any living human. That is unless you find something to feed on in time."

She paused to make sure that Naomi was listening. "And as for our family, your new home, you harm no one; you do not feed off them like cattle. Living with us is simple, the rules are clear. I make the rules and the money so I must be obeyed. If you can't live by our rules, then feel free to pack up your things and leave."

What things? Naomi twisted her mouth into a bitter smile. Julia had left her naked in that alley, stripped of everything she'd walked out of her sister's house with that afternoon. "Why Alaska? You couldn't find a more godforsaken place than that to hole up in? Whose fucking brilliant idea was it to live in that tundra anyway?"

"Mine."

"Figures."

The two women eyed each other over the half dozen feet of tension. Under their feet the engine hummed, taking them farther and farther away from everything that was familiar to Naomi.

"I don't want to make this hard for you."

"Then don't. Send me back to my island, to my mother and my daughter. Pretend that Julia never saw me. Pretend you don't even know that I exist. You say that if I can't obey your rules I can just go. Well, I'm telling you now that I won't obey. So let me go."

"It's not quite that simple."

"What could be simpler?" Naomi prided herself on her rationality. If these creatures thought that she would be such a problem it seemed like a solution they could both be happy with.

"You're dangerous. You can't be trusted around humans. Not yet. Later, perhaps."

Naomi froze. "Am I a prisoner?"

"Do we have to make you one?" The other woman's voice dropped deep into her chest. Suddenly she seemed more alert, more dangerous than before.

Naomi's defenses rose in response. She sat up in the chair. "I think we both know the answer to that question." Her eyes narrowed. "You know, I never asked for this. Julia took advantage of my weakness for women, for my sinful ways"— she couldn't prevent her mother's words from falling out of her mouth—"and made me into this thing. Why am I suffering because of her fuckup?"

"I'm sorry."

"But not sorry enough to let me go back to my family?"

"No." Silvija stood up. "I'm going to lock the door. Buzz Stephen or Ivy on the intercom if you need anything."

Naomi didn't bother to reply. She was cold. Her body was frozen as if they'd already made it to Alaska and she stood naked on the prow of the boat. The door closed softly behind Silvija before the lock slammed home. Her fist clenched. She barely stopped herself from throwing her body at the door and trying to rip it off its hinges. Naomi turned away from it in disgust and went back into the bathroom. A part of her acknowledged that this was strange, that at no time in her life would she have thought that acting like this was acceptable. Fiendish, unconscionable, and deliberately provoking behavior was something that she had no experience with and certainly no tolerance for. But now it was the only way she could react. Naomi wanted to scream and howl and break things. She felt herself sliding away, becoming the animal that they all thought she was. Denial rose up from her in a whimper. She was human. She was kind. She was Naomi.

The human Naomi grew up in Friendship, a combination fishing village and mountain town where everyone knew everyone. An almost daily verbal record was kept of who died, who moved off the island or "a foreign" and who married and under what circumstances. The Bakers had had seventeen children, all of them girls except for Efrain and Augustus. Naomi was the middle girl.

She had been generous, had been sweet, always volunteering to babysit for her sisters because, although she wanted another child, Naomi couldn't bear the thought of a man touching her in that way again. Her experience with the opposite sex was limited to the necessary interactions with the father of her child and several eye-opening experiments with Fitzroy Douglas in basic school, which made her realize that she hungered for something else. And Naomi eventually learned to suppress those hungers and to pour her love into the life she already had.

Kylie loved her and Naomi loved her daughter in return, treasured her baby scent, her laughter at the small wonders of life, the way she reminded her of herself many years ago before she had to grow up and face her own desires. Kylie was her world. And she'd given that world up for what? A small, curvaceous body that held no soul. Visiting her sister, Claudine, in Negril had been her idea. Ever since her younger sister told her about all the foreign women who came off the planes and ships—touching each other like they were already in bed together, laughing, and beautiful—Naomi had wanted to go to Negril. Claudine never said that they were attractive, but Naomi imagined them to be that and more, voluptuous and clever, holding the syllables of their foreign words in their mouth like pearls before letting them fall on anyone lucky enough to hear them. She'd wanted to go alone, to leave Kylie at home with her mother, but Roslyn had insisted on coming too. Then there they all were in Claudine's tiny downtown apartment, each hopping with her own excitement at being in the city overrun by tourists.

While her mother and daughter had gone out to play in town, Naomi snuck away. She went to Claudine's hotel on her sister's day off, dressed in her most sophisticated clothes, and sat in the lobby with a book in her lap watching the women come and go. It was as she expected, and less. Some of the women were nothing more than half-cooked lobsters stumbling in from their fifth cocktail and eighth round of lying poolside in the sun. But some were captivating with their short hair, pale skin, bare legs, long hair, wandering hands, dark skin, reserved smiles, full lips, wicked eyebrows, bare necks, deep voices—everything that Naomi had never seen in Friendship. She watched them in the lobby all day and well into the evening, looking up from her book so often that she knew no one was fooled by her pretense.

Then, at a few minutes past seven o'clock, Naomi saw Julia. She was small and perfect, a body created for Naomi's idea of sin. Although she had no idea what to do with her tongue or mouth or hands or fingers, she knew that she wanted to do *something* with Julia. She followed her through the lobby into the hotel garden with its ripe scent of lilacs, roses, and hibiscus.

Julia looked back at her once, met her eyes, and led her into the shelter of scented petals. Her hands touched Naomi's in greeting. The human woman didn't remember what was said, only that Julia's hands were cool on her flesh, her skin inviting to the touch, her scent the sweetest that she had ever experienced. She never expected to end up in the penthouse suite with its basket of fruits and chocolates, whisper-soft sheets, and gigantic bathtub. Upstairs, Julia talked with her, pulled out the narrative of Naomi's life so far, bathed her in scented water, and then kissed her. Naomi's hands shook in disbelief. She trembled at the thought that finally her desires, rising up inside her since childhood, would be released. Her body was full with that desire, swollen and hot beneath the cool sheet. Julia's hands touched her body, she melted, and hours later her life was gone.

Naomi blinked at her face in the mirror. Agony was written in every line. Agony and loss and anger. She turned away from it and left the bathroom.

Chapter 4

She threw herself off the boat. With a strength borne by anger, she pried out and off the porthole leading to the sea. Although her body didn't seem small enough to fit through the modest hole, she pushed and twisted until it dropped, bloody but already healing, out and into the water. Naomi swam quickly away from the powerful propellers under the yacht. It was dark, still early nighttime, and although this area of the sea seemed unfamiliar with its absence of coastline or lighthouse, she sensed that land was to the east and swam for it. It never occurred to her that she wouldn't make it. Naomi wanted to be gone from the boat and she did it. She wanted to go back to her family and she would be back there soon. Her arms and legs moved tirelessly through the water.

By the time she reached land the sun was threatening to rise. Naomi stumbled out of the water and her feet dragged in the pale moonlit sand. The lights of the city were far off, earthbound stars that beckoned her with the promise of shelter and food. She looked toward the east, trying to peer past miles of trees and whitewashed cliffs to see her girls safe in their house. Over a week. She knew that she'd been gone eight days, so her mother must have taken Kylie back to Friendship so she could go to school and continue with her normal life. A lost mother was incidental to her schooling.

On the beach, she heard noises, soft moist sounds like saliva or blood moving quickly around something solid. Her eyes found the source of the sound, two bodies—boys—fucking intently on clothes spread over coconut tree leaves in the sand. They were quiet, only the sound of their bodies moving together in determined, even strokes, and the quiet crinkle of the green leaves. The smell of their sweat was sweet, but the blood of the one being fucked was sweeter. His lover held his hips as he fucked him, sweat dripping down his face onto his naked chest. His dick slid wetly in his lover's hole as the bottom boy roughly grabbed at his own penis, working it as hard as his lover was working him.

In the dark, his face was a study of pain and pleasure, lower lip caught between his teeth, eyes tight in concentration, leanly muscled arms stretching and tightening with each thrust. His round ass bunched and flexed as his lover moved inside him, filling him with his hot thickness. Sweat covered both their bodies despite the cool night breeze that brushed over all three of them, carrying the scent of sex to anyone paying attention. Their passion, all the hotter because it was forbidden, flared on the dark beach.

Although her body quickened at the scent, Naomi waited until they were finished. She understood now about the fleeting nature of lust, how important it was, sometimes life changing. If this was their first time she did not want to be the one to end it prematurely. Even in her most animal moments, she could not be so wicked. When the smell of spent semen was hot in the air and the boys had collapsed together with soft grunts and moans, she stepped closer.

"Hello."

They jumped up, guilty and embarrassed, scrambling away from each other, although the lassitude in their bones must have made it difficult.

"No, it's okay. I was just wandering by and noticed you. Don't worry about me." She showed her most harmless smile.

They gaped at her nakedness. "I wonder if I could borrow your bike." She gestured to the motorcycle far from the water's edge.

The boys still moved back as if smelling the danger on her. Moving didn't help them. With a slight shake of her head that might have been regret, Naomi ran them down, ripping the sweetness from their eyes with her elongated teeth and talons. They were loud then, shouting at her and each other as they tried to fight. But it was over quickly.

Naomi put on the smaller one's clothes, a crisp white shirt and belted slacks. Both pairs of shoes were too big so she left them there with the drying bodies and took their bike to Friendship. The wind stung her face and eyes as she drove, staring unblinkingly into the night. Trees and bushes and lights sped by her in a blur. She urged the bike faster. The need to see her family, to hold them and tell them that she did not abandon them, rose and ebbed like a tide inside her.

But you did abandon them, her inner voice said. *You left them for a woman. As soon as you stepped away from what your mother taught you about right and wrong, then you no longer deserved to be with your family. You made the choice. It's done. Go back to your monsters. They are your family now.*

Naomi growled her denial and gave the bike more gas. Sunrise found her on the main dirt road to Friendship. Although her skin raced with alarm at the mere thought of sunlight touching it, she denied that instinctive knowledge and pushed herself even faster along the road.

When she was alive Naomi had been in love with the sun. She always woke up in the morning at six so she could watch it rise with its delicate dustings of pink on the landscape, then amber, and after a few hesitant moments, the lushness of blood orange, then finally gold. To see the dark slink away under the power of the sun was as much a part of her day as washing her body or eating food; she couldn't imagine a day without it.

Now the first touch of the sun made her skin crawl. Her flesh quivered over its bones and began to burn. And it was barely sunrise. The sky was still a dusky shade of rose, beautiful and brightening with each passing minute. Her bike rumbled on toward its destination, but her eyes squinted helplessly in the light from the sun, beginning to feel gritty and swollen and wet. Naomi rode the bike on the extremes of the road, sliding off the already rough path to hide under the overhanging trees. The sorely taxed tires kicked up gravel and rocks and they skidded in the rough before righting themselves under her frantic direction. Her body was steaming in the heat. Wetness blocked her vision and she angrily wiped it away. It was blood.

The bike skidded again and ran completely off the road into the vines of an overgrown hibiscus plant. The engine screamed before it flew up in the air, then back to the ground, pinning Naomi's leg and thigh beneath it. The burn from the muffler was nothing to the vicious bite of the sun all over her body. Her face felt swollen, her eyes itched and bled and burned. With a pained groan, she pushed the motorcycle off her and crawled under a cluster of breadfruit trees. It felt like a colony of fire ants was bent on devouring her skin, bite by bite, piece by piece. She curled as deeply into the shade as she could, cursing her own stubbornness, cursing Julia, and even the giant.

The pain swamped her, but angrily she batted it away. To her surprise, it stayed gone, cowered away in a corner of her mind that didn't need to be accessed now. Sequestered away from the pain, Naomi could finally think. But her besieged mind only ran in circles until she simply covered her face with her burning hand and waited for it all to end.

"She dead, man."

"You sure?"

From the depths of her stupor, Naomi heard the voices but could not move.

"Look, she just twitch."

"I think *you* just twitch."

"Shut up."

Something poked her, hands tugged at her clothes and at the arm covering her face. For a moment their bodies shielded her from the sun. She made a noise and turned her head to face them.

"Shit! She look like duppy for real. Look at her teeth dem."

"Them long, man. And skin up like some kind of animal. But she alive. Maybe Ruby can help."

They moved her. Agony. Pain. Flesh sizzling. Then merciful darkness. Some time later she felt a woman's touch on her, felt hands that were warm and gentle on her skin. And she smelled the blood. Her body immediately took notice, warming with the hunger, lengthening her teeth.

"You smell nice," the woman's voice whispered over her. Mango-spiced breath floated over Naomi's face. "Like the sea." A wet rag wiped her throat and chest. "And I can't find anything wrong with you. I don't know what those boys were talking about."

Naomi opened her eyes. And the woman startled, jumping back.

"Sorry. I'm harmless, I swear."

The vampire sat up in bed, then propped herself up against the pillows. The leftover blood from the two amorous boys started to pump harder in her body. The woman was very tempting. She was no one Naomi had seen before. The fiend would have remembered this creature with her bracketed full mouth and eyes deep with childlike curiosity. Her body had reached the full maturity of age, settling into its forties with a plump ripeness that Naomi suddenly found infinitely stimulating.

The hum of the woman's blood just under the skin still held the vampire's attention. But that hunger was manageable. She didn't *need* to leap on the woman and steal her blood. Naomi tamed her smile, made it more friend than fiend.

The woman's smile trembled, then warmed. "Sorry. My cousins scared me a little bit."

"But you still took me in. You're very brave."

"Not really. I just can't stand to see another human being in pain. Even if she's got wild eyes and makka and wildflowers caught up in her hair."

The words of the John Keats poem came to Naomi again, the one Kylie had been singing in her dream. "La Belle Dame Sans Merci." The beautiful woman, a beast, without mercy. What Naomi had become.

"You should watch that urge; it might get you into trouble." The beast softened her words with another smile. "By the way, I'm Belle." Her eyes wandered over the woman, drinking in the soft body under the green dress, the hypnotic throb of blood under her skin, the trust that blossomed in her eyes.

The woman offered her hand with a shy smile. "Ruby."

Belle made an involuntary moan of sensual appreciation. Ruby's hand was soft and scented and warm, like fresh bread. Only much, much better.

"Thanks for fixing me up. I need to get going soon. I have to see my family in Friendship."

"It's not far from here. My husband or one of my cousins could take you."

Hmm, a husband. "What about my motorbike?"

"You had one?"

"I guess I don't anymore." Belle's mouth twisted into a wry smile. "Ah well." *Easy come, easy go.* "Can someone take me there tonight?"

"Of course."

"Good." *So can I play with you now?*

"I'll let you get some rest. I think the exposure wore you out."

No, but you can. Belle controlled the urge to pull the woman into bed with her. "I think you're right."

Ruby left her in the dark, although Belle almost begged her

to stay and keep her flesh warm until she woke again. Eventually, she relaxed against the sheets that smelled like Ruby and someone else. The husband, perhaps? A sensation of loneliness settled in beside her. She wished that she had—not a husband, precisely—but someone to touch her while she slept. The need puzzled and irritated her. Without giving herself time to think any more about it, Belle lay back against the human-smelling sheets, then slipped them over her head, burying herself in deeper dark until the real thing came back with the night.

She awoke to someone sinking into the space beside her in the bed. A fresh mango and blood scent. Ruby. Belle waited until the human woman had pulled the sheet from her face to speak.

"You know, Ruby"—she felt the woman startle—"I wasn't quite truthful with you before."

She waited until the deep brown eyes met hers and the tempting scent of her was draped across her on the bed. "I am *not* harmless."

The sun still surrounded the house, but it was much closer to setting than when Belle had first fallen into sleep. She had three hours until sunset, but until then her death lay outside. What did this woman want? As if Ruby read her mind, she put a light hand on Belle's chest, just above her breasts.

"I want," she said simply.

Belle wondered if it was something about beasts like Julia—like her—that human women found dangerously irresistible. Not that it mattered. Just like Ruby wanted, she wanted too. She wanted the press of flesh against hers. She wanted to feel a woman in her arms again. She wanted blood.

"Where are your cousins?"

"Gone."

"Your husband?"

"Working until nightfall. Far away."

Not that it mattered. Nothing would stop her from taking

this woman now. Her experience with Julia had been vertigo inducing. She recalled the sensations more than the specific acts, and before that she had had no experience with a woman. The only thing to guide her now was her desire. She wanted to inhale Ruby, to take in as much of the woman as she could. And she didn't want to hurt her.

"Take off your clothes," Belle rasped.

Her breasts were tender where they scraped against the thin sheet. Suddenly she wished that Julia was here too. The woman came into the bed, trepidation and excitement in every breath. She gasped when her flesh touched Belle's. She hadn't expected the cold. No surprise there. Neither had Belle before all this started.

She traced the lines of Ruby's skin with curious fingers. Each movement of Ruby's flesh under her fingers sent a lovely answering shock through her body. The human's breasts swung over Belle as she came closer. Lovely. Ruby had taken a bath. Her skin was fresh with the scent of river water and the old-fashioned English soap that Belle's mother still used.

Her hands skimmed the scented flesh and she forced herself to slow down. She wanted to devour and ravage and glut her hunger with Ruby's blood, with her sex, and with her screams echoing in Belle's ears. But she touched her softly instead. She cupped the heavy breasts in her hands and touched the responsive nipples. They hardened instantly, scoring her palm with their firmness. Belle was wet. Her tongue lapped at her own lips. Then at Ruby's. The human woman gasped again from the coolness of her skin, then from the wicked brush of Belle's thumbs against her nipples and the delicate skin of her breasts.

Belle smelled her cunt. It was mouthwatering hot, a sweltering heat that called Belle's hand. She brushed the furred mound, the pink and brown peaking lips. God, she was soft. Ruby threw her head back, her body a symmetry of poetry and bliss. All the shades were drawn. Belle knew the human could barely see. But the darkness haloed her, made her even more luscious. Sparks of life flew from her skin. Each time Belle's fingers slid into her, she moaned, arching back, moving her hips, undulating and sighing in delight.

"Belle!"

When she'd been a human woman, Belle's experience of sex was rudimentary. Only when Julia had taken her into her scented arms, kissing her in places she had no idea were made for pleasure, did her world open up. She wanted to fling that window open again with Ruby, take her to that treasured space where only scent and touch and taste and sensation mattered. She wanted to make her feel.

Belle dipped her fingers deeper into the lushly wet pussy. At Ruby's wail she reached up, covering the human woman's mouth. She bit her. The pain sent delectation and danger bolting deep inside Belle. Ah, that was what she wanted. She wanted the pain. She wanted the lust. She wanted the loss of Ruby's control. Her fingers curled inside the human woman—someone she used to be, someone she could have been had Julia left her alone. The breasts above her shuddered and misted with sweat. Ruby was a flame. A wild dancing light at the end of Belle's hand. She trembled and writhed above her, moaning her pleasure.

When she collapsed in the bed, Belle pounced on her. The scent of her sweat was strong. It was so human, so luscious with its complex makeup of salt and electrolytes and acids that Belle wanted to lick her all over. So she did. The skin and nipples rose up to meet her tongue, goose-pimpling under her hands and blood-speckled saliva. Ruby was a divine miracle of sensation and tastes. Every millimeter of skin on Belle's fingers felt her. Felt her trembling breath, her arousal, the flutter of her pussy in the aftermath of her first orgasm. The skin was heaven, a soft-scented trail leading to tender armpits that Belle bit into, tasting her pungent ripeness, the lift of blood just beneath the skin.

She rolled the small nipples between her thumb and index

finger. She squeezed and Ruby almost came all the way off the bed. *Interesting.* Belle licked under the heavy breasts, still pinching the nipples between her fingers, around the turgid buttons, before finally taking one into her mouth. Ruby's hand clenched in her hair, trying to hold her head fast. The nipple hardened even more under her tongue, caressing each rising taste bud as it too was caressed. *Hmm.* Belle fell into the V of Ruby's thighs and sighed. The scent of the other woman's sex, her arousal, the very reason why she was here in this bed, rose up between them and tugged Belle down.

Yes. This was what she'd wanted to experience as a human. Belle licked the weeping wet pussy and found the heaven she missed when Julia stole her death from her. She dove in. There was the scent of old blood. It slipped between the molecules of female essence that coated her tongue. Belle's fangs lengthened and she went deeper, determined to get more. But she forced her teeth back. And the ache of it was bliss, ricocheting, rocketing through her body. Ruby moaned and thrashed her hips. Her pussy slid and wept against Belle's mouth. The clit was fat and growing fatter. Inside, her pulse raged. The heat flared under her skin. Ruby panted, the breath rising high and fast in her throat.

She felt her peak rushing up. Belle moved her fingers deeply inside Ruby, curling them, instinctively searching for that place that hummed with the most heat. The woman bucked against her fingers, and her breath came more and harder and more again. Belle's fangs lengthened, and just as Ruby's quake took her she sank her teeth into Ruby's thigh. The fat artery pulsing with blood gushed liquid nourishment into her mouth, filling her, sending her tumbling into her own orgasm. Her hips moved frantically against the bed and she felt every scrape of the cotton spread against her skin, each hiss of Ruby's breath in her hair, heard the pulse raging under the delicate skin beneath her mouth. She sucked at the flesh in time to Ruby's pulsing descent from her orgasm. Her own body throbbed with renewed strength, her vision cleared, all sensations came to her needle sharp and immediate. Now it was her turn.

She peeled away Ruby's pleasure slowly, revealing just a bit of pain at a time until glimmers of her bloodlust shone through to the human, but it was too late for her to turn back. Her body was on fire with delight and Belle fed her own with needles of pain—the harsh clutch of her nails in Ruby's skin, the scrape of fangs against soft thighs. The woman cried out.

The blood innervated her, flooding through every piece of her until Belle felt fat with the nourishment. Ruby was a goblet full of endless sweet. It could all be hers. Every delicious drop. And the woman wouldn't even know what hit her. Ruby rode obliviously through the storm of her orgasm, her cunt squeezing Belle's fingers as she tore breathlessly through it. As Belle took more of her, she began to whimper. Her breath became shallow and sparse. *Ah, she's so sweet.* Belle laughed and drank her up.

Chapter 5

Belle left Ruby alive and smiling on the verandah as she rode off in the back of a taxi toward Friendship. The driver was Ruby's husband, Devon. On the ride, he was pleasant and chatty, but cautious. He made sure that Belle noticed the gun he wore in a handmade holster close to his heart. Unlike his wife, he was giving much more credence to the cousins story.

Night was a soothing blanket outside the car, a balm to Belle's abused senses. Her eyes and skin soaked in the darkness, feeling cooler and stronger with each passing moment as if her morning in the sun had never happened. She felt generous enough to let Devon go when he dropped her off at the mouth of the narrow path leading to her house. Though as she watched the white Toyota disappear down the road and felt the first stirrings of real hunger, Belle had a moment of regret. Then she remembered that she had more important things to worry about.

At barely eight o'clock, the path was quiet and dark. As a human, she had been afraid when she walked alone at night to the store or down the lane to visit her cousins. Naomi had imagined all sorts of evils lurking in the bushes, waiting to rip her to shreds. And now Belle was that evil.

Footsteps sounded a few yards down the path. Three people. Belle put on her most human face.

"Mimi? Is that you?"

Her pupils opened up in the dark to see the faces coming up toward her. They were people she'd known her whole human life, three girls she'd gone to school with. That familiarity didn't prevent hunger from tugging hotly at her teeth and searing through her veins like fire. She struggled to remember how she was as a human. "Yes, man," she called back to the girls. "Who else?"

"Miss Roslyn said that somebody took you off in Negril," Daphne, the sable-skinned girl she'd had a crush on in primary school, said. "We thought you were gone for good."

The girls came close, but not too close. They were wary.

"I got lost on a big street and didn't have any money with me, so it took me a while to make my way back up here." *Who the devil would believe that tripe?* Belle almost shook her head at her own stupidity.

"Okay. Good to see you, though," one of the other two women chimed in, but suspicion marked the look she threw Belle's way. In the dark, they thought she couldn't see. "Say hello to Miss Roslyn and Kylie for me," the other said.

"I will."

More people started coming up the path in a steady trickle, old friends or enemies who said their hellos or waved, all expressing their relief that she was all right and hadn't been kidnapped like that Holt girl who'd gone to Kingston for her brother's graduation and gotten picked up, raped, and killed by a taxi driver. The police found the girl's naked body in a gully a week later. Her family members hadn't been the same since. None of them even went to visit Kingston anymore.

Belle was grateful for their concern. She really was, and told them so as she smelled their good, generous blood and hugged them as had been her custom in life. Some exclaimed at how cold she was, urging her to get inside and warm up. Belle said that she would. Her family was sure to warm her when she got home. Then she walked away from their concern.

The house looked the same. Somehow in her yearning dreams it had taken on a glowing quality, like a jewel in a land made exotic and desirable by distance. It had glowed the rich blue of heaven, windows sparkling with some otherworldly cleaning solution, the rock path that Kylie and Naomi had made had become bright like diamonds, and the fence of tall bamboo had become green again, its leaves waving in an ever-present breeze. But reality now asserted itself. The house was the same as when she'd left it over a week ago. Plain and beautiful.

As Belle walked closer to the house one of the dogs started barking. It was Coco, the ghost-white dog Naomi had rescued almost five years ago. The same dog who never left her side when she was home and who always wanted to be under her fingers or her feet. Coco's blue eyes flashed and hardened inside the fence. She rushed up to the locked gate, barking furiously. Another dog—Sasha, Roslyn's favorite—started barking, then both were warning her away.

Their deep growls made Belle want to rush through the gate and dash them all against the wall, splashing blood and viscera against the Caribbean-blue paint and watch it drip down in long scarlet streaks. A light came on in the house and Roslyn's face appeared at the window. She looked delicious. Belle shook her head and pretended to breathe. Then took a step back, then another and another until she was walking quickly back up the path.

But even as Belle ran away from the house where she grew up, the details of Naomi's life overtook her: the way her belly had swollen with Kylie and how it felt like happiness growing inside her, expanding the shallow contours of her life; the rhythm of her mother's voice rising and falling with the accent she'd acquired during a childhood in England; Kylie in her crib, eyes wide and long lashes occasionally blinking as she, with her mouth parted in her baby's burp of a toothless smile, listened to Naomi sing. She would miss these things.

Belle's feet pounded against hard-packed soil and the wind whistled past her ears. Kylie deserved to live the life that Naomi had given her. No one, not even Belle, was going to take it away.

The beast inside her was hungry. Belle didn't fully realize it until she turned away from her old home. The thought that food lay just beyond that front door pricked Belle. Irritated, she shoved it away. Now she felt deprived and raw and hungry down to her very marrow. The need dragged her down, made her want to drop to all fours and howl.

She slunk away to spend the day in the caves by the sea, enclosed in their moist coolness while the sunlight drained away to nothing. The cave's darkness made her feel welcome. She could have spent eternity there, embraced and cocooned in caverns that protected her Maroon ancestors from their British and Spanish enemies. Even as daylight burned outside her aboveground tomb, she could not sleep. She dreamed with open eyes of her past with Kylie and Roslyn, with the girls she went to school with, of her fantasies of leaving the island for wintry England, of so many things that were gone and could never be again. Still, she needed her family. She wanted to have them close. She couldn't imagine an existence without them. Her flesh ached to hold them close, to feel their words wash through her ears. The yearning was so strong. Belle couldn't remember feeling this way before.

At sundown, she left her cave in search of food. A boy found her first. He thought that she eyed his strong body with lust. When he came closer she brought him down in a quick, silent rush. His blood was like sorrel in peak season. She drank him dry and left his body under an ackee tree.

With her skin still flush and warm from her meal, she decided to try and see her family again. Belle cleaned her face in river water and brushed as much dirt as she could from her stolen clothes. In the wavering mirror of the river, she looked almost normal. Then with the moon shining behind her like the light of truth, she saw how she often looked now, face narrow and hungry, coral-brushed lower lip even redder as if touched with blood, the fangs that curved like shiny white daggers over that lip and their twins, smaller and closer together, rising from the bottom row of teeth. Acting purely on instinct, Belle stretched her jaw and forced the hollow canines to retract. They did. She tried a smile. Okay, maybe not.

On her way to the house she saw them: her daughter holding her mother's hand and looking grim. Kylie's small face did grim very well. Roslyn looked even more protective than usual in her prim dress and hat. Ah, it was Sunday. They both looked very human and vulnerable as they walked together, yet alone under the intermittent streetlights.

"Good night, Miss Roslyn," someone greeted from just beyond the light.

Roslyn clutched Kylie's hand tighter before turning to face the source of the voice. Three people walked out of the shadows, all smiling reassuringly at Belle's women.

"Good evening, Deacon Jarvis. Mrs. Jarvis. Harry. I didn't know you were walking this way tonight." A smile settled into Roslyn's voice.

"We weren't but we heard the news of some strange happenings in the district so thought it best to walk you ladies home." The deacon handed Kylie a lollipop and the little girl accepted it with solemn thanks.

"Thank you," Roslyn said. "This is most unexpected."

They all began walking together toward Roslyn and Kylie's house. The house that once belonged to Naomi too.

"Have you heard from Naomi yet?" Harry, the deacon's young brother, asked.

"No, but we are still hoping."

The three shared a look that said they'd heard of Naomi's return to the district. They were suspicious.

"They say that everything happens for a reason, Sister Roslyn," the deacon's wife said. "Just take care of yourself and the little one now. Have faith."

Roslyn nodded. "That is all we can do now, although Claudine is still keeping an eye out in Negril. The last thing she heard was that Mimi was in the hotel looking like she was waiting for someone."

The three nodded as if that meant something to them. They reached the house and guided Naomi's family inside.

"Take care walking after dark, ladies. And don't hesitate to call on us if you need anything."

A frown marred Roslyn's face but she nodded, hugged her escorts, then locked herself and her granddaughter inside the blue house. Belle watched from the shadows, far back from the house so the dogs could not sense her presence. Kylie and Roslyn were alone. Could she resist taking them if she got close? The answer kept her in the shadows. She watched until all the lights were off in the house and traffic along the path trickled away to nothing. As the night grew, so did the doubts about her self-control.

She left the familiar path behind, running in the shoes that Ruby had given her, although she knew that the snarling beast inside her could not be outrun. The smell of food stopped her. The heady scent of blood and pain threw her temporary restraint out the window. In a fever she dropped to one knee, nosing through the bush, heading steadily for the source of that scent. Stifled screams and whimpers guided her to the woman spread out near the star jasmine bush, bleeding and in pain.

She was lovely, with black velvet skin and eyes glazed over with fear and horror. A hand flecked with scars and dirt was clenched tightly over her mouth, muffling her pleas. The men inflicting her pain didn't see Belle. Terror oozed from the woman like raw honey, electrifying Belle's air, her fingertips, her teeth. It was only fair that the men should feel it too. Fire licked through her veins.

The one with his penis inside the woman deserved her attention first. She grabbed him by the throat and away from his victim. Under her claws, his neck burst open like a wine-skin, spurting blood and screams into the bush. The others rose up in surprise, scrambling up from the woman's bleeding and torn body to come after Belle. She almost laughed.

Instead, she cut them down with her claws and new quickness, waiting until the first two were dead, before playing with the last one, cutting at his skin, slamming her fists into him to show him what a real punch felt like. Then she finished it, crouching over his bucking and howling body to rip out his throat and gorge herself on his thickly gushing blood. Her body throbbed with his life.

"Shit! There it is!"

Something knocked her away from her feast. She raised her head, showing a face that was blood-streaked and annoyed. A dozen people at least. The group of men surrounded her. Two others crouched near the bleeding woman, calling a name in urgent, piercing voices. The men advanced on Belle with machetes and sticks, circling and slashing at any part of her that they could reach. She hissed and backed up until she felt trees and ripping branches at her back. Still, they advanced.

They circled and slashed at her through the bushes. Her flesh vibrated with their blows as blood fled to the surface of her skin. It hurt. Hissing, Belle cut at them with her fingers and tried to spin to get away, but the men were everywhere. Their cheeks opened up under her claws; men screamed but came back at her harder until she was clenching her teeth against the need to cry out and scream. Blood splashed over her skin and in her face. Suddenly she heard the sound of more than one screaming, heard agony and surprise in the high shouts and curses. Silvija. Something inside her opened up and purred at the sight of the giant standing there in the moonlight.

Belle saw the beauty of the other fiend without trying to. Silvija burst through the circle of humans, her body a graceful killing scythe. She was a blur of movement and silence, slashing with long claws and lightning knees and fists and legs. Julia was there too, crouched low to the ground and draining the men who fell under Silvija. All the men eventually fell. Before the two vampires could look up from their butchery, Belle turned and ran.

Her long legs quickly took her through the underbrush. When she heard them begin to follow, Belle chuckled. She ran under swaying trees, past dew-flecked flowers and thorns that tore at her flesh like sharp, bloody kisses. Laughter tumbled recklessly from her lips.

Silvija appeared on the path in front of her and forced her to stop. "I never thought you'd come running back to the fold with this much enthusiasm, puppy."

Behind her, Julia laughed, then cowed back at the look from Belle.

Silvija's eyebrow rose along with the corners of her mouth. "Have you had enough of freedom? Are you ready to come with us?"

"I wouldn't say that," Belle said, although going home with her sounded like a much better idea than hanging around Friendship like the pathetic ghoul she was. She looked beyond Julia. "Where are your lackeys?"

"I gave them the evening off and told them Julia and I had to clean up a mess that we caused."

"Are you referring to me, fair leader?" Belle suddenly felt too tired to stand. She sat down cross-legged in the dirt and leaned back against a tree.

"Sadly, yes." Silvija looked up at the sound of running feet and baying human dogs. "Why don't we take this discussion somewhere else?" Without looking to Belle for agreement she turned and disappeared back into the bush. The young fiend had no choice but to follow. A taxi sat in the road with its engine still running. Silvija and Julia got in.

"Coming?" Silvija asked, her mouth curving into a dry smile.

Belle entered the cab.

Chapter 6

"This is a beautiful house."

"I know. It's where I bring all my women."

Belle stood in the hallway while Silvija shut the door. The small bungalow was plush and comfortable with its cozy window seats, cushiony chairs, and warm hardwood floors. The stained glass windows were sealed closed with only the drapes opened to let the moonlight in. The house was a testament to their love of comfort and luxury. With the curtains pulled closed it would be a warm den, suitable for getting close and closer. The beast's warm, clove scent stroked Belle's senses. After a single look at Belle, Julia left them alone.

Silvija turned to Belle. "Go and clean up. There are some clothes in the room at the top of the stairs. Use whatever you like."

Belle nodded, unwilling to thank her for anything. Although she would never admit it, Belle was grateful for the vampires' presence. Some part of her had missed them. Even the little fiend, Julia. What Silvija had said earlier was true. They were her family now, whether she liked it or not. In the bedroom she showered and changed into a loose white dress that gathered just beneath her breasts and fell to her knees.

"Very nice, puppy," Silvija murmured as she walked down the short flight of stairs. "Now I can almost see why Julia took you."

Belle's mouth twisted at the backhanded compliment. "Would it make any difference if I told you my name?"

"I already know your name."

"No, you don't. If you did you wouldn't call me . . . that."

Silvija's eyebrow rose. "Could it be that you're finally learning something?"

"Doubtful." Belle had enough of a sense of humor to smile at that. She sat down next to Silvija on the sofa and curled up to rest her chin on her knees. "But I'm ready to listen to you now." That moment in front of her house—when she'd smelled Kylie's blood and had been titillated by the almost-thought of drinking her mother dry—shook Belle. She didn't want to be that much of a monster. But she could be. "Thanks for showing up when you did, although I was handling it just fine."

Silvija smiled. "You think so?"

"Absolutely. Even with all that blood"—her teeth tingled at the memory of it—"I didn't touch her."

"Can you honestly say that after you were done with those men you would *not* have turned on the girl too?"

Belle opened her mouth to protest, then closed it again. The smell of that woman's blood, of her fear, and her pain, was what had drawn her in the first place. It would have been like dessert or a post-orgasm cigarette to sink her fangs into that woman and suck every drop of fear-flavored blood from her. Belle shivered.

"That is our nature," Silvija said. "The virus takes away our humanity, whatever civilized veneer we had. Many of the newly turned are little more than wild animals who end up getting themselves killed within a few hours or they kill humans for days or months until vigilantes hunt them down and use their carcasses to fertilize the countryside."

Belle stared at her. "Anyone tell you that you have a way with words?"

"I'm just trying to pass on a few truths in a way that you can understand," Silvija chuckled.

"I won't even bother to ask you what you mean by that."

"Good, because I think you know."

The two beasts looked at each other, one warily, the other mildly amused. Belle heard the sounds of another entering the room, Julia, but did not look away from Silvija's gaze. The brown eyes actually sparkled.

"Have a seat, Julia. I was just telling your young convert here all the things you should have." There was faint censure in her voice. "She seems to be in a more amenable mood than last time."

"That's good to know," Julia purred. "I'd love to continue our relationship where we left off. In Negril, that is."

Belle glanced at her. "Not to be melodramatic or anything, but I'd rather crawl naked into the sunlight on razor blades than have you touch me again." Her eyes scraped over the small, curvaceous body draped in a white silk robe. "No offense." It wasn't quite true, but what she just said would work for now.

"None taken."

Neither of them acknowledged what had happened on the boat the night Belle swam away. It was as if that momentary lapse—Belle's—had never happened. Julia turned her eyes to Silvija and seemed to forget all about Belle.

"You are an animal," Silvija continued. "Your self-control is at zero, in your case I'd say less than. Right now, when you want something you take it. Emotions rise up and grab you by the throat and you are absolutely helpless. Eventually, you will learn to control yourself and your emotions. That's where living with the pack comes in."

"Pack? I thought you people were bloodsuckers, not dogs." Belle lifted a mocking eyebrow. "Do we lick each other's assholes in public too?"

"Only if you want to," Julia murmured from her chair. When she saw Belle looking, she wiggled her shapely ass and lifted it slightly in the air.

"Julia, behave." Silvija spoke before Belle could, which was probably for the best. She turned to the younger vampire. "I should have brought you here earlier, instead of forcing you on board the boat. Mea culpa."

At Belle's blank look, Silvija smiled ruefully. "My error. I apologize."

It was starting to be really obvious that the beast was a brain as well. One that didn't lord it over members of the ignorant masses like herself. It was getting more difficult to keep hating her.

"Yeah, you made a big mistake trying to take me away from this place and everything I love, then drop me off in goddamn Alaska of all places."

"It's not as awful as it sounds. This time of year, the sun is only out for about three hours a day and we can prowl freely."

"And freeze freely too, I bet."

"Don't be stupid, puppy. You've been in this new flesh long enough to know that we do not feel the cold as humans do. I daresay it would be a pleasure for you to be there, to learn your new power without the limits of only nine hours of darkness. As for the cold that makes you so uncomfortable, don't worry. We only spend the winters there."

"Then what? You load me back on that miserable boat to spend the summers in Antarctica?"

"We can drop you off there if you'd like," Julia said with a glinting smile.

Belle shook her head. If they took her to Alaska she would stay there. She'd rather that than come back here again and put her family at risk.

"My name is Belle." She said the words softly into the silence so that they both heard. Then she met Silvija's eyes and nodded once. "Belle."

Silvija nodded in turn, accepting the name and the silence that sat around it.

Belle nodded again. "But you were saying?"

Silvija smiled. "Although things haven't exactly gone the usual way for you, I'll tell you how it's supposed to happen."

Her eyes traveled to Julia. "You will come to hate your maker. You'll only be able to see her as the person who knew you when you were human and frail and beautiful, then changed you into this. It becomes painful and you want to escape her, perhaps even destroy her." She pursed her lips. "I think you're already at that stage."

"So it's not just her? I'm programmed to want to ram a steel pike through her chest?" Belle bared her teeth at Julia. "Good to know. So I have an excuse when I actually do it. None of this was my fault. The blood made me do it."

"I'm here to make sure that you don't kill Julia." Sylvija's voice was hard. "Try very hard to resist the temptation."

Because that's exactly what it was. A temptation. The sense memories from that first night snuck up on her at the most unexpected moments. The feeling of sliding against Julia's wet cunt on the beach and the power-thick blood gushing into her mouth. The smaller fiend bucking under her, helpless and small. Her whimpering cries. Horrific pleasures she'd focused on to distract herself from thinking of her family as wild game to be brought down under her savaging teeth.

"Another part of this new existence is your feelings. You may have noticed by now"—Silvija's look was ironic again—"that it's become very difficult to control yourself. It will get easier. But generally speaking, we are very instinctive and passionate beings."

"Animals," Belle said.

"If you like." Silvija nodded once.

"What about you? I don't see you running around here on all fours trying to rip out everyone's throats."

"Because I control myself."

Even when you're fucking? Belle's mouth quirked up at the stray thought.

Their eyes met and Silvija released a small breath as if striving for patience. Belle teased her with an impish smile that Silvija, naturally, ignored.

"We will stay here for one month and teach you some basics," Silvija said. "After that we get back on the yacht and head north."

Unspoken was her permission for Belle to say good-bye to Jamaica and all the things she loved here. One month. The evening passed quickly. With sunrise came the rain, a thundering downpour that seemed like it was there for the long haul. After the other two had gone upstairs to sleep, Belle stood at the window gazing longingly at the raindrops that hit the windowsill and glowed in the pink light from the rising sun as they fell. In her life she had loved the rain almost as well as the sun and tumbled into stupors of joy when it rained on a sunny day. Rain falling on a sun-scorched pavement. The light, brilliant and sure, caught in the tumbling drops as they hissed, splattered, and steamed. Golden drops falling from the skies, splashing over her face and onto her tongue. On those days she swallowed the sun. And it tasted like heaven.

Belle pulled the shades and backed away from the light. The windows were heavily tinted and tightly closed, but it didn't hurt to be cautious. The pain she'd felt on the journey from Negril wasn't something she wanted to experience again. She went upstairs.

Expecting to see closed doors or at least a feminine form under the sheets from the open doorway, Belle was surprised when she peered into the first three rooms and found them empty, their king-sized bedding undisturbed and pristine. There was only one bedroom left. It shouldn't have shocked her that Silvija and Julia slept together, but it did. She felt left out. In the room farthest from the pair, she took off her dress and climbed into the cold bed.

"You never listen when I talk, do you?" Silvija appeared in the doorway, clad in a thin dark robe. "We sleep together. We need to."

With the shades drawn the house lay in perfect darkness. Her skin shimmered in the dark with the promise of comfort and heat. The monster seemed beautiful. Her clove-infused scent—Belle recognized it now—flowed into the room, light as new rain. "I don't—can't—do that."

The prospect of sharing a bed with the two beasts tripped her tongue, made it impossible to speak. Even with her new heightened power, coherent thought was out of the question as well.

The monster laughed. "You'll let go of your human prudishness soon enough." She leaned against the door frame as if settling in for the night. "Don't worry, it's not about sex. At least not completely."

But her slowly slinking scent said otherwise. Although Silvija hadn't moved, Belle felt she only had to turn her cheek to sink into the sweetly spiced reality of her. "No. I think I'll stay here."

Silvija shrugged and gathered herself. "Whatever you say. See you in the evening."

But as soon as she vanished from the doorway, Belle's flesh began to ache. While she lived, she was never one for physical affection. Aside from the stream of never-ending hugs and kisses from Kylie and her mother's occasional soothing touch, Naomi had never cared much for the caress of others. When people were too close, it made her jumpy and nervous, like they wanted something from her that she couldn't give. Belle remembered the unfamiliar yearning she'd felt with Ruby, wanting to just lie with the human woman and feel her blood-scented skin against hers while she slept. The feeling now was similar, but much, much more compelling.

She lay in the cool sheets, listening to the rain beat on the roof. Her eyelids drooped, but each time they lay closed for a moment they instantly popped open and she felt panicked as if she'd forgotten something very important and couldn't get to sleep without it. *Why don't you just get out the fucking hair shirt and roll around in it?* a mocking voice asked. Over an hour after Silvija had left her room, Belle got up, got dressed, and went to find the beast.

She didn't bother knocking. They probably already heard

her reluctant but inevitable footsteps approach the door. It was already open. A commingled scent of sweetness and spice drifted from the room, strong and delicate aromas that together created an odd feeling of peace. The two beasts lay in the bed, naked and pressed close together. Silvija held her body in a soft C, a shallow cup of still flesh and bone that contained Julia, curled and content with her cheek pillowed against her clasped hands and her back pressed to Silvija's breasts. When Belle walked through the door, the giant's eyes flickered open. She watched her come closer, and the young beast could feel the heat of her gaze, the soft considering look that was neither triumphant nor predatory.

Belle was determined to keep her dress on. As her knee hit the bed, Julia groggily opened her eyes. She mumbled something and rearranged herself to accommodate their new bedmate. Belle didn't want to touch her, didn't want to go anywhere near her, but their closeness was seductive. She scooted up behind Silvija, and almost against her will her body wrapped itself around the giant, finding the warmth it had been craving for the past hour. In their oversized bed, scented flesh pressed against scented flesh, generating a phantom heat, not unlike an amputee experiencing sensation from a long-gone limb. Their heat was hallucinatory, but it still felt wonderful. The heated skin acted like a sedative; moments later her eyelids drooped and then she was asleep.

Sometime during the day she woke up and stripped off the dress, impatiently leaving its shredded remains on the floor beside the bed. Then she fell back to sleep. When Belle woke again she lay sandwiched between the two beasts, her head on Silvija's chest, hand snuggled between the soft breasts. Julia lay on Belle's back with an arm flung across the beast's thighs. She wanted to stay like that forever. Between the three of them they had manufactured warmth, a thing they no longer had in their bodies, and slept soundly in it. Her skin felt like stretched taffy, warm and lissome and wonderful. A noise of undiluted pleasure vibrated in her throat.

She wasn't sure whose fingers curled first, whose hand reached out in lust, but she felt a cool palm around her breast weighing its heaviness, then testing the hardness of its nipple. Belle moaned softly but did not open her eyes. Sharp teeth nibbled at the back of her neck while the fingers massaged her breast, teased her nipple, squeezing it. Belle's thigh lifted to clasp another and her wetness scraped across the muscled hardness of the beast's thigh.

Her fingers found harder nipples, then her mouth, until the hard flesh floated over her tongue, in the wet cavern of her mouth. Belle licked the nipple and an answering moan vibrated above her. Fingers glided inside her from behind and she gently pushed back, inviting and sighing. The sensation, the warmth, made her want to sing. Instead she reached for more contact, rolling her body onto the beast's and sinking into the strangely warm flesh while Julia followed hers, gently fucking Belle with small fingers.

She parted her legs and arched her ass into the air for Julia to slide deeper inside her. Below her, the beast was incandescent, head flung back against the sheets and her breasts rising up for Belle's mouth, her throat bare and vulnerable. In this twilight land of half sleep, Belle's desires, her actions, seemed beyond her control and knowledge. All was sensation and yearning toward satisfaction. Her skin flared and tingled, alight with lust.

Between her legs, Silvija was an even greater miracle, cool wet pussy and clit Belle could have feasted on for days, but she would have to make do with her hands. Julia had no such limitations. Behind her, she bathed Belle's clit with her tongue and deeply fucked her pussy, making Belle's hips dance in the air as Belle stroked Silvija's nipple and clit to the same rhythm that Julia set.

Silvija sighed her orgasm into the soft pre-evening, trembling gently under Belle's fingers. Julia flicked her skilled tongue over her, gasping at the same time from her self-induced orgasm. Belle shuddered from her own, clamping down hard on Silvija's neck without drawing blood. All three sighed together as they collapsed back into the bed.

The sun was still up. Belle knew that as surely as she knew her own name. But night would come soon. She licked her fingers, pulling the surprisingly delicate essence of Silvija into her mouth. Then it would be time to get up and begin her "lessons." That time was far enough away. Now there was no reason to leave the warm cocoon of their bed. Not yet. Belle turned into the cushion of Silvija's breasts and drifted back to sleep.

Chapter 7

Hunting was one of the basics she had to learn. When not to, who not to, how not to. By the third waking hour, Belle had learned so many things not to do when looking for food that she began to wonder how these fiends fed at all.

"Some places you can't just take what you want and leave the empty sack for the whole world to see." Silvija turned and pulled on a black shirt in one smooth motion, shielding her heavy breasts from sight. "Others like us live here. Don't make it hard for them."

This experience, Belle thought, looking at Silvija, more than any killing or blood drinking, definitively separated her life from what she knew now. Belle had access to everything female and sensuous she'd ever wanted in her life: lovely women to look at, to look at her and tease her with their beauty and their words. She admitted now that Silvija was beautiful, not in the insipid way that praised frailty and cuteness and lack of intellect. Silvija was truly a beast, with a long and powerful body, muscles singing entire arias under her skin as she moved. She was not kind, she was not small. Her face of all broad angles and planes shouted that she had been born to fight, born to lead. Belle could not see her as some man—or woman's—helpmate. Her eyes flickered over Silvija again; then she looked away.

Belle, already dressed and attentive in well-fitting black

slacks and a button-down shirt, waited patiently for the older
fiend to finish talking and show her what all this was about.
Her hunger slept, but she was eager for a lesson. After waking up a second time earlier that evening, she'd felt the awkwardness. Then, after a low-voiced invitation from Silvija,
she'd stayed to take a shower in the adjoining bathroom and
pick through the clothes in the closet. Julia already went out
to get her own food.

Belle held herself back—but only just—from actually lik-
ing Silvija. That was the slippery slope to becoming her pawn,
her fool. She could never let Silvija turn her into the kind of
beast that Julia was. The little fiend crawled and cowed in
her presence, damn near begging the giant to torture and
torment her. When she wasn't trying to fuck or annoy Belle,
that is.

"Ready?"

Belle answered the question by standing up and gesturing
toward the door. "After you."

The air smelled moist and fresh from the day's rain. Belle
could taste its coolness at the back of her throat. Night was
just as beautiful as she remembered it, a saturating darkness
that enfolded and welcomed her. Each night when she awoke
and walked outside, it felt like the first—minus the pain.
Rich, inky beauty. And her eyes saw it all. The star jasmine
climbing up the railing to the verandah glowed a sharp, stark
white, their green nest of leaves with their veins of a darker
green branching out to track the entire width of the leaf.
Belle rubbed her thumb over the smooth surface. Alive.

"You're not here to stare at the plants all night, puppy. We
have work to do."

Belle glanced up sharply at the returned hate-name, but
Silvija merely curled her fingers and smiled.

"Come, there's food nearby."

"Hmm, is there ever!" Julia melted out of the darkness,
brushing dirt and bits of twigs and leaves from her clothes.
"It's a gorgeous night for a chase too. The moon is such a

tiny little slit." She giggled. "They can't even see where they're going."

Julia fell in step with Silvija and Belle. They walked quickly until they stood on a hilltop overlooking a tiny town. The rooftops were squat and mismatched, some made of zinc and nails, others professionally built and sturdy. The larger, more ornate houses loomed high above the more modest ones with their gated driveways, large burglar-barred windows. They were multistoried, yet not really much of a challenge to get into. Or at least that's what Belle thought as she looked at them wondering which one to visit for her early evening meal.

"Find someone people won't miss," Silvija lectured at her ear. "So look away from those big houses."

Something inside Belle jerked at the tone, but she didn't respond. She knew well what it was like to be poor, when the government preyed on you, so did the police and anyone else who could. With no health care or legal protection, suddenly there were vampires at your door to worry about too. She wouldn't become a part of that.

She blended with the darkness when Silvija signaled that it was her time to feed. Two men walked together, their arms swinging gently together in friendship. Their cigarettes threaded gray smoke in the night around them. Silvija's womanly silhouette interrupted their mundane talk—potholes that needed fixing, the absurdity of bottled water for sale on an island where it flowed pure and sweet straight from Jah's cup.

They greeted the tall woman with respect, inquired after her health, even offered to walk her to her house on such a dark night. Silvija smiled, charming them with her strong looks and faint foreign accent. When they wished her a good night and made to pass her, she brought them down with quick ferocity, hooking her fingers in their necks, bringing them abruptly to the ground and opening them up like presents. They never got the chance to run.

Julia slowly emerged from her hiding place. "I forget how

fun it is to hunt with you, Silvija." She crouched low to the ground, watching Silvija rip into the prey with her mouth. "You don't mind sharing."

With a low, seductive laugh, Silvija crawled over the other man like a spider and fastened her mouth to his gushing throat. Belle watched from the rocky path, feeling the bits of gravel through the soles of her shoes and the gentle lash of the wind against her skin. The smell of the kill was tempting, but pride prevented her from feeding on Silvija's leavings. She wasn't a baby to suck down some other beast's food, too weak to get her own. In Negril she had survived, she had taken the policeman, the woman, and those two boys with no problem. Belle didn't need this charity. So she looked away, down at the quiet district with its faint murmur of voices and the lights coming and going in the windows. Then she looked back and up to the houses higher up on the hill. Belle unhooked her hands from her pockets and walked toward them.

An arc of lightning lit up the sky. Thunder rumbled deep and strong overhead, reminding Belle of the heavy rains from earlier that day. She sprinted toward the closest house. Julia was right. It was a nice night for a chase. A scent rode the wind like a red banner: woman, sweat-infused perfume, and champagne. Sounds poured down from a nearby house— laughter, music from a live band, the trill of voices competing to be heard. Wonderful. She leapt high over the twelve-foot fence, not believing for a moment that she would not clear it, and landed in a crouch before she sprang up and started toward the gathering of humans at a slower pace. Raindrops patted at her shoulders and hair.

The front of the house was a cool wash of light, lines of expensive cars, and the muted strains of music. Belle slipped around the back. Here was the real party. She looked up, blinking the gathering raindrops from her eyes. High up on a large terrace the surging bodies and tippled laughter ignored the fat, fast drops of rain. People in evening dresses stood side by side with jeans-clad partiers who shared drinks with boys and girls in bikinis. No luck there. Belle looked off in the distance toward the gazebo and garden. Human scents floated from there too.

Through the rain and the party and the music, she found her. The perfect treat. She stood alone in the gazebo, beautiful in a way that no one had a right to be with gorgeous copper skin glowing in the rain, tilted brown eyes, flower-lush mouth, and smelling like wine in a damp cotton dress. The woman was steeped in melancholy, a sadness that made her even more beautiful. An empty wineglass dangled from her limp hand. Beneath the draped white dress her nipples stood up pretty and hard. They drew Belle's eyes, then her feet, closer.

Belle called out a name. The woman turned and Belle apologized, saying she had the wrong person, but the lovely had already turned and seen her. In her black clothes and with her hair pulled back in the tight ponytail, she could easily be mistaken for a man. A very attractive man. The woman smiled and put her glass on the railing. She thought Belle looked like someone she knew. Or wanted to know. She'd been over-indulged, given everything she ever wanted. But there was something missing, an unnamed something whose absence turned down the corners of her mouth and made her give herself to strangers.

The woman slipped on her social face, pushing her sadness aside for the attractive stranger. Her body dipped forward and the dress swayed away from her skin, giving Belle a view of soft flesh, the rise of breast, the hint of a nipple. She stepped closer. The woman said something, some flirtatious nonsense that Belle responded to with a closemouthed smile and a touch. She brushed her fingers across the woman's throat and caught the resulting gasp with cool lips. In the rain her touch was especially cold. The woman's lips were warm, then hot as they moved under Belle's.

The woman twined her arms around Belle's neck, pressing

her luscious body closer, opening her mouth to accept the ravenous tongue. Her smell was intoxicating. Wine, desire, perfume, sweat, and blood. Belle backed her up against the rail, sniffing her throat and the valley between her breasts. A high wind came up and blew rainwater over them, flinging it like a cool aphrodisiac over their flesh. Belle nipped at the soft skin, and the woman gasped again. Her desire for blood and for sex commingled. She didn't want to end this yet. She pulled the woman from the gazebo and into the rain, partially hiding them from other eyes in the darkness. Her dress was instantly soaked, plastered to her skin. And Belle drowned in the sight of her, the small high breasts and their dark nipples, tiny panties and long thighs under the transparent dress. She wanted to slip between the woman's thighs, she wanted inside her, she wanted everything. Oh. So. Good. Her teeth slipped into the skin of her neck like twin hypodermics. The woman gasped. Her eyes flew open and the fingers at Belle's back tightened in her fear. And her delight.

"Don't drain her." The voice reached her out of the dark. Silvija. But it didn't interfere.

It wasn't as simple as obeying a command. Belle needed this terror, the pleasure, that this flesh promised. She sucked the woman into her mouth, took the rich red of her in greedy gulps. Belle became heady with the wine the woman had taken and she stumbled. The woman fell backward, limp and gasping, onto the grass. Belle wanted to put her hand under that wet dress, push the panties aside, and feast on her in that way too. Her belly clutched with desire. Her fingers hurried to that destination, diving into the moist depths of her, then emerged to play on her clit. Rain pounded into her scalp, sliding down her cheeks to mingle with the blood in her mouth, dripping from her lips.

"Just a bit more," she murmured to herself against the hot throat.

Belle's fingers moved again and the woman jerked into the bow Belle's body made just for her. The rain continued to pour over them, its spray from the woman's mouth showing the ragged quality of her breathing. Belle sighed. Grass shifted beneath the woman's back and made a soft sucking noise when she left it, sighed when her weight returned. And the rain. Their bodies became iridescent in the wet onslaught. Their separate needs intensified. The woman's body clutched at her fingers, sucked them deeper inside with each orgasmic contraction. Belle tingled and grew flushed. Warm. She felt so warm.

"Belle!"

The rain's insistent beat amplified her hunger, walking over her flesh and massaging out the pleasure.

"Do not kill her." Silvija and Julia stood back, still not interfering. "Take what you need. Leave her alive." Right. This was a lesson. One that she seemed to be failing. "If you like her so much, you can come back and visit her before you leave. You do want to taste her sweetness again, don't you?" Yes. She wanted to have this again.

The woman's pulse fluttered in her throat. Her breath was only a slight mist in the cooling rain. Belle wasn't ravenous, not anymore. She didn't need to kill the woman to feed, although Silvija had no qualms about raping those two men of their lives back there on that path. Despite the intensity of her desire, she managed to pull her prey to her feet and guide her back to the gazebo. The woman was light and swaying, lovely and still humanly scented. She had plenty left to give. If she had the time, if Silvija allowed it, Belle could spend an entire night with this one, drink from her saturated pussy until they were both weak from coming. Then she would fuck her one last time and drain her dry.

The woman slumped against the bench. Her eyes were heavy lidded and sex-dark. She licked her lips and glanced up at Belle as if nothing more ordinary than a late-night fuck had transpired between them. Belle took her hands from the human with regret.

"Good." Silvija was a cool and solid presence behind her. "Very good."

With the giant's words, the bloodlust slowly receded until she became aware of her surroundings again, the presence of humans nearby, some making love in the drier areas of the garden, others taking illicit drugs, and others still simply standing in the rain under the heavy trellises to enjoy the downpour and the lovely smell it pounded up from the earth.

The lust-struck human and the three vampires weren't that isolated from everyone else, Belle realized. There were dozens of people here. They would easily be able to take the three of them, tie them up in the sun to burn away like garbage.

Belle shuddered. "I'm ready."

They turned and walked quickly from the garden, taking the back way from the house and streaking through the rain like ghosts. Once they were beyond the gates, the vampires ran. Silvija attained and maintained the lead, swerving around high bushes that Belle didn't even see. She was a beautiful symphony of movement, their leading string, whipping through the night as the other two followed helplessly behind her. She never once looked back to make sure they stayed with her. When they were high in the mountains, even higher than before, Silvija stopped. Belle smelled the thinner, richer air and noticed just as quickly how far away the human houses were. They were mere pinpricks of light below them.

Silvija turned. "Don't you ever disobey me like that again." Her eyes burned. "I am training you. That means you stay close to me. Watch what I do, then see if you can do it."

So much for their truce. Belle sneered. "So, you taking out those two guys at once, what was that supposed to teach me? Wasn't that waste? That one"—she jerked her head toward Julia—"had already fed. Were you just showing off for me? If that's a lesson, then I wasn't really impressed."

If anything impressed her it was the giant who seemed so calm. Belle vibrated with energy. The new blood ran through her thick and hot, fizzing inside her like fresh champagne. Her vision was clear and dagger sharp. She wanted to touch something new, to feel something, to use this energy, all of it. She wanted to prowl. Shit, she even wanted the beast to fight her, anything that was flesh-on-flesh contact. Anything.

"Julia, go back to the house. The puppy and I need to discuss a few things."

The smaller fiend turned and left them without a single word. So obedient, that one.

"Listen, I know you're about to jump out of your skin, but this isn't the way to go. Believe me." Without seeming to move a single muscle, Silvija grew more threatening. "I told you, drink to kill. Do not leave witnesses behind to ask questions and to show their marks. That girl may not know you for what you are, but her people might when they see your bites on her neck. They are wealthy, they have access to things. They might come hunting after us."

Belle's lip curled. "And they might not. So you wanted me to cut open her throat with a blade, hide my marks, and leave her to rot in the rain?"

Even in the midst of her anger, Belle could see that Silvija was pleased to hear that she had listened earlier and taken that lesson.

"You have to be consistent. Isn't it because she was beautiful that you're filled with mercy and human love? Do you want to sneak back into her house and fuck her as often as you like, to enjoy all the luscious pussy you never could before?" Silvija made a dismissive noise. "There are other women out there. More beautiful women who will see you for the beast you are and still want you for it. They will lift their skirts and bare their necks and beg you to take them. She is not one of those."

Then, because to her the discussion was over, Silvija turned to look behind them. "Come, the night is still new. There are other things to learn."

Chapter 8

They barely made it back to the house before sunrise. Julia had found them again, and while the fiend taught Belle a few basics of fighting—Silvija called them the dirty moves that would quickly get her out of a jam—the smaller beast clapped and laughed, especially when Belle ended up on the ground with some new pain blossoming in her body and the giant standing over her, hard-eyed yet patient.

Despite the approaching heat of sunrise, Belle slowed down as they neared the cottage. There were others inside. She could smell them, a pungent combination of lime, cinnamon, and bergamot. Three of them. Cool-blooded, but not precisely harmless. Belle slowed down even more as the other two rushed ahead. Again, Silvija was faster. Inside the house she heard the hush of greetings, their deference to the giant, and then their inquiry about Belle. The lackeys. She set one foot on the porch steps, resisting the urge to turn and run back into the dark. Was their night of lessons over? She waited a beat, then two. When she heard movement toward the door—Julia sent to fetch her, no doubt—Belle tumbled up the steps and into the house.

"The gang's all here." She couldn't summon a smile to make her words less snide.

Silvija lifted a curved eyebrow. "And I thought we were getting along so well. . . ." Her voice was low and deep, full of the blood she had taken. The night's events had distracted Belle, but now she noticed that everything about Silvija was amplified, from the swell of nipples against the black shirt to the animal gloss and weight of her braids lying against her neck and shoulders.

She forced herself to look at the new arrivals. It was the same threesome from the night of her death. The first two were a matched set. Sepia-toned skin, round faces with a touch of Asia in the eyes. Tall beauties with straight, deadly-looking bodies. The third was a bit of a troglodyte. An almost prehistoric-looking creature with squashed features, a slight stoop, long silver hair in a braid down to her ass. Bright skin with aggressive notes of cinnamon. Her face had a touch of a smile to it. And not a nice one either.

"That one?" the troglodyte asked, responding to what Silvija had said moments before. "The only way you two would be getting along is if she was tied up and you had a cane to her backside."

"An interesting proposition." Julia giggled and slid a sly look at Belle. "I bet her screams would be lovely and loud. Like a red fire engine."

The troglodyte laughed as if Julia had made the biggest joke. Belle walked away from them and left the room. After her talk and sparring session with Silvija she was truly filthy. Her ass had hit the ground more than a few times that night. She left them to their discussions about leaving and what it would all mean for them. For Belle it meant a loss of the home she'd known all her life. Loss of the family that she'd almost killed in her new bloodlust.

Thoughts of Kylie and her mother and her sister, Claudine, haunted her through her shower. After the urgent yearning she'd felt for them days ago—the same yearning that had led her to squeeze herself through a porthole and swim God knows how many miles just to get back to them—this existence felt like a dream. Wake, kill, disobey, sleep, wake. That would be her life now. This was all she would ever know until the end of her days.

Steam misted the bathroom as the nearly scalding water poured over her in healing jets. The borrowed heat felt good on her skin, warming her flesh almost to the same temperature of the stolen blood churning inside her. Kylie. Her baby. The only person who'd given her life meaning. Now she had nothing. No one. There had been times in Naomi's life when it seemed that life was at its lowest. Times when she'd felt that there was nothing for her to do but curl up and give in. And those were the times when Kylie's love had saved her.

One day three years ago, she'd walked down the hill for home with her lip trembling from a humiliating job interview in town when the sound of arrhythmic clanking greeted her. Looking up from her defeated study of the ground, she saw Kylie, three spoons in hand, toddling up the hill toward her. Worry and warmth battled equally in Naomi's chest as she walked quickly toward her child. What the devil was Kylie doing out here by herself? Still, it felt good to see her smiling face after the bank manager's scornful dismissal of her and her qualifications.

Her daughter laughed, still clanking the spoons together, and called out, "Mama!" as if she'd been waiting for Naomi to come home. Late afternoon sunshine slanted over her cherubic bare belly and the cloth diaper fastened with two yellow duck-head pins at her hips. Except for two bare-chested boys scrambling down the dirt-covered hillside with their arms overflowing with mangoes taken from an overhanging tree still thick with fruit, the narrow lane was deserted.

"Mama!" Kylie cried out again as Naomi rushed to her, scooping the child into her arms. The spoons pressed into her neck as Kylie clung to her.

Naomi looked up, startled, when her mother rushed out of their gate a few yards down the hill. "Kylie!" Roslyn shouted, looking frantically around her with a fist clenched to her chest. "Where are you?" Water splashes darkened the front of her green blouse and tufts of graying hair peeked from the edges of her head wrap.

"It's okay, Mama! I have her." Naomi hugged Kylie to her, inhaling the baby-powder fresh scent and spreading her fingers wide over the soft skin at her daughter's back. "I have her."

In the shower, Belle's eyes burned and the tiles slid under her flattened palms. Now she had nothing. As the tears threatened to spill, she closed her eyes and swallowed.

Then she thought of the woman from earlier that night. The softness of her throat. The sea salt scent of her under the dress. If she couldn't be with her daughter she would at least try for that. The woman—Belle didn't even know her name— was in pain and yearned for something. She understood that.

She got into bed with less reluctance at sunrise, even though there were three others making the enormous bed less so. They all crowded around Silvija, touching the giant and making it impossible for Belle to get close herself. The bed was soft and comfortable. She sank down into the mattress and it arranged her, dropping her down between one of the twins and Julia. Belle must have made a noise of protest, suddenly exhausted beyond all thought, because they moved themselves in an undulating wave, adjusted until she was flush against Silvija's broad back. The troglodyte's hip pressed close to her other side, and one of the twins, wearing a long shirt that scratched at Belle's skin, crawled over and settled on top of her, his head in the soft dip between her breasts and hips. Better. Their multilayered scents—lime, jasmine, cloves, bergamot, cinnamon—wrapped themselves around Belle and followed her down into sleep.

The three other vampires weren't just there for company. Silvija set them loose on Belle for the next few nights, to teach her more about fighting and self-defense. After a quick supervised hunt and feeding, the lackeys—Belle couldn't think of them as anything else—took her to an old, crumbling building with vast untamed grounds surrounding it, and wore her out. They taught her to fight with knives, with her fists, with a staff, even with guns.

"We live in perilous times," one of the twins, Ivy, said. "People are dangerous. We must learn to be more so."

Stephen, her brother, agreed, telling her to get a gun as soon as they reached "home." Belle flinched at the word. She was already home. Even with the constant drills and exhaustion and the easy anger always churning inside her, Belle knew she was home. Jamaica, the island of the burning moonrise and silken sway of hibiscus in silver light. The place where her daughter roamed and her mother called to the dogs for their dinner. Belle's chest hurt at the thought that she would never see these things again.

Belle let the twins hit her, take her down to the ground; then she bounced back up. The pain, no matter how fleeting, felt good. She needed it as penance for what she had done, for what she had given up. Crystal water rushing over moss-skimmed black rocks. Sunrise playing over the wet green of the banana trees. June plums swaying gold and heavy on their fragile stems. Claudine skipping across the warm sand on her day off, urging her to hurry up with the sweating packets of bag juice. Pain blossomed on the side of Belle's face and her arm came up, too late to return the blow. Too late. Soon she would be leaving home.

At the end of each night she was too tired to do more than wash the grime from her body and fall into bed. She was even too tired to butt heads with Silvija. Needless to say, the giant was pleased. On her sixth night at the cottage, she woke early. The sky still burned a skin-prickling rose outside the windows, so she showered and dressed, waiting for it to fully sink beyond the horizon before she left the house. Her new family slept on in the bed.

She crept back to the scene of the party on that first night, easily finding the high gates, the plum-colored house, and the gazebo where she'd pressed against that delicious woman.

Her scent still lingered there, smeared across the railing, trailing through the air. Belle followed it. She didn't have to go very far for its source, only to a neighborhood barely half a mile away. Literally, the next hilltop over. The trappings of wealth were no big surprise—the Range Rover, three-car garage, spiraling stairs that led to a fantastic skylight and balcony with a view of the rocky coast. She could see all that from the outside. With all their money they should have gotten a real security system.

Belle leapt up to the bedroom balcony, grasping the smooth iron with her hands and swinging her legs over. This time the woman wouldn't be drunk. She would need more of an explanation. More wooing. Belle had worn black again and had pulled her hair back. After she had her in her arms, melting with lust, perhaps then she would let her know that it was a woman who made her feel such pleasure.

As Belle touched the curved handles of the bedroom's French doors, her nose told her that there was something wrong. The smell was too good. Too immediately tempting. But she ignored the warning. The doors swung easily open. The woman was already on the bed, sprawled out on the burgundy sheets, her face turned away from the French doors.

"It's funny that we keep meeting like this," Belle said, or at least that's what she was going to say until she noticed that the sheets weren't burgundy at all.

A killer had laid the woman open with a knife, spilled her life all over the bed, all around the room. And she made the motivation look like something it wasn't, dragged the woman's skirts up to her waist, ripped the bodice of the expensive little summer dress, baring her top to bottom and bloodying her thighs.

Her dream woman looked empty. Not the drowsy, just-fucked look Belle craved, no look at all, really, just the dead of her eyes staring into nothing. The horror of it clawed up in her throat. That someone could take something of hers when she wasn't finished with it. Belle threw a single hot glance around the room to see if the killer had left anything behind. A clue. Anything. She didn't have to. Belle knew who was to blame.

She was a fast learner. Her nose tracked Silvija, searched out the thieving bitch's whereabouts. Belle ran straight at her, to hell with the consequences. As she came at her with her eyes wild and fingers hooked to talons, Silvija laughed.

"I wasn't even sure that you'd be able to find her." No coyness. No denials about what she had done.

"God damn you." Belle didn't have a name for the churning cold feeling that had taken over her body. It was beyond anger. Beyond any fury she had felt before.

"Perhaps." Silvija smiled.

She flew at Silvija with her newly learned skills. The older fiend only laughed as she blocked the amateurish blows. Then, when she'd had enough, she knocked Belle back against a tree and pinned her to it by the throat. She lifted her so the two of them were at the same height. Belle struggled silently at the weight pushing at her throat, flailing her legs in the air and grabbing at the unyielding hand, even though she must have looked ridiculous. The tree's rough bark scraped at her back, digging in through her clothes. But there was no pain. She was beyond it.

"You do not endanger us. Do not form frivolous attachments. This family of ours is everything. That human was nothing." Silvija stared long into Belle's eyes, still holding her up against the tree, showing her strength and dominion over her. Then the giant shook her once, as if to make sure she understood this lesson, before releasing her. "If you're finished with your hysterics, let's go back to the house."

Much later, Belle would realize that while it was Julia who had turned her into a beast, it was Silvija who taught her how to be cruel.

Chapter 9

She woke up thinking about murder. Well, it really wouldn't be murder since the beast was already dead, was it? Belle stared down at the giant in their shared bed. The beast was beautiful. There was no denying that. In the quiet darkness of the bedroom, Silvija lay with her head back against the sheets, showing off the fine curve of her neck, her strong jawline, and the feathery brush of her eyelashes against her cheeks. Julia lay against her breasts, smiling in her demon sleep, a hand splayed possessively over the beast's muscled belly.

Belle pulled away from them, although her skin nearly groaned at the loss of contact. The sun was still high outside the windows, and the day warm. She knelt in the bed, watching in silence, wanting to rip the skin from the beast's face and feed it to Julia before burning them both to hell. How possible was it? As quickly as the thought brushed through her mind, she was leaning over Silvija and slashing down with a clawed hand. The beast's eyes flew open and she jerked out of Belle's path. Her fingers sliced through the sheets and before she could adjust her balance, the beast was up from under Julia and behind Belle, her hands grabbing roughly at Belle's upper arms and immobilizing her. The other beasts in the bed didn't stir, she was so quiet.

"What am I going to do with you, puppy?" Silvija hissed, her lips a mere breath from Belle's.

Obviously the question was purely rhetorical. In the end, she tied Belle up. She quietly lifted her up from the bed without even a grimace of effort and dragged Belle through the house, past the open doors of the other bedrooms, through the dark sitting room, and down even darker stairs to a room that smelled like blood and iron. She locked the door behind them.

"I've tried to be patient with you."

While Silvija was preoccupied with the lock, Belle twisted away and tried to run. The beast backhanded her and she slipped down the half dozen steps to land on her back. She grunted. Then the beast was over her, lifting her up and twisting her hands behind her back before propelling her backward toward the strong iron smells.

"I've tried to be *nice* to you." With quick, efficient movements, she shackled Belle with the dangling manacles and leg irons on the floor.

"What the fuck are you doing?" Belle looked around in alarm.

She was in a damn dungeon straight out of a horror movie with thick brick walls, a torture rack on the far side of the room, and, near the far wall, two sets of manacles hanging from the ceiling. The iron abraded Belle's wrists as she tugged at them, glaring bloody murder at Silvija. The chains stretched her arms apart and up, just as the leg irons pulled her feet apart. Belle was stretched wide open and vulnerable in her thin, knee-length nightgown. The beast could do anything to her down here.

Belle hissed, "Let me go."

"That's not an option at the moment."

Silvija cranked a lever on the wall near them and the chains holding Belle rattled, then pulled tight, stretching her arms up and back, until she was almost on her toes. Her ass jutted up, her back curved in.

When she'd brought Belle downstairs, the beast had neglected to put on clothes. In the darkness, illuminated only by Belle's eyesight, she glowed. The cinnamon skin radiated strength and power, bringing attention to the impressive muscles writhing just beneath. Against her will, Belle became very aware of the high breasts and their hard, crowning nipples. Her curving ribs and muscled belly slid away beneath them. The curved hips, bushy mound, sturdy thighs and legs all proclaimed her strength. This was not a delicate woman.

Belle knew that she might have gone too far in the bed with Silvija, but she would never admit it to the beast, not even if that was the reason she had her tied up like a slave in this damn dungeon. But the beast had made her angry. She had taken her toy. She had taken her life and was forcing her to go to a place she didn't want to go.

"Is this about that stupid girl?" When Belle didn't answer, Silvija's mouth twisted. "She's not worth it."

"She was worth it to me."

"Worth what? A quick fuck? Or a 'fuck you' to me?" She sneered again. "Either way, trust me, it wasn't. Your rebellion is pointless. You're just going to hurt yourself in the process and make yourself look foolish."

"You mean that *you're* going to hurt me and make me look foolish."

Silvija smiled coolly. "Whichever."

The beast was furious. Belle could tell. The anger simmered just beneath the surface of her skin like human heat.

"Let me go, Silvija."

"No. You obviously cannot handle freedom."

Belle growled. "Listen. To. Me. Bitch." She rattled the chains imprisoning her arms. "Let me the fuck out of these chains."

"Or what?"

"Is that what you want?" Belle rattled the chains again. "For me to threaten you?"

"No, that's not what I want. But that's been what you've been doing since I met you. Empty threats and provocations that have only managed to completely piss me off."

She stalked back and forth in front of Belle, watching her, then looking away. With each provoking word that Belle uttered she grew closer until each motion she made in front of Belle left a slight breeze.

"This is pointless," Belle said, finally calming down. "Let me go."

"Why? Is it because you don't like being under someone else's control? Or because you don't like being under *my* control?"

"You don't control me, bitch."

"What did I tell you that first day?" She didn't wait for Belle to answer. "This is my clan. Julia bit you. She is my clan, so you are of my clan. You are *all* under my protection."

"Do you just get off on this power trip? Is this the only way you can really control your women? To bring them down here and torture them, make them bleed? This is obviously the only way you can think of to control me."

Silvija shot forward suddenly and bunched Belle's nightgown into a shaking fist. "Why do you always take things one step further, hmm?"

Belle spat in her face. Silvija's eyes flashed. She moved back abruptly, taking pieces of Belle's nightgown with her. Cool air washed over Belle's skin. Silvija deliberately wiped the spit from her face with the pieces of Belle's nightgown. Her face was granite hard, and cold. "Is that how you want to play it?"

Silvija's eyes flickered over her face and body, missing nothing. Not her rebellious look, not the scornful twist of her mouth, and certainly not the contempt blazing from her eyes. Pieces of Belle's split nightgown hung limply off her shoulders and hips. One shrug and those bits would fall to the floor, leaving her completely naked. False breath shuddered in her throat and she felt her breasts move, the tips standing up in the cool air.

"You may not understand yourself now, but I know. You

want something from me, puppy. I'm assuming that you find it hard to ask for, but that's all right. I'll give it to you anyway." The cool eyes licked over her again. "But only this once. Next time, next time"—her voice was gravelly and thick—"you'll have to beg me for it."

Silvija walked slowly around Belle, taking her time stirring up the prickles of awareness on the bound woman's skin. The air stilled when she stopped behind her. Belle didn't give her the satisfaction of twisting her head around to see what Silvija was doing. She would be stoic. She would wait for whatever the beast thought would move her. Belle steeled herself against the pain that was sure to come.

A breath of sensation seared down her back. Her skin flinched from it, but the touch was surprisingly gentle. It remained steady and light, threading down the valley of her spine, licking over the rise of her ass, before flaring back up to her shoulder blades. Hands moved through the air, leaving a slight breeze in their wake. The breeze brushed the sensitive skin over her ass; then it was the hands themselves, shaping the rounded flesh, cupping her. Fingers glided down the backs of her thighs and calves. The beginnings of arousal flared under her skin and spread quickly. She shivered.

Stretched as she was, her body anticipating the sting of pain, the gentle sensation was jarring. And much worse. She ground her teeth together and pulled at the manacles holding her arms captive. That pain grounded her, made her rerealize why she was here. This pleasure wasn't real. It was poisonous. As much as the source of it was.

"Stop it."

But Silvija didn't stop. The fingers brushed between Belle's thighs, avoiding her intimate place. Then disappeared. The breeze came again when Silvija stood up. She didn't speak. Belle breathed a sigh of relief. But it came too soon. The fingers came back. This time, they flickered out to stroke her belly from behind. She slammed her head back, hoping to catch the beast in the face, but Silvija was lower. Deliberate breath coated the small of her back.

"Fuck you," Belle ground out between her teeth.

The fingers danced over the muscles stretched tight in her stomach, over the flare of ribs, then up to the sensitive underside of her breasts. Sensation writhed in her belly. Hands cupped her breasts, stroked the heavy globes, but avoided the turgid nipples. Belle looked down and saw her shame, nipples plumping up in Silvija's hands, hard and ripe, mere millimeters from the stroking fingers. She felt the giant's tongue on the small of her back. The tongue dipped lower and then teeth scraped the tender skin at the top of her ass the same time that fingers brushed her nipples. A noise escaped Belle. The fingers tugged and flicked her nipples while Silvija bit her from behind. Belle's mind deserted her. Her hips pushed against the air. She pulled against the manacles, scraping her wrists. Words came from behind her, words muffled by the press of skin. They sank into her, incomprehensible but arousing, stoking the flames of her desire.

"No." *No. No. No.* She couldn't want this humiliation. But the movement of her hips proved her wrong. She didn't know whether she fought against the manacles to kill Silvija or to touch her in return. "No. . . ."

The fingers and tongue disappeared. Belle was breathing heavily, unnecessarily, but couldn't stop herself. When she opened her eyes—when had she closed them?—Silvija stood in front of her. The beast's eyes were heavy-lidded and savage. It seemed then that the lesson was over, but Silvija reached out. Her hands snagged in Belle's hair and pulled her head back. She buried her face in Belle's throat just as her hand grabbed the outthrust ass and pulled it close. Silvija's thigh pushed between hers, slid against the shame of her desire. Her pussy wept. The big thigh muscle smoothly stroked her, abraded the delicate flesh of her exposed cunt lips, and her clit. The echoes of their fucking sounded loudly in the room.

She would not shame herself by begging, but she was so close to it. So close. Silvija licked her throat, nuzzled her, while her thigh worked against Belle. The heated clove scent of her was overwhelming. Their bodies together seemed to generate another kind of heat. One different from the kind expelled when they were piled together in sleep. This heat blossomed under Belle's skin like the sun, incinerating, smoldering. She cried out.

That sound woke Silvija from the trance she had fallen into. The beast moved away from her throat and down Belle's body. The loss of that heat made her want to shout out in pain. This was too much. She tugged harder at the manacles, curling her fingers together so they could slip past the iron. Blood began to seep down her wrists.

Silvija's nose burrowed into the curls at the tops of her thighs. She inhaled deeply and whispered something, something that Belle wasn't meant to hear. But she did. She did.

"So sweet," Silvija said in wonder. "So sweet." Then she took Belle's clit in her mouth. Her world imploded. That's what it felt like as Silvija sucked on her flesh like it was the most delicious thing she'd ever had in her mouth. Belle gasped and her knees went weak. She stumbled against Silvija and the beast pushed her back upright without relieving her of the blissful torture of her mouth. Belle's hands and fingers scraped against the iron manacles as they finally slid free. Her own blood smell threatened to suffocate her, to drown her deeper in the bubbling vat of forced pleasure and pain. Her hands were raw and bleeding, but she wanted them all over Silvija.

She fell, pushing the tall beast from between her legs and flat against the dirty floor. Silvija grunted and dragged Belle beneath her, pinning the shackled body beneath her superior weight. Her flesh was so hot. The beast's naked belly and breasts pressed into hers. Belle did the only thing that seemed right, she grabbed the beast's face and kissed her.

Silvija tasted of wildness and a wind-tossed sea. Her senses

reveled, disbelieving in the untamed thing over her. Silvija
didn't fight her mouth, she fought *for* it, biting at Belle's lips,
forcing them apart to plunder the tender pink flesh within.
Belle bit her back. Their blood bubbled together, melded
until they were both drunk on each other and writhing on the
floor. Why did she taste so good?

Silvija abruptly pulled her up with a grunt and followed
Belle's body with her own. Belle's bare bottom skimmed across
the floor and her thighs strained from the awkward position
of being pushed flat on the floor alongside her shackled legs.
Silvija pulled her back to her knees and thrust her fingers
deeply inside her. Belle staggered.

But she held on to Silvija's face, catching her fingers in the
multitude of plaits, pulling her harder against her ravenous
mouth. It didn't make sense that she wanted the beast so
much. The fingers moved inside her, fucking her with firm,
deep strokes. She gasped her delight into Silvija's mouth,
telling with her nimble tongue how much she loved her fingers inside, how the trembling in her thighs was a good thing,
how fantastic it was to feel her world exploding.

She died again. And it was better than the first time. She
clutched at Silvija and let sensation take her away. Belle
panted in the beast's arms, trembling in the aftermath of her
orgasm. Silvija gently lifted her away and laid her on the
floor. The rough concrete scraped her cheek and her palms.
Dust and dirt billowed up with each exhalation of her
breath. She squeezed her eyes shut. *No. no. no.* The manacles
tugged at her ankles, but she barely felt them.

Silvija stood up and scrubbed her hand over her hair before looking down at Belle. Something in Belle's eyes made
her back away toward the stairs. If she had hurt her, it would
have been better. It would have made sense for her to flare up
in anger and smash everything that Silvija was into the dirty
floor beneath her feet. But she didn't. Instead, she made her
feel. Her body still throbbed with satisfaction and her mouth
was full of the taste of Silvija.

The beast stood naked at the bottom of the stairs with Belle's bloody handprints streaked across her face. She blinked once, twice, then regained her composure.

"I can make your body do anything that I want," she said. "Anything. And don't you ever forget it."

And she left her. Belle blinked at the disappearing figure through the flickering haze of her hatred and lust.

She was a beast. Only one thing could have put her close to humanity again. And that thing was gone, taken by Silvija. Belle freed herself from the leg shackles and crawled upstairs to lie in bed beside Julia, not touching the beast. Hours later, she left the house before everyone else did, braving the last traces of the setting sun to flee into the jungle surrounding the cottage. She'd let Silvija, a thing that she hated more than death itself, touch her. And she'd enjoyed it. The humiliation of crying for release, of wanting to taste the dripping cunt so temptingly close. All these things made her a beast. She'd never been a slave to her emotions. Never.

When she'd decided it was time to have a child, she'd chosen Clifford with a cold-blooded calculation she'd hid even from her mother. He had been attractive, didn't chase anything in skirts, and had a good job. It didn't matter that he'd only dated smaller women before her, or that his preference tended toward lighter-skinned women with connections abroad. She wanted him to be the father of her child.

Naomi had seduced him and held him enslaved between her thighs for weeks. By the time he realized that she was not what he wanted, she was already pregnant and content. She barely noticed when he left. Only her baby, her Kylie, had touched her deeply, had made her feel things against her will that were separate from her destructive desire for women.

Kylie. Her daughter's name sang through her blood as she ran through the woods. She wasn't sure how far her old home was from the cottage, but she would get there. She was more surefooted in the dark now; she was mastering some of the arts of camouflage that the beasts were teaching her. This time she knew that she wouldn't be seen.

The moon was a glowing halo overhead. Without Silvija's presence she felt free to enjoy its luminous perfection against the inky sky. Was Kylie watching the sky like she was? Or was her daughter playing on their small verandah, heedless of the miraculous beauty that shone down on her beautiful face? It didn't matter. As long as Kylie lived.

Belle heard voices approaching from the dusty street. Four men, one woman, and a child between them. Her fangs emerged with sudden awareness of hunger. She'd left the house too fast, neglecting to eat, and now . . . Belle tightened her jaw, pulling the hunger back. She wasn't ready to feed.

At her old house, she watched the women she loved go about their lives. While Roslyn cleaned up the dinner table, Kylie walked outside to feed the dogs leftovers from their meal of stewed chicken and rice. Belle smelled the remnants of the food as Kylie scraped the plates clean, dropping bits of rice and bones to the ground while the two dogs rushed around her small frame to eat. In the two weeks since Naomi had been gone, Kylie's face had fallen. Her mouth no longer pulled up automatically at its corners, and her eyes pointed downward like large brown tears. The muscles in Belle's jaw tightened.

From the safety of a distant tree, their petty routines comforted her. When she was alive, all this had seemed so boring—washing dishes, taking food to the ailing neighbors, locking up the house in preparation for sleep, but of course now she treasured those simple tasks. And hated herself even more for giving them up.

As she watched, a steady stream of people passed the yard. Most went through the gate to pay their respects to the bereaved family of two. Some even brought plates of food, adding to the mound that was already doubtless in the house. Mama wouldn't have to cook for days, maybe weeks with this steady outpouring of charity. While the women went in the house or lingered on the verandah to talk with Kylie and Mama, the men loitered by the gates, watching the dirt road for signs of something that wasn't supposed to be there. Like Belle. She watched them from her perch and sneered.

Fools. Belle tried to tell herself that it didn't matter now. But Kylie laughed at something the dog did, rearranging the somber lines of her face, and broke her mother's heart all over again. Belle laid her cheek against the rough tree bark. Her family wasn't quite happy, but they were healing. It wasn't something she would have chosen for them, but it obviously wasn't a decision that she could take back.

Tears sprang behind her eyes. A faint sting, but they didn't fall. The image of her daughter playing with the white dog blurred before she blinked and set her vision to rights. Belle remembered, suddenly, that it was the dog who had taught Kylie how to walk. When Kylie was nearly a year old, Naomi had stepped onto the verandah to see her daughter holding fast to Coco's neck with both hands and pulling herself up-right. Naomi stopped and held on to the door frame, just barely preventing herself from rushing toward her daughter in case the dog reacted badly to the stranglehold that Kylie had on her. But Coco was patient through the ordeal of Kylie finally standing, then craning her neck to look at her sur-roundings from the new height. Then the dog began to walk off and Kylie stumbled along with her for four steps before letting go to walk two more steps on her own. When she tried a third step, Kylie staggered and fell back to her bottom on the hard tile floor. She looked startled, then vexed with her tiny forehead wrinkled in a frown at Coco, who trotted off into the yard to lie on a soft patch of grass in the sun. Before Kylie could start crying, Naomi ran to her, covering her darling with kisses and worry. But Kylie didn't cry; she only squealed with happiness at being swept up into her mother's arms, her fall and Coco forgotten.

Belle blinked again. This life was the past. It was time that both she and her family learned to live without each other.

* * *

Belle waited until Roslyn and Kylie slept and most of their protectors were long gone before going into the house. With silent footsteps, she went in the back way, careful to walk upwind of the dogs and men lurking nearby.

Her bedroom was empty. When she was alive she and Kylie slept peacefully in it while Mama had the larger room to herself. Now Roslyn shared her room with Kylie. Belle listened to their quiet breathing as she walked through the house, being careful to disturb nothing. There was only one thing she wanted.

Their breaths were spiced with blood, the smell of them so deliciously tempting that she stopped in the hallway to look at the closed door they slept behind. Their rest was peaceful, untainted by knowledge of beasts in their small community.

Her teeth blossomed again to stretch her mouth and jaw. It would be so easy. . . . Belle walked past their bedroom and into Naomi's. The room was painfully human. It held all of her old smells, the Provence-made lavender perfume that she sparingly used to indulge herself with, a lingering scent of the menstrual cycle she'd had before she left for Negril. The old blood smell made Belle ache. She wanted those simple hurts again, hurts that merely signaled another passing month in her human life. But those were behind her. Belle glanced quickly around the room, at the neatly made bed, the dresser with brush, comb, and deodorants, before taking what she came for. She was done and out of the house within seconds, dashing quickly away from the temptation of killing and the memory of Naomi.

She ran through and out of the neighborhood as if she was being chased, but the thing she longed to escape followed her all too closely. Barely eleven o'clock and she was ravenous. She'd done it. She'd proved to herself that she wasn't the beast that Silvija and the others thought she was. Kylie and Mama were safe in their beds and that small part of her humanity was intact.

But that thought didn't stop her from savaging the first person she saw. Belle brought the old man down with vicious efficiency, rushing out of the green to sweep his legs, his cane, from beneath him and drop him to the ground. He barely had time to gasp before she snapped her jaws shut on his carotid.

She was so filled with humanity that she didn't make the old man suffer. Belle brought him down quickly under her clawed hands, giving him only the barest moment to register what would happen to him. His cane fell away, bouncing against the unpaved road. He called out once, but that was all. His wrinkled throat smelled of medicines and camphor, but it was what beat beneath his skin that interested her most.

His life rushed hot and sweet into her mouth. She turned his head out of her way, barely registering the snap of his neck and the brush of his bristly beard against her face. His hands came up to push her off, but she swept them away like bothersome twigs. Belle crouched over him, her senses open and taking in everything—his failing heartbeat, the shallow breaths he took, a faint unthreatening presence in the woods near them. Heat flowed deliciously through her body, warming her, banishing the chill that had flowed into her at the house. The old man's struggles dwindled and the last of his life poured into her. His body shuddered finally and let go.

She looked up and felt the moonlight burrow into the curves of her face, shining over the slackening tension in her features that feeding caused. Her blood-smeared mouth twitched. Belle stretched, elongating her body over him, feeling the life fill her, expand her rib cage, fill her veins and muscles with renewed power. Her vertebrae popped one by one as she stood up. It wasn't quite the same as taking someone young and healthy; the age-flavored blood flowing through him had been a nice change.

Silvija was watching her. She could feel the beast's eyes, but Belle carried on as usual. She snapped the old man's walking stick in half and used the splinted edge of one of the pieces to slash his throat, eradicating her bite marks. Blood splashed up into her face and she licked her lips to bring an errant drop into her mouth. His body barely stirred in the dirt.

For a moment, Belle stood still over him, looking at the gaunt, lifeless frame. Once, she had known this man's name. He was a family friend, someone who trusted the beast who now wore Naomi's face. The moonlight was kind to him in death even after her savagery. Belle touched the small locket dangling from the slim gold chain at her throat, the one she had taken from the bedroom. It held a picture of Kylie and of Naomi, of how they were barely six months ago. Mother and daughter. Inseparable. Human. Her hand dropped from her throat and she closed her eyes. When she opened them, the old man was still there at her feet, and she was still a beast. Belle nodded once, finally accepting. A breeze came up and brought the scent of cloves. She turned quickly and walked into the underbrush, leaving the old man to head back to her new family.

Chapter 10

She stepped into the clearing near the cottage. Behind her, the scent of Silvija wavered in the light breeze, as if uncertain whether to come closer or stay away. But not so with the beast. The origin of that scent had gone downwind, perhaps even circling from the front of the cottage to enter through the back door.

"Are you hiding from somebody?" Ivy asked from the verandah.

Stephen looked at something beyond Belle, then refocused on her. "Or is somebody hiding from *you*?" he asked, his voice barely an octave lower than his sister's.

He lay on the bench swing, his head in his sister's lap, one leg flung over the far arm of the bench as they rocked in the gentle breeze. With his black hair loose around his head, he looked more like a woman than ever, almost identical to Ivy except for a slight broadness of the shoulders and the lightly protruding Adam's apple.

"I hope you and Silvija don't end up killing each other," Ivy murmured, threading her fingers through Stephen's hair. "I was just starting to like you." Her eyes sparkled wickedly in the moonlight.

"Behave," Stephen said, practically purring under her hands.

Silvija emerged from the house. "I'm glad you could grace us with your presence tonight." She lashed Belle with her gaze before looking at the twins. "Get ready. We leave for Port Royal in two hours."

So much for a month.

Chapter 11

The air swept up, salty and wet from the sea, bringing with it a scent of the storm a few hundred miles away. In Port Royal, it was calm. The *Ynez*, Silvija's yacht, bobbed in the water ready for departure save for the absence of one of its passengers. It wasn't Belle. She was rooted by inevitability to the dock where they waited, watching Stephen and Ivy run back and forth on the oversized boat performing last-minute checks while the ashen waters of the Caribbean Sea beat a sad tattoo, a good-bye, against its hull.

The troglodyte, Susannah, was still somewhere in the bush, but no one seemed worried, least of all Silvija, who Belle couldn't stand the sight of just now. She should have let it go—she herself had done much worse—but she didn't.

Belle heard Susannah before she saw her, the heavy footsteps making their way down the narrow sloped path leading away from the house, then on the sand skimming toward the boat. Of course, Silvija had a house here too, posh and palatial, with a humbling view of the harbor town and the sea beyond. Belle watched Susannah lope across the sand with a crocus bag slung across her shoulders. She barely acknowledged the younger vampire, merely nodding once before swinging with a curious grace up the gangplank steps, announcing her arrival to anyone who would listen.

Julia suddenly appeared at the railing high above Belle's head. "All aboard, sweet."

Belle found her room, the one they had locked her in the first time, and sank into the embracing bed. She didn't stir when, much later, cool flesh pressed against hers until the bed was an almost-warm cocoon. Soon, she felt them all—Julia, Ivy, Stephen, and Susannah—drift into sleep. But she couldn't.

"Why don't you come into the control room with me?"

Belle blinked at the unexpected rumble of Silvija's voice beside her. She wanted to tell her to fuck off, but she wasn't about to get any sleep and, strangely, the beast's company was better than none. Belle slipped quietly from the bed; then Silvija did the same, leading her out of the room into an adjoining office and a short flight of stairs going down.

They were indeed in a control room. A half dozen monitors showed different views of the boat—straight ahead where it cruised apparently on automatic pilot, on the sun-washed deck, even behind them where the yacht left trailing ripples in the bright blue ocean. Three computer keyboards, a smaller bank of monitors and switches, and what looked like a joystick for a video game completed the equipment in the high-tech nook.

Belle's eyes swept over the equipment, to the automatic rifles and pistols fitted into brackets on the walls before looking fully at Silvija. "Did you bring me here to rape me again?"

The beast's eyelashes fluttered in surprise, the first emotion Belle had seen other than anger and lust, from her.

"I did *not* rape you," she hissed.

"Say whatever you want, we both know what that day was about and what you did. But since that's not what you brought me here for, get to the point. I'm all ears."

Violence hummed in the body folded into the leather seat next to Belle's, but Silvija didn't approach her. Something else hummed between them too. Something that had more to do with the memory of come and sweat and desire licking over heated skin.

Silvija's jaw twitched. "There are some things that we need to get clear before we get home."

"More rules that I, and no one else, should follow?"

"If you choose to see things that way . . ." She let the trailing silence speak for itself.

Belle clenched her teeth, but said nothing.

"First, Alaska is your home now." She ignored Belle's flashing look. "You have access to everything in the house and on the grounds. This includes the cars, snowmobiles, and airplanes. Don't make me regret trusting you with these things."

"What if I want to fly myself back to Jamaica?" Even as she said it, Belle knew that it was an impossibility. There was no place for her on the island anymore.

"That's not an option," Silvija said. "Not right now. When you're ready, one of us, Liam, will teach you how to fly. If you can't drive, he'll teach you how to do that too." She paused. "I'm telling you this now because when we get home I probably won't have the time. And I doubt that Julia will think to let you know these things."

Her last words fell off into silence. Belle watched her and still said nothing.

Silvija pursed her lips. "I won't apologize for what I did. It was a necessary exercise and, I think, you enjoyed it."

Belle jackknifed out of her seat and came at Silvija.

"*Don't* do it." The giant didn't move. Her eyes flickered over Belle's face. "There's no shame in enjoying your body. Granted, it wasn't under circumstances that you found ideal, but I believe that I made my point." Her nostrils flared. "Know your place. Don't fuck with me. And everything should be more than tolerable for you."

The urge to rip Silvija's face from her bones impelled Belle forward. She stopped just short of the beast.

"One day you'll learn not to disrespect me," she said. "And it won't be a gentle lesson."

Silvija bared her teeth. "Whenever you're ready, here I am."

A growl rose in Belle's throat. She jammed her clenched fist into the pocket of her robe and left Silvija alone.

Chapter 12

Before she knew, Belle thought that vampires weren't supposed to sweat. But here she was with Silvija's pussy open against her own, the beast staring hard into her eyes, their bodies slick perfection as the sheets beneath them ran wet with bloodied sweat. It was an addiction. There was no other name for it. When the beast had walked into the stateroom, she should have told it to get out, to find someone else to play with. But one look from her and Belle reached out, blindly, sinking her fingers into heavy braids and pulling Silvija close, and closer. Her lips were fire and ice. Silvija's teeth scraped her in their haste to mate, to reconnect. They stumbled backward toward the bed, but didn't make it. Instead they dropped to the floor with Silvija straddling her and ripping off her own clothes at the same time to get their flesh where it belonged—together.

All Belle had on was a robe. It was gone in a moment, pushed quickly out of the way so Silvija could cup her breasts and squeeze her nipples with something like awe in her face. Belle's skin sang with sensation. The morning of their confrontation in the control room, Belle had lain awake wondering why she hated and lusted after the beast with equal intensity. But she wasn't wondering now. She just wanted.

Her belly jumped when Silvija flicked her blunt nails down its length and her legs quickly fell open. *Oh!* And she was inside. Being taken had never felt this good. The beast's fingers moved inside her, creating heat and everything else that Belle knew as dangerous. Silvija's fingers slid inside her with liquid accuracy. Each thrust brought her hips up, searching for more pleasure, more contact, more sensation, more of Silvija. The beast's mouth was open. Belle watched her with wonder, with ferocious possession as she fucked Belle's hips off the floor.

"Harder," Belle hissed into Silvija's ear and fumbled up, grasping a hard nipple between her fingers and squeezing. "Yes."

Belle's fingers scraped down Silvija's muscled back, down to the hips and ass that flexed and released, as though the thing between her legs, her clit, the thing that Belle wanted in her mouth, was doing the fucking, was bringing her to that point of—fuck! Her back skimmed across the floor with each movement of Silvija's fingers inside her. Her clit felt thick and explosive with each frictioned caress.

"Now," she gasped. "Now." And the beast reached even deeper, reaching for that place. Her hand moved faster. Her fingers curved. And she found it.

"Oh! Sil—" Her words fell away and her body shuddered inside, the quake spreading from her pussy, through her limbs until the whole of her was shuddering, trembling, and Silvija was over her, inside her, still fucking the sensations out of her. Belle clenched her eyes and saw constellations. Her entire sky lit up with Silvija and the incendiary desire the beast flared inside her.

She panted, still staring up at the beast, who glared at her as if she was responsible for something namelessly horrible. She lifted Belle and threw her on the bed. The mattress bounced once, twice, and then Silvija was on top of her, dropping her thigh abruptly between Belle's.

"Don't say anything," she said. "Just let me fuck you."

Right. Even with Silvija's electricity firing through her body, Belle hadn't lost her mind. She abruptly flipped over and pushed the beast onto her back. Silvija's hands rose to reverse their positions, but Belle slid a hand between the beast's legs and her resistance became a deep moan. Silvija's clit was thick, hard, and distended, wet with her juices that Belle longed to lick. But that was for another time.

The beast's thighs widened and Belle moved her own thigh between them, quickly positioning herself between the beast's spread legs so that her pussy was pushed against Silvija's. She turned her body perpendicular to the beast to increase the contact between them. Perfect. Silvija's leg rose up and Belle grabbed it, kissing the sweat-slick knee, biting it until little blood drops popped up on the soft flesh. The beast groaned again and flung her head back against her sheets. Belle pushed her clit against the beast's in a sweet liquid motion that set her sky on fire again. She reached out, molding Silvija's breast with her hand, squeezing the nipple in rhythm to her leisurely cunt ride.

Silvija growled and reared up in the bed, tumbling Belle from atop her and pinning her back firmly to the sheets. Her thigh moved between the smaller beast's until her pussy was flush against Belle's thigh and Belle's cunt lay under the thigh muscles, lips wide open, clit throbbing again and begging to be touched.

"Give me what I came here for," Silvija hissed in Belle's throat, teeth nipping at the tautly stretched skin as Belle sighed in the bed.

Belle's skin flared with desire, the flesh shuddering as if a thousand pleasure beetles scurried over it, burrowing into it. It was torture, this feeling that she had for Silvija. She pressed up against the thrusting thigh for more. The blood bubbled madly beneath her skin and she fought against the urge to scream. And lost.

The beast grunted as she moved over her, shoving their bodies together in a hard, frantic rhythm that rattled the bed, brought blood-tinged sweat rushing to the surface of Belle's skin, had her clawing at Silvija's ass, her back, the sheets, her own hair. The heat curled up in her belly and slammed into the cradle of her hips. Silvija's eyes bored into hers as she brought them both closer, thrusting her thigh, her whole body into Belle until the weight of it, the heat of it threatened to destroy them both. But she wanted this destruction. She wanted this pain. She wanted Silvija.

Belle's pussy slid hot and wet against the invading thigh, and she arched up, gasping and grasping at the beast that tore her sanity to shreds, making her acknowledge nothing else in the universe but her, nothing on this boat but her, even though everything she hated was her.

The eyes pinned her to the bed. They were hot and heated, watching the blood sweat drip down Belle's face, watching her lick her own lips and gasp as if she needed this air when all she needed was this heat in her belly, this hard flesh against her cunt, this hard body slapping against hers.

Silvija flung her head up and back, baring her gorgeous neck to Belle. Her flesh was sticky with sweat, the pulse thudding at her neck. Her fangs flared out, abruptly piercing the air, and she roared, shuddering against Belle. The smaller woman reached up, tempted beyond reason, grabbed the back of Silvija's neck, and bit her.

The orgasm tore viciously through Belle as Silvija's blood, stolen and still warm, gushed into her mouth. She sucked harder, riding the last waves of her orgasm on the beast's thigh. Silvija grabbed her hair and pulled Belle away from her throat.

"Get your own food," she said. But her fingers lightly caressed the back of Belle's neck before withdrawing, stealing the harshness from her words.

The blood ran swiftly down the beast's long neck and down to her breasts, but in seconds the flow became sluggish, then stopped altogether. Belle flicked a thumb across the ensanguined nipple, then sucked her finger clean.

Silvija looked down at her, at her lips. Her head dipped down and she tasted Belle, flicking her tongue across the open portal of her mouth. Belle groaned as her tongue sought entrance and gained it, dancing with hers, tasting each corner of her mouth. They both moaned. It was starting again, that incendiary flame that caught them both so quickly ablaze. Belle reached for Silvija's breasts.

"Silvija!"

The shout came from directly outside Belle's door and she flushed hotly, shrinking away from the giant. They knew she was in here. Silvija lifted her head and cocked an ear toward the door. She then looked down at Belle with regret.

"Coming." She didn't bother to raise her voice. Everyone on the boat heard her. Belle sat up as Silvija rolled from the bed and tugged her clothes on. Her eyes swept over Belle once. No words, just a promise in the flicker of her lashes. *More. Later.*

But their later did not come. Days later, after a steady diet of prepackaged blood from the ship's galley, the *Ynez* arrived in Alaska. The yacht coasted into the cold, calm waters and Belle could feel the difference. The way the air had cooled and gradually become sharper as the miles stretched between her and Jamaica. This was truly an alien land. She rose from her chill bed—the others had long since gone—put on the flowing white cotton robe that had become her favorite, and slipped outside to the top deck.

The beauty of the landscape surprised her, held her immobile at the high railing, staring up and out. Belle shuddered. She was used to ice in her glass. Not like this, rising up from the sea in jagged arcs of blue bright enough to rival the sky's on a sun-flushed day. The *Ynez* knifed through the water past rising mountains of white, a green landscape mottled with splashes of blue water and teeming with life. Far off on land, she could see a few scattered humans walking on the docks in their fur-lined coats, or walking toward the village of plain single-story buildings near the water. The sun was gone, but she could see remnants of it in the sky, a timid pink rapidly retreating under the full glare of night. She could barely feel the cold. Her skin interpreted it as mild buffeting air only a few degrees cooler than her body's internal temperature.

Belle closed her eyes as she rode into the wind, feeling something loosen inside her. This wouldn't be a place of unrelenting ugliness and strife after all. Almost disappointing that she was being deprived of yet another reason to hate Silvija. Her robe fluttered in the wake of the yacht's journey, flapping around her like the wings of a large bird.

The *Ynez* pulled into the dock behind a long flat house. The Cave, they called it, and Belle had shuddered at the image the word conjured. When she drew closer she saw that more than half the house was buried underground, its façade of glass and metal skimming the surface of the land like the back of a large glittering whale. Not bleak and cavelike at all.

Belle quickly backed out of the way as Ivy, Stephen, and Silvija unloaded cargo, moving to and from the house in a brisk line. For once she was grateful for Julia's presence when the smaller creature tugged her hand and pulled her toward and into the house.

Belle wasn't so far beyond human that she didn't gawk at the opulence of her new home. Everything in sight and within touching distance seemed designed to stimulate the senses. The entire house was the height of sensual indulgence. Only the entrance with its glass and metal was modern and cool. Once inside the Cave, everything was rich color and decadence. Marble, wood, and stained glass all met in a gorgeous harmony of elements that made the huge structure seem homey and welcoming yet very, very impressive. The long narrow hallway inclining gradually belowground was dotted by fantastically carved wooden benches and stretched deep into the house. Painting after painting of sunsets, sunrises, and full sun shone from nearly every wall, making the place glow with warmth. Belle immediately noticed that there were no clocks, calendars, or other timepieces in sight. Who needed those trappings when vampires, by virtue of their blood change, had essentially become timeless?

"The moonroom is my favorite," Julia said, pointing as they passed a set of open double doors.

The richly colored velvet cushions that begged to be relaxed into and the gigantic bearskin rug sprawled before the fire were the only highlights of the moonroom that Belle got the barest glimpse of before Julia led her away. She took Belle around a corner, down a flight of stairs, and into yet another hallway that terminated in a large open room.

"This is where we sleep."

She waved her hand to indicate the room where they stood. Everything seemed to be very much of a grand scale in Silvija's world. The bed was bigger than king-sized, yet still barely took up a quarter of the space, leaving room for all sorts of miscellany, including four large standing mirrors, two wardrobes, a half dozen wooden chests filled with who knew what, a giant television, and a VCR.

"If you want a separate room, there are a few empty ones farther down the hall. Pick the one you want, then let Keiko know which you'll be in from now on."

Belle never got the chance to know who this Keiko was. A young girl flew into the room and flung her arms around Julia. She was small, her waist barely a hand's width wide and her head at least a foot lower than Belle's six feet. Her moon-round face was wreathed in smiles and her eyes sparkled a velvety brown. The sheen of her white teeth was fiercely beautiful against her butter-gold skin.

"I heard the news. Is this her?" The gamine spun to Belle, looking her up and down. Her black hair stood up from her head in six perfectly symmetrical little cotton candy puffs. She held out her hand for an awkward but endearing sideways handshake.

"Hi, I'm Shaye."

Belle had no choice but to take her hand. Up close she

smelled like an herb garden, an ambiguously fresh and multi-layered scent.

The child grinned. "You're pretty. Not what I thought Jules would bring home at all. She has awful taste in lovers. Her last one tried to kill us all in our sleep."

"And this one might do the same." Silvija walked in, shedding her travel clothes as she went. Belle turned away before she could see the beast fully naked and shame herself.

"Julia and I aren't lovers, Shaye." Belle found herself talking to the girl like she talked to Kylie. She had to be no more than fifteen. "We aren't even friends."

"Is that true? You turned someone who doesn't even like you?" Shaye spun away from Julia and flopped on the bed close to where Silvija stood pulling on a pair of jeans. The giant's powerful body bent and flexed in the artificial light. She didn't have on any underwear.

"She doesn't like us as a whole, love." Silvija buttoned her jeans and turned away to rifle through one of the wardrobes. "And right now, I believe she likes me least of all."

"No one could hate you. You're the *best* of all." The girl giggled and star-fished herself flat on her back across the bed. Her mirth seemed genuine, not the put-on emotion that Julia used in her attempts to frighten Belle away. Or was it to pull her closer?

"I am the best, you're right." Silvija pulled on a black tank top, then shrugged a man-tailored shirt over it. "But a lot of people hate me. Not without reason." She leaned over to tweak the end of the child's nose. "You're the only one who loves me in spite of myself." She straightened. "Family meeting in a few." Moments later, she left the room, never once looking at Belle.

Shaye glanced between Belle and the open door where Silvija disappeared with a small frown. Then she rolled onto her side and propped her chin on a fist to look at Belle. "Silvija protects us. You shouldn't hate her. Even when she's mean, it's because she's thinking of us."

It began to filter to Belle that this little girl was a creature just like she was. Why else did Silvija treat her so fondly, not like prey, but like a peer? Or a little sister. Aside from her loveliness and the steady glow of goodness that seemed to radiate from her, Shaye could have been any of the children she'd seen on the streets of Negril. Granted, this child wore clothes that few of those children could probably afford in a lifetime, but her quicksilver energy, her playfulness, were things that immediately drew Belle to her. Even though she insisted that the giant was "the best of all." What did this child know anyway? Belle caught Julia's eye across the room, surprised that the woman was still there. The thought must have shown on her face because Julia winked, then left her alone with Shaye.

"You're Julia's first, you know." The child grinned at Belle, then patted the space beside her on the bed. "We never thought she would make a child."

Belle's annoyance flared. "I am not her child."

Shaye giggled. "You do hate her." She jumped up off the bed to study her reflection in the tall, brass-framed antique mirror leaning against the far wall. "Jules is a pussy cat once you get to know her."

"She killed me. She'll never be anything but garbage."

Shaye glanced over her shoulder at Belle. "We're all the same. Never forget. She's no better than you, and you are no better than her. I'm sure there is someone out there now who hates you as much as you hate Jules. Worse." She looked in the mirror, smoothing long fingers along her neck, admiring the way it dipped into the Peter Pan collar of her blouse.

Belle couldn't dispute what Shaye said. Those two boys on the beach could have parents, other lovers, or children, all who would want her dead. The policeman too. And the girl from the alley.

"But you're not concerned about them. You're not them. And at least you were merciful and killed them instead of making them into what you are."

Belle was taken aback. "How old are you, anyway?"

Shaye giggled. "Older than you, youngling."

Belle looked at the other fiend more carefully, noticing the radiant skin, the bright eyes, and the aura of power that she wore as effortlessly as her Converse sneakers. She still studied herself in the mirror, as absorbed as any fifteen-year-old would be, yet when she looked up, as she did now, centuries of knowledge peeked from behind her eyes. Belle would have to remind herself never to underestimate this one.

After a "snack" of bagged blood from the kitchen, Shaye took Belle into the family meeting, looping their arms together and pressing against her side with a conspiratorial giggle. They were the first there in the soft, inviting room. The long coffee table had a dozen or so chairs stretched around it, armchairs, lushly upholstered sofas, and a black velvet love seat. Wood-paneled walls with their paintings, vases of dried flowers, and walls and walls of books made it seem like someone's living room, a cozy one that invited shared secrets and soft-voiced confessions, all with the promise of an understanding shoulder to lean on afterward.

Belle gently—she didn't think that she remembered how—disengaged herself from Shaye and headed for a butter-gold leather armchair. It would be a mistake to think that the girl was on her side. Belle was alone in this. The imp passed her an understanding smile touched with a hint of mischief and sat in a neighboring love seat. Her skin glowed softly in the light.

Shaye, like the rest of the beasts, was almost too good-looking. They all burned, mythlike and beautiful, like newly risen phoenixes in Belle's universe. Even Susannah with her misshapen face and rude manners had a certain appeal of her own. No wonder humans—and especially her on that warm evening in Negril—didn't stand a chance.

The other beasts streamed in one after the other, each glancing at Belle before taking a seat or joining others in a huddle to talk like friends, touch roughly like family, or lovers. They were all shades of dark, beautiful well-fed bodies and shining eyes that flickered immediately to Belle before moving on to someone or something else. But she felt their gazes return, and like children they did not shame from staring. She noticed their faces, the fact that they had no features in common, except the four pairs of prominent canines when they smiled.

Shaye quietly named the beasts as they settled into their chairs or the familiarity of each other's embrace. The tall one, taller than Silvija even, but with little of the giant's obvious strength, was Keiko. She didn't have much of a sense of humor but was a good soul. *Did vampires have souls?* The round one with the neatly shaved head and wearing an off-the-shoulder blouse, short jean skirt, and tights was Violet. She spent so much money on clothes and other frivolities that Silvija had sent her off to New York to earn a degree of her own and accompanying skills. Now she was an engineer and brought to the clan almost a quarter of the money that their caretaker did. Shaye called her a genius of mischief.

Liam was her easygoing twin who existed for pleasure's sake alone. The scruffy one with hair tangled in dreads down to his ass was Rufus, a front man for a band popular in England now. And he was also psychic. Shaye named everyone in the Cave—eleven of them including Silvija and herself—until Belle's head was full of the identities and proclivities of her entire new family. There were more females than males, although somehow she'd expected that.

"Welcome to the cold."

The one Shaye had called Eliza stood before her. Small and beautiful with a long neck and a smooth, ageless face, she smiled boldly at Belle. But the new beast had noticed how her eyes skittered, then stayed away from Shaye the moment she noticed the child nearby.

"Thank you," Belle said.

Masochistic, the child had said, but nice to everyone with all that. Sometimes almost unbearably so.

"I'm not as young as you, but I know what it's like to come here without preparation. Alaska will grow on you. The people are delicious."

Belle laughed. The demon smiled, then wandered away to her chair at the opposite side of the room. Then the three lackeys, Ivy, Stephen, and Susannah, came in together, laughing and jostling each other for a place on the largest sofa. Their clothes were wrinkled and wet and their bodies radiated a flickering temporary heat. They'd just fed. Belle couldn't help but notice Ivy's and Stephen's linked hands. After getting themselves satisfactorily situated they turned as one to Belle with her name on their lips. A chorused greeting that made them laugh. Not so serious up here in the wilderness, then.

Shaye was apparently familiar with this side of them. She crawled into their consecutive laps to be tickled and coddled. When Silvija walked into the room, all that stopped. The vampires slouched down into their chairs to stare unblinkingly at her, or sat up, giving her their undivided attention. She too glowed with the vitality of fresh blood. Her eyes rested on the eleven fiends, one after the other, gathered in the room before she smiled, a quick movement of her lips, and sat down.

"As you all now know, we have a new addition to the family." She gestured to Belle. "If you have any questions concerning her, come to me."

A rustling of noise broke out in the room.

"Has Julia refused to care for her?" Rufus asked.

"No, but what happened is her business so you can ask her about that. Belle is to be cared for by all of us until the time she says otherwise and means it. Susannah and the twins will see to her martial training. Everyone else, do what you can to make her feel welcome. In the meantime, I'll be in

Anchorage for a while beginning tomorrow. Call me on my mobile phone or at the office if you need anything important. Keiko will stay behind for everything else."

Belle sat sprawled in her chair, her pose one of gorgeous indifference while Silvija talked about her yet managed not to look at her at all. She felt like she had on that first day when the giant had introduced herself by knocking Belle flat on her ass. Anger. She held the emotion tighter to her breast.

The beast's eyes rested on her only once. They floated over Belle, really, not actually resting at all, before moving on to someone else. It was only later in the meeting that she felt Silvija look at her. The beast's expression was enigmatic to say the least.

Just before the meeting ended, Belle slipped out. Shaye followed closely behind her. "Silvija seems troubled by you," she said.

"Really?" Belle asked. "I hadn't noticed." If anything, the giant seemed completely unconcerned, more than ready to go off to Anchorage. "Why is Silvija leaving? We just got here."

"She's usually gone. Either to New York or Anchorage or somewhere else to deal with family business."

"You make it sound like she's head of the Mafia or something."

Shaye shook her head, smiling. "It's not anything like that. The family has a lot of its money sprinkled in investments all over the world. Some real estate, soda, even computers. Silvija handles all of that."

"So I guess I shouldn't take it personally that she's just dumping me in this wasteland and then taking off?" At the child's questioning look, she shrugged. "It's been a long night and I'm getting hungry."

Shaye rolled her eyes but didn't pursue it. "That snack didn't do me much good either. Let's go out."

Despite the cold, the night was perfect. Only a few hours lay between them and dawn, but the newness of the country with its pines and bears and crispness disoriented Belle. Everywhere she looked, she couldn't help but compare this new land to Jamaica, how it lacked in color and rhythm and spontaneous beauty. They walked for what seemed like miles in companionable silence, their feet moving quietly over the snow-dusted ground.

"It will get better for you," Shaye said. Her eyes flickered over Belle and seemed to see through her like glass. "You won't always feel like a stranger here."

Belle nodded, but her new home distracted her. The night hissed and whispered with unfamiliar, yet beguiling sounds. Its touch on her skin, the way the breeze toyed with her hair, the animal noises beyond the trees, were almost presumptuous in their intimacy.

"Silvija didn't like Alaska either when she first moved the family to the Cave. Coming here was her idea, and because of the freedom that the twenty-hour winter nights bring us, I think it was a good one." Shaye's eyes wandered briefly from Belle to take in the forest around them. "But the adjustment from Jamaica was a big one to make. Silvija tried to shield it from us, but she was unhappy for a long time."

The beast was from Jamaica? It seemed impossible. She was so cold. So wintry. This place suited her more than Seaforth, Albian, or any other district Belle knew back home. But she said nothing to Shaye.

"Do you hear that?" A sound pricked her ears. The sound of something heavier than human in the icy forest.

Shaye grinned. "Oh yes."

Whatever it was breathed heavy and loud in the night, its breath mini explosions in the night air.

Shaye grabbed her hand. "Come."

The night glowed silver and perfect. Belle's new eyes were exquisite magnifying lenses, picking up everything around her. The flashing lives of insects, their industrious scuttling about in the dark, the dew swelling on the grass and on the limbs of overhanging trees. The bear—because she finally saw that the hulking creature was a huge brown bear, a PBS program come to life—swung to face them as the two vampires burst into its path.

Shaye dropped Belle's hand and grinned. "Isn't it gorgeous?"

And in enough time for Belle to realize that the creature was furious at them for barging into its territory, Shaye leapt at it, eyes and teeth flashing, laughter tumbling in her throat. Looking as startled as Belle felt, the bear reared up to its hind legs and bellowed. Its breath reeked of fish and cold water. The bear stumbled and reached desperately behind to bat the vampire off its back, but Shaye clung leechlike, her taloned fingers digging into it. She ripped at its neck, tearing away a patch of hair, then skin. The bright red smell of the bear's blood splashed into the clearing. At last the beast found purchase and spun, throwing her off its back. Shaye landed in a thorny bush and cursed. She was still laughing.

"Come on!" she called to Belle, brushing dirt and bits of debris from her face as she rose again to face the bear. "It's not as much fun to watch."

The bear turned with her, not allowing Shaye to get near its back again, and swatted its giant paws at her, growling low in its throat all the while. Its blood scent was dizzying. The smell flowed richer with its struggle, an unusual but intoxicating perfume that tugged on Belle's teeth, brought them abruptly out with the sound of a switchblade. A growl of excitement rose in her throat.

"All right. That's what I like to hear." Almost as an afterthought, Shaye jumped out of the bear's slashing reach, her quick agile movements more than a match for the lumbering giant and its claws. "Don't you think this would make a much better meal than some sagging bag of plasma in the fridge?"

Much better. Belle leapt for the bear's throat, sliding up between its paws to hook her fingers into the furrows that Shaye had already made. She pushed herself off its chest and somersaulted backward, taking most of the beast's neck with her. It was much easier than it looked. The blood rushed over her, bathing her face and throat. She dimly heard Shaye's laughter as she charged back toward the spray, elbowing the dying animal's gaping jaws out of her way to get to the red gush of fluid. Belle followed it down to the ground as it toppled and shuddered, giving up its wild blood to her mouth.

The beast's thick fur scratched her as she fed, devoured its deliciously spiced and thoroughly inhuman blood. Shaye's head nuzzled close to her when she too moved in to feed. The place where their flesh met tingled with warmth and shared pleasure. Shaye sighed.

They left the drained and cooling body on the banks of the gurgling stream. Shaye wanted to stay at the stream to bathe and wash the blood from their faces and hair, but Belle was uneasy about the upcoming dawn.

"You'll see. Even though it's nearly spring, the winter nights here are much longer than you're used to in Jamaica. Like I said before, about twenty hours of darkness. That's why Silvija brought us here."

Perhaps. But Belle would rather see the proof of that from the safety of the house than huddled beneath a tree waiting to be burnt to a true death. Walking up to the house, she felt an irrational feeling of safety and welcome. The doors opened automatically for them—a sensor attuned to current members of the family, Shaye explained—and Belle immediately excused herself from the young girl's presence to gather her thoughts.

Exhausted, but not quite ready to sleep, she spent the rest of the evening wandering the confines of her new home, peeking into all the hidden corners she found, and trying not to think too hard about her indefinite Alaskan exile. The Cave, she discovered after careful counting, was a mostly underground structure with eighteen rooms including a moonroom—Julia's stated favorite—with a massive skylight and bearskin rugs spread over most of the hardwood floors.

As sunrise drew closer, she chose a room that was farthest from the others, tucked away at the top of the house and looking out on the frosted landscape with the sleek, snow-washed mountains that loomed over the Cave.

Belle curled up in her new bed. It was warm. But not warm enough. She cursed Silvija again as shivers of discomfort and unease rippled through her. She didn't want to go to them. A scratch came at the door, then a smell of herbs and the out-doors and soap. Shaye. The child slipped into the bed with her, pressing her forehead to the tight muscles in Belle's back and slipping her arms around her waist. Belle almost wept with relief.

Chapter 13

Silvija floated in and out of Belle's life like fortune. The mystery of where the beast went and why everyone seemed content to have her gone was unsettling. Belle slipped quietly down the hall, minutes to sunrise, with her body already refreshed from sleeping between Shaye and a playful Violet. They still slept while Belle wandered. She found Silvija's office. The unobtrusive wooden door was dark and rough like the beast, the gateway to a room far away from the rest.

Belle slipped in, greeted by cooler air and cold modernity. Dark wooden floors, a black desk with neatly organized ladders of paper, a blank-screened computer with its silent keyboard. Belle sank into the thick chair behind the desk. A scent of leather rose up around her as she leaned back into it. Her eyes flickered to the wall. This was where all the timepieces in the house were kept. The white wall before the desk was a modern piece of installation art, clocks telling the current time and date in countries all over the world—Kingston, Auckland, Tokyo, Fairbanks, New York, Sydney, Los Angeles, Honolulu, and some cities she'd never heard of. Framed in white oval, the clocks mercilessly ticked away the time, the names of those cities in stark black and white below them.

She imagined the beast sitting where she sat now, her long length relaxed and easy in the black leather, eyes surveying

the bone-white and earth-black severity of her domain. Belle
pressed the power button on the computer, and the machine
flickered to life. While she waited for it to open its secrets to
her, Belle noticed the only spot of color on the desk, a framed
photograph of two perfect, bursting hibiscus blossoms, their
hearts a pulsing red that gave way to soft white, then an explosion of yellow. Their backdrop of moist green leaves only
made the blossoms more beautiful. Jamaica. The flowers reminded her of Jamaica.

There was nothing hidden on the machine. Even Belle's
limited computer skills easily brought up the spreadsheets,
the correspondences between families and vice presidents
and everyone in between that showed just how busy Silvija
was. There were companies, banks, restaurants, and fashion
houses, even farms that generated income for the family and
had Silvija's fingerprints all over them. This responsibility
was what took her from the Cave so often. And this was why
Belle and the others were able to have the Cave with the
planes in the hangar, the silk on their beds, and their peace of
mind. Did anyone else have to deal with these financial reali-
ties?

"What are you doing in here?"

Keiko's voice sliced through the quiet. Her scent, peonies
in a cool breeze, eddied lightly over Belle as she stood rigidly
in the threshold, watching. Her fingers gripped the doorknob
while artificial air from the vents above stirred the long thick
hair that bracketed her face like dark water.

Belle looked up with her gaze carefully neutral. "Finding
out what I've gotten myself into," she said.

"You won't find that here."

"I already have, actually." Her eyes flickered back to the
screen, to the cold facts of Silvija's wealth. Her responsibility.

"You need to leave now." The tall beast pushed the door
open wider. "This is Silvija's place alone."

As Belle slipped from behind the desk, Keiko looked

around the room as if checking to see if anything had been obviously stolen or destroyed.

"Don't worry, I haven't taken anything," Belle said.

The forbidding woman closed the door behind them. "Not yet."

Chapter 14

Belle was restless. She hovered near the exit to the Cave. Waiting. After countless nights of being gone, Silvija was still not back. The heavy glass windows and doors coated by layer after layer of UV-protection film looked out on the frozen dock and hillocks of icy snow. Beyond that was the sea and around the bend, the small human town of Wildbrook. Outside, the sun submitted quietly to the darkness while the ice grew colder, more firm. Belle had rushed from the cloying phantom warmth of their communal bed as soon as she opened her eyes, pausing only to pull on jeans and an old T-shirt. Whose, she didn't really know. Strange as it was, she missed Silvija. She could finally admit it to herself. She could even say it out loud. Not to the beast, of course. That time probably would never come.

What was it that she missed? Her cruelty? Her mocking presence? Either way, her skin craved the giant's. It still wanted to lose itself in the rich clove scent, to press against Silvija's until they both burned.

Belle jumped back from the glass as a heavy wet sound jolted her out of reverie. Blood and flesh smeared the surface before her eyes. The thing that was once human stared with one remaining eye, the skin on its face ripped and gouged to show the tissue and muscle underneath. Belle swallowed as hunger tugged at her teeth. Two figures in white filled her vision for a fraction of a second, then were gone. They were too quick to be human. Her pulse leapt to life as she jumped to the control panel on the wall. The ID laser scanned her hand with a deathly slow pass of its ice-blue light.

"Access denied. Sunset still in progress."

She stared at the panel in disbelief. Then up and out past the glass where she could barely make out two shapes blending into the snow in their white clothes.

"Fuck!"

Belle turned and ran back into the bowels of the house. Noises—the minute creaks of bedsprings, kisses, and moaned greetings, husky laughter—told her that the beasts were just beginning to stir. Didn't these damned creatures have alarms? Belle ran for the other communal bedroom. She knew Stephen and Ivy would be there. Searching for them with her sharpened hearing, she found that they were still in bed, wrapped in a cozy tangle of bodies with Violet and Keiko. Belle burst through the heavy double doors.

"Get up!" She looked reflexively behind her. "There's someone outside."

Ivy shook off her lethargy first. "What?" Her eyes quickly cleared.

"There's a body outside, and I just saw the things that threw it there."

With a quick shake of her naked body, Ivy was up out of bed. Her brother, wearing pajama bottoms and a slim-fitting shirt, followed quickly behind. The others in the bed eyed Belle with various looks of disbelief and irritation. Then Keiko, as if remembering her position as second in command, hopped from the cozy nest of bodies and grabbed a robe. Ivy did the same, then ran with Belle and Stephen up the steep incline toward the main entrance of the Cave. Others emerged from their beds as the three of them dashed past, brought to full wakefulness by the urgent footsteps. The twins' clothes flapped wildly as they ran. As the sun fully retreated, the glass on the outside of the compound cleared, opening up to a vast view of the snow, the sea, and the beginning glitters of the night sky.

The body was right where Belle left it, smeared across their front door like the remnants of someone's early night snack.

"It's a human," Eliza said, stating the obvious.

Even Belle could tell that from the lingering scent of food on it, and from the way that its skin did not fight to knit back together as hers had so many times. Ivy quickly scanned her palm print and rushed outside with her brother following closely behind.

"We need to clean this up now," Keiko said, coming up quickly behind them in her billowing black robe.

"If the humans found this . . ." Eliza trailed off, then stepped back to allow Shaye to come through. The child was already dressed. She ran through the open doors with a thick, heavy-duty plastic bag and instantly stooped in the bloodied snow to help Stephen and Ivy with the pulverized body. They poured the body, along with the bloodied snow, inside the bag. The twins gave it to Shaye and she took it up as if it weighed nothing, heaving it over her shoulder before jogging up the hill, away from the water and toward the vast wilderness behind and beyond the house.

"What did you see, Belle?" Stephen asked as soon as Shaye left.

She shook her head. "Why wasn't I able to go outside after them?"

"You would have burned up," Keiko said.

"No. The sun was going. I would have been able to follow them safely."

"It was going but not gone." The tall woman crossed her arms. "That would have been suicide."

"I'm dead already," Belle growled.

"Fine," Julia interrupted. "Change her access. Silvija won't miss her that much anyway."

At Belle's contemptuous look, she stuck out her tongue. Beside her, Eliza giggled.

"No." Keiko's look was implacable. "Until Silvija says change her access, it will stay the same. It was for her safety and ours."

"What the hell does that mean?" Belle asked.

Keiko shot her a hard-eyed look. "You're so damn smart, you figure it out."

Susannah finally spoke. "We need to find out what happened and stop messing around."

"Then let's look at the footage and stop arguing with her," Keiko said.

Belle looked at them all in disbelief. "You had cameras but no sensors to tell you that those animals were coming near us?"

"We do have sensors." Keiko turned to Stephen. "Don't we?"

He shook his head and put up his hands. "We can't afford to be divisive in this." He looked at his sister. "Ivy, Susannah, and Keiko, meet me and Belle in the security room. We'll have an update for everyone else within the hour."

In the security room with its monitors flashing scene after scene of the perimeter and interior of the house, the vampires gathered.

"We have the footage," Ivy said.

She put in the tape and they watched silently as two pale figures appeared from the snowy background carrying something between them. They were heavily covered in thick thermal layers, with their eyes protected by dark goggles as they approached the house in the last rays of the setting sun.

"Vampires." Stephen's voice echoed dully in the room.

"Humans would not cover themselves up so completely," Shaye said as she came into the room and stood close to the monitors. "The cold is not that severe now."

Ivy nodded, not taking her eyes from the screen. The creatures in white stealthily approached the house, neatly avoiding the motion sensors that self-activated after sunrise. They seemed familiar with the layout, as if they'd watched or walked that path many times before. Belle's eyes narrowed. They did not hesitate. With long, swift steps they rushed up to the glass doors and swept their cargo from the bag.

Was Belle the only one who leaned closer, mouth open and teeth lengthening when the formerly human thing, incredibly, still alive and twitching in its last moments, was thrown with inhuman force against the glass? In the monitors, Belle saw herself jerk toward the impact, eyes already searching for what might have been the cause. She was a blur of motion, swiping her hand against the sensor for release from her glass prison, then slamming her palms against the glass in frustration as they ran quickly away and out of sight.

She realized then that Keiko was right. If she had gone after the beasts she would have been burned. But she had been through an exposure before and survived. She shuddered. It wasn't an experience she wanted to repeat.

"That didn't tell us too much," Belle murmured.

"Only that they were other vampires." Keiko stared at the monitors still. "They want the humans to come here. There's no other reason they would leave that trash at our front door."

Stephen's jaw flexed. "They might have already alerted the humans to come and search the house."

"We need to let the others know about this." Susannah's quiet voice brought the attention back on her.

"Another meeting?" Belle made a rude noise. "We need to act, not meet ourselves to death."

"We need to let everyone know to be careful," Keiko said.

"If they have sense, they will. Almost everyone was there tonight when we found the dead body." Belle's gaze slashed to the family's protectors. "We don't need to have another damn meeting."

"Tell you what." Keiko looked hard at Belle. "You stay here and do whatever you like. If you want to take part, the meeting will be in a half hour in the usual place."

*   *   *

Of course, she couldn't stay away. At first she lay in the bed that Silvija had left cold for her, listening to the voices—some raised in alarm, others simply humming in curiosity—ebb and flow in the meeting room. For the most part, they all seemed to be waiting on Silvija to come and save them. A very useful meeting indeed.

Stupid. She lay there with contempt for them trapped behind her teeth, imagining some greater beasts breaking down their glass tower to devour them, and no trace of Silvija in sight. When she walked into the meeting, the entire room instantly focused on her. She sat on the arm of Shaye's chair, and the smaller vampire smiled, gently nudging Belle with her braided head. She was a child again.

"What did you see?" Rufus asked Belle.

"A dead human. Maybe from Wildbrook. Someone wants the humans in town to come looking."

"It sounds like a prank to me," Liam said.

"A prank?" Belle asked before she could help herself. "What the hell kind of prank is that when something ends up dead?"

"Somebody got bored." Keiko looked around the room with her eyebrow raised in question. Most shrugged dismissively, denying any responsibility.

Stephen hissed, "That's the kind of prank that we can't afford to happen. We've worked hard to build peace with the humans in town. If we are to remain here we have to keep their deaths to a minimum."

"I know I won't kill mine," Julia said. "She's too cute."

Keiko sucked her teeth. "Pet humans. What the hell are you thinking?"

"You used to do it too, Kei. Don't get all high and mighty on us now."

Belle didn't bother to ask what they were talking about. It just all seemed too strange and macabre. If there was something for her to know, she'd ask Shaye.

"But prank or no, if someone here did this thing, own up

to it," Susannah said. "That shit wasn't funny. And it wasn't safe."

Ivy nodded in agreement. "In the meantime, assuming it wasn't a prank from one of you young idiots, everyone needs to take extra care. When you take from the humans in town, be careful, don't drain them completely. Don't kill them. And watch out for strangers. Those were vampires on that tape."

The others in the room nodded or quietly voiced their assent. Would these fiends do this sort of thing as a prank? Belle shook her head.

"It's probably nothing," Shaye said. "We've had pranks get out of hand before but in the end turn out to be harmless, really."

"We'll talk to Silvija about this when she gets back," Keiko said, dropping her hand on the table with finality. "The decision on what to do next is hers."

Voices rushed up to ask questions, but they only buzzed incoherently in Belle's ears. She turned to Shaye. "Why would other vampires try to hurt us?"

"I don't know." Shaye shrugged. "We have a decent relationship with the other clans. Silvija is a wonderful diplomat. She makes it very peaceful for us here. No one bothers us. Those who she cannot make peace with, she destroys. We have few enemies."

Few enemies? Belle could easily see Silvija's attitude spawning *many* enemies for the family.

Shaye patted Belle's hand once with the same finality that Keiko had touched the table. "All this is probably nothing. Or it could be someone sending us a message. When Silvija comes back she'll tell us how to handle all this."

"So we're just going to wait until she gets here?" Belle asked. "What if she doesn't come for another month or two?"

"Keiko will call her. She'll come back soon." Shaye stood up. "Anyway, forget about all this. We're all going to the beach tonight. You should come."

Just that quickly, the dead human and the clan's fears were dismissed.

"The beach?" Belle looked at her.

Where would they find a beach here in Alaska of all places? When she thought of the beach, the images of sunlight, women in bikinis, and powder-white sand came to mind. There was none of that here.

"Of course. That's one of the best parts about living on the coast." At Belle's disbelieving look, she grinned. "Come on."

The sun was completely gone now, and with the dismissal of the impromptu meeting, everyone rushed outside apparently with a destination in mind.

"I wish we had horses," Liam said, rushing by with Violet in tow. "That would make it even better."

"I won't even ask what he's talking about."

"Don't. Your delicate sensibilities couldn't take the answer."

Belle rolled her eyes. In the room, Shaye grabbed two bathing suits and a fishing gun.

"Who keeps a fishing gun in their bedroom?" Belle muttered in mild disbelief.

"I do." Shaye laughed and tugged her out of the room.

They went out the back way of the house, pausing only to pick up bagged snacks from the kitchen. Outside, the snowfall was steady and relentless, tumbling from the skies with a mesmerizing, reckless abandon. Each snowflake fell, lilting and tipping gracefully down before landing on Belle's skin. They did not melt. Beside her, Shaye danced in the steadily falling powder with the fishing gun a dangerous attachment to her arm.

By the time they arrived at the beach, crunching through snow, ice, and everything in between, the party was already on. A boom box set up on a platform of rocks played Lena Horne's sexually charged version of "Honeysuckle Rose" while Violet lay naked under the eddying snowflakes on textured red velvet. The comforter from one of the beds, it looked like. Rufus, Eliza, Liam, and Julia ran naked into the water, laughing as they splashed among the tiny ice islands floating on the ocean's surface. Moonlight danced over their forever young bodies.

"Here."

Shaye thrust a bathing suit at Belle and she began to unself-consciously change her clothes right there on the snowy beach. Her body was slim-hipped and beautiful in the way that newly formed teenagers were with sparse body hair and a coltlike awkwardness that made Belle think of her own child. She followed Shaye's lead and shimmied out of her clothes and put on the one-piece bathing suit that fit remarkably well considering who she borrowed it from.

"I still don't understand all that's happening," Belle said, reaching back to their earlier conversation.

"There's nothing to understand. If anything all this is a big *mis*-understanding. I don't think that there are any big bad vampires out there trying to harm us." Shaye picked up her fishing gun. "Just as human countries exist mostly without conflict, vampire clans do as well. Sometimes we do business together. Sometimes we're friends. But mostly we stay away from each other. Too many (nonfamilial) vampires in one area would lead to a scarcity in food. Competition."

Belle smoothed her unruly Afro back from her face and se-cured it with a rubber band. "Why doesn't somebody de-velop artificial blood so we won't have to kill or feed on the humans?"

"Someone has. It's only in case of the direst emergency. None of us wants to drink water when we crave wine. Besides, the stuff is revolting." Shaye looked at her. "We have some here if you want to try it."

The thought of no chase, no fangs slicing through human or animal flesh, no whimper of fear or arousal, made Belle a little sick. She shook her head. "No, thanks."

Shaye laughed. "Come on, let's go look at the fish. I like hunting. It's one of the best things to do out here."

"But we don't eat fish."

"Their blood is sweet, like the humans' candy. Pixie sticks." She licked her lips and smiled.

Belle followed Shaye up the beach and onto icy rocks nearly ten feet up from the sand and jutting out over the water.

"Look." Shaye pointed.

Below them, the water shimmered silver and cold. A quiet school of fish with scales glittering rainbow and white skimmed below the surface. Their scales flashed in the moonlight, beckoning Shaye's gun. Belle couldn't imagine sucking on the pretty fish, no matter how hungry she was. She wasn't that nostalgic for candy.

A flash of fire sparked in her peripheral vision and Belle looked up. Seconds later a roar of flames and a heaving splash came from below.

Nearby, Eliza twisted in the water and came up screaming. "Fucking asshole! You could have toasted me!"

The rocket exploded harmlessly in the ocean a few hundred feet out. Violet chuckled with fiendish delight and dropped down on her ass in the snow-covered sand.

Shaye rolled her eyes. "They're such kids."

Belle smiled. Rufus, Liam, and Julia ran from the water yelling as they rushed toward Violet. The merry-eyed girl jumped away from her homemade rocket launcher tilting drunkenly in the snow and ran. They dashed down the beach, running and sliding in the snow, as if the human's body hadn't been found, as if Ivy and Stephen hadn't warned them to be careful. Belle wasn't surprised. She could not imagine such magnificent beasts on a leash of fear.

Rufus skidded, naked, in the snow, and sailed into the thick piles of powder high on the beach. He quickly formed a snowball and threw it at Violet. She sensed it coming and dodged it, dipping gracefully to the side and laughing at him.

Liam and Julia quickly followed suit with the snow, scooping up wild handfuls of the white stuff and throwing it, hard and soft, at the blatantly unrepentant Violet.

"That looks like fun," Shaye said.

She glanced down at the flashing fish, then back at the fight winding up and down the long stretch of snow-covered beach.

"I'll be right back," Shaye said, and dropped her fishing gun beside Belle. In moments, she was down the slick rock and running after the string of imps of the beach, shouting their names and scooping up her own snow as she went.

The fish, frightened off by the loud noises, flashed under the water, quickly turning their glittering bodies and dashing for deeper waters. A few feet away, Eliza swam noiselessly beneath the ocean's surface, her eyes wide open to look at the distant stars.

Chapter 15

"Tell me what happened with this dead human," Silvija said.

She appeared in the bedroom, seemingly from the ether, her clothes smelling like the city, of smog and perfume and air-conditioning. Belle looked up from her game of chess with Shaye—the little imp was beating her shamelessly—and hid her smile. The beast looked good. There was no other way to say it. For a dead woman, she positively radiated disgusting health with her glowing skin and effortless grace. Her hair was loose around her face in heavy kinks and curls serving as the perfect background to blazing dark eyes and her voluptuary's face. And she managed all that while wearing dark slacks, a black turtleneck, and boots. Belle bit the inside of her lip.

She barely noticed when Keiko, Stephen, Ivy, and Susannah sailed in behind Silvija, like the floating tail of a giant cat.

Belle put one of her knights at the mercy of Shaye's queen, rolling her eyes at her own stupidity as she did. "Two vampires broke a human against the outer glass. It was very messy. They ran away after they did it."

Shaye smirked at Belle but she ignored her.

"That's it?" Silvija asked.

"Yes. Didn't you see the footage?"

Silvija pursed her lips. "I did." She turned to the cabal behind her. "Since that's all there is, we need to be careful for the next few days. The humans will come searching, so make the place look human enough for them, and if you haven't already done it, clean the front glass very carefully."

The twins, along with Susannah and Keiko, nodded as one before they quietly withdrew from the room.

Belle laughed. "Feeling queenly today?"

"Always," Silvija said, playing along. She dropped down on the floor beside them and sprawled out her long body on the rug.

"I was the one who threw the body away," Shaye said suddenly. She toyed briefly with Belle before capturing her knight.

Easy come, easy go, Belle thought with a shrug. She moved her eyes over the board trying to calculate her next move. Games of logic weren't quite her thing.

"Good," Silvija said. "At least we know the humans won't find it, then."

Shaye smiled. After a few moments of staring at the ceiling in contemplative silence, Silvija rolled over to her side to watch the quiet game between Belle and Shaye.

"You're not really good at this, are you?" she rumbled quietly at Belle's side.

"If you're going to be a commentator, you might as well go back where you came from," Belle said without looking up.

She started to move her bishop, but Silvija's hand moved out, captured hers, and moved it with the chess piece still clutched tight between her fingers to a more advantageous spot on the board. Her hand tingled. Belle still didn't look up, so she felt rather than saw Silvija's smoothly raised eyebrow, her wordless stare. Across from her, Shaye's mouth twitched but she remained silent.

"I'm going to look into this thing with the human," Silvija said quietly, as if talking to herself. "It seems a little strange."

"That's a good word for it," Belle said. "Strange."

Silvija smiled briefly at her, then went back to watching the chessboard. Later, after she helped Belle hold her own at least twice more, Silvija's hand, the one that had helped Belle stay in the game, drifted to her thigh, and stayed. Shaye won the game.

Chapter 16

The expected visit from the humans came a few days later just past two in the afternoon. Belle struggled from the bowels of sleep at the distant sound of the doorbell and then fists pounding on the door. Violet's body moved against hers and her head popped up from where it rested on Julia's chest. The pale-eyed imp blinked sleepily.

"What was that?"

Belle shook her head in reply, reaching automatically for Silvija. But the beast wasn't there. She'd spent a long night in conference with her second in command and her three lieutenants, but during the day she lay pressed against Belle's back, warm and still. In their waking hours, she watched Belle strangely as if the new vampire were some unexpected thing she encountered, but in bed they flowed toward each other, perfectly.

Silvija's soft footsteps sounded down the hall accompanied by the light whisper of silk as if she was slipping on a robe. Belle fought lethargy, looking around for her discarded clothes from earlier that morning. With a wiggle and shrug she was in the white wrap dress and following after Silvija.

Outside, the sun was at its highest. But inside the Cave she only felt the usual tiredness from want of sleep and a mild irritation that something had taken the beast from her side too soon. As she approached the main double doors, Ivy ran past her in the hallway, moving as fast as her sleep-laden limbs would allow.

There were humans at the door. Police. Two men in ear-muffs and heavy jackets worn over their street clothes and another four officers, one woman and three men, in weather-ready beige uniforms under matching jackets. All had their guns in plain sight.

"We have a warrant to search the premises, both the house and the grounds," one of the plainclothes men said in a low voice. He presented an official-looking paper to Silvija, but she looked at it without reaching out her hand.

As Belle approached the door, Silvija, still safely protected in darkness thanks to the heavily tinted glass, stepped back and allowed the small party of humans to walk into the Cave. Only then did she reach for the document. Ivy, now alert, stood just behind Silvija.

"May I ask what this is about?" she asked, reading the warrant.

"You can ask but we don't have to tell you a damn thing." The second plainclothes officer propped his fists on his thick waist and leveled a cutting glance around him.

But the woman shifted her gaze to look at Silvija. "A local man was reported missing a few days ago. A witness said they saw him head up here."

When Belle rounded the corner, stepping fully into the humans' sight, they turned. The woman's eyes flickered over her body before coming back to rest on her face. Belle smiled at her in greeting.

"How many of you live in this house?" the second officer asked.

"Twelve," Belle supplied softly, at her most nonthreatening. "But not everyone is home at the moment."

The human woman watched her closely as she spoke. Silvija smiled.

"And you think that we have this missing person hidden here in our home?" she asked, getting back to the previous conversation.

"Or at least evidence of what you did to him."

"So if you please, ma'am. Just step back and let us do our jobs."

"Of course." Silvija's voice was a soft invitation. "Search anywhere you like. We have nothing to hide."

A sweet enough lie, but Belle could hear the others rustling around in the house, putting away things that the police didn't need to see, like their supply of human blood in the fridge.

"What's going on?" Shaye appeared from behind Belle, looking at the police with curiosity.

The officers paused in the act of pulling on their gloves long enough to assess that she was no threat, then ignored her question to follow their own agenda.

"These nice men will just be searching the house for a while," Silvija said. "Looking for dead bodies or evidence of them."

Shaye grinned. "Sounds like fun."

As the police trooped down the hall, Silvija came closer and furtively touched her breast, smoothing a hand down the front of the white cotton, then down to her hip. Belle's nipple instantly hardened.

"You look like an angel in that dress," Silvija murmured. "I'll have to make time to rip it off you later."

Hiding her surprised smile, Belle turned away and followed the humans into the great room. She felt Shaye's gaze on her back, but didn't turn around to see the child's face. *Later. When would that be?* Would "later" for her and Silvija really come? Her womb felt hot and molten, her attentions fast-forwarded to that "later." She almost bumped into one of the uniformed officers. His mouth literally dropped open when he stepped past the double wooden doors that were the true entrance to the Cave. Belle could almost see his mind calculating how much all this must cost.

"Excuse me," she said, and he blushed before quickly moving on to what he came to do.

With their latex gloves on, the humans searched through everything, the bookshelves, desks, behind mirrors, under chair cushions. They could easily have split up into pairs to have the search go faster and perhaps more efficiently, but they stayed grouped together as if frightened to be separated from each other. Even the belligerent one. At this rate, by the time they finished searching it would be nightfall.

"You don't have to follow us," the policewoman said. "We promise not to break anything."

Silvija's mouth twisted into something that passed for a smile, but it was Belle who spoke. "Things can be replaced. We're not worried about that. I'm here just in case you have any questions, or run into a locked door."

As they searched every nook and cranny of the enormous rooms, leaving cushions tossed and paintings pitched crookedly on the walls, Silvija dismissed Ivy with a slight tilt of her head. The amazon flickered her jaundiced gaze over the humans before she quietly withdrew from the room.

After they were satisfied that the missing boy was nowhere to be found in the moonroom, it was on to the next. Belle sat on the chairs of one of the lesser used bedrooms and watched them search, rubber gloved, through the chest of drawers with its cache of unworn unisex clothes. The officers looked behind the mirror, knocked on the floorboards to check for basement storage, even asked Belle to get off the chair so they could check that too.

The woman's eyes kept coming back to rest on her, and Belle met her eyes with a curious look of her own. She was attractive enough in that insipid way that human men seemed to love their women. Petite frame, big brown eyes under a wealth of black hair she wore pulled back from her face in a soft version of a ponytail. Wings of hair drooped down to cover her ears and brush her shoulders. Despite her small size, the woman seemed very comfortable in her uniform and gun. It was hard for Belle to imagine her in a dress.

"What's your name?" she asked the woman.

Her partner looked up sharply at Belle as if she'd broken some strict item of protocol. He continued his search but pointedly slammed the drawers shut as he went.

"Officer Lovelace," she said, pausing over a collection of black-and-white photos she just unearthed from a drawer.

"And your first name, in case I have questions about this search later on?"

The woman looked at her suspiciously before answering. "Tamsyn."

Belle nodded. "Thank you."

They moved on from the bedroom with obvious looks of disappointment.

"Sorry to disappoint you, Officers," Silvija said. "We lead fairly ordinary lives up here."

Humans and vampires walked as one down the quiet hallway leading to the bedroom that Ivy usually shared with Stephen, Keiko, and Rufus. The room smelled of interrupted sleep, as if the four beasts had gotten up with all the commotion at the front door, then fallen back into slumber after only a few moments. Ivy was not in the bed.

"Ordinary, huh?"

There was nothing more scandalous here than three people asleep. Belle could see his point if they were fucking, but their nude bodies were still, entwined gently with each other under the thin cotton sheet. They did not stir when the humans started to search. Eyebrows rose even farther when the humans discovered the sex swing and the assorted toys scattered around it at the back of the room. The woman's eyes found Belle again and her skin darkened to an even deeper shade of copper.

"It's all relative," Silvija murmured.

Soon enough, they finished the search and headed, empty-handed, for the front door.

"It was a pleasure, gentlemen and lady." Silvija handed the belligerent one a card. "If you have any further questions for me, I'm usually available by phone."

Belle tucked her hands in her pockets and watched as they all took turns getting one last look at the Cave before walking out into the sun. The woman was the last to go.

"By the way," Silvija said, catching her attention before she could leave. "We're having a party at some point. Next year, I think, or perhaps the one after that. Belle will be there." She took out another card and scribbled something on it before handing it to Tamsyn. "It's costume and starts at nine. The other necessary information is on the back."

The human looked startled, then pleased. "I'd love to come. Thank you."

After she disappeared and Silvija locked the door behind her, Belle asked the question. "Are we really?"

"Oh yes. And I think you'll have a good time." This time her smile was absolutely devilish.

The house was quiet once again with the source of their disturbance gone. But the last thing that Belle wanted to do was sleep. The woman had oozed desire from every pore, practically licking her lips every time she looked at Belle. And Silvija loved it.

"The woman liked you," she said, plucking at the flimsy belt holding Belle's dress together.

"Did she? I hadn't noticed."

"Yes, you did." She pulled harder at the belt and it gave way, letting the dress fall open to show off her breasts, the nipples that were already hard with anticipation, and farther below, the clit thickening with want. "She was dripping for you. Don't tell me you didn't smell her pussy."

Silvija's own scent washed over Belle's senses. She was the one dripping with want. The giant backed her up against the glass, and she gasped at the coolness of it through the thin dress. Silvija effortlessly found her clit, slid below it to find the wet folds of her pussy, then inside. Belle gasped.

Silvija widened Belle's thighs and thrust deeply inside with her fingers.

"You know she's watching now, don't you?"

A humming pulse began in her throat, threatening to choke her.

"You want to see?"

Before she could assent or deny, Silvija abruptly spun her around, withdrawing her fingers from the wet pussy. The cool glass connected with a slap against her bare breasts, belly, and thighs. Silvija pulled the dress from Belle's back, ripping the soft cotton.

Tamsyn and her colleagues ambled down the snow-covered walkway to their twin police trucks. As Belle watched, she turned to look back at the Cave, heedless of whatever her colleagues were saying. Her eyes were wide as she looked back. But she couldn't see beyond their heavily tinted glass. *Could she?* Heat flooded into Belle's face.

"Open your legs."

Belle blindly did as she was told, and she gasped again, breath misting the glass, when the giant thrust long fingers into her pussy. She hissed. Silvija twisted Belle's hair out of the way and bit the back of her neck. Her body settled against Belle's back as she fucked her deeply with skilled fingers.

At the truck now, Tamsyn climbed into the driver's seat, but something made her stop and get back out of the truck. She said something to the man beside her and started walking back toward the house. Belle groaned. Her pussy was overflowing. She felt her wetness dripping down her thighs, staining the remnants of her dress.

"You want more, don't you?"

The pleasure rolled inside her, churning her insides and her breath, raking her clawed fingers against the unyielding glass. Her belly was on fire with lust. What else could the giant give her?

"Yes," she choked out. Whatever it was, she wanted it.

Silvija's fingers slid even deeper and Belle felt a curling, felt herself stretch. She lifted her ass up and back for more of the sensation burning her to cinders. Tamsyn came toward the house in slow motion, each footstep echoed by the movement of Silvija's hand inside Belle. The human's face was a mask of duality—purpose and confusion, want and repulsion.

"Yes!" Belle pressed her hands against the glass and slipped lower, bracing her legs even wider apart. The giant moved deeper inside. Belle closed her eyes.

"Do you want this?"

"Yes. Yes." She felt a fullness inside her like never before, a stretching that was almost pain, heard Silvija sob behind her in gratitude. Outside, the human approached, but neither paid her the least bit of attention.

"You really want this. God, you really want this. . . ." There was wonder in Silvija's voice. Then she was silent, and her curled fingers, her clenched fist began to do all the talking. It was vicious and it was tender and it was merciless all at once, Belle's cunt swallowing Silvija's fingers, and threatening to swallow all of the giant, her energy, her power.

"Ah, fuck!"

Silvija's fingers raked her back, then jumped to her ass. She began to grunt again as they moved faster together. As the pleasure built inside Belle her head flung back and a wordless cry escaped her. It was like nothing she'd ever felt before, and everything. This moment was her reference point for loving. For lust made flesh. Her knees weakened, and threatened to buckle, but Silvija grasped her hip to hold her up.

"Just a little more. Give me just a little more."

Belle felt her sweating too, felt her effort, and her passion. Silvija trembled behind her, but held on. The doorbell rang. Its sound echoed in Belle's head like a gong, like the permission she was looking for to come.

Fire and heat and destruction and completion burst inside her belly, in her thighs, into the deepest part of her that Silvija held tight in her fist. Too much. She shuddered around the giant. Sound trembled in her throat. It wanted to come up, but it was too much. A sob rose inside her, and her sweat dampened palms banged against the glass. Once. Twice. Then another. The glass bowed beneath her hands. Her knees buckled and she went down. Silvija came down with her, their knees hitting the marble with a final sounding thud. The giant's fist slowly released inside her body. Belle felt each minute movement of her lover's hand before it finally emerged with a soft pop.

Her palms lay flat against the glass as she knelt in Silvija's cool embrace, panting uselessly. The doorbell rang again, and she shivered.

Silvija cleared her throat. "Do you want me to invite her in?"

Belle was too spent to answer. She opened her mouth, but could only manage an incoherent whisper.

"I guess we'll save her for another time, then." She kissed Belle's shoulder, then slowly stood up to answer the door.

"Officer Lovelace, did you forget something?"

The woman hesitated, as if she had been expecting some-one else at the door. "Yes. Can I bring a guest or is the invitation for me alone?"

Belle could almost see the smile on Silvija's face.

"You can bring anyone you wish."

"Thank you." Tamsyn smiled, clasping her hands behind her back.

"Does that mean you'll be joining us?" Silvija asked.

"If I'm not working, then yes."

"Good. We look forward to seeing you." Silvija closed the door softly after the woman's good-bye.

"You have a new fan who's dying to get to know you," she murmured above Belle with a smile in her voice. Her scent, then her body came closer. "In the meantime, let's get you to bed."

Her powerful arms lifted Belle until she was cocooned in her scent of cloves, power, and satisfied desire. Silvija's breasts felt soft beneath her cheek. Like home, like everything. If she'd thought too hard about it, Belle might have fought to be put back to her feet, but all her thoughts had been crushed by Silvija's fist inside her, leaving behind nothing but warm satisfaction and a feeling that there was nowhere else that she needed to be. Belle breathed herself into sleep.

Chapter 17

"Silvija?"

Belle barely whispered the name in her half sleep, suspecting that, even as she opened her mouth, her lover was already gone. Julia made a low noise in her slumber as she snuggled closer, wiggling her backside into the cradle of Belle's hips. Violet slept peacefully beside them with her face buried in Julia's breasts and Eliza's leg flung over her. Silvija was not with them. Sifting through the layered scents in the room, of apples, sage, and jasmine, then deeper in the Cave, bergamot, cinnamon, lime, peonies, Belle realized that Silvija wasn't there. She sagged back into the bed and closed her eyes. Sleep didn't come. Instead, she waited.

And then she got tired of waiting.

"Teach me to fly," Belle murmured to Liam one evening.

He lay seemingly exhausted on the sandy beach while Violet played a short distance away in the waves. His smile was sweet and slow as his eyes flickered under the bright half moon. "Whenever you're ready, let me know."

"How about now?"

He laughed.

They started the next night, going through the basics of the single-engine Cessna, until Belle knew what each switch, display, and button on the futuristic instrument panel was responsible for. It was tedious, but after a few nights Belle learned it all. She focused her energy, her anger, and her need into learning all about yaws, induced drag, airspeed, and the exhilaration of flying. Belle learned to handle the small plane like it was an extension of her body, gliding through the clear starlit skies with Liam by her side.

Although she didn't want to admit it to herself, she learned to fly so she could escape. Not from the Cave and all the monsters inside it, but from herself. From the person she became when Silvija was at home. Then not at home. Weeks later when the time was right, she flew away from the sun by herself. The plane's engine hummed softly under her as she sailed toward the place that, according to Liam, was the least likely to yield boredom. Belle swam through the air in the Cessna until she lost an hour, then two, then four and she was on California time, hovering in the air over Los Angeles. She felt like one of the angels as she descended into the brilliantly lit city.

Belle emerged in L.A. a new beast. Away from the clawing needs of her own body, she felt strong. The city was vibrant and beautiful, nothing like home, but as Belle lifted her nose, all the better to smell the blood in the air, she suspected that it had its own charm. Every human here seemed beautiful. On the surface, certainly, with their gym-hardened bodies, perfect complexions, sculpted noses, and the scent of sex rising from them like steam.

There were vampires here too. She smelled their particular odors and consciously steered away from them. Belle wanted to feed tonight, not compete. As she walked down Santa Monica Boulevard brushing against tempting bodies and soft looks, a familiar scent reached her nose. Ah. The place that Liam had told her about.

"I think you might like this," he'd said with a knowing smile.

Despite his vague directions, she found the place. The door was easy to miss. Iron-worked and heavy, it nearly blended in with the graffitied wall. Mina's Chamber, as Liam called it, was a dungeon. Inside, the luscious girl by the door who seemed like a pixie with her tiny red mouth, brown skin, and red vinyl tube dress, looked Belle up and down before wearily holding out her hand.

"Twenty-five dollars, please."

Belle gave her some of the crisp bills Liam had given her and walked down the dark, candlelit hallway. A song she recognized as Prodigy's "Firestarter" from Rufus's eclectic collection of music beckoned to her from inside.

The dungeon smelled like blood, sex, and tears. Belle's hand fluttered to her stomach and a smile came and went on her face. The night was looking up even more.

When Belle had told Liam that she wanted to go out for fun, he told her to wear leather.

"The humans love it," he'd said. "If you don't get food, then you'll at least get fucked."

For Belle it wasn't really an either/or proposition. She wanted food, but she also wanted to be with people enjoying their bodies. She wanted to be among those fucking and being fucked. So what if their pleasures reminded her of Silvija? Some days, her very own existence reminded her of the beast.

Belle walked down the tunnel with its flickering candlelight, aware of the eyes that brushed over her leather-clad skin, lingering on the tight black pants sitting low on her hips and the leather blouse, also black, with its crisscrossed lacing over her cleavage. The eyes made her flesh tingle.

A very forward girl walked close to Belle, caressing the beast's ass as she passed, then after she was sure that Belle had noticed the sensation, turned around with a flash of dark eyes and white teeth to look back. She wore an electric blue-rubber dress that clung to every well-made piece of her. The stilts she wore as shoes easily brought her up to eye level while her pale skin, bright blue eyes, and scarlet hair flashed in the dim light. Belle smiled back at her with moist lips.

Perhaps this one would be good for a little nibble later on. The girl slowed down enough for Belle to catch up.

"I'm Natasha and"—her eyes danced over Belle's provocatively bared skin—"I think I'm in love."

Belle's mouth twitched with the beginnings of a smile. "Just because you like how my ass feels?" she asked, deliberately not offering her name.

They walked toward their shared destination, weaving through the crowd and keeping close to each other.

"I like how it looks too. Not to mention the way that sexy accent of yours wraps around every word that comes out of your mouth."

Belle's smile burst free, taken off guard as she was by Natasha's unexpected charm. "It's good to know you're not superficial."

"You don't need to see under my surfaces to know that I'd like to play with you tonight." Her soft mouth opened again to smile and Belle caught a flash of silver in her tongue. Some sort of jewelry. Ah, she could take pain.

"So, may I play with you?"

Belle tilted her head as if considering. "Maybe. I'm really just here to watch tonight."

"Are you new to the scene?" Natasha asked.

"Very."

"Delightful. A virgin. Welcome."

"Thank you. I'm looking forward to what the night will bring."

The woman smiled. "So am I."

They stepped deeper into Mina's Chamber. As the seductively dressed crowd promised, there was a lot to see in the lower levels. From the main entrance and hallway, the Chamber split into several arteries of rooms, with the main room being the focus of attention. Some sort of show was already taking place on its stage.

A human woman straddled a long red chair that was velvet, padded and shaped like a tongue. She was leaned forward away from the audience so everyone gathered could see her long white back bared in a floor-length leather halter dress slit all the way up both thighs. Someone had strapped her arms wide apart in shackles that hung low from the ceiling.

"Oh, they already started the show."

Natasha tugged Belle through the enraptured crowd and up a set of side stairs until they stood on a balcony overlooking the stage. A couple and a threesome—two men in rubber and three women wearing leather in various shades of red—were already there. The monstrously tall boy with bloodred contact lenses and teeth sharpened to daggerlike points greeted Natasha with a kiss and smile. She hugged him and his tuxedo-clad boyfriend in turn, before slipping a hand around Belle's waist.

"Pretty," she said about the scene unfolding on the stage below them.

Belle was inclined to agree. All the players on the stage were human. Their intoxicating smells rose under the hot stage lights like perfume. Sweat. Arousal. Fear. Excitement.

Natasha leaned closer. "That's a corset piercing." Her warm breath rippled over Belle's ear and neck. "Ellie is the girl getting it done. It's her first time."

Ellie was taking the pain well for a novice. She writhed only a little when the thick hypodermic needle pierced her skin. It was only the second of fourteen. Her long, elegant back was dotted with marks, apparently guides for the needles that together formed an hourglass shape from her shoulders down to the top of her hips. The piercer looked competent and sexy in her sky-blue plastic gloves, knee-high Doc Martins, and a small rubber dress showing off what looked like a two-headed dragon tattooed over most of her café au lait skin. As she bent over to grasp a bit of flesh between her fingers in preparation for the needle, her dress lifted above plump ass cheeks showing off the bright red slit of her panties.

Only a few drops of blood rushed to the surface of Ellie's

skin in the needle's wake, but Belle smelled it. She also smelled the scent rising from beneath Ellie's dress as her hips rode the chair with each wave of pain the needles brought. The girl was enjoying herself.

"She's being so good," Natasha murmured. She moved even closer to Belle, rubbing her rubber-clad breasts against Belle's back as she spoke.

Belle hummed in agreement and leaned slightly back into Natasha. Could she take her? Did she really want to? Did this affect what she wanted from Silvija or what the beast wanted from her? The human's scent answered no to all those questions. Belle felt the others' eyes on her as she leaned back even more and Natasha's hands snaked around to rest just above her zipper.

But their companions' interest in them was fleeting. In the next moment, their eyes were back on the stage, on the prettily pierced Ellie, who whimpered softly now as the pain and her pleasure grew in equal measure. The piercings were only halfway done.

"After this"—Natasha's hand gently stroked the cool leather over Belle's belly, then wandered lower—"they're going to replace the needles with captive bead rings, then slide a ribbon through them." Two fingers skated between Belle's thighs and toyed with her through the leather.

Belle dropped a hand on top of Natasha's. "That could be interesting," she said.

The hand beneath hers tried to move, but she tightened her fingers. On the stage, blood rose up on Ellie's back. The scent caught Belle before the capable piercer could wipe it away. Belle sighed, feeling the hunger flow into her like wine. Her canines tingled. She threaded her fingers through the human's and turned until they were face-to-face. Her other hand fell to Natasha's ass and she brought the woman closer. The edge of the balcony caught Belle at the small of her back and she felt velvet from the curtain's brush against her side, her face. A gentle throb began between her thighs.

"How hard do you generally play?" she asked the suddenly trembling human.

"As hard as you've ever played. Harder," Natasha said, chuckling deep in her throat. Her eyes flared an even brighter blue. "I knew you were special the moment I laid eyes on you."

"Laid eyes on my ass, you mean."

Natasha laughed again. "Exactly."

Then Belle was done laughing. She lightly nipped Natasha's chin with her sharpest teeth, tasting blood. The human's eyes widened in surprise, but she stepped closer. Belle licked Natasha's chin, lapping at the faint drop of blood there, then at her mouth eagerly opening up to taste. The delicate flavor of anise lingered on Natasha's tongue.

Beneath the faintly musty balcony curtain was a solid wall. Belle leaned into it, taking Natasha's weight with her. The woman was slight, nothing like Silvija's solid weight at all. She chuckled as Belle's hands moved over her rubber-encased ass. The dress was too long to simply shove out of the way. Belle grew impatient and quickly lengthened one fingernail, pushing it out past the cuticle until it emerged, blood-flecked and sharp.

Natasha gasped when she felt the rubber give and pulled back away from Belle. The scent of talc rose up between them. It was an expensive dress. Her eyes snapped, but Belle's hand moved into the hole that her fingernail made and touched Natasha's bare ass. The human woman's hands tightened on her shoulders, scored her skin, in retaliation perhaps for ruining her dress, but Belle only smiled.

"You are very surprising," Natasha murmured.

Natasha wasn't surprised. She was excited. That was apparent enough with the growing wetness between her legs and the sighing looseness of her body. But her fingers clung harder still until Belle's blood rose up under her sharp nails.

"Are you sure you want that?" Belle asked.

"Absolutely."

The others on the balcony watched them, unashamed and interested. The tall man licked his lips and the other four crept closer.

"Care to go somewhere more private?" Belle asked.

"No." Natasha's voice was low. Rough.

Could this human really handle what she wanted from Belle? It wasn't really a question. Belle was going to give it to her anyway. Give her everything that she asked for with the fingers scraping blood up from Belle's skin, with her burning eyes, and with her red, red mouth.

"Can you trust me?" Belle asked.

She knew it was the wrong time to ask that question. The woman was already imagining their sex, was already wet for it.

"I shouldn't." Natasha's eyes glowed blue and aware. "But I do."

Perfect. She stripped Natasha naked. The others watched, eyes alight, as the pale woman's flesh was revealed. She didn't have a mark on her. No tattoos, no bruises, no scars. She was a blank canvas waiting for Belle to perform a night's work on. Natasha stepped out of her shoes.

"Anyone have a knife?"

The man in the rubber tuxedo quickly offered Belle his switchblade, releasing the wicked edge with a soft click. On the stage below, the show continued with Ellie's soft cries and the minute sound of the needles gliding into her flesh. But they were all much more interested in what was happening here.

Belle cut the tasseled tie-backs from the velvet curtains, two long pieces that were perfect for the idea taking shape in her mind. "Unpin your hair."

Natasha seemed to take as much pleasure in performing this little foreplay as Belle did in watching it. She plucked the pins from her hair, and the heavy red rope unwound, sliding down her neck and breasts, picking up glimmers of light as it went. The blush in her small nipples perfectly complemented the shimmering red in her hair.

Belle stepped closer to Natasha. She deeply inhaled the smell of sweat and the remnants of an earlier bath—cucumber melon soap and a lighter scent of apricots—that clung to her skin.

"I'm glad that you trust me," Belle murmured, allowing the woman to feel her cool breath against her neck. Natasha's blood beat quickly beneath the fragile skin.

"Whatever happens," the human said, "I know this will be unforgettable. And that's what I want. That's what you want too, not trust." She bit Belle's ear.

Belle lifted her to sit on the metal balcony railing. She heard a low gasp behind her but paid it little attention. Natasha watched her, lips slightly parted as she waited to see what Belle would do. With a sweep of her hands, Belle widened her legs, lifted and spread them wide enough to see her shaved pussy, the thickening clit and the moisture already seeping from inside.

"How flexible are you?"

Without answering, Natasha firmly grasped the railing beside her hips and lifted her feet higher to the same rung as her ass, spreading her legs wide until she balanced perfectly on the balcony edge facing Belle, thighs spread, and knees only inches from her shoulders in a lovely design that reminded Belle of a cat on its perch.

"Perfect."

She tied the woman's legs to the railing, then her hands. With a quick pull at the rope, she tested the strength of the bonds. Then after a moment's consideration, she anchored Natasha with a strip of the thick velvet curtain tied around her waist and secured it to the balcony railing at boot level.

Belle gathered the woman close to her. The pomegranate-scented hair was heavy over her fingers as it slithered through them and down Natasha's back. An artificial breeze blew from a vent above them, ruffling the soft hair, blowing it slightly back and over the crowd still entranced by the show taking place on the stage.

Ellie was now completely pierced with all fourteen needles and the patient piercer was already in the process of replacing the white-capped hypodermic needles with captive bead rings. The holes in the human's back looked painful, but she seemed to be in a state of near ecstasy.

Natasha vibrated gently in Belle's arms. The human was excited. On edge. Belle kissed her. She licked the soft lips until all Natasha's lipstick was gone, until the slightly bitter taste of the color blended with the anise on her tongue and the essence of her desire.

Belle wanted to taste her pussy. Not with her tongue, but with her hands. Belle's fingers fluttered at Natasha's opening. The human gasped softly in her mouth and the pussy clenched eagerly, nibbling at Belle's fingers. Hm, she was soft. A softness that seemed even more seductive with Natasha's hard teeth nipping at her lips. But that wasn't what she wanted. Belle grasped Natasha's hair, jerked her head back to bare the long neck, and slid her teeth into her.

A sigh left Natasha's mouth the same time that her hot blood rushed between Belle's lips. Warm breasts thrust against her. More wetness poured out of Natasha. Belle staggered at the surge of pleasure, the heat, and the nourishment flooding into her open mouth. She gulped greedily and closed her eyes at the spreading warmth in her body, the feeling of every molecule plumping, strengthening, and bursting with life. Her hand tightened in Natasha's hair. The woman whimpered. Belle pushed her open palm against the dripping pussy and the human moved against her, trying to scratch her own itch. It wasn't her turn, but Belle let her. It felt good, that wet movement against her hand, the soft pussy lips and the slick opening that begged to be penetrated.

She barely stopped herself from draining the human. Belle slowed her gulps down to sips, then to the barest taste before she licked the wound and drew away. Natasha trembled. Satisfaction suffused her languorous blue eyes and she smiled. Did she think it was over? Belle shoved her away.

Gasps. They came from all sides. From behind her, chorusing from the five onlookers and from Natasha herself as she pitched backward and off the balcony toward the floor twenty feet below. But the rope jerked around her hips, on her hands, at her feet, and held. One by one, heads began to look up, and more gasps came. A scream. Flashes of widened eyes, of terror and curiosity, looking up at them, at Natasha with her long banner of scarlet hair waving as she swayed above them in the air, a tightly held pendulum, suspended by the ropes. The balcony groaned.

"Do you still trust me?" Belle asked.

"Yes!"

The word burst out of Natasha, past the heaving chest and the cold fear raising a stink on her skin. Belle heard movement behind her. She felt a rush of air.

A hard voice said, "Don't mess with the scene." And everything quieted.

Natasha's skin reddened from the pressure of the ropes. Her eyes were wide and afraid. But her cunt still dripped, its moisture still begged for Belle's fingers.

"Good."

Her pussy was pink, purring perfection. Nothing like Silvija's, of course, but it was certainly gorgeous. Belle touched the moist opening with tender fingers, lightly stroking, spreading the wetness up and over Natasha's clit. The electric feeling of her intimate flesh sent a charge into Belle's own pussy. She was wet, anticipating the full feel of Natasha around her hand, the sound of her coming, of what she would do to her after.

Belle moved her fingers inside Natasha. She curled them and began to stroke. The human's body was beautiful as she forgot her fear. Her hands loosened from their death grip on the railing, her eyes fluttered closed, and the striated muscles relaxed, retreated to rest once again beneath the skin of her neck, shoulders, and belly. Her clit plumped beneath Belle's thumb, soft noises began to leave her throat, then hard ones, gasps of pleasure. Her muscles tightened again. Her belly flexed.

Belle grasped the rope tied at Natasha's waist. She pulled it, jerking the woman against her as she fucked her. She fucked her sweetly. She fucked her hard until Natasha's voice rose up higher to the ceiling, flowed down to the stage, into all the rooms of Mina's Chamber. Until her voice was the only thing anyone could hear. No one heard the liquid fuck of Belle's fingers inside her miraculous human cunt. That sound was for Belle alone. The noise that quickened her clit and had her fucking the air as she was fucking Natasha.

"Yes! Oh!"

The human's cries grew louder. Her voice roughened until all that came out were sounds, not words. But everyone understood. Her delight was gorgeous to see. Gorgeous to feel pulsing around Belle's hand, squeezing her fingers, bubbling up from her juicy pink cunt, flooding down into her ass, and sending sensation rushing over Belle's skin. Natasha's voice rose in a climactic shout, then quieted. She hiccupped and sighed. Her breath flowed down over the crowd. A smattering of applause sounded below as Belle slowly began to pull her up.

On the stage, Ellie was finished. Her corset piercing glowed silver and red under the hot lights. All fourteen captive bead rings were in, hooked just beneath her skin in a gorgeous hourglass shape made even more lovely by the red satin ribbon threaded through the rings to make it indeed look like the laced back of a corset. Ellie was flushed with satisfaction, while her piercer stood by her side, smiling proudly.

Natasha panted. As much from the renewed fear at her dizzying height above the crowd as the orgasm still sending tremors through her body. Belle grasped the knife and released the blade. She cut Natasha off the balcony and the human staggered against her on weakened legs, stumbling with her fear-scented breath and her nearly feverish body. Her wrists, ankles, and waist ran hot with rope burns.

"Thank you," Natasha sighed.

"You're welcome." Belle gently leaned her toward her friends and the women took her, their eyes flickering between Belle and the weakened woman. "Can I keep this?" Belle held up the knife. When the tuxedoed man only nodded, she smiled her thanks and left the balcony.

A smell had come to her in the middle of fucking Natasha. It was a smell that Belle recognized. A smell that had distracted her from the human. It was blood. Vampire blood. Suffused with the scent of jasmine. Natasha had been sweetness itself, gushing pleasure in hot spurts that made Belle's pussy slick with appreciation. But when the smell of jasmine rose up in the club's heat, she suddenly wanted something harder than the human. She wanted something that only another beast with a strong, relentless touch could provide.

Belle cut quickly through the mostly human throng in their slippery costumes. It didn't take long to find her. The beast was stripped and tied to an X-shaped cross in a small room. A dozen or so looked on while a human woman took a whip to her. It was a long mini bullwhip that snaked out gracefully before lashing against Julia's back with a sound like a bullet.

Julia jerked in pain, each lick of the lash bringing up a crimson stain and a gash against her brown flesh that quickly healed leaving only its bloody shadow.

Belle pushed past the closest spectators and grasped the hand of the woman expertly wielding the whip. The human turned, the whip lashing in the air above them, caught in midstrike.

"What the fuck?" The woman struggled in Belle's grasp.

"You're done."

As much as Belle relished the sight of Julia in pain, she had a better use for the beast. Belle shoved the woman back, not watching to see if she fell or merely stumbled against the people gathered close. The room was hot, nearly claustrophobic with so many humans and their needs. Vampires who had gathered—Belle smelled at least two—lent their coolness to the air but it didn't help. In the light, with the heat racing through her from the encounter with Natasha, Belle saw Julia's tight little body, and hungered. Her small bottom and thighs with their disappearing lines of pain excited her. The muscled back, dimpled cheeks, and the moisture leaking from between her legs all made Belle ache. She snapped the chains holding Julia's arms captive to the iron cross and swung the smaller beast around.

"Fuck me," Belle said.

The fiend stumbled off the cross and into Belle's eyes. Her own eyes blazed with want and her breath had already started, shuddering so deeply in her chest that the small breasts heaved with it. Julia's sable skin shimmered with bloodied sweat.

"Now," Belle hissed.

Julia didn't hesitate again. She ripped down Belle's zipper and plunged down into the cool leather. Her small fingers quickly found Belle's clit, slid against it firmly, parted plump pussy lips, and teased the soaking hole. The taller woman gasped and stumbled until her back was to the cross. Julia tugged down the pants and then her fingers weren't teasing Belle anymore. They were fucking, slipping with cunning ease into her wet pussy, thrusting and fucking, her thumb roughly jerking at Belle's thickening clit until she gasped, lust and desire and the need for satisfaction crawling inside, scalding the heat up between her legs. Julia dropped to her knees, taking the pants with her, baring Belle's cunt to the warm air, then to her cool mouth. *Fuck!*

Belle's head fell back, her thighs widened as far as the pants would let her. She gasped. Julia moaned, her mouth full of pussy, her fingers again inside Belle. She fucked and sucked while Belle grasped the back of her head, pushing the little fiend's face deeper into her pussy, into that hole that begged to be filled even more.

With one hand, she gripped the dangling remnants of the chain that had just held Julia captive, clenching the heating metal in her hand tighter as the band of sensation inside her tightened, as tightly as Julia's curled palm and fingers fit inside her needful pussy, fucking the pleasure in, pulling fulfillment out. Julia sucked hungrily at Belle's clit, lapped greedily at her gushing cunt until Belle completely forgot the eyes on her, until she closed her eyes and let the tide claim her. The orgasm bolted through her like lightning. Her hips jerked against Julia's mouth and the chain groaned, snapped, in her hands.

When she opened her eyes, the fever inside her was gone. Julia stood up, licking her lips and her fingers. Her eyes still burned. Beyond her, the crowd watched them, waiting to see what they would do next. Especially the full-bodied woman who had used the whip to such good effect on Julia.

Belle's mouth twisted. "I'll let you get back to your fun." She wiped a spot of her come from the corner of Julia's mouth, then licked her finger. "See you at home."

Chapter 18

The snow swirled up in thick white strips, whipping wind and cold into Belle's face. At one o'clock in the afternoon it was still dark with not a sign of sun in the sky or people in the streets.

"I love Christmas in Alaska," Shaye said with a delighted laugh, twirling like a snow angel in the white drift. "Jamaica is beautiful but you can't hunt a human under the afternoon sky there."

Belle had to agree. Wind howled around them, whistling through the wide, friendly alleys of Wildbrook, through the snow-laden trees standing still and white in the small park a few feet away. Behind her sunglasses, Belle squinted. Before they left the Cave, Shaye had told her to wear them, and at the time she thought the idea was stupid, but now in the lashing snow that would have blinded her eyes and led her stumbling into parked cars, houses, and even boats frozen to the dock, Belle was grateful.

After being in California, it felt good to be back home. Among the plentiful warmth and excess, Belle had thrived, glutting herself on disposable humans until she thought she would burst. But she wanted someone to share that plenty with. The beast. Or even Shaye. On the plane ride home, she indulged in fantasies of living someplace warm with the family. A place with a regular sunrise and sunset, where the food was as plentiful as air and the family bed always warm with Silvija.

Belle shook herself. But that was a fantasy, and this was now. They were here in the snow to hunt. Any human out at this time of day and in this weather was fair game. As far as their family knew, a bear could have gotten them or even a hungry wolf sprung snarling from the snow. Behind her mask of white, Belle smiled. It was hard to see, but not impossible. She and Shaye left the small main avenue to walk the backside of the town near its bordering wall of snow-covered pines. A flash of dark caught Belle's eye and a strong scent distracted her nose. Pine. *It must be the trees.*

No scent of humans teased the air, no sign of a feast; still, it was good to be out of the Cave, good to not wait for Silvija and wonder when the beast would come back into her bed and give her something to scream about.

A dark flash against white caught Belle's eye again and next to it a dense white, thicker than the swirling snow. Both shapes moved quickly, silently. Warning prickled the back of her neck.

"Shaye—"

Her back exploded with pain. She gasped and spun. Naked air against her skin. The sound of her tattered sweater fluttering in the harsh wind. Another slashing pain tore down her arm and blood splashed on the snow. Hers. Shaye was gone. A noise like triumph rippled close and Belle ducked on instinct, falling flat on her belly into the white powder. Her body sang with pain. A sharp thing whistled in the air above her and Belle rolled across the ground, biting back a curse as a jagged rock stabbed into her side, ripping her sweater and her skin. More pain. She came up alive and spun, kicking out, moving in a deadly arch toward the white thing she thought she saw through the snow.

Her skin was already healing. Before she could focus on the presence, a dark shape darted close and slammed into her jaw, knocking the shades off her face. *Fuck!* Another blow to her belly and Belle sank into the snow but rolled quickly away from the rushing shapes. She couldn't see them clearly. But she heard them and smelled them. A scent of pine more malevolent than that of the trees bruised her nose. And another essence under it that didn't belong. Something sweet, like overripe fruit.

"Shaye!"

Her shout brought the vampires close again and Belle rose up in a crouch, moving as quietly as she could close to the ground. She was suddenly very grateful for her white clothes. The sharp blade swung toward her, its high whistle cutting through the howling wind. She pivoted away and grabbed for the stone that had rammed into her side and threw it— hard—toward the strongest smell. A grunt and a soft thud told her the strike was good. The smell of stolen blood bubbled up in the air.

Belle stayed low to the ground, fumbling in her pocket for the switchblade she'd gotten from Mina's Chamber and recently started carrying with her everywhere. The handle felt solid in her palm. A touch of her finger released the blade just as the scent of pine and a pair of cold green eyes came close. Belle slashed high, reaching for the throat. The blade caught. A gurgle of sound. It pulled jaggedly against flesh and she forced it deeper, pulled out, then thrust back, this time aiming low.

Cool blood poured over her hand. She retreated from the wounded beast with a high whirling kick just like Ivy had taught her. A gasp. The sound of bones breaking. A body fell heavily to the ground. She struck quickly, landing on a surprisingly slight body, slashing with her knife at any part she could reach. More blood on the snow. Her fingers ripped at the mask covering the vampire's face, taking flesh and more blood with them. Dark hair spilled out from the mask and cap. It was hard to see anything else through the wind-whipped snow, but the face was soft under her fumbling hands. They found the gentle symmetry of a female face. The body bucked under hers, dying but soon to revive. She needed to find Shaye. Belle leapt up, eyes squinting by habit against the lash of wind-carried snow.

A few feet away, her foot struck something heavy. She bent. It was a blade. A big one. Belle grasped it, her naked switchblade in one hand and the machete in the other. Snow whipped up to blind her but she blinked against it, twirling, waiting for another attack. The smell of the beasts was thick, wounded, but they were healing even now. Had they killed Shaye?

"Belle!"

The child's voice came from far off, was faint. Belle turned and ran blindly toward it. She found her near the water, bleeding sluggishly from her side and slumped half in, half out of an anchored boat that was nothing more than a cold white shape in the moonlit dark.

"Are they gone?" Shaye gasped, fighting for air she did not need.

"Yes. For now. But we have to go home. Very quickly." She put her knife away, tossed aside the machete, and swung the small body up into her arms. "This is going to hurt, but I need to run."

And she did. All the way back to the Cave.

"What's wrong?"

Keiko greeted her at the glass door, alerted by Belle's pounding footsteps and the sight of her carrying Shaye in her arms, running all the way from the bend in the landscape leading from Wildbrook. A heavy frown sat between her eyes. "Stephen saw you in the monitors."

"We were attacked. Vampires." Belle lightly dropped Shaye to her feet. "There were at least two of them." She quickly told them what happened.

Stephen and Ivy appeared abruptly behind Keiko. "They didn't follow you. I didn't see anything on the monitors coming from behind."

"But we need to go after them." Ivy was dressed for the snow in goggles, a thick jacket she zipped up, putting a dark gun sitting heavily in its holster out of sight.

Shaye leaned against Belle. The wound on her head was already healed, leaving only a thick smear of blood. "I think they're dead." Her voice shook.

"We need to be sure." Ivy pulled out a walkie-talkie and spoke briefly into it.

Moments later, Susannah pulled up outside close to the doorstep on a buzzing snowmobile. "How many?" she asked, raising her voice above the engine and the wind.

"Two." Ivy stepped past Stephen and Keiko. "We can handle them ourselves." Then she jumped on the back of the snowmobile and took off with Susannah, roaring in white powder toward Wildbrook.

But they didn't find anything. Just the machete that Belle had discarded, a jagged rock covered in blood, and an expensive ski mask abandoned in the snow.

"They're long gone." Susannah walked into the control room with Ivy at her heels, her cheeks covered with a fine layer of frost.

"We searched damn near the entire town." Ivy sat down in a swivel chair next to Belle. "No sign of any other vampires."

Keiko's jaw tightened, but she said nothing. The monitors showed scenes of the entire compound. Frame after frame of the quiet perimeter of their home. Snow and wind played roughly with each other, piling up high drifts of powder, then blowing them down. Naked trees at the end of their forest whipped back and forth in the restless gusts. Silent.

Shaye sat huddled in one of the tall-backed leather chairs, her arms clasped around her knees. "There was nothing on the monitors."

"Nothing but us running," Belle said.

They checked their perimeter security. None of the cameras showed anything. Whoever it was hadn't left the town to find them out here. Neither had they come from this direction. According to Susannah's tracking reports, only two other vampire families lived anywhere near Alaska and they were both based at least four hundred miles away from the Cave. The nearest group was across the border in Canada and they were nothing but friendly with Silvija.

"I don't know what to think." Susannah shook her head as if her reports had betrayed her.

"Silvija already knows about everything," Stephen said. "She's already looking into it."

Belle looked up, but it was Shaye who spoke. "Is she coming back early?"

"It depends on what she finds."

Chapter 19

Belle's sense of time was no longer the same. She didn't know how long she'd been in Alaska, or even how long she'd been dead. But she knew that Silvija had been gone from the Cave a long time. The attacks in Wildbrook didn't bring her back, they only brought a restlessness to the Cave, spilling a few anxious others into the small town from time to time to search. They found nothing. Susannah went farther, leaving Alaska altogether in her own investigation, and still hadn't returned.

Belle didn't want to notice the length of Silvija's absence, but her body betrayed her. She counted every peaceful hour, each false start of breath, every anticipatory tightening of her muscles. Strangely, that absence left her more agitated than the sudden presence of enemies in the nearby town. So when she could, she flew away in the Cessna. But Silvija's absence always awaited her in the Cave.

"You need to learn how to relax," Shaye said one evening as she watched Belle give the twins a run for their money in the training room.

Everyone's disquiet had subsided or been channeled into more productive activities, leaving only Belle obviously on the edge of uncertainty. In the training room's cool silence, Stephen came at her again and Belle easily dodged his blow, coming up quickly to slash her elbow, then her clawed hands across his mouth. A long arc of blood flew from his lip and splashed on the floor near Belle's foot. She didn't have the time to admire it. From the corner of her eye she saw Ivy coming at her with the staff aimed at her legs. Belle leapt up and threw out her foot. Ivy fell back and collided with her brother. They made a loud snapping noise as their flesh connected. Belle quickly landed on her feet, then twirled abruptly when she thought she heard a noise.

"Relax," Shaye said again and laughed.

"I *am* relaxed," Belle hissed, not even convincing herself. She was waiting for Silvija to come back. The beast might be the only one who could solve the mystery of who had attacked her and Shaye in town. There were unresolved things between them, she rationalized. Before she could irritate herself any further about it, she pushed the irrational need aside and focused on kicking ass. It was so much more rewarding.

"You're doing well, puppy."

She turned around. Pain exploded on the side of Belle's face and back simultaneously. Her ass connected with the hard floor. *Shouldn't this thing be padded?*

"Shit!"

Shaye and Stephen laughed. Ivy helped her up with a teasing smile before she turned toward the doorway.

"Good to see you back in one piece, Silvija," Ivy said.

The giant was filthy. Her face, hair, and clothes were all smeared with dirt and grass stains. Dried blood dotted the paler red of her mouth and the collar of her cream turtleneck sweater. A line of flesh under her cheek still held the fragile hue of newly healed skin.

"One of your girlfriends got rough?" Belle asked.

"Not quite. You're the only one who bites this deeply."

For a moment, Belle thought the beast's eyes sparkled, but it must have been just a reflection of the overhead lights.

"It looks like you were hunting," Stephen said. The laughter was gone from his face. "Did you catch anything?"

"Nothing worthwhile." Silvija made a dismissive motion. "I stopped in Whitehorse where I'd heard about a loner prey-ing on humans and familied vampires alike. But he was mostly harmless and not the one who came to Wildbrook."

A frown marred Ivy's normally smooth brow. "So we still don't know who's trying to harm us?"

"Not yet, but soon." The heaviness of the words settled in the room, pressing everyone into silence.

"I need a bath," Silvija said abruptly. She looked at Belle. "Join me?"

The question surprised Belle into saying yes and she barely waved good-bye to her playmates and Shaye before follow-ing Silvija out of the room and deeper into the house. Her fears, her resentment, even all thought of the possible danger in Wildbrook fell away in the wake of the giant's scent.

In their suite of rooms, the older vampire swept off her sweater and close-fitting tank top. She spared a moment to pry off her running shoes and socks before shimmying out of her jeans. Belle didn't look away. She savored the sleek lines of the beast, the lift of her breasts, ribs, muscle, bone, all moving with liquid ease under her skin.

Silvija wasn't fragile. She wouldn't break if Belle touched her. Rope burns wouldn't stay on her skin.

"Coming?"

Belle followed, hypnotized, as Silvija went, naked, toward their bathing room. The room was more of a Turkish bath with its ornate mosaic tile decorating the walls and bottom of the pool and the bits of glass winking high on the ceiling that reflected the water, the color, and the steam. Belle had never visited this part of their suites. She'd taken baths, dressed, killed, even laughed in the presence of the other beasts, but had never made time to explore the luxuries of the house. Perhaps she had been waiting for Silvija to come home and show them to her.

The water kissed Silvija's feet, slid up her muscled calves, to the backs of her knees and—Belle swallowed—up the clearly defined thighs and the high, firm globes of her ass. The wetness licked at her back and the beast sank deeper into the water with a decadent growl of pleasure. Steam rose from the water, curling around her shoulders and face. Then she disappeared beneath the surface. Belle released the unnecessary breath she was holding.

She sat on the warm marble bench built into the wall and watched the still water over what she assumed was the beast's head. As a human, she thought that she'd known more about suffering the needles of unwanted emotion, of wanting something so badly even though she knew that the receiving of it would hurt much worse. But now, waiting in the steamed room with her desire drumming in her ears like her lost pulse, feeling the fullness of want between her thighs, she knew what she felt, then was nothing. Did the beast know how badly Belle wanted to touch her? Of course she did. Belle wanted to reach out and take, just like Silvija had taken her. But, despite everything she'd done between death and now, she was afraid.

When she had seen Julia in that hotel, she never thought she would find a more beautiful woman. But she was wrong. True beauty was what snaked beneath the water of this private bath. True beauty was what made her skin feel like it would burst. True beauty was going to be the death of her.

The warm marble skated beneath her fingers and her bare feet. She curled her toes against the floor.

"What are you waiting for?" The question came from the glistening goddess rising from the water. "Take off your clothes. Come."

"Do you get off on ordering people around?"

"No. I just want to forget about those damn interlopers for a moment." A smile toyed briefly with Silvija's mouth. "Besides, I know what you want."

"Really?" She let the doubt color her voice.

"Of course. You want the same thing I do."

Belle was grateful of the respite from Silvija's eyes as she closed them and sluiced water back from her face. Was it that simple? Want and take? Give and get?

Silvija shook her head as she stepped out of the steaming pool to walk down two small steps leading to a smaller bath, a tub made for three instead of thirteen with water already drawn and steaming in it. She rubbed her hand towel with a bar of unscented soap and began to lather herself.

"I want—" Belle stopped.

"It's nothing to be ashamed of," Silvija said within Belle's silence. "We've shared each other before, under ideal circumstances"—her glance clouded as if remembering the day in the basement—"and not. It's no shame to want." Her eyes flickered over Belle's face and body. "In this life, all we have are sensations. So long as only a few, if any, are hurt, we indulge our senses to the fullest here. You know this by now. There's nothing taboo about sex, about our sex, about the things we think about. If you want to fuck, you fuck. If you want to make love"—Silvija's voice dropped deep into her throat—"we make love."

Belle stared at the luscious brown flesh kissed by pale bubbles and a layer of wet. She licked her lips. Silvija smiled, then dipped beneath the surface of the water. Seconds later, she emerged, the bubbles washed from her skin, the lush surface glistening.

Silvija climbed out of the tub and walked toward her. "Is that what you want, my Belle? To make love?" Her damp feet kissed the tile a few inches from Belle. "I enjoy you, you know. All those times when you've allowed me to touch you. Even when you've fought me. I enjoyed you. It's been a long time since I've fucked someone like you who fought so badly not to want me. Would it make it easier if I took you again?"

"I want you to fuck me," Belle said. The decision made itself as the words tumbled from her mouth.

Silvija looked surprised. "And then?"

"And then nothing." Belle held Silvija with her eyes. "I want you. Give me what I want."

Silvija's eyebrow rose. "All right."

She took her time toweling her body dry, lingering over the swell and arcs of flesh, over the heaviness of her hair, all while calmly watching Belle. When she was finished, or sure that Belle was well and truly under the spell of her divine body, she hung the towel back on its rack and walked into the bedroom.

The large bed, the sleek wooden floor with its gigantic bearskin rug and damp-looking sheen, the heavy double doors that had no lock, all took on a lilting eroticism the moment Silvija stepped into the room. Belle's flesh began to weep with desire. This was what she wanted. This was what she'd asked for in that cavernous wet room.

"Get on the bed."

A part of her wanted to say no, to tell Silvija to fuck off and tell her where to stick her orders and authoritative tone. But that small part of her whimpered and quickly slunk away. She walked backward to the bed and sat down.

"Take off your clothes and lie down. In the center of the bed."

Silvija watched Belle, her eyes dark pools of purpose as she walked around the bed to the massive trunk at its end.

"Did you enjoy being fucked by men?" she asked.

After a moment's hesitation, Belle answered, "One man. And sometimes."

"He didn't always do it for you?" Silvija bent over the trunk and rummaged through its contents.

"I didn't always take the time to prepare myself." Belle drew off her shirt and bra in one smooth motion. Her pants and panties followed a few seconds later.

Sylvia's mouth quirked up. "How?"

"With fantasies. Of women." Belle's eyes flickered to the

floor but did not stay there. "Fucking each other. Fucking me. Touching each other's breasts, kissing."

"Ah." Silvija drew a harness from the trunk and fitted a small black dildo into it before strapping it to her body. It fit snugly to her lush hips, transforming her into a hermaphroditic Priapus. Silvija stroked her penis and watched Belle with a heavy-lidded gaze. "Nothing too deviant."

Silvija closed the lid to the trunk and approached the bed. Something deep inside Belle trembled, shuddered, and took notice of the beast. In the middle of the bed, she held her head up and watched Silvija, eyes deliberately traveling the sleek body, lingering on the phallus strapped to her hips. Silvija's knee sank into the bed. She leaned in and stroked Belle's foot.

The caress was nothing. No more than a set of fingertips on the slope of ankle, the combination of flesh and bone. But Belle felt it like a lash. The touch traveled the length of her foot, to her knee, before lightly skimming the outside of her thigh. Breath trembled in her throat and tumbled from her mouth in a sigh. Longing. Desire. She knew what it was now. She knew.

Silvija bent her head and kissed Belle's foot, the smooth line of flesh just above her toes. Belle flinched at the light pain, at the pinprick of sensation from Silvija's teeth sinking into her skin. A cool tongue washed away the pain. She kissed higher on her foot, another sting, another lick. And higher until the length of Belle's foot was a path of pain and kisses, her blood and Silvija's saliva. Her thighs loosened and she sighed, helpless to the swell of her pussy lips, the heaviness in her breasts, and the tightening of her nipples.

Silvija's cool tongue lapped at the inside of her knees, and her tongue nipped at the tender flesh there while her hands trailed a path of fire up the back of Belle's thigh. Her head bowed close to Belle, her scent washed lush and untamed over Belle as her intent, one of seduction, not simply to fuck, overwhelmed Belle, made her release her guard against the beast and allow her between her thighs.

Belle shuddered at the first touch of Silvija's tongue on her clit. It wasn't as if Silvija had never touched her that way before, only that she did it so gently. As if gauging Belle's response to her, and waiting for . . . something. Belle didn't want her to be gentle. She didn't want this light stroke of tongue that could make Belle think this was more than it was, or possibly less. Had their midday fuck against the glass meant anything to Silvija? Belle grabbed Silvija's hair and pulled.

Silvija jerked against her, flashing a look of fire. She growled. Her grip on Belle's thighs tightened enough to bruise.

"Fuck me," Belle hissed. "Don't pretend that I'm someone else or that this is something more. If I wanted fake tenderness I would be in Julia's bed tonight."

The beast suddenly rose up above, her nose only accidentally nudging Belle's clit as she emerged from between her thighs.

"Trust me when I say you don't want the kind of pain I can give."

"I don't want your pain," Belle growled, equally fierce. "I want this." She grasped beyond the thick jutting dick to cup Silvija's pussy, the soft bare expanse of flesh that slid wet beneath her palm. The beast jerked against her, a gasp tumbling, uncontrolled, from her mouth.

Belle shuddered at the knowledge that Silvija wanted her too, that this was more than just her delirious imagination and lust. All that was finished. It was desire now between them, laid bare and honest perhaps for the first time. Silvija grasped her jaw, pulling her roughly forward for a kiss. Her mouth swooped down to cover Belle's, lips parted, teeth sheathed, and eyes ablaze. She had killed something tonight. The taste of it hovered on her tongue, a light flavoring over her taste buds, a gentle breath of chase and capture and conquer that flooded like memory from the beast. And Silvija's skin still smelled like it, despite her earlier bath.

...

Their mouths met and dueled and took into each the flavor of the other. Their tongues slid and met and licked and their dull human teeth bit into wanted flesh, tearing only a little when the desire became too rough. Belle raked her fingers over Silvija's chest, flicking over hard nipples, heavy breasts, and down to the flat belly that danced beneath her hands. The beast growled into her mouth, pushed her back, and nudged her thighs open.

She moved into Belle like a dream. Like coming home, like the noonday sun through flesh. Belle arched against the sheets at that first stroke. The beast settled into Belle's pussy like she planned to be there for a long time and wouldn't leave it until she was good and ready. Belle widened her legs for more.

"I want you to know," Silvija hissed, pulling completely out of her and taking the smaller beast's breath with her, "that I'm fucking you because I want to." The dick rubbed against her cunt lips, teasing. "Not because there's someone else I'd rather fuck." She thrust deeply back into the pussy, bringing back breath, and sensation, and the beginnings of heat. "Not because I'm pretending that you're someone else." Her strokes deepened, quickened. "Not even because you asked me to." Belle gasped again and wrapped her legs around Silvija, pulling her close. "Only because I want to. Understand me?" She fucked her slowly, deeply, keeping her eyes on Belle. Above her, she was gorgeous, wet hair sliding over her shoulders and breasts as she moved, her flesh steaming with desire, the long muscles in her arms hard beneath Belle's hands as the two women came together. Again. And again.

"Understand?" she asked, using her dick to make the point for her, moving quickly now inside Belle as she waited for the answer.

"Yes." Fuck. "Yes."

Belle clung to her, mouth open, pussy wet and filled, begging with her body for Silvija to give her what they both wanted. They slid together, churning sweat up on their skin.

Her hands skimmed over Silvija's arms, up to her shoulders, and down to the snaking hips.

"Fuck me harder." *This* was what she wanted.

Silvija grunted and sped her movements, deepened her thrusts until they both made needful animal noises, grunts and gasps and yeses and please and fuck me and now. Belle opened herself as much as she could, spreading crablike under her lover, grasping her tighter to hold the sensation of heat and of pleasure curling up inside her. Slick and hard and aching. Her entire body, her breasts, her clit. Her mouth opened for something to taste and found Silvija. She swallowed the giant's grunts, muffled the sound of need as they fucked. Harder. Deeper.

She felt Silvija shudder, felt the orgasm ripple through her beast as Silvija's hips jerked and her gasps rose to near full-throated roars. The giant bit her mouth, her throat, and clutched at the back of her neck. Belle moaned hotly as sensation glided through her. She pulled Silvija's head closer and their mouths meshed and parted, allowing room for sound and killing teeth that suddenly flared free. Belle gasped and quivered against Silvija. It was coming. It was—Belle gasped as Silvija abruptly pulled out of her. Her body clutched at the sudden emptiness.

She licked her dry lips. "What?"

"Turn over." Silvija's voice was low and rough.

Her thighs spasmed and trembled with need. Blindly, she did as the beast asked, turning over and tilted up her ass. Cool air brushed over her exposed wet pussy.

"Perfect. That's exactly how I want you."

Silvija's hands drifted down to cup, to press, to part Belle's pussy. Belle shamelessly thrust back, wanting to feel more of that pressure, wanting Silvija to finish what she started. Fingers flickered across her clit and she moaned, widening her thighs. Silvija chuckled deep in her throat. She whispered something, a light brush of sound against Belle's back that triggered a shudder in her. The shudder became a groaning gasp when

Silvija slid into her. The giant built speed, slipping easily back into the rhythm they shared before, the same pleasing stroke that stirred heat in Belle's insides and had a scream crawling up the walls of her throat.

"Do you like this?" Silvija grated against her ear. "Do you?"

"Yes, oh!" Belle gasped through her wide-open mouth and licked her lips.

The dick moved inside her, sliding deeply into the slick cavern of her pussy, tilting into her, sweetening her. Her fingers tightened in the sheets and she blinked at the headboard as sweat dripped into her eyes. The bed shook as Silvija fucked her, slamming the delight into her body from behind. Sensation built inside her, roiled and tumbled until she was shuddering and gasping, clawing at the sheets and completely under Silvija's power.

Silvija pulled at Belle's nipples, twisted her own hips, fucking the pleasure into Belle until they were both moaning and gasping on top of the sheets. The bed shook as they moved as one, flowing with the liquid fucking of Silvija's dick inside the swimming heat of Belle's pussy.

The orgasm slammed into them both, tumbling the two beasts down into the bed. Belle's scream rose up in her throat, rocketing into the room joining Silvija's roar. Their two voices melded, echoed, tapering off into panting gasps that were suddenly very necessary for two beasts who didn't need to breathe.

Silvija withdrew and tumbled to the side, relieving Belle of her body's weight. She shivered as Silvija skated her hand down her back and dropped a heavy palm on her hip. Their breaths slowly subsided into quietness before disappearing altogether. Belle blinked at the bedroom wall as everything inside her fell back into place. It felt absolutely right to have Silvija at her back, to have the giant's comfortable weight behind her in the sprawling expanse of the bed. She fumbled back for Silvija's hand and put it on her breast, reaching out for the gentleness she had denied herself when they first started.

"You two are done, right?" Julia asked as she crept in, smelling of shared blood and limes. "I need to sleep."

She dropped heavily into the bed, eyes scorching over Belle's nakedness. Her body slipped up behind Silvija, and Belle could only watch as Julia unbuckled the giant's harness, took the dick that was still wet from Belle's body, and tossed it behind off the bed. A deep purr vibrated in Julia's body as she cuddled closer to Silvija.

Belle fell into the beast's loose embrace, her strength completely depleted. As she sank deeper into sleep, she thought she felt a kiss, a damp float of lips across the back of her neck. But it couldn't have been. She must have already been dreaming.

Chapter 20

Belle dreamt. The forest spun with indefinable shapes, deadly pale and dark forms that threatened with their eyes and hands. She took out her blade, a long machete the size of her body, pulling it up from the sheath slung across her back, and whirling as the snow whirled, her teeth clenched together ready for whatever the creatures would throw at her.

"Come with me." The words came from beyond the forest, and the shapes before her shifted again and became like mist.

Belle shook her head but the voice insisted again, whispering low and soft at her ear. "Come with me."

She opened her eyes. Silvija hovered over her in the bed, a dark shape in the darker room. Beside Belle, Julia and Violet still clung to sleep and to each other, their limbs only twining incidentally with hers. Belle sat up. Silvija held out a hand rusty with the smell of blood and Belle took it, sliding from the bed wearing only her skin. She released the beast's hand to pull on a robe and followed her silent form out of the room and down the hallway. With the light and the mists of sleep washed from her eyes, Belle noticed that Silvija was wearing black. A turtleneck that fit close to her long body, skimming the lush curves without clinging, and slacks that did her thighs and legs the same favor. Thick-soled boots muffled her footsteps down the hall. She smelled like pain.

They swept through the silent Cave, past rooms with sleeping beasts and others who were simply being quiet. At nearly five in the afternoon of another completely dark day, most slept, either by habit or because they'd worn themselves out staying up for days at a time, hunting pleasure or hunting food. Belle hadn't been able to hunt.

Silvija led her up a surprising set of stairs ending at a room with no ceiling. Shaye stood silently in one bare corner with an equally quiet Keiko next to her. In the center of the room, sitting on the floor with her arms and legs stretched uncomfortably before her into a shallow pan, sat a pretty vampire. She was a cliché of their kind with thick black hair hanging to her waist, pale skin, and red lips that glistened wetly under the naked sky. A crisp pine scent hovered around her.

"This is Colleen," Silvija said, as if introducing them at a garden party. "Is she the one you saw in Wildbrook?"

Up close, Belle saw that Colleen's hands and feet were trapped in a block of dried cement. The skin at her ankles and wrists were bloody and raw from when she'd tried to free them. A shudder of fear, then satisfaction, rippled through Belle. The vampire's face was a mass of healing bruises and cuts. A thin line of crusting blood ringed her neck, and what Belle initially thought was a fashionably asymmetrical blouse had actually been ripped to expose her shoulders to pain.

"I'm not sure," Belle said.

But a flash of the captive's eyes, fearful, defiant, and brilliantly green, confirmed it. Belle moved forward in shock. *This was the one who had attacked—?* A sharp slap cut her thought short. Colleen's mouth was redder now, with blood and the mark of Silvija's hand across it.

"Were you sent to kill them?" Silvija looked at the captive now, her mouth held in a tight, hard line.

"They're still alive, aren't they?"

Silvija grabbed one of Colleen's hands just above the wrist
and jerked. The sound of tearing flesh, breaking bones, and
vampire's screams ripped through the quiet. Blood sprayed
across Silvija's face and chest.

"That's not what I want to hear," she growled.

She held Colleen's arm firmly in her hand, the mangled
flesh with its protruding twin bones hovering above the
blood-slashed cement block. The vampire's eyes were wide
pools of pain, no longer holding defiance. Her screams ricocheted through the room. She panted between screams, even
as the pink and white flesh of her arm wriggled like blood-fed
worms, reaching toward the wrist and hand still trapped in
the cement, trying to heal itself. Belle crossed her own arms,
hugging herself and recoiling in reaction.

The skin in Colleen's face was taut and white, the eyes ter-
rified. "I—don't!—I don't know anything—" Her eyes swiveled
around the room as if looking for mercy from somewhere.
She shook her head. "Please—please!"

"That's not it either," Silvija said. She dropped the vampire's bloodied arm in disgust and stepped away, wiping her
face with her sweatered arm. "Keiko, shut her up. She's not
saying anything useful."

Her second in command was immediately there, kneeling
close. She snapped Colleen's neck, abruptly cutting off the
captive's screaming pleas.

Belle looked at Silvija. "Did you find out anything from
her at all?"

"Only that she's very loyal." A sigh of irritation hissed
from her mouth. "We've been at her for a long time. I doubt
she'll say anything." Silvija turned to her second in command. "Finish her, Keiko. Unless you think you'll have better
luck. I'm tired of playing."

Belle watched as Keiko shackled a limp Colleen to the
floor with a heavy chain, triple looped around her waist. Her
neck was broken, but she would revive soon enough. If the

sun returned before Keiko was through with her, the vampire would burn away to ashes and bone under its unforgiving heat. Belle shuddered.

"Come with me," Silvija murmured, her voice distant. "I'll take you back to bed."

But as they walked quietly back down the hallway toward the main bedroom and a sleepless day staring at the ceiling, Belle realized that she didn't want to go back there. In the room, when the giant would have led her to the rumpled sheets, Belle took Silvija's hand and walked past the still slumbering Julia and Violet. The bathing room was quiet. She bypassed the hot pool and Jacuzzi in favor of the simple oversized tub. There she released Silvija's hand to turn on the hot water and sprinkle unscented bath salts under the steaming gush.

A muscle ticked in the giant's jaw. "I don't have time for this."

"You do."

Belle started to undo Silvija's slacks but the giant stopped her. "I don't. People have threatened us. They harmed you and Shaye. If I rest they'll think that we're weak and that they can keep doing this. Then we're finished."

"That's not true. Colleen and the other one came. Shaye and I got hurt, but we're fine. It's only a matter of time before you find the other one and sort this all out. Susannah is looking for them. Ivy and Stephen and everyone else is keeping an eye out at the Cave and in town. There's nothing more to be done now. Tomorrow you can burn and kill and fight. For today, just give me this."

With each word Belle spoke, Silvija softened, her stance relaxing until her hands fell back to allow Belle what she wanted. Her head rolled back and she sighed. Belle swept off Silvija's bloodied turtleneck, the heavy boots and dark slacks before pulling off her own robe and tossing it aside.

"Come with me." She echoed the giant's earlier command, holding out her hand.

Silvija came. She put her bloodied hand in Belle's and they sank down into the far end of the bath together away from the streaming tap. Silvija watched her tiredly, as if to see what she would do next.

"Lean your head back."

And Silvija did, resting her head back against the soft pile of towels Belle put there just for that purpose. Another shuddering sigh escaped her lips. She looked beautiful. Strong. Exhausted. She lay limp in the tub with faint ribbons of red— Colleen's blood—already threading from her skin through the water.

Belle soaped a small towel and began to wash Silvija, starting at her feet, massaging her tense calves, thighs, her belly, breasts. The giant relaxed even more, lifting her arms for Belle to wash, one after the other. Her face, Belle lingered over, wiping away the blood and tension, smoothing the towel over the soft skin and closed eyes until Silvija pushed it away, smiling tiredly.

"Enough."

She pulled Belle against her and with a small splash, the smaller beast came, turning to press her back against Silvija's breasts, her head relaxed against the scented curve of the giant's shoulder. Belle's knees rose up in the tub, water sluicing off them like tears.

In the spacious room with the Mediterranean and sky-blue mosaic tile, with the winking pieces of glass on the ceiling reflecting their stillness, with their bodies bare and steaming in the wet heat, and with nothing between them but exhaustion, frustration, and fear, Belle felt more intimately connected with Silvija than ever before. She closed her eyes to enjoy the moment before it ended.

Chapter 21

Belle had fallen in lust. There was no other way to put it. She had tumbled from the relative safety of her hatred for Silvija to a place where she could do little but crave her. Their quiet moment together in the tub had only made it worse. In the forests of Jamaica, and even on the boat, their encounters had been so separate from anything else she'd known. They were isolated from the rest of the world. Nothing had existed but them and a few forgettable others. Lust had seemed a logical respite. But here, it was different. There were distractions and people she could be friends with and confide in. There was danger in the town and food, new skills to practice. Belle had other things to do besides fall under Silvija's spell. But she realized that none of this mattered.

When Silvija walked into the bedroom with animal grace, Belle's body sat up and took notice. Her legs unwound from their lotus position on the heavy cedar chest at the foot of the bed and her bare feet fell lightly to the furred rug. Belle swallowed. She could see the impression of nipples through Silvija's dress, feel the long cool body as it brushed through the air and made its way toward her. An image of the beast at work, her blood-splashed face hard as she growled at Colleen, flickered in Belle's mind. Her thighs pressed tightly together. Silvija didn't have pleasantries in mind with this visit; that much was obvious. Her eyes flashed with the hunger that Belle had come to know, had come to anticipate and crave.

"You look good," Silvija said. And Belle was caught off guard. What was this?

Belle put her already neglected book down beside her. When she was just a few tempting inches away from her, Silvija smiled.

"What are you reading?"

"I can't remember." A tingling wetness settled between Belle's legs.

She could smell Silvija. The beast's clove scent rose and expanded in the room until it nuzzled against Belle's face, brushing against, then into her to gain access to all her orifices. And Silvija's woman scent. It rose up too, unfettered by underwear from beneath her dress. Silvija lifted her hand to Belle's face and the smaller beast moved her head abruptly back.

Silvija smiled. "You don't trust me?"

"Do I look like a fool?"

Silvija only laughed. Then completed the motion with her hand, lightly stroking Belle's cheek. When the fingers grazed her lips, she started to quake inside. Why was she so weak? A thumb flickered against the side of her mouth and, Belle couldn't help it, really, she licked her lips. Inadvertently wetting the beast's finger. Silvija growled. The thumb brushed Belle's lips again and she opened her mouth, inviting it inside. Silvija accepted the invitation, slowly moving the thumb past her damp lips to stroke the tender flesh inside, then her sharp teeth. She touched the smooth front teeth, playing with them before caressing the sharp lower canines. She cut herself. Now it was Belle's turn to groan.

Her tongue licked at the bloodied finger, then cupped it into the sensitive thick trough. It felt like the beast was touching her clit, rubbing her finger over and beneath it, stirring up pleasure with every movement. Silvija stroked her tongue with the finger, her own mouth open and avid as she watched Belle take all of her finger and begin to suck it. She had to close her eyes. It felt so good. The finger moved inside her mouth, rubbing against her lips with each pass. Belle's legs opened of their own volition. The sensations between them were too much to keep in. Her pussy lips plumped and grew tender with wetness. Silvija took her finger back.

Belle's eyes flew open. Would the beast tease her and leave her like this, flushed and feeling foolish? Silvija moved to sit behind her and, with a quick lift of her powerful leg, was behind Belle, her lush woman's heat against Belle's backside and her breasts a cool weight pressing at sighing shoulder blades. She felt Silvija's hand at her neck, sweeping the braided hair away from it. Electricity fired through her as she sat, immobilized, beneath the magic beast.

"What have you been doing in here all by yourself, hm?"

The words hummed against her exposed throat, sending vibrations along her skin and between her thighs. Silvija licked her throat. The beast's rasping tongue made Belle shiver, made her head roll back, and her lips part. A gentle suction of Silvija's lips joined the electrifying caress of her tongue. The whole of Belle tingled and swam in desire. It pooled between her legs, threatening to spill out on the floor and wash her away. She whimpered deep in her throat. And in the next instant cursed herself for the weakness.

But Silvija didn't care. Her teeth scraped Belle's neck, bringing up twin lines of blood, she was sure. And Silvija licked her, made her wet, made her want. She needed to touch herself, to anchor herself *to* herself with the sure stroke of her clit, controlling her own pleasure as assurance that Silvija did not control her.

"Don't do it."

The harsh command stopped her before she could completely lift her skirt out of the way. But she touched herself anyway, and it felt so good. Her clit was hot and hard and wet.

Silvija pulled her hair, dragged her head and neck back until it hurt. "What did I say?"

It didn't matter, because the pain felt good too. She gasped and pressed harder against her clit, dove deeper into her own wetness.

"Julia," Silvija growled against her throat. The sound carried beyond the bedroom, and soon the little fiend came running. She stuck her head into the room.

"No." Belle shook her head. She wanted this fake intimacy, this tearing inside for Silvija, but not with Julia watching. Not with her in the room.

Julia smiled when she saw what they were up to. She came deeper into the room looking intently at Silvija, then Belle, then back to Silvija again. The beast gestured her even closer and, with a flick of her fingers, told her to get on her knees. Julia dropped to all fours, then crawled the rest of the way to them, licking her lips as she drew closer to the sprawl of Belle's thighs. Belle made to slam them together, but Silvija gripped her knees with powerful hands, holding them apart.

"Be still, puppy." Silvija nuzzled her throat. "Be still."

Julia crept closer and fanned her breath against Belle's bare cunt. Her flesh jumped. She didn't want that foul beast to touch her, but the more she protested, the more her skin wanted it.

Silvija lifted the skirt completely away from her thighs and up to pool just beneath her stomach. "When will you learn never to disobey me?"

"Never."

Silvija chuckled against her throat and licked her again. "Maybe that's why I can't get enough of you." And she sank her teeth into Belle's throat.

Belle screamed. Too much. It was too much. She felt her blood spurt hotly into Silvija's mouth, felt the beast open even wider and suck more strongly on her throat. And she felt pain. It flung her head back and opened her up. Julia's mouth opened over her pussy. It floated over her heated lips, over

the wetness pouring out of her like a river. Just as Silvija
sucked, Julia sucked. The lips on her clit and on her neck
worked in unison, milking her, drinking her until her hips
writhed against the thick oak chest, against Julia's mouth, in
the V of Silvija's hips.

The giant's hands fumbled for her breasts, searching blindly
over the dress for buttons to free them. When she realized
there were none, Silvija ripped the cloth. Belle's breasts tumbled free, the dark hardened peaks becoming harder under
the pinching and stroking fingers. Silvija made hungry animal
noises as she suckled from Belle's throat, her mouth wide, her
hips moving in rhythm with Belle's against the solid oak
chest. She felt Silvija's wet pussy against her ass, felt the fat
clit as it strove for satisfaction against her skin. The beast's
teeth released Belle's throat, but her lips stayed to suck at the
sensitive skin.

It was Julia who held her thighs apart now. The fiend
lapped at her pussy and pushed at Belle's thighs until they
made a nearly straight line. Her hungry mouth was loud and
savage as it slurped Belle's pussy, as her long tongue delved
inside Belle's weeping cunt. She pressed her open palms
against Julia's head, pushing her deeper into her cunt, urging
the fiend to fuck her harder, to eat more of her, to make her
come.

Belle felt rather than saw Julia's hands delve between her
own thighs. She felt the hot flush rise up in Silvija and the
deepening guttural cries Julia made against her throbbing
flesh. Silvija squeezed her breasts, pulling at the already distended nipples until Belle was crying out. She didn't want to
want it, but she did. The pain, the pressure of the beast
against her back, the relentless mouth working on her pussy.
Fire shot through her. Silvija's hand tightened across her
chest, crushing her firmly against her.

"Belle." Silvija's hips moved harder against her ass. "Belle!"

Silvija's fingers squeezed her nipples even harder, and then
they were coming. All three of them. Belle grunted like a

ravening beast, her fingers tight against Julia's scalp, bringing up blood. Julia grunted, then groaned deeply, her lashes fluttering against Belle's skin, before she collapsed in the V of her thighs. Belle sagged back against Silvija and her head fell forward.

Silvija brushed blunt-tipped fingers down the curve of Belle's neck, ruffling the fine hairs that grew there. She said nothing. Not even when Julia crept up from the floor to tumble into the bed next to Silvija. Although she didn't turn to look, Belle knew that the smaller beast had her head on Silvija's thigh, her eyes closed in bliss.

Chapter 22

"I have something for you."

Belle turned from her contemplation of the snow to look at Shaye. She hadn't even noticed when the child appeared in the hallway. Grinning, Shaye held a clumsily tied rectangular package in her hand.

"Here." Shaye sat down beside her on the bench. "Take it."

With one tug, the rough cord loosened and fell from the package. The brown paper wrapping came off easily too. Belle crumpled them in her lap as she stared at the back of some sort of picture.

"Turn it over, silly."

Belle turned the frame over and stared. A human shudder rippled through her face and she turned it back over. "Where did you get this?"

"I took it."

"Where?"

Belle's hands trembled around the framed photograph. Although she stared at the plain brown back of the frame, the image behind the glass was already etched in her mind. It was unmistakably Kylie. Her child was older now, maybe nine or ten, taking on the look of her mother in her height and slashing cheekbones. The photographer had caught her running. With a smile as wide as the sky behind her was blue,

Kylie ran in the direction of the photographer, her two Afro puffs caught in midbounce. Her blue school uniform looked clean and well pressed, and it fit her tall form well. She looked happy.

Blood-flecked tears splashed on the back of the photo. Belle blinked and looked at Shaye. "Thank you."

Shaye smiled, showing off her pretty white teeth. "You're welcome."

Belle barely noticed when the smaller vampire left. She turned over the framed photograph and stared at her daughter's face. Her little girl was so beautiful. Belle's trembling fingers floated over the glass, then into the space marked with her deep dimples, gifts from her long-gone father.

She looked up from the photograph back to the snowy landscape outside. Everything was different from what she used to know. By the look of the photo, over five years had passed since her death at Julia's hands, but her homesickness for Jamaica hadn't lessened. Neither had her contempt for her impulsive decision to go off with Julia. The tears tracked down her face, and Belle did nothing to stop them.

Sitting in that bright hallway with the moon a steady constant presence, Belle felt utterly alone. She was dimly aware of others passing by—Keiko and Liam—but she did not acknowledge them.

"I know you miss Silvija, Belle. But there's no need for tears."

Liam abandoned his companion and sat down gracefully at Belle's feet. His eyes flickered to the miles of white snow and ice beyond the glass. Before Belle could respond to that bit of nonsense, he angled his long neck up to look at the photograph. "Nice human. Is she yours?"

"Yes," she murmured. "My daughter."

Liam looked surprised. "Really? You're not hunting her?"

"Hunting? No. Why would I do that?"

He shrugged. "For fun, of course."

At Belle's horrified look, he grinned. "Sometimes we get

bored. As I'm sure you've already noticed, there's not too much to do up here. When it gets really bad, or whenever the mood strikes, a few of us have chosen humans to watch and sometimes steer them down or away from a certain path— for maximum amusement or accessibility. Then when the time is right, after we've gotten all we can out of it, we kill them."

Belle's eyes widened.

"Don't look so disgusted. Sometimes it's all that saved one of us from going on a rampage in that stupid little town around the bend, or doing something equally unfortunate."

Belle held the picture closer. "There's nothing human in any of us, is there?"

"Of course there is. One's digesting in my tummy as we speak." His smile was pure mischief. Then something beyond the glass distracted him. Liam blinked once, batting his beautiful long lashes at her before sliding bonelessly to his feet. "See you later."

As he walked away, Belle pushed the photograph of Kylie under the bench and leaned back against the cool glass. A deep breath filtered through her, a needless exercise that she sometimes indulged in to try and recapture the feeling of being human, of needing something other than blood to keep her alive. She closed her eyes.

"I hear you've been crying tears over me, puppy."

"You shouldn't trust your sources," Belle murmured without opening her eyes.

Everything in her universe snapped securely back into place, though a part of her vehemently denied it. The air around her shifted as Silvija took a seat on the bench. The beast's clove scent, delicate and almost tentative today, nuzzled even closer to Belle. Any moment now she would be able to taste it on her tongue. She opened her eyes.

Of course, the beast looked good. That last night, Belle had woken up and felt an absence in the bed beside her. When she rolled over, her body eager for the press of Silvija's skin against it, she realized who was gone. No one told her where the beast had taken off to, only that she had business in the city.

The last time Belle saw Silvija she had been naked. Today she wore some designer business suit, charcoal gray instead of the usual black. With her seated, the skirt flirted with the top of her knees. Smooth, elegant knees that had never known what it was like to bend to someone. Belle's eyes skimmed over that part of Silvija's anatomy to meet her laughing gaze.

"So, if not for me, then why the tears?"

"None of your business."

"Come on, puppy. Haven't we gotten past that stage already?"

"Just because you fuck me"—Belle ignored the faint stirrings of heat that her words brought—"and say that our animosity is over doesn't make it so."

Silvija reached out to touch Belle's face, and the smaller woman flinched back. The fingers hovered in the air, waiting, then slowly reached out and brushed Belle's cheek. Memories of the recent night in their bedroom—of Julia's tongue lapping at her pussy, of Silvija's cool heat behind her—clutched at Belle with the giant's familiar motion. Electric sensation shuddered under Belle's skin, but she tried not to let it show.

"My daughter," Belle said.

"What? Is she dead?"

This time Belle flinched and moved back from Silvija. The beast's hand fell away.

"No. Someone gave me a photograph of her. She's growing up without me. It was only human to cry. Do you even recall what that's like, to be human?"

"Once or twice I get an unpleasant reminder." Something clouded the beast's expression. "This photograph, do you have it with you?"

"No."

Silvija's look said that she didn't believe her, but what could she do? She nodded. "Stop thinking about the child. It will only make things worse." Silvija stood up. "When you're finished basking in your warm memories, come to the bedroom. I want you to hunt with me tonight."

Belle swore that Silvija waited until she heard her footsteps outside the bedroom before she started to take off her clothes. As she walked into the spacious room filled with the scent of a half dozen beasts, Silvija put her jacket in the closet. The fur rug burrowed up between Belle's bare toes and stroked her feet as she walked deeper into the room.

Silvija didn't acknowledge Belle's presence. Instead, she unbuttoned her blouse and shrugged it off, revealing a muscled back and soft skin. Belle couldn't blink. The skirt disappeared, slid off her hips, and bared the lush ass, her muscled thighs and long legs. Temptation. It was a small bit of relief when she tugged on the black slacks and turtleneck sweater. When the beast turned, tucking her business-braided hair into a tight French roll, her eyes rested on Belle.

The languorous gaze moved over her body as if touching her skin through the dark jeans and fitted thermal shirt. They hadn't seen each other in at least a week. They hadn't touched, fucked, or bled each other in those long days. Silvija blinked, and Belle felt the air between them change. She backed away. *Not now.* Silvija nodded. She put on a pair of shades, dropped a wicked-looking switchblade into her back pocket, and tilted her head toward the door, indicating that she was ready.

"Unless you see one of those bitches who attacked you and Shaye, killing here is not often an option for us," Silvija said when they were beyond the house.

Belle nodded though she already knew. Even though they hadn't found out anything new after Colleen's capture, Belle had gotten over her terror of Wildbrook and its unseen things. She'd gone back on her own, then with Shaye. The older vampire had taught her well what to take, and she'd learned, sipping from the few homeless in town, those who lived on the fringes and survived. Belle had killed only once here. The temptation then had been overwhelming with the woman's heavy thighs and cruel hands reminding her too much of Silvija.

Snow swirled lightly around them, catching in their hair and eyelashes, on their cool skin. At the beginning of night, Belle could still hear the people in the town, easily fifteen miles away, begin their evening rituals—taking dinner, doing homework, getting ready to settle in for another harsh winter's night. The air was chill and sharp. Taking it into her lungs felt like breathing icicles, so Belle stopped breathing.

The thick snow swallowed her feet up to the knees as she stepped through it at Silvija's side. The beast floated easily on top of the snow, watching Belle with amused eyes.

"Around four hundred humans live here. Not all of them are well liked, but their community will definitely notice if we take one."

Belle nodded but didn't say a word. No one had noticed when she took the woman. She had made it look like an accident. A bad fall in the snow near too many sharp objects. Anything was possible, right? Silvija looked at her as they continued walking, but said nothing else.

For another eight miles, they walked in silence before Wildbrook appeared abruptly around the jagged cliffs. One moment it was simply them, their quiet footsteps, and the whisper of the waves on the snowy shore. Then a feast.

It was different sensing their presence from so far down the beach, with their human warmth dulled by the miles of chill air, blustery wind, and Silvija's incendiary presence at her shoulder. Belle blinked through the swirling snowflakes and *saw* them. Their little bodies inside the steaming gingerbread houses throbbed with delicious life. Wildbrook was idyllic. Even with the snow and the mountains jagged with ice, it was classic Americana come to life. From their human warmth in the cozy houses with the chimneys puffing white smoke to the snow-covered dock, its dozens of anchored boats, and the ocean beyond. It was too much. Belle smiled.

"We do not kill them," Silvija warned. "Watch, and do nothing until I tell you."

This was different too, walking this road with Silvija. Everything seemed new again. Like the first time. Only now her senses were working overtime but seemed less capable. The snow was deep, but Silvija held herself perched on top of the thick mass, a graceful butterfly, while Belle, overset by the nearness of the beast, floundered foolishly, sometimes floating, sometimes tumbling deep into the snow that grabbed at her ankles and knees.

"You know," Silvija murmured, "I can help you with that."

The thought of Silvija touching her out here in the snow was too tempting.

"Tell me."

Silvija ignored her. And put her hands on Belle. She lifted her out of the snow, hands burning where she grasped Belle's arms.

"You're not human. You skate on the surface of all things. Remember that." She released Belle. And for a few precious seconds, Belle balanced on the top of the snow, lightness itself under Silvija's penetrating eyes. Then the giant looked away and started walking forward again. Belle stumbled. The snow grabbed her knees.

Silvija laughed. "And if that doesn't work, remember what it's like when we're fucking. That feeling right before you come. When you feel suspended on the edge of everything."

A hot flush took a hold of Belle. Other than when they were in bed fucking, Silvija didn't often acknowledge that there was something between them other than their passionate dislike for each other. Belle looked after the beast. Something was changing between them. She shook her feet free of the snow and followed.

Silvija had already chosen her prey. The girl was plump and appealing in that pale, milk-fed way with big breasts, big eyes, and a mouth that was perfect for eating pussy. She sat in her room, eyes skimming over the pages of a romance novel while her feet tapped an impatient rhythm on the bedroom floor. The rest of the single-level house was silent with the two other humans cuddled together in their bedroom and the younger daughter watching television from the living room floor.

Silvija made no attempt at stealth. She tapped lightly on the girl's bedroom window before opening it and climbing through. At the sound, the girl jumped up and ran to Silvija. What Belle initially thought was a dress was actually a sheer nightgown, high-necked with tiny buttons running from the neckline to just below her healthy breasts. The girl looked like she had the starring role in a gothic film. She greeted the beast with a slow lingering kiss that ignited the burn of jealousy in Belle's gut.

She watched as the beast transformed herself, shifting her facial muscles, softening her presence until she was no longer a powerful beast, but a seductive one, a soft and pliant creature with desire shimmering on the edge of her smile.

"I wasn't sure you'd come," the girl said.

"How could I stay away?" Silvija's voice rumbled in its deepest registers.

The girl shivered against the giant, her hands sliding up over her back and under the light sweater. She tilted her neck for Silvija, and Belle noticed bruises, days old, that dotted her throat. The beast had been feeding on this one for some time.

"I waited for you."

"You're a good girl, Marie."

Belle rolled her eyes. With a delicate press of her hands, Silvija guided the girl against the far wall so Belle could watch them. She traced the plump little neck with her hand, brushing the pale hair out of her way. Even from the window, Belle could smell the human's excitement at Silvija's touch, could hear her frantic pulse beat, and the shallowing of her breath. Her lips parted for Silvija again, but the beast kissed her neck instead, peppering the soft curve with stinging bites that pulled little noises of pleasure from her.

Unable to resist the sight, Belle climbed through the window and came closer. Marie's eyes fluttered closed as she leaned back against the wall. Silvija bit delicately into her neck until blood bubbled up from the pinprick holes. She licked the pale throat. The girl trembled and her thighs fell open, allowing Silvija between them. She cupped the girl's face in her palm, gentleness itself as she suckled from the tiny holes in her throat, building the girl's excitement with each wash of her tongue. A heated river began to flow between the girl's legs.

"I have a friend with me tonight," Silvija murmured. Her thumb brushed across the girl's nipple.

The soft thing moaned, a parting of her pink lips, the flickering of dazed eyes. Her lashes fluttered open. She barely registered Belle's presence, as if the new beast was no more unexpected than the wind or Silvija's desire for her.

"Can she touch you?" Another brush of her thumb against the cloth with the distended nipple pushing against it.

"Yes." The word pushed softly against the air.

She smelled delightfully human and warm. The scent of her arousal was lush and full, permeating the room with its loamy essence. Belle wanted to burrow beneath her dress and find the source of that smell, to bury her nose in it, to bite into it. She licked her lips. It had been a long time since she'd had a human so thick with sex.

Silvija reached for her. "Be gentle."

How else could she be with this miraculous creature? Marie lay back against the wall, as pliant as a newborn kitten, her delicious breath panting softly from between her pink lips as she stared at Silvija. The giant moved aside.

Belle's body was a confliction of needs. Her mouth hungered to taste the human's blood, to sate the night's hunger on the healthy cornucopia before her. But her hands wanted to touch that body, to explore it to see if it really was as soft

as it looked, or as lush. She kissed the girl's neck. She burrowed her nose into the scented trail left by Silvija, the line of
cool clove scent and saliva, of devilish intent and anticipation. The girl's soft dress interrupted her exploration so she
ripped it. Marie gasped. Buttons went flying in the room,
pinging across the hardwood floor and settling into the plush
rug.

"Gentle." Silvija's voice was a buzzing interruption at her
ear; then the beast's lips pressed closer, just beneath Belle's
ear and against her neck. "Remember?"

Yes. She remembered what it was like to be gentle. But that
was a lifetime ago. Before Julia. Before she knew about the
power of blood. Marie's breasts jutted out, pale and tipped
by deep pink nipples. Her agitated breath made the soft flesh
shudder. Belle kissed a nipple to quiet her, licked the hardening tip, and took it into her mouth. Sugar sweet. A ripe plan-
tain fresh from the frying pan type of delicious. Belle's teeth
flared out in an uncontrollable thrust, piercing the soft breast.
The girl whimpered. Belle retracted her teeth and sucked the
nipple again to soothe her. Silvija kissed the back of her neck
in reward and moved back. But only one step. The girl kept
her eyes fixed on the beast.

In another life, she had been this girl. Seduced by a being
with all of temptation at its fingertips, a victim to desire and
the pulsing song between her legs. Belle dipped down, gently
ripping the cloth as she went, until all of Marie lay bare to
her gaze. *Ah yes. This is what Silvija came for.* Not the blood,
but Marie's sighing acquiescence and the heady scent of passion between her legs. Her tits weren't bad either.

Belle's teeth easily pierced the skin like moonlight through
silk. She tasted like youth. Like her lost humanity, like sex in
a pleasing package that she needed to unwrap, with or without Silvija. The girl gasped again in Silvija's direction. The
giant came closer, brushing her lips over Marie's as Belle fed.
The hot blood rushed into her mouth, sainted and sweet. She
pulled the girl roughly against her, her passion-wet pussy

against her belly. The girl gasped again, her breath coming roughly in her throat as Belle drank her up and rubbed her pussy against Marie's stomach. The girl's breasts trembled against Belle's throat with their scent of milk and sweat and blood.

"That's enough."

It wasn't, but it had to be. This was Silvija's pet. Belle didn't want to damage it. Perhaps later she would come back and play. She licked the girl's throat once and pulled away. For a moment, she leaned back against the beast's solid coolness, feeling tension in the long body. The beast wanted something else tonight.

Before Silvija could complain of her weight, Belle straightened up and moved from between the two women. Marie still only had eyes for Silvija. The beast kissed her mouth and peeled her from the wall. Silvija was gentleness itself, taking the scraps of Marie's nightgown from her body and folding it neatly over the chair near the window. Then she dotted the human girl's face with kisses as she pressed her into the bed.

Marie sighed in pleasure, as if the whole world was becoming right again. She twined her arms around Silvija's neck, inviting the beast to kiss her throat, to come between her thighs. And Belle watched. She watched as Silvija trailed tender hands down the girl's body, making her moan with delight. Watched her squeeze those farm-fed breasts, squeeze the dark nipples until they stood out even darker against her Alaska-pale skin. Watched her drink deeply from the veins cupped in her elbows and then, with bloodied lips, kiss every inch of the girl's body. Her eyelids, her mouth, the nipples Marie held up to Silvija's mouth, the curved fullness of her belly, the hot slit of her pussy, her knees, the curling toes. Belle watched.

The girl cried out softly as Silvija sipped delicately from between her legs, burrowing deeply with her tongue for the treasure of her orgasm. Then she found it. Belle leaned against the wall, watching her lover make love to another woman, felt the jealousy churn her belly to soup, felt the arousal pool between her legs like molten lava. Unable to help it, she touched herself, unbuttoning her jeans and shoving them out of the way so she could massage the ache that could only be soothed by one person.

"I see that you brought a friend with you this time."

The low voice came from the door, a human woman wearing a pleased smile and a blue terry cloth robe. She came into the room, closed the door behind her, then locked it. Belle straightened from her passion-dazed slump against the wall and slowed the movement of her fingers against her clit. This was interesting. The woman was older than the girl Silvija eased gradually down from her orgasm. The girl lay there, eyes blurred and unfocused beneath the giant's attentions, her body splayed across the bed, smears of blood and the outlines of Silvija's mouth swirled across her pale body. Even as the woman walked closer, she didn't stop what she was doing, didn't pull her mouth from the moist and twitching pussy until she was good and ready. The woman didn't seem in any hurry herself. She waited.

When Silvija straightened to her full height, the woman sucked in a deep breath. She was not as young as the girl on the bed. Lines of experience and laughter pressed into her skin. Belle could tell that the woman's face had been unremarkable in her youth, but with age, beauty had taken up residence in her features, creating a pleasing harmony of narrow lips, heavy-lidded eyes, and high cheekbones. Her blond-streaked white hair lay in neat curves on her shoulders. She was undoubtedly the girl's mother.

"Was she sweet?" she asked Silvija, brushing her thumb across the giant's damp lower lip. "Did you enjoy her?"

"As always, Lily."

At the sound of her name, the woman's eyes flickered. Her hand fell away from Silvija's face and she dropped both hands to the giant's shoulders, sliding behind her to caress her back, her waist, before sneaking in front to stroke the

long belly. Silvija stood there and let her. This was very interesting, indeed. If this was what Silvija called "hunting" in
Alaska, Belle could easily get used to it.

The woman slipped her hands up Silvija's sweater, caressing her belly and breasts. "It wasn't that long ago that I was
the one in that bed, Silvija. Was it?"

Beneath the sweater, the woman's hands tugged down the
cups of Silvija's bra to touch her breasts, to squeeze the nipples that Belle knew were already hard. And still the beast allowed it. She didn't slash and slap the woman away, instead
she closed her eyes and parted her lips with pleasure.

Lily sighed. "You know I want that again. It's been so long
since you came."

"And I've told you that you don't need to use Marie to get
me here. You're still beautiful to me."

"Then why did you take her? Why do you take her every
time?"

"Because she wants me to."

The woman laughed. "When did someone else's wants
ever determine your actions?" She raked her nails down
Silvija's belly, heading quickly south.

The giant stopped her hands. Belle knew the answer to the
question. Only Silvija's wants ever mattered, and in this case
she was just being greedy. She'd lectured Belle on the danger
of becoming attached to humans, but she was hypocrisy itself
with her mother-daughter tag-team fuck friends who already
knew her name and probably where she lived.

When there was no kill, the blood was sweet, especially if
it was taken during sex when the pulse pounded like war
drums, pushing the blood into the mouth in eager, hot spurts.
But it wasn't enough for a good meal; this was a snack at
best. But now with two women, the possibility of a full, satisfying meal was much more real.

Silvija turned in the woman's arms. "Where is your husband, Lily?"

"In bed. I gave him something to sleep. He won't bother us."

Silvija chuckled. "You're a very wicked woman."

"I learned from the best."

How long had they been lovers?

Lily rested her cheek against the giant's back. "Can I have you like I used to?"

"No. Nothing can be like it used to be."

Still, Silvija dipped her head to kiss Lily. The human growled low in her throat, opening her mouth wide for Silvija's teeth and tongue. She clawed at the back of the giant's head, low desperate sounds ratcheting up in her throat. The giant took off Lily's robe, baring her slim, spare body with its delicate skin and sprinkling of freckles. Her desire was heavy in the room, a pungent, aromatic musk that was much more substantial than the pale scent her daughter exuded.

Silvija's nostrils flared, and she pulled Lily roughly down to the rug. The girl on the bed stirred from her postcoital stupor and began looking around for her lover. Lily groaned, drawing the girl's attention to the writhing couple on the floor. She made a distressed sound.

Belle touched her back. "Don't worry, honey. Silvija has enough to go around."

The girl didn't seem convinced and only whimpered more, seemingly incapable of adult speech. She started to get off the bed and go to her preoccupied lover.

"No, darling. Stay with me."

Belle pulled Marie and the human easily acquiesced, almost falling into her arms, weak from the blood loss. Her lashes fluttered weakly at Belle.

"Silvija, come back to me," she moaned softly.

Belle almost hissed. The child was redolent with the scent of Silvija. Bound in her pores, in her breath, in the blood staining her white skin. Belle wanted to eat her up. Not because of any great desire to have the girl, but because Marie seemed to have the giant, have her in a way that Belle could not, in that weeping, needful way that some women managed effortlessly. She wanted the giant's strength over her, but she wouldn't weaken herself for it.

Belle sniffed Marie, taking her Silvija-tainted smell into her nose. On the floor, the two females writhed against each other. The human lay naked and bucking as Silvija's hand burrowed deep into her pussy and her mouth fastened, sucking, on the frail neck. Is this how Silvija made love to these straight women, with her clothes on and them panting only for their own pleasure? How pointless. And pathetic.

Marie whimpered beneath Belle's hand, the scent of her resistance and yearning for Silvija a ripe stink on her. Belle nuzzled her throat, licked the wound she left earlier. The girl flinched, but with her head nearly hanging off the bed, she didn't take her eyes from the giant. The scent of her was an intoxicant, blood, sex, satisfaction, fear, yearning, everything.

Belle lowered her body onto Marie, feeding her the weight of her presence one ounce at a time until the girl was used to her. And her blood was ambrosia. It slid like wine down Belle's throat, igniting her hungers and satisfying them at once. She sipped the weak girl, mindful of how much she took.

Both pairs of eyes, Belle's and Marie's, lingered on the figures on the floor, drank up the bare skin, the liquid kiss of flesh on flesh, Lily's moaning cries, and Silvija's quietly intense fucking. Marie's lashes flickered in the dim lamplight, then closed. A trembling sigh left her mouth and her soft wet breath fluttered against Belle's face. The vampire drank her up until she was full.

Their walk back to the compound was a silent one, with Silvija striding by Belle's side lost in thought, hands in pockets, eyes flickering up ahead in the snow before them. The scent of both women, mother and daughter who lay replete and nearly bloodless in their beds, drifted from Silvija on the chill breeze. Jealous. Belle was jealous. She swallowed and kept walking.

Chapter 23

Belle was warm. The body next to hers, Violet's, shifted in sleep and she turned into it, throwing her hand over a solid hip. Her nipples scraped over a muscled back and automatic arousal shimmied along her skin. She moaned softly.

"If I didn't know any better I'd be jealous." Julia hung over her, smiling. She was fully dressed.

Belle batted at her in annoyance. "Go away," she muttered.

It was barely eight thirty and the sky was almost dark, but Belle didn't feel like getting up yet. Sparring the night before had been hard, with Stephen and Ivy pushing her until she nearly collapsed with exhaustion. At this point she couldn't even wrestle a baby to the ground.

"Silvija is gone," the fiend whispered in her ear. "And I know you're bored."

Belle opened one eye. "What?"

"Come out to the city with me?"

"Why?"

Julia giggled. "Why not?"

Belle shifted in the bed again. The prospect of sparring with the twins again tonight had little appeal. They were entertaining, but only up to a point. Ivy shifted in the bed again but didn't wake. Why not, indeed? Within moments she was out of the bed and dressed in jeans, a tank top, and a leather jacket. Julia was dressed in her huntress getup—asymmetrical leather skirt, a silk blouse that clung to her soft breasts and nipples, and a tight matching leather jacket that looked like it had just been skinned from its original wearer.

The two beasts quickly left the compound for the small airstrip outside the Cave. Of course, Julia expected her to fly them wherever they were going. After quickly getting the details about their destination and how to get there, the two women were off in the small twin-engine plane. Six hours later they floated above a city of lights and darkness.

From afar, it looked like Los Angeles, but as they flew closer, it became apparent that the two cities were nothing alike. New York, at this distance, sounded strangely like Jamaica. Patois and bullets, sex and dominoes, laughter and knives. Belle even heard the skin-pounding music from clubs and dance halls. She heard quarrels and babies crying. She heard women making love. Julia glanced slyly at her as if to say, "See, I am good for something after all."

After Belle landed the plane, Julia wasted no time in getting them out of the tiny little airport and into the belly of the city. There was a cab already waiting for them at the airport and it took them straight into downtown. Into New York City.

When the cab dropped them off on a crowded street with the scent of the gutter and the people and strange foods threatening to overwhelm her, Belle shuddered. The city was sensual overload. Its lights, the people with their fiercely beating blood, their smells, the way they looked at each other like prey. It was all too lovely. Human corruption and decadence pushed hotly against her skin. Belle rolled her shoulders in pleasure. Even her trips to L.A. hadn't felt like this.

"Come."

Julia tugged her toward an impressive building with marble steps and a sharp green glass façade. Belle wasn't surprised to see Silvija walk out of the building. The beast was crisp and cool in a black pantsuit that fit her body well, tailoring her sleek killer's physique in civility and making her look almost harmless. She walked out of the building with three men and another woman. She walked with them to a limousine, shook each vampire's hand, and stepped back to let the car drive off. Her eyes scoured her surroundings, yet she seemed indifferent to the energy vibrating off the street, off the very air around her. After the limousine pulled off she walked in the opposite direction toward the teeming life deeper in the city.

Belle sniffed the air, imagining that she was pulling the tall beast into her. Halfway down the street, the beast stopped and looked around. Julia pulled her back into an alley. After a pause, they followed after her, using the humans to shield their progress down the street. Four blocks down, Silvija veered off into a restaurant and sat down at a table separated from the sidewalk by an iron railing. A waiter came to take her order and when he came back with a bottle of wine and three glasses, the two vampires stood back and waited.

Who was she here with? What was she waiting for? Belle became caught up in the beauty of Silvija's movements, the sure way her lean frame folded into the elegant but uncomfortable-looking chair, her quick flickering glance over the patrons in the restaurant, the way her power seemed contained only by the sheer force of her will. She and Julia stood at the opposite side of the street, watching. Then Silvija's cool glance sliced through the crowd and found them.

"Why are you following me?" she asked softly.

Belle sighed, feeling like a mooning fool. "Come. She knows we're here."

Julia grinned as if it had all been one great joke and jogged lightly across the street, dodging cars that would not stop for her. Belle followed at a more sedate pace. She waited for the light to change; then she too came to heel at Silvija's summons. The beast's eyes brushed over her. There was gentle irony in them as well as something else that Belle couldn't read.

"We're not following you," Julia said, sitting down at the table. "Belle was. She just dragged me along for spite."

Belle didn't bother to comment at that blatant lie. Neither did Silvija. In what universe would she blindly follow after the beast like some besotted puppy dog? She drew up a chair and sat down.

Silvija poured wine for her two unexpected companions and smiled. "Are you having fun, Belle?"

Her smile was teasing even as a long finger casually circled the rim of her wineglass. The burgundy wine was nothing like blood; still, it made Silvija's full mouth glisten in the city lights.

Belle wondered what it would be like to bite into it. "Not really. Julia promised me an interesting time. And all I see here is you."

Silvija chuckled. "A terrible disappointment, aren't I?"

"You said it, not me."

The waiter came back. "Can I get anything else for you ladies?"

Then Belle noticed that under those slacks and man-tailored shirt, the waiter was a woman. A very pretty one. Of course, Silvija noticed her wandering attention.

"Yes, you can." Silvija rested her hand on the table, spreading out her long, graceful fingers with their clear pink nails and soft, accessible fingertips. She gave the waitress a moist-lipped smile. "May we have your phone number?"

The young girl looked startled, then pleased. A blush stained her pale cheeks, and the hand holding the notepad trembled. Her pulse began a rapid beat in her throat. She opened her mouth to speak. Silvija's hand drifted out to touch the waitress's thigh through the slacks, a casual movement and a light brush against flesh through cloth that Belle knew from very personal experience had the girl trembling deeply inside.

"I don't mean to be too forward, but my darling here"—it

was Belle's turn to startle as Silvija looked briefly at her—
"would dearly love to see you naked tonight."

Belle could practically feel the girl's thigh, her whole body,
shudder beneath Silvija's hand. Her eyes swept to Belle and
lingered. The blood rushed up inside her, into the hard points
of her breasts, down to her clit.

"Ah," Julia murmured beside Belle. "Good choice."

"I . . . um." The girl cleared her throat. "I don't get off
until four." Two hours away.

"Why wait when you can do it now?" Silvija asked.

Julia giggled. Belle didn't even look her way. She pursed
her lips and watched the mesmerized girl. The flow of traffic
in the restaurant had slowed down to a trickle until their
table and another with a balding man and his giggling young
tartlet were the only ones occupied. Pedestrian traffic was
heavier, but the people passing by with their singing laughter
barely paid attention to anything or anyone not walking with
them.

"Do you get any sort of lunch break?" Julia asked with a
hopeful lilt to her voice.

"And the place is not so crowded that you can't step away
for a few minutes," Silvija murmured.

The hand on the waitress's thigh was implacable, undeni-
able. If Belle had been human and in that position, she would
have done anything to keep Silvija near and to have that firm
hand of power on her.

The waitress cleared her throat again. "Give me a few
minutes."

While the little morsel disappeared inside, Belle sipped her
wine, wincing at the unappetizing bitterness. Silvija smiled
benevolently at her two charges while the waitress made her
excuses to leave. A few moments later she was back.

The hotel was only a couple of blocks away. The suited
prig behind the high marble front desk only smiled at the
four women as Silvija took the key cards and nodded in

thanks. Belle wanted to eat up the little waitress. She was just too adorable. Of course they wouldn't kill her. That plump mouth of hers and the way she submitted so sweetly to Silvija's will were beyond compare. She reminded Belle too much of herself, but that was another matter.

The suite must have been posh and properly turned out, but that wasn't what Belle was here for. Before the door was completely closed behind them, Belle was on the girl. She tasted like sugar, like the sweet brown crystals Belle had loved to eat by the spoonfuls as a child. Her mouth devoured the girl with kisses while Julia and Silvija tugged her clothes off and guided them both toward the gigantic bed against the room's far wall.

The girl squirmed under her, trying to get her hands free to wrestle off Belle's jacket and jeans. Behind her, Julia helped with the process, tugging off her clothes until Belle was naked on top of the girl and pinning her hands to the bed as her mouth wandered all over the soft skin. Belle knelt over the girl, sniffing her throat with the blood rushing so savagely beneath the skin. The girl gasped as Belle nipped her throat with sharp teeth, then sighed when a wet tongue replaced teeth. A softer sigh rippled through her when Belle's mouth claimed her nipple, covering the hot little nubbin. She swirled her tongue around the deep pink nipple, then sucked it into her mouth. The little waitress squirmed with pleasure under her hands and mouth while the sweet disbelieving noises she made burned the fiend's flame even hotter. Belle sighed.

Julia crawled into the bed, naked except for the two platinum rings in her nipples. She walked over Belle and the human, bathing them in the scent of her cunt as she went toward the top of the bed. Julia bent at the waist and grasped the low headboard, waving her dripping pussy in the air over the waitress's face. She turned her head to look at Belle, her smile all mischief and lasciviousness. Flicking out her pink tongue, Julia reached between her own legs and bent deeper, showing off her luscious pink pussy as she touched herself, spread her lips. She was wet and becoming even wetter. Belle licked the human's nipples, squeezing them in her eager hands, then moved lower. The scent of her hot pussy called to her.

Still watching Belle, Julia slid two fingers inside herself, her lashes fluttering in bliss as her fingers went deeper.

"Hmm." Her deep moan made the waitress look up, suddenly very interested in the show going on just above her head. Julia fucked herself slowly, slipping the fingers deeply into her wet pussy, then out, moving her ass in a snakelike rhythm above the girl's head. Belle bent to taste the girl.

So very human. Salt and wet and passion. Like candy. Just a little snack. Belle licked the already stiff clit, bathed it with her tongue, once, twice, before dipping low. She lapped up the girl's wetness, getting the slick heat all over her face and chin. The girl gasped as Belle dipped her tongue deeply inside her.

She felt a tongue inside her own body too. Belle gasped and thrust back against it, and pushed her own tongue deeper into the waitress at the same time. When she felt the firm, sure fingers on her clit, she knew it was Silvija. Belle groaned.

Pleasure skinned her alive, leaving her nerve endings open and raw to everything. Julia crouched over the human's face, her wet pussy wide and well tended to by the gasping human girl. The soft slap and slurp took Belle's arousal higher. Silvija sucked her clit deeper into her mouth, sucking and licking until Belle was light-headed, and only kept feeding the human girl's desire by instinct, her awareness of the world sharpened down to the mouth on her pussy and the fingers squeezing her nipples.

Belle's belly was tight with arousal and her thighs shuddered with the need to come. But Silvija's mouth abruptly left hers. Belle groaned in protest and the beast slapped her ass. The sensation ricocheted through her body, flinging up the tension in her cunt. She was dimly aware of the human girl's body pulling away, then disappearing from hers, of Julia snagging prey. Silvija captured all of Belle's attention. Her fingers teased the opening of her pussy, then fluttered over her clit. The beast's cool breath grazed her ass a moment before she felt sharp teeth nip her flesh. Her body jerked with gluttonous satisfaction.

Fuck me. Please. Fuck me. She wanted to say it. She needed to. But Belle bit into the sheets and clenched her hands against the words. Behind her, Silvija laughed. Belle pushed her ass higher in the air and widened her legs. And because she was not always cruel, the beast gave her what she wanted. Belle heaved a ragged sigh with the pleasure of feeling Silvija slide millimeter by millimeter inside her body. Lovely. It was so lovely. The heat crawled up inside her, burning away everything but Silvija, everything but the slow movement of her fingers in Belle's pussy. Her body clenched around those commanding fingers, wanting to keep them inside, to keep them close until Silvija became a part of her, and stayed.

She was distantly aware of Julia and the waitress curled in a sixty-nine position on the bed, slurping hungrily at each other and moaning, spiraling aural delight into the air. But their noises were inconsequential to the slow fire Silvija lit inside her, pulling the fingers slowly out of her pussy, before pushing even more slowly back inside. *Faster. Please. Faster.* The sheet ripped beneath Belle's teeth. She felt her jaws widen and her teeth extend. Belle closed her eyes against the torture of the emotion, the sweat, the desire being pulled from her like blood. Silvija's claws raked gently down her back, stirring up the muscles that coiled under the skin. Helpless, she moaned.

Silvija's movements sped up. Her fingers dug into the flesh of Belle's ass, and her hand moved faster. Breath churned in Belle's throat and she abruptly tried to stop it, but it was too late. Silvija had heard her moan, had heard her lose control. Heat rippled deep inside her. It radiated up until her entire belly, her clit, her world was incandescent. Silvija moved faster behind her, grunting now with her efforts; the thrust and liquid slide of her hand were thunder in the room, the sensations in Belle's body, lightning. She reached down to touch her own clit, to give herself that push that she needed, but Silvija batted her hand away. And touched her. The fingers moved over her slippery little button. Her hand curled deeply inside Belle and she was coming.

She reached out with a hoarse shout as her body went up in flames, as Silvija pounded still inside her and her body gave up everything it could, the sensation, the orgasm, the liquid spray of blood-tinged fluid over Silvija and the sheets. Her body shuddered and danced around Silvija's hand and still the giant moved inside. She milked her until there was nothing left, until Belle trembled and fought to get away from the overstimulation. She panted and clawed the sheets to escape. But she didn't beg.

Above the noise of the other two fucking and watching them, above the pounding of her still functioning pulse, she heard Silvija sigh. It was a soft sound. A noise of completion that she would have missed had she not been waiting for it. Belle released her own sigh and collapsed in the bed. Above her, the two women finished each other, but the girl wanted more.

The waitress crawled away from Julia toward Silvija. "Can I eat your pussy?"

She begged prettily enough with her already come-stained face and bare breasts rosy from Julia's teeth and tongue.

Silvija's white blouse was stained pink with Belle's come, but still neatly tucked into her black slacks, and she looked for all the world that she'd gotten into some civilized ladies' quarrel and been splashed with pink lemonade. She shook her head to the girl's request but allowed her to leave the bed and come close. With her pussy still tingling from the aftershocks of her release, Belle watched Silvija lift up the girl and drape her across a high console table, all the while still smiling benevolently. The girl's eyes were big, excited as she watched the beast finally drop her pants. The dildo she wore was big. Easily the width of one of Belle's wrists.

"I'm going to fuck you," Silvija murmured to the girl, and proceeded to do just that.

She swept the girl's thighs wide, baring her wet, pink pussy. The girl sighed and dropped her head back against the wall. Silvija licked her lips at the sweetly offered bare neck, but she only licked the expanse of pale skin once before sinking deeply into the plush pussy. The girl rose up with a pleased gasp. The beast sank deeply into her, fucking the willing and wet pussy with a gentle leisure, as if inviting Belle and Julia to stare, to admire the graceful flex and release of her ass muscles framed by the jock-style leather harness, the way that she effortlessly held the girl's legs open with one hand while the other braced against the wall next to the human's head.

"You smell so good," the girl gasped. "So good."

Near the peak of her passion, the waitress shuddered, her breathless mouth open to kiss Silvija, but the beast grasped her jaw and turned her head away. Her movements sped up and the girl gasped, panted, and clutched at Silvija. Her sweat poured over them as the table knocked against the wall. A low wail sounded as the waitress reached her peak and the blood rushed its fastest through her veins. Silvija bit her. The blood gushed into her mouth and Belle watched her lover gulp down the rich nourishment, the taste of the human blood immediately giving her skin a soft, ethereal glow as she fed.

"I love you!" the girl cried, clutching harder to Silvija. "I love you."

From the bed, Belle watched them. *I know how you feel.*

Silvija sent the little girl away with kisses a little after five in the morning.

"Can I see you again?" she asked, looking Silvija over as if she owned the six feet of rangy flesh. Her hand flickered out to stroke the white cotton over her breast.

"No." Silvija kissed the pulse point in her wrist again to lessen the sting, but the waitress still flinched.

"Okay." She slowly backed away from the door. "Bye."

Silvija smiled at her, baring her bright white teeth before closing the door in her face. She turned. "Are you having an interesting time yet, my Belle?"

Belle smiled at the endearment. "Something like that."

She watched Silvija from the bed, feeling that familiar flush of heat, that wash of pleasure that came from filling her eyes, her senses, full of this creature.

"You want more?"

"I always want more. You should know that by now." Belle held Silvija's gaze steadily with her own.

The giant smiled. "How do you like New York so far?"

"Too . . . busy. Not somewhere I can picture us living."

"First impressions can be deceiving." Silvija flashed her teeth again. Her eyes flickered over Belle, then the nude and still lounging Julia as if an afterthought. "Get dressed, we're going out."

Julia grinned. "Fabulous."

Within moments, they were all wearing their dark clothes and leaving behind the twirling gilded doors of the hotel. Belle had no idea where they were going, but Julia was excited and eager as she loped gracefully on the other side of Silvija. They left the glittering part of the city behind, slipping into darkness, through fetid alleys with bracketing fire escapes and the murky streets beyond. Away from the shimmer of exclusive hotels and restaurants, from the sidewalk cafés and the well-fed people, the city was a beast. It uncurled dark and snarling before them, its underbelly rumbling with violence, unanswered cries for help, pleas for mercy, and all manner of viciousness that made the beast inside Belle growl with pleasure.

"Feeding here is always fun. You can give yourself full rein. People disappear here all the time." Julia grinned.

"And there are bad humans here," Silvija said. "Worse than us, that others would like to see disappear." Even in her sleek two-thousand-dollar suit, Silvija managed to fit in to the darkness there.

She did not blend in, a creature like her never would, but the darkness settled like familiar clothes around her shoulders, and her prowling gait was the perfect thing. In this between time—that time between deepest dark and the fledgling light of morning—most humans were still asleep. Everyone else, the ones who crawled or limped through the streets, prowling in their own way, they were the ones about to be prey.

Belle chose a gang of privileged boys for her hunt. They were four healthy specimens who smelled like money, like drugs and sex, and of a well-spent night. Their laughter trilled through the early morning air, curling around Belle's ears like invitations to taste. She licked her lips.

Julia made a noise that distracted Belle from her fun. The little beast looked worried; then she looked at Silvija. "They will be missed. I've seen those two"—she pointed to the blondest ones, the ones with well-satisfied smiles and their arms draped across their friends' shoulders—"on the television."

"This is a place where people go missing every day. Isn't that what you said?" Silvija teased with a smile. "You're right, they will be missed. But it's nothing that their police will be able to trace back to us." Belle heard Silvija's voice float closer as the giant began to follow her and the prey. "Let the girl have her fun."

Belle wanted to be naked and barefoot. She wanted to feel everything about this moment, the breeze, dirt coating the sidewalk, their breath on her face as she drank them up. She shrugged out of her animal skin jacket. The shoes quickly followed. Belle let them hear her approach. One looked behind, saw her solitary figure, and smirked before turning back to his friends. One after the other, they turned to look at her, before dismissing her presence. *Good.*

They were walking toward their car, to the limousine waiting not far away, and to safety. She wouldn't let them reach it.

"Can I have your autograph?" she asked with a breathless laugh she'd learned from Julia.

They turned and looked at her again, at her bare feet, her breasts moving, braless, beneath the white blouse and the jeans sitting low on her hips. The slender one with a girl's red mouth was the first to stop and really look at her.

"When I see a girl like you, the last thing I think about is an autograph," he murmured with a charmer's smile.

His friends stopped to watch the action.

"Oh, good."

And she pounced, leaping gleefully at the human buffet with its scent of decay and overindulgence. She wanted nothing more than to glut herself on them, to feast on their blood and their cries until she was covered in them and they were nothing but dying sounds and a burp rising up in her throat. Belle felt the wind whip over her face as she sprang up from a crouch to land on the startled face of the girlish one. She slashed his throat, pulled him close, pressed quick kisses to his mouth before whirling for the gaggle of friends, rooted by fear and surprise to the spot where he lay bleeding and already dying.

Before they could move, Silvija was there. She smiling, whipping close to bring one of the boys down from behind with a red kiss to the side of his neck. The other boy closest to him tried to run, but her hand flashed out and caught him in the throat, holding him immobile, struggling and tearing at her arm. He gurgled uselessly and grasped with desperation at her vise grip. The pitter-patter of his friend's fearful feet sounded in the alley as he dashed toward the car waiting out of sight. A hoarse shout shot into the night. Julia brought him down quickly, leaping up and landing on his back with a light thud. They fell on the dirtied and moist pavement. She sat on his back and held his mouth shut with one hand. Her head turned first in one direction, then another, looking at Silvija and then Belle.

The pretty boy was a delight to drain. He bucked under Belle, giving her an exquisite ride as his blood rushed past her lips, stroking the pleasure centers in her mouth, gushing over her tongue, and filling her up. She moaned against his throat. His biceps flexed fiercely under her clenched hands as he fought her. His champagne-scented breath misted her hair and made her sigh.

When she stood, Belle stumbled. The air rushed fresh, steady, and clean around her. The new blood thrummed in her veins, brimming with energy and something else. She saw Julia feed too. The little fiend licked her lips and grinned as she stood up from the dead boy.

"Oh, that was magic," Julia squealed. She spun, staring up at the sky. "I wish we could do this every night."

Belle wanted to spin beneath the stars too, she wanted to howl at the waning quarter moon, and she wanted to kiss Silvija where she stood. But she did none of these things. Instead she stood over the boy whose drug-flushed blood was giving her such lovely feelings and wept.

Through her tears, she saw that Silvija still fed. The beast had a tremendous appetite that she loosened freely on the boys beneath her. One was already empty with nothing but a faint nosebleed on his pale and still face. The other still struggled feebly beneath her as she suckled from the artery throbbing beneath the skin on the inside of his arm. Her body undulated over him as a purr vibrated from her.

"Something tells me," she murmured, standing up, "that these boys were high on something other than life." Silvija chuckled. "So sweet. I haven't had one of these in a long time, Belle. Thanks for the suggestion." She licked a deep red stain from her finger and laughed again.

The sun was near rising. New York flushed a lightening

gray, a sure sign that the time of darkness was coming to an end. Awareness of the time flickered over Belle's skin and she searched through the gray sky for some sign of the sun.

"Pollution," Silvija said. "Sometimes it's a friend to us."

The boy's blood rushed through Belle's veins like lightning. She felt energized. Her head swam with the possibilities of this strange super blood. Julia came close briefly, dropping Belle's shoes and jacket on the ground. Distractedly, Belle put them on.

"We can do anything," she said. "Even stay out for as long as we want." Her eyes flickered around the alley, landing on the dead boys, the trash cans with their crooked lids, the rats scurrying under the thin cover of darkness. "This place is amazing."

"It's the spiked blood talking." Silvija signaled to Julia. "Come on, let's go."

And she did something that she'd never done with Belle in her life, she shoved her, nudging Belle playfully out of the way before taking off at full speed out of the alley. Only when Julia bumped her too on her way behind Silvija did Belle lurch out of her surprised stupor to run after them. The New York air slapped hotly against her face as she bounded after them. The passing buildings were trails of brilliant light, intangible ropes of illumination that tried unsuccessfully to hold her to the ground.

The city landscape was a jungle of another sort, one with its own beasts and its own dangers. But the freedom, the stretch of her muscles, the unrestrained joy of releasing her full power on the streets was the same. The three beasts easily slid through the crowd, only lightly nudging some of the humans as they passed, phantomlike through the last moments of the night. A few people turned their heads to try and watch them pass, but that was it. No alarms raised, no police called, no sensibilities bruised. Belle laughed.

They slowed down at the entrance to the hotel, jogged into the gilded lobby, before taking the elevators upstairs to their room. The beasts collapsed on the bed, already tugging off clothes and snuggling into each other. Belle kicked off her shoes and was happily naked within moments before reaching over to take off the rest of Silvija's clothes, her pink-stained white blouse and panties.

"Hmm."

A noise of contentment rumbled through the room from their collective throats. Daylight was approaching but the curtains were already safely pulled. Belle rubbed her cheek against Silvija's bare back and draped her leg over hers. Sleep came quickly after.

Someone was watching. Belle's eyes flew open and her muscles tensed.

"Steady," Silvija's cool voice said. "It's only me."

Silvija's motionless presence was only a hairbreadth away. Her dark eyes were open and staring. "Do you want something from me, Belle?"

"Yes." Her answer was immediate. "Everything."

"I don't have that to give you," she said. "No one does."

"That doesn't make me want it any less."

A wave of a movement flowed from Silvija, like a sigh without breath. "I want you," Silvija said.

Finally.

"And I'll give you what I can in return."

Belle nodded in the dark, knowing Silvija could see it. For now, that was enough.

Chapter 24

New York had been perfect. Even with the mini hangover she had from the boy's drug-infested blood, having Silvija close and hearing the beast's late morning declaration made the entire experience unforgettable. The city had been nothing else that she'd ever experienced. Not Jamaican television with its constant feed of American and British programming. Not even Los Angeles could have prepared her for the reality of the city that never slept, that had almost an infinite supply of food, and that brought out the impish side of her lover's personality.

Now New York was thousands of miles away and even though their visit to the city was long ago, Belle felt its effects resonating inside of her like it was yesterday.

"It's almost summer."

Belle stirred from her contemplation of the lushly green landscape washed under moonlight outside the bedroom window and turned to look at Shaye as the young-looking beast walked into the room.

"I noticed," Belle said. "Where are we going this year?"

The girl giggled and sprawled in the middle of Belle's bed, shoes and all. "Guess."

"The only place I want to go is Jamaica, and if we can't go there, then I'm not interested." Belle knelt to pull on her boots.

Something about Shaye's silence made her look up. The imp was smiling.

"Are you interested yet?"

Belle sat down on the floor. "Yes?" She felt a smile taking over her face. "Yes."

Shaye giggled.

They left a week later, loading up the boat with blood, Violet's favorite clothes, and Silvija's laptop. The beast was nowhere to be found during the preparation for departure but for once Belle didn't mind her absence. Their journey across the seas was swift, one moment Belle was sinking into the scented bed with anticipation, a gently smiling Silvija at her back, and the next, they were pulling into the Kingston harbor at night. The rough smell of the city rushed in to meet them.

"The hunting," Silvija murmured, her deliberate breath teasing the back of Belle's neck, "will be good here." Her nipples prodded gently against Belle's shoulder blades.

Only Silvija's presence in the bed had kept her there. Otherwise she would have been watching the island approach, getting larger and more beautiful after so many years' absence from her sight.

"You can go up if you want." Silvija's hand rested lightly on her belly, possessive, but ready to move at any moment.

Belle turned to face Silvija in the bed, her shoulders brushing against Julia's back as she moved. "Thank you for bringing us here."

"I figured it was time," Silvija said.

Their mouths moved toward each other and met. A gentle exchange of suction. Parted lips. The sweep of tongue. Their breasts slid together and Belle moaned softly as arousal trickled low in her belly.

"Am I finally going to see you two fuck?" Violet's bright eyes appeared over Silvija's shoulder.

"I know we've heard them a lot. Especially recently." Liam laughed, popping up in the bed beside his sister. "You know that normal people get bored of the same piece of ass after a while."

"Who's normal here again?" Belle asked, reluctantly letting go of Silvija.

The beast's hand drifted down her back, settling on her ass. She smiled. "When someone answers that question you let me know." She patted Belle's flesh then got out of the bed. "I'll be on deck if you need me."

They all watched her pull on jeans, boots, and a light shirt before disappearing out the door. Outside, Belle heard Keiko and Ivy's voices raise to the giant in greeting. It was time to get up.

"Are you glad to be back on your island?" Liam asked, a wicked glint to his purple eyes.

Belle jumped from the bed and flashed him a smile. "What a question."

By the time she was dressed and on deck, a taxi van was already waiting to take them to the house. The pavement burned with remnants of the sun and the salty breeze licked at her neck, plucking at the shirt and slacks she wore. A sigh loosened from her lips.

"You keep on looking like that and someone might get the wrong idea." Silvija stepped up behind her. "Or the right one." She dropped a heavy hand on Belle's back, dragging it slowly down between her shoulder blades then along her spine to rest finally on the swell of her ass.

"And what's going to happen?"

Silvija laughed and stepped closer. Nearby Shaye, Ivy, Keiko, and Susannah loaded up the van with their belongings, only occasionally flicking their eyes toward them.

"You know," Belle said before Silvija could reply, "Once I took two boys who were making love on the beach."

"And then . . . ?"

"Nothing. I killed them." Belle leaned back into the giant's sure embrace. "But before that, the sound of their bodies meeting, the smell of blood and sex—it was beautiful." The memory of it sparked and caught fire in her mind. "I've thought about you fucking me like that."

"Ah."

And the sound from the beast's throat slid into Belle like first blood, pooling between her thighs. Her nipples peaked beneath the thin shirt.

"Is that an invitation?" Silvija asked.

Belle turned her head only a little to look at her lover. "What do you think?"

They didn't bother with coconut leaves in the sand. While the taxi took the others away to the house in the hills high above Kingston, Belle and Silvija snuck away. They fell onto the first stretch of sand they found, never mind that it wasn't that far away from discovery or from the water splashing up close, nearly to their feet. Belle kissed Silvija roughly, bringing the parted lips down to hers. Their teeth clicked. Silvija moaned, opening her mouth wider, hands ripping away Belle's shirt from her shoulders, knees sinking into the sand. Silvija's thumbs brushed her nipples, her fingers squeezed them. Lightning bolted into Belle's pussy. Her thighs widened.

"Fuck me," she panted. "Fuck me now."

But Silvija wasn't ready for that. She fastened a ravenous mouth on Belle's breasts, licking them hungrily, slurping against her skin. Her teeth scraped Belle. They both growled as blood scent flared up between them. Her fingers fastened in Silvija's hair, pressing the giant to her breasts. Silvija burrowed into Belle's pants, teased her clit. Belle jumped. Gasped. Burned. Two fingers dipped inside, fucking her shallowly, once, twice. Then retreated.

"I need—" Belle's voice broke off in a gasp.

Silvija licked her nipples, clenched one between her teeth, drawing blood and moans. "I know."

Belle ravaged Silvija with her hands, squeezing breasts, her ass, gripping the flesh that she wanted badly, feverishly. Silvija's clit moved under her fingers, a cool and hard invitation. She stroked as Silvija licked her breasts and teased her clit. Then Silvija fell lower, roughly pushing Belle's pants out of the way to lick the crease at the top of her thighs. *Oh God!*

And her mouth was gone. Silvija pushed her, turned her around. Bared her bottom to the breeze and—oh! Her fingers slid abruptly into Belle's pussy. A cry rang out, a praise. Belle's thighs fell even wider apart. Silvija's fingers drove deeper.

"Sometimes you can be so sweet," Silvija rasped. Her hand gripped Belle's hips, sinking into the flesh like love. "Why can't it always be like this?"

Breath trembled in Belle's throat until she was gasping, her hands gripping fistfuls of sand. "Because—" The fingers fucked her harder, blazing fire into the pit of her belly. She bit her lip. Her body moved over the sand back and forth like a frantic rocking horse. "You wouldn't—you wouldn't know what to do—" Her head flung back and her fangs flashed out. "With me." The last was a low growl. Belle's knees sank wider and deeper into the sand and seawater splashed over them.

Behind her, Silvija shuddered with her fucking motion, and laughed hoarsely. "You're probably right." Her fingers curled inside Belle, fucking harder, faster, deeper.

And Belle was coming. Stretching. Howling under the spilled moonlight with Silvija's fingers flashing inside her cunt and her hand tight on Belle's hip. Belle shuddered, her body flickering with electricity, her breath slowing. Silvija spun her around and shoved her down into the sand. The rough grains stuck to Belle's skin, slid between her toes and against the backs of her thighs.

"Now—" Silvija panted. "Don't bite me." She shoved off her jeans and crouched over Belle's face. Her knees sank into the damp sand on either side of Belle's head. A growl of appreciation rumbled inside Belle. The wet cunt above her smelled as welcome as home with its salty tang and ripeness, its flavor of drizzling honey and cloves, its aroma of lust.

Silvija gasped when her lover's breath washed over her cunt, when the hungry tongue snuggled against the swollen clit and woke it up even more.

"Oh yes," Silvija murmured. "That's right."

Her hands clenched in Belle's hair, sparking trails of pain along her scalp. Belle moaned. Silvija's soaking wet slit coated her mouth with desire and Belle's tongue slid deep into the damp hole, fucking, savoring, loving. Juice slid into her mouth and over her chin. Belle swallowed Silvija's nectar, moaning with the pleasure of it. She lapped at Silvija's clit and fumbled up blindly for her breasts, but encountered her lover's hands instead. Their fingers tangled and together they squeezed the turgid nipples, roamed over breasts until Silvija was gasping and bucking on Belle's face.

"That's it, baby . . . that's it. Eat this pussy." Her hands clenched harder in Belle's hair. "Yes!"

The slick flesh slid faster over Belle's mouth and tongue while the air and the beach churned hotter with their lust, with the uncontrollable breaths that Silvija took. Water rushed over Belle's feet and legs. Silvija's body shuddered over her, shaking in the breeze as she came with a deep-throated roar. Belle felt her lover's body sag, like a puppet suddenly without strings, then fall heavily into the sand beside her. Silvija panted. Belle laughed and reached for the giant. Her fingers tangled in the soft cotton shirt then moved over the belly still moving with breath.

"I thought I heard something."

Belle stiffened at the sound of the unfamiliar voice. She sat up. On the breeze she suddenly smelled humans. Three of them, creeping closer to where the two vampires lay. Her senses had been so full of Silvija that she hadn't noticed their approach, and now they were almost on top of them. The giant stirred from her lethargic sprawl in the sand and smiled crookedly.

"I guess we better get out of here, huh?"

Or we could stay and get a proper meal. But Silvija was already standing up and dragging Belle with her. They quickly pulled on their clothes and dashed across the sand, getting only a lightning glimpse of the three humans—two men and one woman in startled, wide-eyed poses—as they ran. Briny water, traffic, billboard-littered streets. They left that behind them, running with Silvija in front, before they stopped, finally, in front of a pretty two-story house with bursts of pale pink hibiscus flanking the tall front gate. The two beasts looked at each other and, overcome with the absurdity of running away from three puny humans armed only with flashlights, burst out laughing.

"Do you think they would have clubbed us to death or something?" Belle asked, still giggling.

"You never know." Silvija smiled.

She swayed lightly on her feet as if nudged by a firm breeze. With her dark plaits snaking over her shoulders and her teeth a brilliant white against the dark skin, Silvija was easily the most beautiful creature Belle had ever seen. She shook her head.

"I thought you knew everything."

"Not quite," Silvija said.

Belle stepped close to the beast. She sniffed the perfect clove skin with the scent of their sex still lingering on its surface. With the briefest smile, she pressed her mouth to her lover's. "Good. I don't want you to be too perfect."

Silvija's face lost its smile, but her look remained soft. "Come on," she said. "The others are waiting."

And they went on.

"We were wondering if you two were going to show up before sunrise." Julia looked up from the couch when they walked in.

"I think we can take care of ourselves," Silvija said. Her hand lightly brushed the top of Julia's head as she ambled deeper into the house. "Why aren't you out hunting?"

"The others went, but I didn't feel like it."

Meaning she wanted to wait for Silvija to come back before she made any move on her own. Belle's mouth twisted.

"Go," Silvija paused in the threshold. "You need to eat."

"Will you come with me?"

"No. I'm going to shower." Silvija turned and kept walking.

"I can wait." But the giant wasn't listening. She ran up the stairs and disappeared into one of the rooms.

"You won't be her favorite for long, you know," Julia said.

"I'm not her favorite now," Belle said, barely paying attention to the little fiend.

She was torn between following Silvija into the shower and exploring Kingston on her own. Julia's derisive laughter made the decision for her. Belle walked out of the house and kept on going.

Kingston. She'd only been there a few times in the past. In Friendship, the city was considered one of the most dangerous places to be. Gunmen. Kidnapping. Rape. Rampant tourism. It all happened here. But she went down the hill and past gated houses and tall mansions feeling that nothing ever happened in this neighborhood.

This was where the privileged raised their children, hired their live-in maids and compared their newest American imported toys. But this was still Jamaica. Extending out all of her senses, Belle could smell all the things she'd adored about her island as a human—the salt-scented breeze, ackee and salt-fish simmering on a nearby stove, the tempting smell of a woman fresh from her bath, a Guinness stout foaming in a glass and ready to be drunk.

The flowering myrtle trees waved in the breeze as she walked by, tickling her nose too with their fragrance. But the closer she walked to the pier and away from the human-scented houses, the more she saw of what everybody in Friendship had warned her about. Fire-gutted buildings. Skulking humans. Rats the size of crawling babies.

It seemed that no matter how poor someone was in Friendship, they never had cause—unless they insisted on it—to sleep out on the street or go without a hot meal. Even the local madwoman was offered food and a place to sleep, if even on someone's verandah, as she passed mumbling scriptures or some other unintelligible thing beneath her breath. But not here.

The humanity crawled out of her as she passed bodies huddled in ramshackle doorways for shelter, bodies that under the thin covering of plastic bags and filth-darkened rags were nearly skeletal from missing countless meals. There was barely enough blood trickling through them to make leaning down for the kill worthwhile.

"You shouldn't be wandering down here alone at this time of night, darling."

The Jamaican-accented voice pulled Belle away from her study of a figure sleeping in the doorway. She had been aware of the foreign scent long before but paid it little attention. Now, the figure emerging with a smile from the dark had *all* of her attention. The girl's scent was sharp, cutting through the tang of the gutter and the briny sea air. Tamarinds. She smelled like tamarinds.

"Neither should you," Belle murmured, watching her come closer.

The girl's smile was concerned, but the teeth beyond it were predatory. Jeans, a tight blouse, and high heels packaged her slight body for sex and vulnerability. If Belle had been human she would have felt hulking and plain in her black slacks and man-tailored shirt.

The stranger laughed. "I am not alone."

As she spoke, the other scent Belle noticed on the breeze drew near. Fresh milk?

"Somehow I'm not surprised," Belle said.

The two strangers, obviously vampires and obviously young, were beautiful together. Like a small family. Had they met each other after the change? How did they survive on the island, the island that Belle was taken away from after her change? Envy squeezed her chest. She could have stayed here too.

The tamarind-scented girl and the man creeping fully into the light with deliberately casual movements, tried to corral her between their bodies and the graffitied wall. She didn't move. As they came closer, Belle slid her hands in her pockets and braced her legs apart, waiting to see what they would do.

"I'm Belle," she said.

They stopped, not quite exchanging puzzled looks, but close enough. The night, warm and ink-dark, was the kind of night that Belle had missed while being in Alaska. It wasn't so much the temperature but the way that scents carried more easily in the heat and the gentler caress of the humid air against her skin. Sometimes she was in the mood for gentle.

"I should warn you," she said. "If you try to drain me for food, I'm not going to play nice."

The surprise on the girl's face was comical.

"Are you one of us?" The man, a boy really, emerged fully from the shadows, although he had already marked the details of his moon-gilded form. Strong face, trim body, another pretty beast. Yet his maleness would have alarmed any lone human woman in this part of town.

"You don't smell me?" Belle asked.

"The sea is all I smell," the girl responded. "And unless that's you—" at Belle's upraised eyebrow, she stopped.

"Amazing." Her friend moved even closer, close enough for Belle to kick, visibly sniffing.

"You don't have to work that hard to take me in, baby," Belle murmured, looking down at the boy. His fresh milk scent butted against her nose.

"I think you're worth the work," he said with a grin.

His girl didn't appreciate the joke. Belle presented them with her own smile and pulled her hands from her pockets. The girl still looked hungry perched on her high heels and with nothing helpless to kill. Belle looked at the homeless man huddled underneath his rags and felt the other two beasts do the same. No. He could barely sate his own hunger, much less theirs.

"Take a walk with us?" the boy suggested.

Belle nodded and fell into step with him. The girl, with her lips held tight with something like irritation, moved to Belle's other side. They smelled cool, like old blood. Their most recent feeding was at least a day before. It wouldn't be worth it to drain them either. Well, maybe not just one.

"This is Adele," the boy introduced his friend. "And I'm Byron."

Adele, whose eyes hadn't once left Belle, smiled briefly but said nothing. She obviously wasn't the warm and friendly type. Whatever happened to the little girl who had been concerned about her welfare? Ah, she longed for the civility of deception.

"Do you live in Jamaica?" Belle dropped her innocuous question into the murky silence between them.

"Of course," Byron answered with a flirtatious look. "Did you think we're just here looking for you?"

At Belle's fixed stare, he laughed. "You're one of those intense ones, yeah?" The laughter shook his slight frame. "We live here. Why else would we be here, especially in Kingston?"

"Because you love the island and can't stand to be anywhere else?"

Adele finally spoke again. "Please. We not tourists. We stuck here."

Stuck? Belle stared at them in disbelief. "You don't seem like you're suffering. And I don't understand how you feel stuck when you could do almost anything. This world doesn't hold us."

Adele sucked her teeth. "*This* world," she indicated their surroundings "holds us."

"How long have you been dead?"

"We're not—"

"Eight years," Byron interrupted.

That's no time at all. Had they been on the island the entire time? "And you hunt here, too?"

Adele's look was scornful. "Where else would we hunt?"

Belle didn't trust them. Adele still eyed her with an inhuman hunger, as if Belle was somehow inferior, and therefore food.

"How can you kill here?" she asked, knowing she sounded naive even as the words left her mouth. "All the time?"

Adele stopped. "We need to eat."

"And you live with yourself after?"

"Like you said before, we *aren't* alive." The girl tilted her head, looking at Belle from beneath lowered eyelashes. "You can't have it both ways, you know."

"I think," Byron said, "because you don't live here, Jamaica is a dream. Everybody is good. The world is perfect and we all live happy. But what we live is real."

"When I lived here, things were good. Not perfect. But I still can't bear the idea of feeding off my people."

"But I'm sure you did it," Adele said the same moment Byron laughed at Belle, calling her a country girl.

Belle chose to ignore Adele. "What does that say? Everywhere—country, city, cruise ship—Jamaicans are beautiful and they deserve everything. Including the right not to be eaten by monsters."

"But the monsters are Jamaicans too. And we have to eat." The boy flashed his teeth. Smartass.

The streets passed quickly under their feet and they ended up on the pier, dangling their legs over the side and watching the water ripple under moonlight. Salty, sea smell blanketed the air around them and Belle breathed in its comforting familiarity. Despite their hunger, Adele and Byron stayed with Belle, taking turns teasing and challenging her. She found out that they were from Portmore and bitten by the same man they later killed and feasted on.

"I thought this was what I wanted," Byron said. "To grow old and die wasn't something that I saw for myself." Moonlight glimmered in the boy's eyes as he looked out to sea. "A girl was taken from town almost sixty years before me and was turned. I saw her and she looked the same. Her grandchildren looked like crones compared to her."

He had followed the vampire to get what he thought was the answer to all his problems, but her lover found him instead. The older beast was happy for the gift. He fucked Byron, tied him to a bed and kept him human and bleeding for weeks before finally turning the boy after he was almost too weak to drink blood.

Belle easily imagined the violence of the scene. The rusty smell of the metal headboard under the boy's sweaty palms. An immortal beast with a tireless dick riding Byron until his voice was gone. The blood snaking down the back of the boy's neck into a waiting mouth. She felt both his terror and his maker's pleasure.

"I thought this was what I wanted," Byron said. "But I was wrong."

Adele's story was different, yet the same. She saw the man, the vampire, who would be her maker and lover. She saw him and wanted him. His other lovers—the boy with the wounded gaze and the round fleshed woman who seemed like little more than a child—didn't concern her. Tall, with the burning eyes of a zealot and a finely muscled body that made hers weep in response, the vampire had been everything that Adele ever wanted in her short life. She got what she wanted. And more. After he had her, the beast went to Adele's house and killed everyone there. Her parents. An elderly aunt. Her twin daughters.

The wind, sea-scented and soft, ruffled their clothes. Beside her, Belle felt Adele tremble.

"I have a child," she said. "A human."

For a moment there was silence between them. Then Adele turned to her, dark eyes blazing. "I'm sorry."

Belle's fingers clenched into the wood beneath it. "There's nothing for you to be sorry for."

* * *

She left Byron and Adele with their hungers. The sun would rise soon and she wanted to feel Silvija's warmth tonight, not the pain of strangers. On the way back to the house, Belle found food, a muscled youth and his friend who tried to sell her drugs. She took them both and left their bodies cooling near the bottom of the hill.

Her lover was already in bed, alone and reading in the dark. The smell of the others, delicately spiced and on the verge of sleep, reached Belle from another room in the house. Her eyebrow rose.

"What? I'm not allowed to read in bed?" But Silvija's mouth quirked up.

Belle pulled off her clothes and the giant watched her, gently closing her book and putting it aside on the bedside table. All impossibly commonplace. If they had been human.

"We're on a vacation of sorts," Silvija murmured. "So I'd like to do some unusual things."

"Like read in the dark?"

"And have you to myself for a night or two, yes." Silvija pulled aside the covers for Belle to slip beneath them.

Belle's skin instantly began to hum with warmth at her lover's proximity. A low growl of pleasure escaped her lips as Silvija's belly and breasts slid against hers. So warm. She could easily get used to this.

"I'm enjoying this far too much," Belle murmured against Silvija's lips.

"Speak for yourself," Silvija said. "My level of enjoyment is just perfect." Her tongue lashed Belle's mouth. "Hmm. You fed well tonight."

"Yes. Very. And now I'm ready for my dessert."

Laughter rumbled in Silvija's chest and they sank deeper into the sheets, drowning in the perfume of their growing desire.

Chapter 25

All too soon, summer gave way to winter again, and the family was back in Alaska, basking in the glow of a solstice moon. Travel clothes unpacked. Boundaries reestablished. Silvija gone again.

Belle stood in the middle of downtown Wildbrook looking for something to distract her from her loneliness. In Jamaica, she'd gotten so used to having Silvija close that she needed this distraction. Desperately.

Eyes followed her down the wide street, taking in her thin winter clothes, aimless stroll, and dark skin color that was very different from the Inuit brown and Anglo white that they were used to. Belle smiled at a very young girl who was nearly swallowed in a pale blue fur trimmed parka. Her big eyes blinked at the beast as she held on to her mama's leg.

At just past eight, everyone was still out and about in the little town—children, kittens, grown-ups, and tasty, nubile little things waiting for a beast like Belle to take advantage of them. Belle couldn't pinpoint the precise time that she became so cavalier about taking human life and seducing human women, but it was easier now, often done before thought. Now, standing on the sidewalk surrounded by innocence and corruption alike, Belle felt no urge to distinguish between them. She could ravage them all and drink them up like fresh milk. Thoughts of her own child, her family, and her own humanity were so far away as to have been a dream, nothing real that she could relate to now. Some nights it was appalling what she'd become, other nights it was just another fact.

A sound overhead interrupted Belle's thoughts. Her gaze drifted skyward and she smiled. In another moment, she turned from her contemplation of the fresh blood of Wildbrook and walked quickly out of town in the direction toward home.

Belle walked nonchalantly into the Cave, as if she was only incidentally there. Anticipation curled inside her, loosening her movements and stance. The mirrored hallway reflected an image back at her, hands thrust deep into the pockets of her slacks and her hair a loose, snow-dusted halo around her face. She strode down the hall, then through the heavier wooden entrance to the warm sanctuary of the Cave. The plane had already landed and the engine was quiet. A strange scent reached her. Human. Belle's steps faltered.

Did Silvija bring a human here? That couldn't be. She wouldn't dare to bring one of her prey to the Cave. But the scent wasn't wrong. The human smelled of a recent meal, of filet mignon and asparagus and potatoes. Of expensive French wine and Silvija's kisses.

Belle turned away from her original destination and went instead to her bedroom, her solitary one, not the cavernous room she shared with Silvija and the others. She pulled off her sweater and threw it on the bed. The joy and anticipation she had felt at Silvija's return turned to acid in her belly.

She sat down at the dresser, stared down at her neatly arranged collection of toiletries. After all these years, it was the same arrangement she'd used at her human house. Comb, brush, and hair lotion neatly arranged on a white lace doily she'd found in a local shop. The empty jewelry box with its single resting place for the pendant she wore around her neck was on the opposite side of the dresser. Why did she rush home when there was nothing for her here? Why was she a fool?

"There you are."

Belle didn't look up at the low sound of Silvija's voice. Instead she stared even harder at the empty jewelry box, unwilling to look her embarrassment in the face.

"Why won't you look at me, my Belle? Afraid to show how much you missed me?"

The teasing tone brought her head up and her gaze met Silvija's.

"I'd hate to think that you're not talking to me." The beast's smile widened.

"Do I have anything to say to you?"

"I hope so." Her eyes flickered over Belle, to her agitated face, her tight mouth, the fist clenched on the dresser. "Poor Belle." She walked deeper into the room, bringing the scent of the human with her. "I brought something for you."

Belle's lashes flickered. "You did?" Yes, she was officially a fool.

Silvija nodded. "You want to guess what it is?"

"I don't—"

The beast put a finger against Belle's mouth to stop whatever she was going to say. "Shhh," she murmured, looking intently at Belle's lips. "For once, don't be difficult."

Belle bit Silvija's finger. "You brought a human with you."

"Got it on the first try." Silvija took her finger back and licked its bloodied tip.

Belle stared blankly at her. "What?"

"Whatever happened to 'thank you' or 'you shouldn't have'?"

"You shouldn't have."

"Ah, but you'll thank me for it later." Silvija chuckled before turning slightly toward the door and raising her voice. "Come here, Rayne."

The girl was a gorgeous flower of caramel skin, dreamy brown eyes, and a slender, boyish body beneath a long-sleeved shirt, argyle sweater vest, and khaki slacks. Her hair fell to her shoulders in shiny black braids and her mouth was red, passion-bitten and full. Up close, she smelled like drugs. Like X. Belle leaned back against the dresser, curious to see what her lover had in mind.

"Is this her?" Rayne asked with an equally lovely voice, dreamy and American-accented. She was somewhere from the South.

"Yes."

"She's pretty, like you."

"I know." Silvija held out her hand and the girl came deeper into the room to take it. "She thinks you're pretty too. Don't you, my Belle?"

"She's lovely," Belle murmured, more to please the girl than to answer her lover's question.

The human was a tamer, smaller version of Silvija, with a body built on the more modest side of the scale while Silvija's was all marvelous excess. Rayne moved with the loose-limbed grace of an acrobat. Belle stood up from her chair and took the girl's other hand.

At first glance, the human seemed like one of those narcissistic types, but more charming than most Belle had met before. Her smile was dazzling.

Rayne slid her hand from Belle's to trail her fingers up the sensitive skin leading to Belle's shoulders, neck, and face. "You're gorgeous."

She leaned in to kiss Belle. The taste of the French wine still lay on the girl's tongue. It was infused with the light bite of an intoxicant and Silvija's rich clove flavor. And her lips were soft. Soft and delicate and bitable and nearly perfect.

Belle slipped her arms up the fine cotton of her girl's shirt-sleeves, over the argyle sweater and the material covering her breasts.

"Is your bed big enough for us?" Silvija asked from behind the girl.

Belle didn't bother looking at the queen-sized bed that came with the room. If that small thing could handle her and Silvija rolling like ships in a wind-tossed sea, then surely it could take the addition of one small human who weighed next to nothing. In answer, she reached past Rayne for her lover, tugging at Silvija's sweater to lead them all to the item of furniture in question.

Rayne smelled beautifully of intoxication and of want. Whatever Silvija had given the human made her ravenous for sensual attention. She moaned softly beneath Belle's mouth, a soft lovely sound that intensified as Silvija kissed the back of her neck and began to tug the clothes from her body. Soon she was naked, sandwiched between Belle and Silvija, who touched her slim, scented skin, cupped her breasts, squeezed her nipples and her ass.

"I'm so hot for you," the little human said, gasping into Belle's mouth.

"That's perfect," Belle said. Rayne's heat was exactly what she wanted right now. That and Silvija's hands on her. But she knew she would have to wait for the latter.

She pulled back from the girl. "Get on the bed."

While the human lay back, still watching with hungry eyes, Belle quickly took off her own clothes. Silvija disappeared from her field of vision, but she still smelled her lover, knew she was behind her and to her left, rummaging in the top of Belle's closet.

Before she could join Rayne on the bed, Silvija came up behind her. "Get on your knees facing me, Rayne."

The human's eyes glittered as she looked beyond Belle to the giant. When Rayne did as she was told, Silvija knelt on the bed with four loops of thick, silken rope in hand. "Spread your legs and keep them open."

Silvija tied a length of rope around the human's ankle and anchored the other end to the middle of the bed frame under the mattress. She did the same to the other ankle. A groan of excitement left Rayne's mouth as she watched the giant work. She swallowed. The wetness between Belle's legs grew at the sight of the human spread out and damp, even more helpless than before.

"Now bend backward for me, love."

After the flexible human slid easily into the position Silvija wanted, the giant moved up behind Rayne to do more work, but Belle couldn't watch her any longer. She crept toward Rayne's heated pink pussy and pulled its scent deep into her nose. A moan escaped her. The human jerked at the feel of her cool breath on her pussy, and then she was moaning as Belle stroked it with her tongue, bathing the hot-pink and caramel flesh with slow, deep licks. Even down here she tasted like the drugs, of ecstasy and coke and something else that made Belle's head swim and her mouth open even wider for more. Rayne moaned again, moving her pussy in rhythm with Belle's movements.

"More, please." Rayne gasped when she got what she asked for. "More. Oh yes. Yes."

"That's enough."

At Silvija's order, Belle grasped the human's hips even tighter, feeding more on her pussy, until she felt Rayne's orgasm tilt close, and closer. Belle gasped as a rough hand pulled her hair, jerking her up from her feast.

"I said, enough."

The hand gentled and released her almost at once.

Silvija was naked now, and fearsome; at her most powerful with her breasts bared, her sleek body on display with a dick strapped to her hips and ready to fuck. Belle sprang at her, hand raised to slap the arrogance from her face. Silvija never learned to control her dominatrix tendencies where Belle was concerned. It was time she was taught. The giant easily grasped her hands, restraining her hands behind her back. Even with Belle struggling, Silvija kissed her throat, lingering at the sensitive spot just beneath her jaw. Her dick nudged Belle's stomach.

"Teach me a lesson later, my Belle. The girl is awaiting your pleasure. And hers."

She turned Belle around to look. Rayne was bent over backward and laid out like a holiday feast, her pussy wet and pink under a sprig of dark curling hair. Her hands were tied and spread wide on either side of her. Obviously ready for whatever the night might bring, she licked her lips and lazily watched them.

An antique mirror rested on the wall, seven feet long, four feet wide with a view of most of the room, including the bed. It was homage to the vampires' general narcissism but Belle's in particular, since she never actually slept in this bed. The mirror reflected the three women. Silvija and Belle pressed together, the giant's dick pushing into the small of Belle's back while her hands lightly caressed her breasts. The two of them watched the human girl with very real hunger.

Lightning flashes of pleasure flared through Belle's body at Silvija's touch. The sight of them in the mirror, the heated gaze her lover bestowed on her, the uncontrolled shudder in her breasts as phantom breath shivered through her, all made her legs fall open.

Silvija touched the wetness between her thighs, slid an electric finger against her clit. "Do you want her, my Belle?"

What she wanted now more than anything was Silvija. The human girl was a temporary accessory that she could live with if she had to.

"She'll do," Belle murmured with her lashes hanging low and heavy over her eyes.

"Good."

And just like that Silvija kissed the back of Belle's neck and nudged her forward. "Take her. I brought her for you. Rayne is a good girl. She'll do anything you want."

"Really?"

Belle climbed over the girl's curled body, kissing the soft lines of her flesh as she went. Rayne was salty and wet, her body damp with that heady combination of fear and arousal Belle had felt with Silvija on many occasions. As she climbed over the girl, she made sure to slide the cool wetness of her pussy over the girl's skin, to allow Rayne to feel how badly Belle wanted this.

"Touch me," Rayne pleaded. Her voice was low and hoarse, as if everything about her existence depended on the next movement of Belle's hands. Belle skimmed the girl's cheeks with her palms, lightly brushed her lips with those hands before replacing them with her wet pussy.

"Drink up, honey," Belle said. "I know you're thirsty."

The girl made a low, urgent noise in her throat before she opened her mouth wide for Belle. Her hot breath scorched.

"Slowly, honey. Slow."

Rayne lapped obediently at the damp flesh, washing her tongue over Belle's clit and making her sigh at the lush delight of it. Behind her, she knew Silvija watched her, watched the slim line of her back, the thick curve of her ass from its crouch over Rayne's mouth. She wanted to see her too. Belle turned around.

The girl gasped with the momentary loss of the flesh over her mouth before sighing again when it returned. Belle sighed too. Rayne had a wonderful talent. The slim girl fluttered her tongue at the entrance to her pussy, stimulating the hypersensitive nerves there. Then she took Belle's clit in her mouth. *Ah!*

Silvija knelt between the girl's legs watching Belle intently even as she played with the girl's pussy, stroking the tender flesh, making the girl jerk and gasp at the electric contact. Silvija's eyes played over Belle's face, watching its every rictus of pleasure, every sigh that left her lips. It was as if Silvija was the one sucking her pussy, as if she were the one making her feel such decadent things. Sensation shivered in Belle's belly as the girl lapped her up.

Silvija put two fingers in her own mouth, sucked wetly on them before she inched them into Rayne's pussy. The human moaned against Belle, distracted from her rhythm by this new sensation. The rising inside Belle receded until it was ordinary pleasure again. Belle held Silvija's gaze for a moment before her eyes slid away to the giant's dark-tipped breasts, her tight belly, and the deep fucking motions of her fingers inside the girl's liquid cunt. The girl's belly trembled, her skin grew wet, she moaned deeply under the rippling gag of Belle's pussy. As Silvija sped her motions inside the girl's pussy, the girl's tongue on Belle sped up. She was licking her clit, then sucking it, then plunging her tongue deeply into the sopping wet cavern as far as it would go. Silvija watched her and Belle almost cried out.

Silvija stopped. She pulled her long fingers from the girl's clinging hole and sank her dick deeply inside. Rayne gasped under Belle's clit. Then the girl began to eat Belle's pussy in earnest, sucking on her clit, fucking her with her thick tongue. The bed groaned as the girl pulled against the ropes and arched up against Silvija. All three women groaned. They became a chorus of pleasure; Silvija moaned and grunted as she fucked the girl and the leather strap rubbed against her clit; Rayne panted and moaned at the building friction in her pussy, the heat flinging up into her belly, Belle's elixir coating her tongue; and Belle—she felt everything.

Belle's body was bathed and bubbled in lust, her skin fiery and heated over Rayne's mouth, the heat of Silvija's gaze on her body, the scent of their combined efforts, cloves, pussy, the sea, sweat, the anticipation of blood. She skimmed her hands over the girl's sweat slick belly and thighs, stroking her clit. Silvija grabbed Rayne's hips and slammed even harder, and more deeply into her, fucking her, shaking the bed. Her mouth fell open as she grunted even harder and louder. Blood-tinged sweat coated her skin and she glowed, incandescent and lovelier than Belle had ever seen her.

"Kiss me," Belle begged. "Kiss me."

She leaned forward, suddenly desperate to feel the giant's mouth on hers. Her body stretched and reached out. Silvija leaned toward her, still pistoning her hips. Belle grasped her slick neck, slipped her fingers under the heavy snaking hair, and brought her closer.

Their mouths connected with a hot gasp from one or both or all three of them. The heated mesh of tongues and sensa-

tion and the frantic movement of their bodies sent Belle tilting over the sharp edge of orgasm. Her fingers sank deeply
into Silvija's neck until she felt blood. She knew that Silvija
had come at least twice already just from the friction of the
strap against her clit, but still she was insatiable. They both
felt Rayne buck beneath them in orgasm, her shuddering
breaths and gasping sips at Belle's clit. Belle slowly released
her lover.

Silvija pulled out of the still gasping girl with a liquid,
sucking sound and bent to place a delicate kiss on Rayne's
clit. She freed the girl's legs and motioned for Belle to untie
her hands. Rayne shuddered and stretched out on the bed,
mouth still gasping and eyes staring wide at the ceiling.
Silvija stroked the girl's damp belly.

"Do you still want this?" she asked.

"Oh yes, yes." Rayne's eyes searched quickly for Silvija as
if she was afraid she would take away whatever it was that
she had promised her.

"Good." Silvija kissed her on the mouth. "Very good."

Belle put her jealousy aside long enough to look at the two
in speculation. What wicked thing had her lover planned for
this little girl?

"Lie down on your side," Silvija instructed. "Face the
wall."

When the girl did as she was told, the beast brought Belle
up against her. Her eyes searched Belle, caressing her face,
her mouth.

"I hope you're not tired yet," Silvija said.

Belle squeezed the dick pressed between them. "Not even a
little."

"Good, because you haven't tasted her yet and that's the
best part."

Silvija's raptor smile made Belle's pussy jump. Her fangs
stretched in her jaw, and just that quickly her mouth was wet
and ready for a taste of blood. Rayne moved restlessly on the

bed. She dropped her fingers between her thighs and began to leisurely touch herself.

"Are you going to bite me now?"

"Not yet," Silvija said. "Good things come to those who wait. Remember?"

The human smiled, still lying on her side but with her head turned back to watch the beasts and with her fingers slowly circling her clit.

"Keep your hands off the pussy," Silvija gently ordered. "If that's what I'd brought you here for I would've left you on the plane by yourself."

The girl shuddered as she drew her hands away from her cunt. Silvija nodded in approval. What had she promised Rayne? The human seemed slavishly devoted and ready to do anything that Silvija asked. But wasn't that always the case with any woman the beast encountered? Silvija tipped Belle's head back to whisper hotly in her ear, to tell her exactly what she wanted. Belle's body grew even more saturated, her nipples became pebble hard, and her legs shook. *Oh yes.*

Belle kissed the beast and lay down on the bed behind the human. She kissed the back of the human's neck, raking the pussy-scented hair out of her way. Rayne whimpered softly and tilted her ass up and back for Belle. The vampire growled. She'd always enjoyed humans. They were so sweet to the taste, their passions bubbling up hot enough to scorch and raise desire from the coldest corpse.

When she felt Silvija's breasts against her back and the beast's hands on her hips, her body nearly had its own meltdown.

"Open your legs for me, my Belle."

Her thighs parted at the heated words and had barely touched the air above the bed before the beast's dick moved slickly into her from behind. Phantom breath shivered in her throat, her body moved with agitation, and her own hands drifted forward in their desire to touch. A soft moan left

Rayne's throat. Belle grasped the girl's breasts, playing with the subtle mounds. The nipples were firm and succulent beneath her fingers. She wanted to suck on them, to feel their hardness beneath her tongue. But she couldn't, not yet.

Silvija's dick stirred agitation in her, called up sensation and breath and gasps as its strokes grew longer, went deeper. Belle's hand moved between Rayne's open thighs and stroked her thickening clit, slid her fingers inside her pussy, fucking her to the same rhythm that Silvija was playing so well behind and inside her. The girl moaned and dropped her head back.

"Suck my neck," she begged in her husky voice. "Please, suck me. Please."

Her clit was hot and wet under Belle's fingers, the thighs wide open and already shaking with the promise of coming.

"You heard the girl," Silvija whispered above her in a not quite steady voice.

Her dick moved with liquid ease inside Belle as her fingers grasped tightly to her hips, holding her steady for the perfect strokes. Flames danced in Belle's belly. They licked lower, flaring hot in her pussy. Rayne shuddered against her breasts and belly, her breath uneven and hot. Her smell was perfect. Belle sniffed her neck, sinking her nose deeper into Rayne's scent. The girl's gasps grew louder.

"Bite me," Rayne hissed. Her hips churned faster under Belle's hand. "Take me, drink me up."

Belle took her. Rayne gushed into her mouth like love, like passion, like everything that Belle wanted from Silvija and more, more, more. Liquid, chemical, and sensation overpowered Belle until she gasped as loudly as the human. And she was coming wildly, her insides bathed in the scarlet glow of satisfaction, the churning inside her rushed to its highest high. Still, she swallowed more of the human's blood.

Rayne shuddered against her. The human's passion completed itself in a lush aural orgy, moaning and gasping, begging and thanking as her hands reached up, grasping the headboard until the muscles in her arms sprang out like strings over tapered wood.

"Yes . . . yes." Her voice grew weaker as her orgasm burned itself out and released her body from its grip.

Belle slid her teeth free of Rayne's neck, then licked the twin drops that followed from the pulsing artery. Silvija still moved inside her, but slower now, her strokes mindful of Belle's rippling orgasm. She twisted her head back to kiss the beast, and at the press of Silvija's mouth against hers, spilled some of the girl's sparkling blood into her mouth. Silvija swallowed and sighed.

"How do you feel?" she asked, still fucking Belle, holding her hips.

"Perfect," Belle murmured, closing her eyes. "I feel perfect."

"That's what I want you to feel," Silvlija whispered. "I want you to know how good you make me feel."

She nipped the back of Belle's neck with her teeth, then licked the bite.

"Oh!"

Belle felt another blaze building inside her, but the slowness of the strokes held it at bay. Her body floated on an island of ripe sensation, taut and suspended. It didn't matter that Rayne was lying there before her, drained of everything but her ecstasy. Her blood was full. Light danced behind her eyelids, Silvija whispered of desire at her back, the room pulsed with energy, and her whole world was sublime.

"Is there anything else I can give you?" Silvija's mouth scraped against her neck again. "Anything?"

"Just you," Belle gasped. "You."

Silvija moved deeper inside Belle, sped up the movement of her strokes. "That's all you want?" Her voice was sandpaper rough.

"Yes."

She turned Belle over to her stomach without pulling from the cool sheath of her body, and pressed her into the bed. The blaze inside Belle flared hotter and she gasped again. The girl watched them with eyes like mirrors. In them Belle could see their beastly bodies reflected back, their twin lusts, and her own love for the beast that made them luminous. Tears choked at the back of her throat.

"Is this what you want?" Silvija's hips moved faster against Belle's ass, stirring the dick, and her pleasure, and the fire, the lust.

"Yes." The word shot past her wide-open lips into the sheets. She pushed her ass back for Silvija until she was meeting the beast thrust for thrust.

"Give me what I want," she gasped.

The hard nipples pressed into her back like bullets, forcing her over the edge again. She fumbled for the scrolled headboard, grasped it in her hands, and held on as Silvija fucked her, slamming deep into her pussy. The bed shook with each thrust and retreat, pounding against the wall again and again. Silvija's fingers slid against her clit, then squeezed.

Belle threw her head back and howled as the hurricane of their desire took her. The feelings, all the sensations, built up inside her until they had nowhere else to go but in her throat and up and out into the room that she knew was not soundproof. *I love you. Damn it, I love you.* She kept the words behind her teeth, biting her tongue until she felt blood spill from her mouth and trickle down her chin. The beast's hands held her tight as they collapsed into the sheets.

"Did I give you what you wanted?" Silvija asked, licking at Belle's bloody mouth and chin.

"Yes," Belle laughed breathlessly. "Thank you." She stretched beneath the giant and their bodies moved wetly together.

"Can I have some more?"

Belle looked up at the sound of Rayne's voice. She had forgotten that the human was still in the room. She opened her mouth to answer.

EVERY DARK DESIRE   237

"Yes, you can." Silvija's hand drifted over to stroke the girl's back. "But not from us. We have some friends who'd love to have you."

Rayne purred beneath the giant's touch. Her eyes grew bright at the mention of others. Silvija motioned the human to the door and Rayne sat up in the bed, apparently eager for something new.

"Thank you." Rayne dropped a light kiss on Silvija's hand before walking out the door. She didn't look back.

A few moments later, Julia's light voice reached them from behind the closed door.

"What do we have here?" she asked.

The little fiend had obviously been listening to their energetic fucking and was ready for her share of the action. Belle tuned her out and rolled lethargically from beneath the giant. Silvija unbuckled her strap and tossed it behind her to the floor, then followed Belle with her body until the smaller beast lay on her back and Silvija looked down at her with grave eyes. All night, it seemed, Silvija had been searching for something in her eyes, or perhaps searching for something in particular to say. She smoothed the hair away from Belle's face with a cool hand, allowing her fingertips to linger along the jawline and throat.

"Do you want something from me?" Belle asked with a tentative smile.

"Everything," Silvija answered with a smile of her own, echoing her part of their New York conversation.

"I think you already have that." Ever since that day in the hotel in Negril, she'd belonged to the Clan and, by extension, to Silvija.

"If only."

Silvija's lashes fell briefly to shield her eyes, as she hovered above Belle; then she looked fully at the conquered beast—Belle couldn't think of herself of anything but—and kissed her. She kissed Belle tenderly, with a molten core of passion

that made Belle want to rip into her back with her fingernails, to force her to give her what she wanted to, not what
she thought that Belle wanted.

Her lips were melting and sweet, tender in that insincere
way that Belle hated. She bit into the lush bottom lip and
growled.

"No," Silvija said. "I won't let you do that again. *This* is
what I want."

And she persisted with her tenderness. She nibbled gently
on Belle's lips, stroking her belly and thighs until Belle melted
too with the kisses and the two beasts became like waves of
water finally flowing in the same direction. Silvija turned
them until they were facing each other on their sides, mouths
sliding together, limbs intertwining like so many times in
Belle's schoolgirl fantasies. Silvija took her hand and guided
it over her belly, then to the damp spot between her thighs.
She pressed Belle's fingers against her, inside her. "I want you
to fuck me."

The words resonated between them, vibrating until Belle
felt the echo of them over her skin, in her blood. Belle didn't
ask Silvija to repeat herself. That would have made a mockery about what she was offering her. Would have made it less
perfect.

Silvija's flesh under her hand was divine, a complex pattern of regenerated tissue with texture that sent sparks of
awareness dancing through Belle's body. The times they'd
fucked before now were nothing compared to this moment,
this sensation of deep connectedness with her lover. A tremor
shook Silvija.

"Harder," she choked. "Don't be scared. Let me feel you."

Belle gasped and pressed the beast onto her back. Beneath
her Silvija was incandescent, lovely in her breathlessness, her
lips damp and red, and eyelashes fluttering with each movement of Belle's fingers inside her pussy.

Belle's fingers were dipped in silk. Silvija's flesh slid wetly against her hand, against the nerves that suddenly felt as if they were on the outside of her skin, connecting with each electric part of Silvija. She felt each of her lover's moans before they started. Felt them being born from the movement of her fingers. Felt Silvija's lips part and the sound ready itself to blow past soft flesh. Her giant vibrated with pleasure.

Belle's fingers moved deep into her lover's pussy, into the overflowing cavern, into the wetness that was Silvija. And all around her, swallowing her senses, was the liquid sound of her fucking the best pussy she'd ever had.

Silvija stretched back against the bed, her long legs taut with muscles striated and rigid. "Harder."

Belle fucked her harder, thrusting three fingers deeper into that wet slit, grunting with her efforts. Silvija's hips rose from the bed to meet each stroke, with her belly taut and sweating. Her head moved against the bed and she gasped, fingers clenched in the sheets, lips skinned back from her teeth.

"Yes." The word trembled past her lips.

Silvija gasped again when Belle dipped her head to take a nipple in her mouth. She pressed her tongue against the hard nub, sucking and licking at it while pressing her fingers deeply into her lover, fucking her to the hard and harder tempo that her lover demanded. The giant came with a roar. Her body rocketed from the bed, nearly tossing Belle to the floor.

"Thank you," she moaned, moving her head slowly from side to side and licking her lips.

Belle smiled, still shivering from her own sympathetic orgasm. "My pleasure."

The room settled into calm. Instead of passion, lassitude and satisfaction became its new perfume as the two beasts uncoiled from each other and lay back against the sheets. Silvija lay beside Belle, blinking slowly at the ceiling, her body beautifully sprawled in the bed. Her hand drifted out to touch Belle's stomach. Despite its recent orgasm, Belle's body still responded, thrilling to the light touch and curving toward it.

"I'm glad Julia took you," Silvija murmured. Her lashes fell down to shield her eyes. "I can't imagine being anywhere else right now."

Chapter 26

Belle stared at the giant in surprise. But Silvija was paying more attention to her breasts than her eyes. A hand lightly touched one, then the other before settling down to cup the closer one. The beast moaned deeply in her throat, a sound of contentment. She seemed completely unaware of what her words had done to Belle.

Except for her fruitless lingering thoughts about Kylie, Belle hadn't thought about that awful night in Jamaica in a long time. It was in the past and she preferred to leave it there. Nothing could be changed now. Lingering on the past would only cause resentment and anguish, two emotions she rarely had time for these days.

But Belle thought about that night now. She remembered how afraid she had been and how she had raged against Julia, then been abandoned to her own terror, forever changed into something that she hated. The thought crept up on her: did something like that happen to Silvija? It was hard to imagine the giant being at some other creature's mercy.

"Tell me about Jamaica," Belle said.

Silvija turned to look at her. "You already know about it. Weren't you born there?"

"No, I mean about your Jamaica. When you were alive." Her words carved their own space in the room with them, finally voicing a yearning, a need to know more about the beast she desired so fiercely.

Silvija was quiet. Then she shifted next to Belle, stirring up her clove scent and the aroma of their sex. "It was hard. But it was also a kind of heaven. It was a long time ago."

"How long?"

"Three hundred and fifty years, give or take." The corner of Silvija's mouth quirked up.

Belle didn't bother to hide her surprise. "Seriously?"

"Why would I joke about something like that?"

"You don't look bad for someone who should be nothing but dust and memories."

Silvija chuckled. "I know." At Belle's intent gaze, her laughter died away. "I had a hard life, Belle. It's not something those who live in these times can understand. Even before I was made, I had killed." Silvija looked at Belle. "We were Maroons."

Belle startled again. She had heard about Maroons in school, former slaves and their families—some who had never known the lash of captivity—who lived in the hills of Jamaica as free people, terrorizing the English and trying to drive them from the island. And here she was, living with one of them.

"When I was born, Jamaica had a Spanish governor, but that changed soon enough. Almost my whole life in Jamaica, we lived under English martial law. Nothing was soft for us. Nothing was easy. Yet I loved our life in the mountains. We lived to terrify the English and route them from Jamaica. Most of my family had been used to better treatment by the Spanish. They had been slaves, but valuable ones, not to be carelessly cut or beaten like dogs."

Silvija looked away from Belle into emptiness. "An Englishman took my life."

It seemed then that she wouldn't go on. That the memories and the drugs from the young girl's blood had met each other and lay down in the road in mutual surrender.

But . . . "I was thirty and had nothing of my own except a

woman who still belonged to another. In the time that she was my lover, I had taken her family as my own, sat with her as she gave birth to her husband's children, waited through the healing of her womb before I was allowed back into her bed again."

An unfamiliar accent began to creep into her words. "When the English raiders came that night, everyone else was on guard except for us. She had named her child after me and we were now to be a family. Ynez, me, her husband, and the two children who already were as strong as young bulls.

"I wanted to fight the English, not raise children, and that's why I had no true home of my own except for the one between Ynez's thighs. When her husband would allow me there, of course. That night they surprised us. They surprised me. While everyone else was burning down our settlement before the English could do it, while the family escaped, I was drowning in her sex."

Silvija licked her lips and cocked her head. The faraway look in her eyes almost frightened Belle, but she wanted her to go on. "I knew that I should have been more alert to my surroundings, but it had been so long. I remember not knowing what I wanted to do first, taste her pussy or fuck her. There was no bed for us. I was taking her in the woods, with her legs wrapped around my waist, the scent of wood smoke and green ackee from the tree overhead almost as intoxicating as the feel of her cunt around my hand." Silvija cursed. "I was so stupid."

She sat up in the bed suddenly to stare down at Belle. "I swear she came. I'd like to think that she did before they dragged her away from me." Silvija looked down at her hand as if she could still see the smear of her lover's juices on it. "Then that English bastard took everything else away."

In the afterglow of their own lovemaking, Belle saw it all through her lover's eyes. The images swirled in Silvija's gaze like poisoned smoke. The Englishman in a red militia jacket with his long rifle pointed at Silvija. The moon glimmered on his black hair and pale skin as he ordered his men to tie Silvija to the tall ackee tree. He waved a hand at them: they could have the other woman. He wanted this one. And he paid no attention to Ynez's screams as the men dragged her away to a more convenient place. He paid even less attention to Silvija's shouts as her woman was violated by white beasts.

"I like a bit of cunny, too," he breathed the words as if they were meant to excite Silvija.

Her body went stiff as he approached, sniffing at her skin. When he got nothing but scornful indifference from her, he ripped away the front of her shirt with abnormally strong hands.

"You're looking at me now, aren't you?" He dropped his gun. "Look carefully, I don't want you to miss a thing."

Silvija couldn't hide her terror as his face transformed, his mouth widened, and the false English civility fell from his features. Long, slashing teeth thrust out from his mouth and made him into a beast. His eyes burned with hunger.

Belle flinched from the image of the man she now knew as intimately as Silvija had known him. She felt his teeth invade Silvija without permission or enticement. Her neck jerked back in resistance and a scream rose up in her own mouth. He clapped a hand over Silvija's mouth, but she bit him. He loved it. She felt his dick rising against her as she bucked against the ropes lashing her to the tree.

He drained her. The ropes creaked as Silvija's body sagged in defeat. Her pulse fluttered weakly in her throat and she heard him moaning, ripping her pants out of the way before shoving his dick roughly inside her. He was filthy, filthy as he thrust inside her, grunting. She smelled him, a scent like daffodils and earth. There was a cut on his face and the thick blood smell of it blended with the sticky sweet odor of his body. Silvija gagged and a silent howl filled her head. In the bedroom, Belle's fingers curled tightly with Silvija's as their eyes met and held.

He finished with her, leaving her body stained and naked for any to see it.

"Maroon bitch." He hauled up his trousers and spat on her. "That should teach you not to mess with your betters."

Her body jerked at the insult. She felt empty. The healed cut on his face still had blood surrounding it. This animal bled. Just as he was making her bleed. A sob rose up in her weak body. Behind the monster she heard a new noise, a crawling noise that had the Englishman looking behind him and cursing. Rapid gunshots sounded in the trees around them. A shot spun the monster toward, then against, her and his heavy body fell on hers, startling her out of her stupor. One of the ropes holding Silvija upright snapped as the Englishman's hand caught it to balance himself.

She swayed from the tree, hanging by one hand, her shoulder groaning in pain at the pressure, pulling her even more awake. His blood gushed over her face, and her eyes fluttered open, sticky from the red spray. She licked her lips, and it was as if a bolt of lightning surged into her. Her body jerked with awareness.

The Englishman pushed away from her, or at least he tried. Silvija's hand hooked in his neck, pulling him heavily back against her mouth. Her body shuddered and began to warm, to feel mobile and loose again.

"Release me." He tried to push away but she held fast to him with her building strength. "I'm finished with you."

But *she* wasn't finished with him. Her long arm wrapped completely around him and she drew him even harder against her and bit into him, marking his face with bites that fed her small amounts of blood. The hole was in his chest. She felt it as the wound bled sluggishly and was well on its way to closing. Silvija dug her hand into the mangled hole.

The monster screamed and tried even harder to pull away from her, but she pulled him in, ignoring the screaming pain in her shoulder as the need for blood overtook her like a

fever and all she knew was that she had to have this repug-
nant creature under her mouth and into her body. But not the
way that he wanted.

Chaos reigned in the small clearing. Silvija could hear
screams, of men now, as Maroons exploded out of the woods
with their own weapons at the ready. They fired with deadly
accuracy, piercing English flesh. Silvija tugged her other arm
free of the rope and she fell fully on top of the Englishman,
her mouth open and searching for a richer source of blood
than the gaping wound in his chest or the tentative bite
marks on his face. She bit into him, his flesh sucking liquid
and slick at her still blunt teeth. Her hands were red with his
blood, but that didn't satisfy her.

He struggled, his strength rearing up suddenly to take her
off guard. His fists caught her in the face and belly. Silvija
bore down on him, snapping his arms back. A new wound
opened up then, gushing up blood toward her face, and
Silvija pounced on it. She muffled his cries with a hand over
his face, not flinching when he bit and continued to gnaw at
her hand. While she fed on the fat vein pulsing in his arm, she
slammed his head into the dirt again and again, barely breaking her sucking rhythm.

In the bedroom, Silvija reeled at the remembered taste of
first blood. She touched Belle's face with gentle hands as she
subsided beside her in the bed. "It was so wonderful. There
was nothing else like it. Nothing."

The Maroons didn't interfere with her feeding. They'd
seen others driven mad by grief and wild by the thrill of bat-
tle. That's all they thought of it. Silvija's lover was dead, her
family was fractured. She deserved this revenge, this taste of
blood. But they soon found out that it wasn't just the enemy's
blood Silvija was hungry for, and they chased her from their
camp one night after she'd nearly drained her dead lover's
husband.

"I was so hungry. And I didn't know what I was. Only that
I needed blood to live and the sun was my new enemy.

Eventually I figured out what I was and the best way for me to live. But by then, two years or so later, I had killed hundreds, even thousands of humans—British, Spanish, and African alike. My blood thirst didn't care how it got satisfied."

Then something changed. Belle knew it before the words left her lover's mouth.

"Then something changed. It wasn't long before I realized that what I needed was a family of my own. I know I needed permanence, but I also had no idea how to find it. That's when Shaye found me."

"Shaye?"

"Yes. She looks like a child, but she was the one who found me huddled next to the naked body of a woman I'd taken for companionship but used for food. Shaye laughed at me, but she stayed. She and I built a life in Port Royal where Rufus found us only a few years later. As night creatures we were never out of place in a city that made most of its money from piracy and death.

"The town was at its most wicked then. You could buy or steal almost anything. Especially a human life. Nothing was taboo there, and we blood drinkers fit right in. We stole to afford our modest house on the outskirts of the town, and although slavery was very legal and very prosperous, they left us alone. Living there was a lovely respite from the struggles of mountain life. There was no clinging to a fear-frozen human on the dirty floor of a mountain cave, no stealing pigs for blood or luring fat plantation daughters into the bushes. In Port Royal the food came to us. When you're pretty and rich, everything falls into place. People came in and out of that town almost every hour of the day and night. No one noticed when strangers went missing, so we gorged ourselves nearly every night. But of course, all that had to come to an end." Silvija trailed her fingers along Belle's belly, watching how the flesh moved in reaction to her touch.

"The night before the 1692 quake happened, Rufus had a vision and we left. We packed up all the money and goods we could safely carry, and by sunrise the next day we were safely asleep in the belly of a mountain over fifty miles away."

Silvija's head slowly turned to look at Belle. She smiled, a tentative thing of pearly teeth and moist lips. Belle didn't smile. Port Royal could have been a worse disaster. From her school textbooks, Belle knew that the earthquake had come out of nowhere at noon on June 7, 1692, killing over two thousand humans in three minutes. The sleeping vampires would have been swept into the sea and into the heat of the sun, their lethargic bodies burned into unrecognizable piles of ashes and scattered out into the Caribbean Sea like old dust.

Because of Rufus, the beast was here today. Because of Rufus and his unpredictable, unmanageable gift, this creature, under the influence of sex and intoxicant-infused blood, was in her bed trusting her with the tapestried details of her past.

"I wonder what my life would have been like if you had died then."

Silvija brushed her thumb along the full curve of Belle's mouth. "Boring."

Chapter 27

"Why did you invite the humans to come?" Belle asked.

"Because it will be fun." Silvija adjusted the last pin in her hair and turned, smiling, from the mirror. Her reflection had been blinding before, but now the direct heat of her shining eyes and teeth sent a pulse beating furiously in Belle's clit. Why did she only seem to grow more beautiful each day?

The dress Silvija wore was ridiculous. Why would someone that wickedly lovely and tall need to wear the sleek black rubber that hugged her thighs, caressed her ass, and cinched her waist? Belle fought a sigh. The rich bounty of Silvija's breasts rose high and cresting above the red underbust corset with its two side buckles and red silk laces trailing down the back to brush against Silvija's ass with every step she took. The red wasped waist should have made her seem feminine and vulnerable. But it only emphasized her power. Made her seem like more of a superwoman, a sex goddess, risen from the mists.

Tonight, her hair was loosened from its customary plaits and scraped back in a severe bun that left her long neck and assertive jawline open to admiration.

"You look very edible," Belle said.

The understatement of the year. It was all she could do not to jump up and devour the taller beast, to wrestle her to the bed and pop her breasts from their alluring prison and suckle them, riding her rubber-clad thigh and making the material slick with her juice until she came. Belle adjusted her own simple red halter dress and fluffed her haloing hair one last time.

"Thank you." Silvija's eyes caressed her. "I could say the same of you, and more."

They reached simultaneously for each other. Silvija's hand fit in the cool curve of Belle's shoulder and neck. The gliding fingers sent tingles of awareness down her spine and legs. Her own fingers tested the resilience of the rubber over Silvija's breast. The material squeaked softly beneath her touch.

Ever since the night with Rayne, things had been very different between them. They were more open with each other, even loving, and Silvija had become the lover Belle always wanted but had been afraid to ask for.

Shaye poked her head in the room. "While you two stand there mooning over each other, there is a party going on strong in the rest of the house."

"I need to get ready, don't I?" Violet murmured absently from the bed, not looking up from the complicated formation of purple yarn spun between her fingers and Liam's.

One corner of Silvija's mouth turned up. "Only if you want to."

She caressed Belle's skin again, then slowly pulled away, trailing her fingers from the sensitive flesh over her shoulder and throat to Belle's breasts swelling against the bodice of the draped dress. Her nipples came to immediate attention. Silvija's eyes caught the response and she smiled.

"Later," she mouthed.

As the host to a houseful of guests, mostly vampires with a generous smattering of curious and enraptured humans, Silvija had duties to fulfill, never mind that what she really wanted was to fuck her lover all night. At least that's what Belle hoped that Silvija wanted. She nodded and backed away from the temptation. Silvija smiled regretfully and walked out of the room, switching her ass like a tempting metronome purely for Belle's benefit.

The noise from the rest of the room came rushing back to Belle—Julia and Liam giggling behind them about one of their new guests, who they both badly wanted to fuck. Shaye joined Julia, Liam, and Violet in the bed, looking on with some curiosity at the game Violet and Liam played.

"Bondage games?" she asked.

"Only to the twisted," Liam deadpanned.

They'd given up their private rooms to their guests from New York, Shanghai, Suriname, Guinea Bissau, and other parts of the world. These exotic creatures spoke with different accents and were even more interesting than the family here. In the days since they'd arrived Belle often stumbled upon them fucking in corners of the Cave, the air spiced with the smell of blood, their laughter, or urgent voices raised in excitement. They were too beautiful not to watch.

They were here for the party, a rare gathering that Silvija had organized in celebration of this, the longest night of the already dark winter. The beasts would have twenty hours of full dark to play and feast. And Tamsyn, the policewoman from the human search-party that raided the house so long ago, would be here tonight. Silvija hadn't promised her the woman in so many words, but it was a treat Belle was certainly looking forward to.

"You two are completely inseparable these days. Is it the Jamaica connection?" Shaye joked as she turned over in the bed, her upraised feet rocking back and forth in the air.

"She's a good lay." Belle shrugged and sat on the bed to watch the dance of hands between Violet and Liam. "You all know that already."

"Not all of us." Liam glanced at her with his sloe eyes. "Whatever happened to her as a human finished her with men."

"Can't help you there," Belle said.

Violet released the looped string between her and Liam

with a slight sigh. "These days it seems like she's finished with us, too."

"She hasn't wanted to play with me in ages," Julia pouted.

"Maybe she just hasn't been in the mood to play," Belle said.

"Not true. Don't think I haven't noticed the two of you. How she gives you lots of playtime and kisses."

"You've put a spell on our Silvija, Belle." Shaye smiled with her mouth while her eyes burned a melancholy brown.

"I doubt that. Silvy just likes my skin." She leaned in to tease them with her laughter. "See how soft it is, smell how sweet."

Liam grabbed at her arms and pulled her, laughing, into the bed with them. Julia, used to Belle's shunning, automatically moved away from her, allowing Shaye to tumble against Belle. The smaller beast's skin did not warm against Belle's.

"Stop it, you'll ruin my dress," Belle laughed.

But they paid no attention to her. Liam and Violet dragged her down between them, determined to drown her in tickles.

Their house was nearly overcrowded. The halls where Belle had once walked in relative solitude now overflowed with beasts of all kinds, elegant, striding beasts with carmine lips and the scent of sin in their clothes. It was a beautiful sight. They brushed past her in the hallway, twining their scent with hers for a lovely moment. The unfamiliar smells were like intoxicants in the house, thick and heady.

The largest hall in the house had been transformed into a ballroom. Under the lights of the crystal-dipped chandeliers with their winking bits of light, the beasts danced and flirted and greeted each other and fucked. Some wore their favorite costumes. With just one glance, Belle saw fairies and goblins, a Princess Leia, a flapper, an Indian matron, and a rock star. Although, truth be told, it was hard to say who was in costume and who merely came in the clothes of the time period when they died.

She had chosen to wear something simple and light, easy to take off if the need came. Only when she passed herself in one of the room's many mirrors did she notice that she'd worn the kind of dress she always wanted as a human. Floor length, bloodred, gathered below the bust, and fastened at the neck. Retro mid-1990s. Belle chuckled. Like so many of the beasts she lived with, Belle was nostalgic for the time period of her death. It was official. She was now one of them.

Everyone in the family seemed determined to have fun tonight. Not far away, Ivy and Stephen danced with Liam, creating a six-legged beast that was both clumsy and graceful at once, with their bodies moving in sensual rhythm to the bhangra beat pouring from the speakers. The twins created a lovely sandwich with the purple-eyed Liam. They danced as if they were already in bed together, naked and sure of what pleasure they would create. Belle smiled.

Nearby, Silvija's pet humans from town, Lily and Marie, floated about the room in sheer dresses, their arms and throats already dotted with bites from the evening's lovers. Their lips were wet with welcome. Violet, elegant in a form-fitting, vintage 1940s black dress and a white camellia pinned in her shining hair, moved toward them with hunger in her gaze.

"Enjoying yourself?"

A vampire with the scent of lilac and sun-kissed grass stopped at Belle's side. Her hand gently trailed down Belle's arm. The touch was not unwelcome.

"I am, and you?"

"Very much. Especially now that I finally get the chance to talk to you." The woman smiled. "I'm Olivia."

"Belle."

Earlier, Silvija had said that Belle should indulge as she would like. The woman's scent was tempting and the contact with someone other than her clan acted like an aphrodisiac to her sensitized pleasure centers. But the woman was a vampire and thus, Belle decided, off-limits.

"Olivia."

Silvija emerged from the gently murmuring crowd to kiss Belle's new acquaintance on both cheeks. "I see that you've met my . . ." She looked at Belle for a moment. "Belle."

Olivia laughed. "I have met your Belle. Is that how it is with you?" Her hand drifted out to touch Belle's. "She is very delightful."

"Very. But be careful, she likes to scratch and bite."

Belle's eyes narrowed. She gently took her hand back from Olivia and moved away from the two beasts. Silvija called out her name, but she ignored her lover and walked instead toward the smell of human blood that had been tugging at her senses the moment she walked into the room.

It was easy to find the human policewoman. All Belle had to do was follow the scent of fascinated fear. There was already a crowd around her, male and female beasts alike who wanted a little taste of her. Tamsyn seemed overwhelmed by the attention. She had a half-finished drink in her hand and a suitor waiting nearby with another. Bureaucracy had washed nicely off her. The dress she wore was very flattering. It brought out the copper lights in her skin and showed off her curvaceous hips. But she seemed uncomfortable in it as if she'd rather be wearing slacks.

"Tamsyn," Belle called out as soon as she was within the human's range of hearing. "You look wonderful in that dress. Who knew you'd clean up so nicely?"

"Or attract all this attention." The petite woman slipped through and past her companions, murmuring excuses and pardons as she made her way toward Belle.

"You're a beautiful woman." Belle kissed her on the cheek in welcome. "Of course we'd notice you."

"Your friends seem a little intense." Tamsyn swallowed the last of her champagne, then abandoned the glass on a nearby table.

Belle laughed. "A little. Sometimes we just can't help ourselves." The scent of the human was almost overwhelming.

The rich blood smell, her sleeping sex under the thin dress, her excited sweat and fear, all made her infinitely appealing and seductive. If Belle had been half this enticing when she'd walked into the Garden Hotel and into Julia's clutches, no wonder the other vampire had been unable to resist taking her.

"I'll get you another drink." Belle started to walk toward a waiter with a tray of wine gracefully balanced on his upraised hand.

"No." Tamsyn's hand landed gently on hers. "Maybe later."

Belle smiled. The human's touch sent a shiver of awareness racing along her senses. Tamsyn wanted her. It was only a matter of time before she would show it in other ways.

"How are you enjoying the party so far?" Belle walked slowly beside the human woman, guiding her through the swirling party with its trance music, through the beautifully dressed beasts and the occasional human toy. She consciously made her voice lower so the human had to lean close. Belle's movements softened and she became the very embodiment of tame sensuality. When a slim vampire looking like an anemic Billy Idol jostled the human on his way out the door, Belle steadied Tamsyn with a firm hand on her lower back and pulled her a little closer.

"I'm actually enjoying myself," Tamsyn said in response to Belle's question. "Your friends are strange, but fun."

"Good. It was a nice surprise to see you here, especially after how things ended the last time you were at the house."

"There was no body to be found, thank goodness. It was all just a terrible misunderstanding." Tamsyn sounded convinced of their innocence.

Belle nodded. "Exactly. There's no reason for any of us to harm someone in town. But mistakes are made all the time. This one was corrected before anyone got hurt, so it had a happy ending after all."

"Except for that poor guy who disappeared."

"Except for him," Belle agreed.

They stepped out the back door and into the cold. A breeze came up and fluttered Belle's dress. She breathed in the crisp air and smiled. Alaska wasn't so bad, really. The verandah was open and exposed. The long row of bench swings, seemingly out of place on the ultramodern compound, swayed gently in the breeze. Snow hung heavily on them.

"There's so much perfume in that house. Everyone seems to have their own really strong scent."

"They do."

It was the height of inanity to be talking with this human about vampires and their smells when all she wanted to do was press her down into the snow and drink her up. An awkward silence descended between them; then the woman turned suddenly to Belle.

"I think you're very attractive."

Ah. Here it is. She had a brief thought of why the creature didn't find the others similarly appealing, but it was perfectly okay that she didn't. Belle wasn't ready to share yet. If she couldn't have Silvija tonight, then she'd make do with this human breath of fresh air.

The human's head barely came to her shoulder, but she was reaching for Belle like she could handle what was in front of her. She brushed her palm against Belle's cheek. She was used to being in control, then? Good. Belle leaned her cheek into that palm and gave Tamsyn that control. Belle kissed the salty flesh and breathed her cool breath into it. The elixir in the human's veins called out loudly to her and Belle's blood answered. She gently bit the human's finger, then sucked it with its pinprick cut into her mouth. Tamsyn trembled.

"Can you handle that by yourself, Belle?"

Silvija and Olivia emerged slowly from the house. They walked one behind the other, looking predatory and seductive in their dark clothes. The beasts smelled like each other. The beloved clove scent was wrapped up in lilac and grass as if the beasts had been rolling around together. A growl vibrated in Belle's chest. She nearly forgot about the human.

"Did you just fuck her?" she asked her lover.

Silvija glanced at her in surprise. "Yes."

"Why?" The word choked past her tight throat.

"It's a party. Why not?"

Belle pivoted, ready to slap her face. "You and I are—" She stopped herself with an abrupt motion. "You're right. Why not?"

Tamsyn looked from one to the other with dawning awareness on her face. "Sorry. I didn't know."

"There's nothing for you to know." Belle turned from Silvija and the other beast as if they didn't exist. She smiled at the human, showing the vulnerable pink of her inner lips and her white teeth. "Come, let's continue what we started elsewhere."

"Belle," Silvija said. "Don't walk away from me."

Belle pointedly took the other woman's arm and led her away from the verandah, back inside the house. Behind her, she heard Olivia murmur, "She is magnificent. And a challenge."

"Are you sure this is okay?" Tamsyn asked with a slight quaver in her strong voice. "I don't want her to come after me."

"She wouldn't dare touch you," Belle said.

"You shouldn't say things like that, love." Silvija's breath brushed the back of her neck, stirring the small hairs there. Belle didn't turn around. "Especially when you know it's not true."

The warmth of the other beasts—Silvija and Olivia—washed over her once they were back inside the house. With Silvija at her back and the human woman still deeply under her spell, Belle felt hot.

"She's harmless," she reassured Tamsyn, leading her to the moonroom. Belle looked up at the retractable glass ceiling.

The moon was out and full tonight, hovering in its bed of clouds like a plump pearl while its silver light flooded over the women's shoulders, illuminating the decadent room. The chaise longue lay empty, its fringed throw tumbled half on, half off the deep mahogany velvet.

Belle pushed Tamsyn down into the chair and sat beside her. "Just relax and have fun. That's the reason you came here tonight, isn't it?"

Silvija was coming through the door any moment. She would pause at the door and watch them. She would pick Belle up from her slow slide down Tamsyn's body and take her away so they could be alone together and fuck each other's skins off. The door creaked as someone else came into the room. Belle filled her senses with Tamsyn, drowning in her lush human scent, the arousal seeping like honey from between her thighs. And all the while, she listened for Silvija.

The beast finally approached and she melted inside, maddeningly, disgustingly. But that was what she wanted. It was what she was waiting for. But the scent was wrong. Tamsyn was drowning in her. The human stared into her face, captivated and completely hers, but her focus was on the scent coming closer. Until a hand touched her shoulder and the scent of lilacs overwhelmed her.

"You're lovely." Olivia's voice scraped against her expectations, rubbing them raw. Belle's hand stopped its ascent up Tamsyn's dress.

"Don't stop." Silvija appeared on the other side of the chaise, her mouth set in a hard, seductive curve.

But it was Olivia's hand that smoothed down Belle's back and loosened the clasp at her neck. The straps of the dress slithered down her chest but caught at the fullest point of her breasts. Her senses took in everything at once—Tamsyn's compelling scent, the sound of Olivia moving closer toward her across the carpet, Silvija's quiet and steady presence near the human's head.

Tamsyn's breath shivered in her throat as Belle's hands

drifted up, on automatic pilot, and snagged on the thin silk of her panties. She dragged them down and Silvija gave a low hum of approval. The human's eyes were full of Belle. She didn't look away once. Behind her, Olivia chuckled and stroked her back, tugging down the zipper of her dress. The material fell away from Belle's body and pooled around her waist. Tamsyn moaned as Belle's fingers combined through her fine pussy hair. With the other hand, she flipped the dress out of the way so that Silvija could see what was happening. Belle's lover smiled with approval.

Tamsyn reached up to stroke Belle's breasts. The peaks hardened beneath her warm hands and Belle sighed. Although it was Tamsyn's hands on her, it was Silvija's touch she felt. The beast's eyes flickered over her breasts and belly, licking up flames of desire, encouraging her without words to taste the human.

There were things she'd always wanted to do with Silvija that she never dared, as bold as she often was when she had the beast on the floor, writhing beneath her. She never dared to be gentle, to touch her with love. She did so now with the human, gently filling her pussy with one finger, then two, sinking into the lush, welcoming heat that opened even more for her. Tamsyn groaned. Her pussy was a wonder of pink and wet. Her small clit fattened and slipped under Belle's thumb.

Olivia's mouth trailed down her spine, kissing fire down to her ass. The other vampire struggled with her dress, lifting Belle and tugging the dress away until she was naked except for her high heels and stockings and the clips in her hair. Olivia lifted Belle's ass in the air, poised her on hands and knees in readiness for pleasure. And Belle let her. She let Olivia lick her from behind, let the stranger taste the fruits of her desire for Silvija, and groan into it. Belle spread her knees in the sofa, giving Olivia better access while she slowly fucked Tamsyn with her fingers. Her mouth opened on the human's breast. She tasted the salt of Tamsyn's lust, her fear

of being in a houseful of dangerous beasts. This was a foolish
woman. She lusted more than she wanted to be safe. Belle
knew that kind of foolishness very well.

She bit into the full nipple, thrusting all four of her killing
teeth into the tender copper flesh. Tamsyn gasped and her
fear-scented blood flowed into Belle's mouth. The spice of her
lust tingled over Belle's tongue and the vampire moaned
against the soft flesh and bit down for more. Tamsyn's legs
widened for Belle's fingers and she moaned when those fingers dipped even deeper inside her, filling her to bursting.
Belle remembered the fantasy that Silvija had spun the day
they met Tamsyn. She remembered being fucked against the
glass wall, being so full of Silvija that she'd felt empty for
days afterward without the beast's thick presence inside her.

Olivia's tongue licked her asshole, flickered around the
sensitive pucker before it burrowed inside. Belle felt the other
beast's delight in her, could smell it rising up from behind her
as distinct from Tamsyn's arousal as strawberries were from
peaches. Both scents mingled in the air, creating a delicious
perfume that drew a moan from her. And then there was
Silvija.

The beast watched her steadily with the downward flicker
of her lashes and her slightly parted lips the only signs that
she wasn't quite an impartial observer. Olivia's fingers teased
the opening of Belle's pussy from behind, teased the slick wet
hole, and sent quivers of sensation bolting into her.

"Put your hand inside her. Make her feel you."

Silvija's quiet words sent breath rushing through Belle.
Her entire body was goose-pimpled and flushed cold. Her
nipples suddenly felt unbearably hard and sensitive. They
scraped against Tamsyn as she moved against the human's
body, licking her blood-flecked nipple, then sucking it deeply
into her mouth. Olivia fucked Belle's pussy, licking her ass in
a sweet rhythm that made her hum with pleasure and push
back for more. Tamsyn stretched out even more on the

chaise, flinging her neck back, stretching out her hands to grasp at anything—the back of the sofa, Silvija's hand.

The beast smiled as she captured the taut hand. She licked Tamsyn's wrist, brought its scented weight to her nose. Still, her hawklike eyes watched Belle thrust her troughed fingers, then her palm into Tamsyn's sopping pussy. They shone with approval and desire. The human's warmth swallowed her hand, enveloping it in liquid desire. Belle's eyes rolled back into her head. Overload was close, the fingers in her pussy, the tongue in her ass, Silvija's eyes on her, licking her face, her breasts, her belly as Tamsyn bathed her with heat, eagerly opening up to take all that Belle had. Tamsyn's eyes were wide and startled, beads of sweat dotted her face, and her mouth opened even more with each gasp.

"Oh my God," she breathed.

Belle felt it when Silvija bit into the human's wrist. She felt her get wetter and allow the widest part of Belle's hand into her pussy. Her cunt clenched around Belle's hand and they both groaned in reaction. Tamsyn was so wet. So hot. It was as if she lay at the core of the human, feeling all her body's movement, its rushing blood, its breath, and pleasure—its life—around her hand.

Silvija licked the wound she made on Tamsyn's wrist, then dove in for another bite. Belle began to move her fist.

"Oh. Oh!"

Tamsyn watched open-mouthed, gasping breath tumbling from her throat, as Belle fisted her, fucked the bliss into her with deep sure thrusts until she had no words left. Was that how she had looked when Silvija fucked her against the glass that first time? As if she'd lost hold of the earth and traveled to a place where nothing else mattered but desire? Pain was nothing. Death was nothing.

The woman's rising gasps became screams. Her loud, vibrating shouts seemed to spur Olivia on. Her fingers moved faster inside Belle, her tongue slid deeper in Belle's ass until

Belle joined Tamsyn on whatever plane she had escaped to in the name of pleasure. Olivia hummed her delight into Belle's flesh, taking the sensations even higher. The orgasm caught her by surprise. It shook her body, trembled her thighs and squeezed her eyes tightly shut. Her fist loosened and slipped back, then forward. Her body's uncontrollable shudders repeated the motion.

"Yes, oh my God!" Tamsyn's shouts poured out into the room. "Yes!"

Tamsyn squeezed Silvija's hand in hers as she approached her own nirvana. Her hips bubbled against the settee and a clear liquid squirted from her pussy. The sharp scent of cloves and blood rose in the room. Her fingernails had pierced Silvija's skin. The squirt became a gush and Tamsyn rode the fist harder. The human threw her head back and shouted out to her God one more time. Her pussy clenched hard around Belle's wrist, squeezing even as she gushed even more over Belle, spraying her chest, neck, and face. Belle licked her wet lips.

"Easy," Silvija rumbled from above them as Belle began to pull her hand from inside the human. "You don't want to break her."

Belle slowly pulled out of Tamsyn, withdrawing her wrist, her hand, then her fingertips. The woman sighed and shuddered once, twice, beneath her.

"That was nice," Silvija said with her voice still gravelly from arousal. She looked at Olivia. "Can I do anything for you?"

"I don't think so." Olivia kissed the curve of Belle's ass and rose. "I don't think your lady would appreciate it."

Belle turned around at the stranger's remark but didn't bother to correct her. She sat down on the chaise in the sprawl of Tamsyn's legs, doubtful that her unsteady limbs would be able to support her. The human looked worn out. Her once neatly French-twisted hair was a fuzzy halo around her beautifully satisfied face.

"Belle is no one's lady."

The three vampires turned at the sound of the new voice. Shaye stood in the doorway with Julia and at least half a dozen others. She was the only one not smiling.

"Nice job, Belle. I didn't think the human would come back just for you."

Belle ignored Julia and set her dress to rights. It took her only a few moments to help Tamsyn dress and pull her to her feet. Olivia moved aside to let Belle and Tamsyn pass, but Silvija deliberately put herself in the way.

"You won't stay with me?" Silvija asked.

"I think you have enough company for the night," Belle said.

"If it's not you, then it's never enough."

Belle looked at her, checking for the jest in her face. She found none. "Find me later."

The giant nodded once and moved gracefully out of her way. Belle couldn't help but watch the liquid sway of Silvija's backside as she moved.

"Come," Belle said to the quiet Tamsyn. "I did promise to get you a drink, after all."

But Tamsyn didn't want a drink. She wanted more.

"That was . . . amazing. I've never—" Her eyes swung from the beautiful crowd to Belle. "Do you do this kind of thing all the time?"

"*This* sort of thing?" Belle's mouth twisted into a half smile. "You mean enjoying myself? Enjoying you?"

"It didn't seem as if you were really into it." At Belle's sharp glance, Tamsyn looked down and stammered, "What I meant to say was we weren't the ones you really wanted. You were hot for us." Tamsyn blushed in memory. Perhaps at the look on Olivia's face as she'd taken Belle from behind, burying her face in the hole that Belle only used for play. Or maybe it was Belle's face that she remembered, her look of almost-divine pleasure when her hand dove all the way inside Tamsyn's warm, wet pussy. "But," Tamsyn continued, "you would have truly enjoyed yourself if it had just been the two of you, you and the one who just watched us."

The woman's look was sympathetic. Belle didn't want her sympathy.

"Hello, beautiful." Rufus emerged from the crowd behind them. "This party is *nice*, you hear me?" He moved close to Belle. "I haven't had this much new ass since the eighties."

Rufus looked especially like a rock star tonight with his oversized belt buckle, gay boy jeans, and tight T-shirt. His dreadlocked hair flowed loosely down his back and over his ass.

She turned to look at him, grateful for the distraction. "I don't believe that for a minute. Human groupies count as new ass, Ru."

"If you say so."

He chuckled. "So, who is this darling right here?"

"This 'darling' is Tamsyn."

"Lovely name." He extended his hand. "I'm Rufus."

Tamsyn looked at him, as if trying to figure out where she'd seen his face before. "Are you on television?" she finally asked.

He laughed. "I am everywhere."

"Don't let him tease you. Rufus is what we like to call a gyrating rock star. He shines the brightest in Europe."

"And on VH1." Rufus laughed again.

Tamsyn turned to him. "Do you live here too?"

While the human was distracted by Rufus's androgynous sensuality, Belle walked away.

She hunted for Silvija. The house had never been this abundant with motion and life. Though Belle's mind was full of Silvija, she allowed herself to be distracted, to stare at the beautiful bodies on display, at the humans who dropped, shamelessly, to their hands and knees just to please these bewitching beasts.

No one bothered to close doors tonight. Excess and lust burned beautifully on display for anyone to see, even if they didn't want to. Nearly giving up on finding Silvija, Belle went back through the crowded ballroom, expecting to see Rufus and Tamsyn. But there was no sign of the human or the musician. She wandered into the training room. And blinked.

Stephen leaned back against a stack of bright blue gym mats, his lean body rippling with muscle and awash in blood-streaked sweat, while Rufus knelt between his thighs. The musician gave the most thorough blow job that Belle had ever seen, diving into and away from the heavy bobbing dick with enviable skill. What truly made his expertise so apparent was that he was fucking Stephen's pussy with his fingers in a pleasing enough rhythm that had the twin grimacing in delight, his eyes star-bright and his mouth parted and wet as he watched Rufus. Stephen had a pussy too?

Keiko and the human stood on either side of Stephen with legs spread wide, sucking on his beautiful breasts while leisurely touching themselves. His hand tangled in their hair, encouraging their sweetly moving tongues and sharp teeth. Tamsyn's eyes were closed in rapture.

Their mingled scents made a fine bouquet in the room, a lovely arousing scent that unexpectedly sparked heat in Belle's pussy, licking her thighs with a telling wetness. She drew in a surprised breath.

Everyone except for Rufus looked up at Belle in the doorway. Tamsyn blushed but continued sucking on Stephen's breast. She didn't stop the motion of her fingers between her thighs.

"Join us?" Keiko pulled away from the succulent-looking nipple wet with her saliva, and smiled at Belle.

Belle shook her head and backed out of the room, closing the door. Behind the door, she heard them go back to their pleasures, not at all fazed by her interruption.

Stephen liked boys? Stephen was—what was that word?—a hermaphrodite. An image of his sloping breasts, lean and muscled stomach, and thick penis took root in her mind. Why hadn't she known this? Belle shook her head again.

Newly inspired to search, she found Silvija in deep conversation with the Billy Idol look-alike and a pretty nymph on his lap. When the beast noticed Belle, she turned to look directly at her.

"Finished with your little copper piece?" She smiled, leisurely caressing Belle's body with her eyes.

"Are *you* finished with your . . . whatever?"

Billy and the nymph shared a laugh. Belle couldn't help but notice his long white hand resting on her bare thigh, while she leaned into him.

"She's just killing time with us, love," Billy said. "Talking about old times and all that."

The nymph's musical laughter chimed again. "Very old. Way before you were born, I'm sure."

Never mind that she didn't look any older than twenty-five. Despite her claims to old age, she lacked that aura of power that came with longevity, that very aura that Silvija and Billy had.

"Are you trying to tell me that she's fucked you too?" Belle asked.

Billy laughed again, then looked at the creature in his lap to see what she would say. The nymph shrugged and managed to look coy.

"I'll never tell," she murmured.

"I think *that's* my cue to leave." Silvija stood up, more like ascended, in the tight rubber dress that made her movement a slow, sensual wriggle to an upright position. Even though she'd seen it at least five times tonight, the red cinch of her underbust corset still made Belle's mouth go dry.

Billy pursed his mouth. "You've never said a truer thing."

"What do you bet that we won't see them again until the next party?"

Belle ignored the nymph's mock whisper and walked out ahead of her lover. She gently cut a path through their guests, taking Silvija toward a less crowded part of the Cave. Both their bedrooms were out of the question since guests were fucking in them.

But there was nowhere in the house they could go. The closets, the Turkish bath, the kitchen, all were filled with vampires and humans in various stages of undress or conversation. They merely looked up in curiosity at Belle and Silvija, noticing their coiled silence, the sense of sweet urgency surrounding them, and smiled. Translation: find somewhere else to fuck.

At the fourth occupied room Belle felt like a pissed-off Goldilocks. She closed the door and leaned back against it, her mouth plumping out in a childish pout.

"Who are all these damn people?"

The answer didn't really matter since all she wanted them to do was disappear, or at least leave one room empty so she and Silvija could . . . talk.

Silvija smiled down at her. "They are our friends." Her eyes dropped to Belle's still pouting mouth. "Come on."

Belle allowed Silvija to take her hand and tug her through the house, through the crowds of fiends that didn't seem to thin out, beyond the kitchen and their meeting room to a quieter but still occupied suite of offices. These creatures were everywhere. Never mind that a few days, even hours ago, Belle had been happy for their lively and cosmopolitan presence in the Cave. Now she just wanted them gone.

"Where are you two going?"

Shaye sat in a plush leather chair with her feet curled beneath her like the child she resembled. The conversation taking place in the small group she sat with ebbed at the girl's apparent curiosity. They were an eclectic mix of young and old-looking fiends, twin beasts in matching pink tutus, a silver-haired Paul Robeson type, a Goth girl in an Elvira dress complete with the extravagant cleavage, all discussing what sounded like the role of sex in sixteenth-century monastic literature.

"Out for a bite," Belle answered with a weak smile.

The group smiled politely, but Shaye looked pointedly at their joined hands.

"Are we going to see you two before the end of the night?" she asked.

They looked at each other. "We'll see."

Shaye wrinkled her nose and finally smiled. "I see you two have a long night ahead of you. I'm heading into town later to meet up with a hot boy, so I won't be in today."

Shaye, with a boy? With anybody? "Is he a friend?"

"A fuck friend, yes."

Belle wanted to close her ears. That didn't even sound right. She looked at Silvija, but the giant simply shrugged.

"Okay, if that's what you want," Silvija said. "Just be careful."

She pulled Belle away from the vampires and their knowing looks to a space behind a wall of books and up the short flight of stairs hidden behind it.

"I feel like we're running away," Belle said.

"That's the point, isn't it?"

The stairs led to an attic door that Silvija reached up and pushed back with a flick of her wrist. As she disappeared up the narrow opening, Belle looked down and behind her at the books, the burnished hardwood floors, and the flash of bright costumes from the beasts who still prowled below. They paid her and Silvija little attention. Apparently even they understood the need for privacy. She swung up into the attic space.

With her legs tucked beside her, Belle watched Silvija close the small door, then look across at her. The giant reached up to press a button on the wood-paneled wall. The roof slid away, transforming the small room into a sky-view retreat. Stars winked down at them from a clear black sky. Noises from the party—laughter, the clink of champagne glasses, the lush contact of flesh against flesh—sounded faintly beneath them, but that was all.

"Welcome to my refuge," she said.

And it *did* feel like a refuge, a place of relative silence with thickly piled wolf and fox furs on the floor, and only a long storage chest for furniture. On top of the trunk lay a stack of books by Jamaican writers and a black iPod tucked into its Bose speaker cradle. There was barely enough room for them to stand to full height. But they didn't need that room.

"Is this where you disappear to when no one can find you?" Belle asked.

"Sometimes."

"Do you hide from me here?"

"Never."

The furs smelled of the wilderness, of pine needles, of the animals who once wore them, and of Silvija. Her clove scent permeated all of the small space, down to the wood. Belle wanted to be like this place, wholly imprinted, owned, and claimed by Silvija; the beast's own tiger on a leash and her safe haven. She knew she was in trouble. This thing she felt for Silvija was different than anything she'd felt before. It was raw and primal. It made her want to eat the beast up. Her hands ached to sink into Silvija's skin, her teeth protracted at the thought of biting into the beloved flesh, tearing her outer covering away so she could fit them neatly together, raw nerves to raw nerves. It was an obsession fueled by images of merging, melting into one so they would never be apart. Belle swallowed.

"Have I been a good lover to you?" Silvija asked.

Belle couldn't hide the sudden heat in her face. "The best."

"Then is there something that you want from me that you haven't been able to get?"

Ah, the real question. Belle pursed her lips. "I think the problem is that you've made me feel too good. I feel things for you that I thought that this blood-sucking urge was supposed to kill." She felt Silvija's hesitation. "You don't have to say anything. Or be anything different than what you are. I'm just—" She paused. "I'm being greedy."

"There's nothing wrong with wanting more, my Belle."

"Of course, you would say that. But can you give more?"

Silvija moved closer. "Ask me and see."

Wicked creature. Silvija knew what Belle wanted. How could she not? Belle opened her mouth. And Silvija kissed her.

Silvija's mouth lit on hers, gently, like a butterfly touching a flower. A sigh, an affirmation. Her beast didn't have to say the words, because they were inside her mouth and she pressed that mouth to Belle and released them into the smaller beast, made her feel them with each slide of her tongue, each movement of her lips.

Belle felt caught in some romantic drama where the crux of the action depended on the hero—Silvija—confessing her love for the panting heroine, played imperfectly by Belle. But it wasn't that. She knew how Silvija felt; she didn't have to hear it from her lips to be sure. As certainly as they were here now, pressed skin to skin, Silvija's sure hands pulling the dress from her body, her lips pressing to her throat and down to her breasts. As certain as these things she could feel and knew to be true, she knew that Silvija loved her.

The question of love had been a mask for the real question. Could the beast be faithful to her, emotionally and physically? Could she forsake all other beasts but Belle?

"Yes." Silvija's mouth trailed to the fullest part of her breast. "If that's what you want."

Her cool flesh, still clothed in its rubber dress, lay over Belle's, pressing her into the furs. Belle's head fell back as the mouth closed over her nipples, both at once, pressed together, and nipped with playful teeth. The sweetness flooded into her and she gasped in wonder and delight. Above her the stars winked and flashed. Their light fell inside her, illuminating her pleasure, searing her from breast to clit.

"Silvija." The name was starlight and passion spilling from her parted lips. It was her love and her lust. It was her reason.

"I'm here, baby." The soft voice trembled at her belly. "I'm here."

*   *   *

Sometime between the last time they touched and sleep, Julia's scent reached Belle. Moments later, she heard the attic door slide back and felt the small fiend's body drop into the furs behind Silvija. Belle's eyes flickered open. Julia looked back at her, sleepy but content.

"At least I waited until you were done fucking." She scooted closer to Silvija's back.

Belle nuzzled closer to Silvija, and the giant's hand scooped her closer, falling lightly on her hip. Wordlessly, she kissed Belle's forehead and pressed her face once again into the full pillow of Belle's breasts. Moments later, they all fell asleep.

Chapter 28

"We have to get out of the house. Now!"

Belle felt more than heard the urgency in Silvija's voice and she responded to it as if it came from inside her own head. She sat up in the furs.

"Julia. Wake up!" She grabbed at the fiend and shook her. Once Julia looked at her with something like awareness in her eyes, Belle dove at the chair to retrieve the clothes she had shed the night before.

The red dress was barely on her body before she shoved back the attic door and dropped down the stairs, running for the nearest exit. The blood pumped in her veins as she heard other footsteps coming hard at her heels. She didn't bother to run for the main door. In the emergency escape plans that Ivy and Stephen had drilled into them, the main exit was the last one to head for. She quickly scanned her handprint across the panel and flew between the slowly parting panels, scraping her sides on the thick glass as she squeezed through.

Belle heard a deep rumbling behind her and felt a flash of heat at her back. A buildup of pressure shoved her high into the air, then into the snow.

"Shit!"

Julia's small body flew at her, propelled by the massive explosion from the house. Shards of glass and bits of wood rained on them from above. Firelit pieces of debris flew through the air and they scrambled frantically toward and under the snowbank to escape them. The smell of burned wood and plastic, of everything that had become familiar to her in the past few years, drowned out everything else. She heard panicked cries coming from the house. Screams. Some-one—Liam—called out Silvija's name. Belle looked franti-cally around her. Where was Silvija?

"Where is Silvija?" Julia screamed, her leather-clad body a dark slash against the snow.

She scrambled up on all fours, blinking in confusion. She stared toward what had been their home and the fire-ravaged remnants of it burned a reflection in the dark pools of her eyes. Sudden flickers of movement in the snow distracted Belle from the fire. She blinked and looked away from the house. Three figures—Ivy, Rufus, and Stephen, it looked like—ran across the ice and snow toward them. But no Silvija. Belle pulled Julia to her feet. The three beasts came closer. Thank God. Maybe now someone would tell them what was going on. But the figures coalesced into strangers wielding crossbows and guns. An arrow darted out and pinned air to the ice. Fortunately their sight was greater than the cross-bow's reach.

"Some are back here!" they shouted back to someone be-yond Belle's sight.

Julia grabbed her hand and pulled her away from the blaze and the three beasts chasing them. Belle tripped over the long hem of her dress and cursed, ripping at the red cotton until the dress tore and its shredded ends flapped against her knees. The piece of red scrap dropped away in the dirty snow as rapid gunfire kicked up ice and water against her feet. They ran. Belle felt a sharp sting against her arm, then her side. As soon as the sensations came they were gone. She ran even faster. She didn't need Julia's tugging hand to tell her the urgency of this anymore. The bullets were enough.

They flew across the snow, cold wind rushing across their cheeks as they ran into the snow-blanketed trees away from the beach and the fire-gutted house. With each step they put between them and the creatures with weapons, Belle's mind chanted an important question: where was Silvija?

She and Julia ran through the snow-covered forest, dodging the towering white-weighted trees and the three terrors with the crossbows and guns. They ran until Julia finally stopped, putting out her hand to stop Belle from going any farther.

"I don't hear them anymore."

"But that doesn't mean that they aren't there."

Still, they stopped in a clearing. Belle pressed her palms against the cool bark of an evergreen as if she could hear it tell her that it was okay not to run anymore. She was frightened. For the first time since her change she was frightened by other creatures. And she was frightened for Silvija. Where was the giant? Where were the others? A sound reached her ears, bringing the answer to her questions. It was limping, whatever creature was approaching. No breath pushed out against the air to announce the intruder as human. Belle didn't know if that was better or worse.

"Climb!" Julia hissed to her.

She wasted no time in clambering up the tree, grasping its few and far between snow-covered limbs until they hovered above the clearing, watching for what might come. The branches hid their presence, Belle knew, but not their scents.

After a few tense minutes of waiting, Ivy limped into the clearing carrying Stephen in her arms. Most of him was in pieces. He lay scattered in bits of flesh over his sister's arms. Half his face had been blown away, leaving only teeth, bits of his nose, and exposed brain beneath the few remaining patches of hair. There was only enough of him there to let Belle know that it was Stephen. The carcass in Ivy's arms did not move.

She heard Julia make a noise from her perch in the nearby tree, and then the beast dropped the twenty feet down to the ground, reaching out toward Ivy and Stephen with tears shimmering in her eyes.

"No," she murmured as Ivy stumbled to a halt in the clearing. The amazon fell to her knees in the snow, shaking.

Belle pressed her cheek into the bark of the evergreen. Was the news of Silvija's death waiting for her like this? The bark scraped away pieces of her flesh, but she couldn't feel it. And where was Shaye? Belle watched them down below, pantomiming loss and sorrow while regret twisted her human insides.

The scent of cloves teased her nose. Belle leapt down from her perch in time to see the giant walk into the clearing. She was naked and covered in blood.

"They're still hunting us," she said. Her voice was rough, as if she'd been screaming.

The deep gouge in her side, probably from an arrow, was already healing. Blood caked around the tender wound with long sluggish trails of red running down her bare hip and thigh. Silvija's hands were wet with fresh blood. She looked down at Ivy crouched over her brother in the snow. Her jaw tightened. Silvija's presence suddenly made Belle feel shy. Even in the midst of all this violence all she could think of was what came between them before. The heat of the giant's mouth, her thick fingers preparing her, Silvija's quiet declaration.

"We must find shelter. The sun will rise in a few hours and if they don't kill us, it will." Silvija dropped down on her knee next to Stephen and Ivy. Touching what was left of his face, she bowed her head. "I'm sorry."

"There's nothing to be sorry for," Ivy said. "We had a long life and death together." There were no tears inside Ivy. She tried to find some, but all that surfaced were harsh, gagging noises, as if she'd swallowed something too large for her throat.

The others moved away to give her privacy, but only within a few feet. Enemies still walked in the forest. If Silvija and Ivy could find them so easily, then so could the other beasts who wanted to kill them.

"Where are the others?" Belle asked.

"I saw Rufus and Violet after the fire." Silvija's eyes roamed the perimeter even as she spoke to Belle and Julia. "They are out there somewhere. When I got shot, I lost track of them." She looked down at her side, as if just remembering the wound. "If they survived, they'll find us."

If. There had been two explosions, one following quickly after the other, that had swallowed the house and the land around it. The town's isolation from them had been its salvation.

"They blew up the bedrooms first," Silvija said.

Belle blinked. "What?"

"How could outsiders know where we sleep?" Julia asked. "It wasn't our humans, was it?"

Silvija shook her head at Belle's question as if it was too much for her to think of now, then turned to Ivy. "Take your time."

"No." Ivy stood up. "We don't need it."

She put Stephen's body beneath a snow-weighted spruce. The icicled needles bowed over it. Already the shell that had been Belle's trainer was starting to disintegrate, the flesh turning to jerky, the limbs falling away like dead leaves.

Ivy stood up, wordlessly swept her long-sleeved sweater up and over her head before handing it to Silvija. The giant covered her nakedness with it, nodding once in thanks. Ivy resettled the bag she carried across her shoulder, over the dark long-sleeved shirt and black pants she wore.

With a face wiped clean of all emotion, she handed each beast three packets of blood from her bag. The liquid swam in red under the clear plastic.

"Drink only when absolutely necessary," Ivy said. "I don't know how long we'll be out here."

Belle took her share of the blood even though she'd rather

feed on the wild game in the forest if her hunger became too much to swallow.

"Thanks, Ivy," Silvija said gravely. She palmed the blood, looking quickly around her. "Let's go. We don't have much time."

That galvanized the others into action. Leaving what used to be Stephen hidden in the underbrush under snow and Ivy's parting kisses, they ran for the hinterlands. The area was a remote area populated by trees, bears, deer, and little else. How many enemies were there? Did they come prepared with an army to take out everyone who lived in the house? The answer to that question was obvious. They had, and damned near did.

"Step lightly," Silvija said. "I don't want to make it easy for them to find us."

The beasts flew across the ice, past trees and snowbanks and naked branches that waited for the sun to melt their ice prison. The forest bled away under their feet. Snow, trees, more snow. Even with the miles passed, the menacing presence behind them felt stronger than ever, so they ran on.

"This is useless, we have to stop," Julia said.

"I'm not ready to die," Belle hissed. "Keep going."

"There are too many of them." Julia's steps slowed. "And they have guns. We will never survive it."

Ivy's silence was telling. She didn't want to survive it. Her brother was gone. To her, she was already dead.

"The sun will be up soon," Silvija said.

And they would roast. When the giant's cool gaze slashed Julia the smaller fiend sped her pace. There was nothing around them now. No trees to shelter in, nothing but the cold ground, the naked spring-starved trees with their spindly limbs. The relentless presence at their back would find them and kill them as surely as it had killed Stephen.

The powdery snow, fresh from the night before, crunched under their feet as they ran out of the forest. The wind clutched at their clothes and hair, plucking at skin that was impervious but still shivered with fear. Belle grasped the blood packets against her belly.

"Fan out." Silvija stopped. Her eyes roamed over the seemingly endless snowy landscape glittering under the silver moonlight that would soon give way to deadly sunshine. "It will be harder for them to kill all of us if we separate," she said.

"No!" Julia stared at Silvija. "I'm not leaving you."

Ivy and Belle looked at each other. The plan didn't make much sense to them either. It was just as easy for the hunters to find one as well as four. And at least they would be together.

"They are driving us into the sun." Silvija looked at each of them with narrowed and determined eyes. "Dig. Find a place to hide until sunset. They will be bored of their sport by then."

Belle wasn't so sure.

Ivy grabbed Julia's hand. "Come with me."

The smaller beast pulled away. "No. Silvija?" She stared at her mistress.

"Go with Ivy. We will meet up after dark."

The little fiend wasn't buying it. But she had spent a lifetime doing what Silvija told her to. Not even imminent death could change that now. Ivy dragged Julia away, and the little fiend stumbled, unresisting but staring back at Silvija with her bruised gaze. The giant was pitiless. She looked at Belle.

"Come," she said.

Belle followed. "You know that wasn't necessary," she said.

"It wasn't necessary for our survival, but it was necessary for me." She didn't say anything else.

The wind whipped around them as they ran. It tore at their clothes and hair, slid into Belle's nose and mouth until she couldn't even *think* of talking.

Suddenly Silvija stopped. "We will take shelter here."

Here was nowhere. Except for a few snowbanks, ice stretched flat and unwelcoming for miles. Only the forest that lay beyond them with its very real threat offered any sanctuary from the sun.

"Dig." Silvija fell to her knees and began digging with her clawed hands. She sketched out a rectangle, a guide for Belle's own efforts, and dug, hands blurring through the air until they were raw and blood-flecked the snow. They were building a coffin in the ice. "As deep as you can."

Belle dropped the bagged blood in the snow and dug in. Working quickly, Silvija shaped blocks of hard-packed snow, then put them aside before digging deeper and more frantically to make a space for both their bodies to fit. And Belle copied her. Silvija didn't look up once, though they both knew, and worked swiftly with the knowledge, that at any moment their pursuers could fly out of the forest. Or the sun, already a threatening shadow of light on the horizon, would incinerate their furiously working bodies. Daylight would only last a few short hours, but it was no less deadly. Wind lashed fiercely around them, flinging up snow and hiding their already sparse footprints.

"They're not coming after us," Silvija rasped in the silence punctuated by their frantic digging. "The sun. They want the sun to finish us."

Belle remembered the stench of burning flesh, her own, as she'd lain on that Jamaican road all those years ago trapped under a motorcycle and its heated muffler. The searing burn on her leg was nothing compared to the sun's bubbling heat that rose up her skin, crisped her to a darker shade of brown, then black. Belle shuddered and dug even faster.

They dug into the snow, then under, tunneling as deeply as they could before the sun found them. Not quite a neat rectangle but more of an angled six-feet-plus hole where they both could hide. Prickles of discomfort danced across her

skin as the sun asserted itself over darkness and began to
climb into the sky. The discomfort soon became very real
pain.

At Silvija's terse instruction, Belle got into the grave while
the other beast resituated the blocks of ice over them before
slipping beneath them to join her. The cold lapped at her
skin. But she only felt it as breath. Air and sun were at least
four feet above them, but they felt like only inches. Pressed
this close to Silvija, Belle felt cold. She was frozen, not by the
sun, but in fear. The sun was so close. It would be so easy for
someone, anyone, to discover them and sweep their frozen
shelter away, leaving them to burn and melt away into the
snow.

"We'll survive." Sylvia's hand moved through the softened
snow to touch the bare skin at her wrist.

And Belle believed her. The sun was up. It swept above
them in a killing arch on the ice. But they were safe. Down
here. Belle's body sagged into Silvija's. She tucked her face
into the beast's throat, and the warmth in her lover took the
fear away. And brought sleep.

Belle felt like it had been a hundred years, but she had only
been asleep for a few hours. The cold lay on her like a blanket and Silvija slept. The sun was going. Its journey left a trail
of warmth overhead that she could feel, a trail of unease.
Silvija's face lay near hers. She opened up her senses and took
the giant in. Her skin twitched from the memory of running
across the ice, of being chased, of almost meeting her death
at unfamiliar hands.

But Silvija had comforted her. Before the very idea had
been laughable, but now . . . Belle moved her hands through
the snow to touch Silvija's face. Her lover slowly stirred. And
the smell of cloves grew stronger until it surrounded Belle.

"Try not to be frightened," Silvija said. Or perhaps that's
what she opened her mouth to say. But Belle kissed her instead. The phantom heat of Silvija's mouth incinerated her. It

seared along her jawline, nibbled on her lips before sinking deeply against her mouth. Belle gasped, because it felt good to let that small amount of control go. She kissed Silvija, and her mouth was softness and perfection and everything else in between. Her giant tasted like blood, exquisitely and perfectly like all the nourishment Belle needed.

Silvija's gentleness undid Belle. The guns, the fights, the explosive fucking, all faded under the caress of her lover's lips. She opened up under Silvija's tenderness, and flowered. The packed snow shifted against her cheeks, and miraculously did not melt. Under the ice, everything was silent.

The wet snow seeped into her skin, into the thin material of her dress, but she didn't feel the cold. All she felt was Silvija against her, the lean length, the unyielding strength that had so often called up her own. She felt the cool wash of Silvija's gaze through her. It braided under her skin, pebbled her nipples, and brought the spill of arousal past her vaginal lips to coat her already wet thighs.

Silvija's tongue swept inside her mouth, bringing more fire. She yielded and gladly went up in flames. Belle wasn't sure if it was the live wire of her imagination or the powerful hold that Silvija had over her, but their snow bed vanished and it could have been just the two of them anywhere else, in any of the places they'd had each other before. Sensations crowded her until she couldn't tell suggestion from reality, desire from the concrete touch of the beast pressed against her.

Fingers squeezed her nipples, spread wide over her chest and rib cage, and drifted down to touch her throbbing clit. False breath welled up to form a gasp and her legs widened. What was it? Why was she feeling these things from just a kiss? Did it matter? Hands seemed everywhere at once. The liquid crush of the snow was like a wet tongue on her breasts, hardening the nipples even more, licking the deep valley in her back, the curve of her neck, the back of her knees. Belle made a low, needful noise.

Julia had introduced her to sex and death, but it was

Silvija who taught her about passion; about how it didn't matter how much you hated someone, that hate could transform lightning quick into desire and that desire could tear your skin, and dignity, to shreds. The cold licked at her back, her sides. And the fingers, oh, the fingers . . . They moved between her legs and touched her aching clit. The snow crunched as she jerked.

"Silv—"

The giant silenced her with a deeper kiss. Her eyes flew open and she stared above into the whiteness. Although she couldn't see it she pictured the deadly sun above them with its killing heat. But it was nothing to the heat the giant generated between her legs, in her cunt, through her entire body with hands and mouth. Powerful fingers stroked her clit again and she trembled. The cold tongues licked at her flesh, massaged her turgid nipples in time to the delicious assault on her most intimate flesh. Then Silvija was inside. God! She was inside. The long fingers curled within her, stroking and pressing, lavishing her body with sensation and rich, undiluted pleasure.

Snow fell into her eyes, into her mouth. Her lashes fanned against the coldness as she stretched, body curving, toward the source of her desire. Her legs spread wider and she swore she heard the liquid sound of Silvija's fingers, three at least, plunging deeply into her pussy. There was no effort from her lover; this act of lust she did not strain, did not sweat, did not cry out.

Belle clutched at Silvija's sides as the orgasm swept through her. Her nails dug into the beloved flesh and she felt Silvija's skin give way, felt the blood rush over her fingers. It was then that Silvija hissed with pain and Belle truly felt the peak of her satisfaction. She bit her tongue against words that crowded up and threatened to spill into their small place. Quiet. They must remain quiet. Her body sagged against Silvija's and she sighed. The two beasts trembled together in their tomb. Stillness took them, and for a moment their bed of ice with the quiet whisper of the wind above and the slow movement of the vermin in the earth below were their welcome companions. They lay still, together, silent and listening.

Gunshots. Belle heard gunshots. Semiautomatic gunfire peppering the snow above them woke her from a dreamless sleep. Her body froze from the inside out.

"Calm." Silvija put a hand on her belly. "They are not shooting at us. Listen."

When Belle stilled her panic enough to pay attention, she heard a helicopter, its blades chopping at the air as it swept close, then away. The sound of bullets chased after the aircraft.

"Still, they must know that we are down here," Belle said.

"Not necessarily."

It was night. The snow had hardened slightly above and around them but not enough to immobilize their bodies. Belle's hand swam through the snow to grip Silvija's. "We need to leave here."

She felt rather than saw Silvija nod.

They slipped up through the snow, the wetness sliding off their faces as they emerged above ground. The wet sweater clung to Silvija's breasts and hips, showing clearly that she wore nothing beneath it. Belle stared, for a moment forgetting about the bullets, and about the chopper coming to either rescue or annihilate them. She and Silvija crouched beneath the moonlight, fresh from their afternoon snow sex with the scent of Belle's satisfaction and Silvija's unfulfilled arousal still floating in the air. The chopper's insistent noise snapped her out of her stupor.

Silvija's eyes searched the sky and she squinted toward the helicopter, making sure to keep low to the snow and out of sight of the shooters. Belle did the same, but she got no new information gazing at the skies. There was a chopper all right, but she could not tell if it was friend or foe.

"The chopper is for us," Silvija said. "It's Killian."

The moon was a full flush of light across the sky. A trailing curtain of stars winked dimly beside it.

"How can you be so sure?"

Silvija lost her patience. "Give me your necklace."

"What?"

Without bothering to answer, Silvija reached for the pendant around Belle's neck, but the smaller beast backed away.

"Just tell me what you want and I'll do it," she said.

Her lover stared at her for a long moment. "Use the mirrored side to signal the helicopter. Flash it up so he can see us."

Belle's hands trembled as she opened the locket, something she hadn't done in what felt like years. The mirror winked moonlight at her. Crouched low in the snow, she threw her light up at the aircraft, twisting the locket again and again to manipulate the light. The chopper was coming closer. And closer. She heard a shout of voices from above, but couldn't make out what they were saying.

"He's coming," Silvija said.

And he was. The helicopter dove neatly out of the cloud-strung skies. A long rope tumbled from it, wriggling madly in the wind generated by the propellers. They waited until the rope came closer.

"Go!"

Silvija pushed her toward the aircraft first before swiftly coming up behind her. Belle heard gunshots, then felt them swiping at the air as they ran in a zigzag pattern for the rope and rescue. Stinging heat slapped against her leg. A bullet grazed her. She leapt for the rope and grabbed it, clambering quickly up its chafing roughness toward the gaping entrance of the chopper. Belle felt Silvija grab the rope below her. The chopper started to move with them still clinging to their lifeline. Wind whirled fiercely against Belle's face, scraping through her hair as she pulled herself up the rope. Her belly dropped with each dip and soar of the chopper.

By thirty-year habit, Belle was panting when she finally collapsed in the rear seat of the chopper. As soon as Silvija scrambled in beside her, Julia shot from a seat in the cavernous helicopter and pressed herself to the taller beast's side, as if determined never to leave it again. Silvija grabbed her in a rough embrace and closed her eyes tightly.

Belle looked down at the cool white landscape falling down from them, the ribbon of an icy river through the trees and the sea lapping on the frosted shore. The gunshots were a distant sound beneath the blades of the aircraft. They seemed determined to shoot them down. But it was too late.

Killian turned out to be the Billy Idol look-alike from the party. He handled the helicopter well until Wildbrook was a miniature of houselights and faint human activity, then a pinprick image, a bad memory Belle would soon escape. The shell of their house still burned near the sea. Not even the people from the town had come to put out the blaze, although they must have known about the fire from the long plumes of smoke and floating ashes that trailed the sky.

"Thank you, my friend." Silvija rested her hand briefly on Killian's shoulder.

The nymph, his woman from the party, sat in the seat next to him. She watched them with hard brown eyes, but said nothing, merely adjusted the automatic rifle to a more comfortable position on her lap.

Silvija rummaged through a pile of clothes until she found a pair of jeans and a sweatshirt to replace her soaking wet sweater.

"Thank Ivy," Killian said. "It was because of her that I found you. She signaled me with a mirror first and told me to wait for you."

The other beast sat subdued beside them, staring into the space between her knees. Inside the huge military-style helicopter with space for at least ten people, their loss was suddenly unavoidably real. Killian had come expecting more survivors. Belle couldn't even look at Ivy. Stephen was gone.

And Shaye. Eliza. Susannah. Violet. All the beautiful beasts in the house. The litany of losses echoed dimly in her mind.

"I got your call when we were nearly halfway home," Killian said from the cockpit. "Sorry it took so long to reach you."

"There is nothing to be sorry for," Silvija said. "I'm just glad you came."

When had she had time to call for help? Everything happened so quickly. Then again, Belle assumed that the beast had fallen asleep after the last time they made love in the attic.

"Did you see their faces?" the nymph asked with the strain of a long night and day in her voice.

"No," Silvija answered. "They hid themselves from us and from the sun."

Killian turned briefly to look at them. "They are not human, then?"

"No."

Humans couldn't have done this. Only a cabal of beasts, one with a grudge against the family, could have done this. But who? Which one?

"Is it to the island, then?" Killian asked. He didn't bother shouting to be heard above the chopping blades of the aircraft.

Silvija nodded. "Yes. The island."

Killian dropped off the chopper at a small airport shrouded in darkness but still bustling with activity. Vampires and humans moved almost soundlessly through the evening, loading and unloading the various choppers and planes. The little carts slid along the tarmac, only adding to the busy, hivelike activity.

"Our ride is over there." Killian pointed to a quick-looking plane with a narrow nose and its steps already out waiting for them.

The women walked quickly to the aircraft. They buckled

in and minutes later were in the air flying toward their destination. The Point Faith Airport flew away beneath the wings
of the plane and the women sat in the simple cabin, lost in
their separate thoughts. Belle's eyes flashed over her companions, over Ivy's drawn face and Julia's contented figure curled
into the seat nearest Silvija. Her lover looked thoughtful. She
only spoke occasionally to her friend in the cockpit.

"There's someone," Killian said, "who knows you a little
too well."

Belle heard the words but didn't quite know what to make
of them. The expression on Silvija's face was grim as she listened to what else Killian had to say. Belle's body throbbed
with the beginnings of hunger, but she pushed it aside. She
glanced at Ivy again, but had to look away. She'd never lost
anyone the way the warrior had. She'd only lost herself. And
that had been a death she'd stupidly walked into, practically
giving her life away to Julia in that hotel room in Jamaica.
Her mouth tightened and she stared out the window for the
rest of the flight.

The plane touched down in a small, unfamiliar airport.
But the city itself was very familiar. Belle took a deliberate
lungful of the balmy Jamaican air. Many years had passed,
but the scent of her country—textured, sweet, with an edge
of blood—remained the same. It was deathly quiet at four
thirty in the morning when Killian dropped them off on the
nearly empty tarmac, and while Silvija and he talked briefly,
Ivy, Julia, and Belle went to a waiting taxi. A few minutes
later, Silvija came to sit with them in the car that smelled of
old perfume and expensive humans. At a few brisk words
from her, the taxi began to move.

"Will we ever stop running?" Julia asked.

Silvija nodded. "Yes. Just not right now. Someone wants
to finish the clan, and until we know who, it's not safe for us
to be on familiar ground."

"But isn't it obvious for us to be here on the island?" Ivy looked at Silvija. "Everyone knows how much you love this place."

"That can't be helped. We'll find a new place to plan and regroup. I want whoever it is to come and find us, but not walk in on us until we are ready. They will come and find us, I have no doubt about that. It's simply a matter of when and how."

Belle's skin prickled at the dangerous tone in Silvija's voice. With the death of so many of her clan, the beast was dangerously wounded and angry. If this enemy was familiar with Silvija, then they must know that as well. They would strike with deadlier accuracy the next time.

"So, in the meantime, where will we stay?" Julia's voice climbed into a high, whining register.

"That's not something that you have to worry about," Silvija said in cool comfort.

The taxi dropped them off in front of a hilltop neighborhood. The houses loomed large and stately with their high, barred windows, lavish balconies, and odor of foreign money. As the taxi pulled away, Julia looked at one house after another, her eyes blinking in confusion.

"We don't own a house here," she said.

Silvija's mouth twisted. "True enough. But it's not too late to get one."

She and Ivy leapt over the high gate and toward the houses, signaling the other two to wait for them. Julia blinked after the giant as if lost. She stared into the darkness, like a guard dog on the watch for the moment when Silvija might return to tell her what to do next. Belle looked at her in disgust.

She walked away to look down at the quiet houses carved in the hillside below. When they were younger, she and her sister used to ride into the hills of Negril, Kingston, and Montego Bay to look at the big houses. The sheer opulence and size of the homes in Jacks Hill, Red Hills, and Summit

Gardens always awed them. They watched with confused
envy as the Benzes and Jags rolled past them to disappear
into the high, polished gates.

The people who lived in these houses always had access to
visas and money. They often traveled abroad and brought
back presents of Nikes, perfume, American jeans, and other
unnecessaries for everyone in the neighborhood. Belle and
her family had never been the recipients of such largesse, but
her sister had, many times over, since she worked in town before as the "helper" who also took care of rambunctious
children and was thought of every now and again by her
traveling employers. Yes, the houses were very large and
smelled so very richly of money and privilege, but, Belle
thought with a wicked grin, their blood ran just as hotly as
their poor counterparts'. She looked forward to tasting it.

A few seconds later, the sound of a high, piercing whistle
interrupted her hungry thoughts. It was Ivy. Belle went back
to Julia and together they jumped the gate and walked to a
stately salmon and white house with a two-car garage and a
high hedge made up of white and red hibiscus plants. Silvija
and Ivy were already inside, exploring the house in darkness
and looking for anything that could be of use. Somewhere, a
dog barked.

"The sun will be up soon. We sleep in this bedroom."
Silvija pointed to the largest bedroom upstairs, obviously expecting them to hop into bed and wait for her, then walked
across the hall to the office. She sat down at the desk in the
neatly kept room and turned on the computer. Ivy floated
like a ghost behind her. Belle looked at her lover's ramrod-
straight back and tight mouth, then went to find herself
something to do.

Before she'd gone to live with the beasts, Belle had never
even dreamed of being in a house like this. The home where
her sister had worked as a maid before moving on to the
hotel was much smaller than this place. Here, they had a big-

screen TV, computers in nearly every room, and beds almost the size of the one they left in the burnt-out and smoking Alaskan compound.

The house smelled like its owners had recently left. Every surface was freshly cleaned, strong with the scent of Murphy's Oil Soap or furniture polish, while the dishes, linens, and clothes had all been put away as if they would be gone for a long time. These were things that Silvija had seen when she looked into the windows.

They'd accessed the house from a high balcony, climbing in and stepping on the cool tile floors. A breeze came into the house, balmy and salted, off the water. It ruffled the leaves of the giant blooming Royal Poinciana tree and nudged the delicate blossoms in the garden stretched across the entire front of the house. The flowers were sweet.

Dressed in clothes she'd found in one of the closets, Belle walked the length of the house, leaving Silvija and Ivy to their plotting and Julia to whatever it was that she was doing. The calendars in the house told her it was June 2007. Fully thirteen years since she had died. It didn't seem that long. In the Cave, time had felt suspended in amber—glimmering, ornamental, and meaningless—with every experience as close as the most recent touch. Now, back in Jamaica, it resumed its swift movement forward. Belle slipped through a doorway into the living room.

She traced each piece of furniture she passed with her finger, taking the time to savor this small bit of peace. It wasn't their house. It was obvious breaking and entering, illegal through and through. But Belle felt safe. The white curtains on the windows fluttered up, waving their pale limbs in the breeze. Moonlight twined with the ghostly whiteness of the drapes, creating the mirage of a snowy night and memories of safety in the Cave. Belle stopped and turned to look back the way she had come, as if she could see the tall beast and better recapture the feeling. It didn't work.

* * *

"We need food," Belle said.

Silvija, alone in the office, looked up from the computer. Her eyes were intent with concentration. "Then go. I have work to do here. Take the others with you. They need to feed too." She looked back at the screen, then looked up again before Belle could say anything. "My Belle, I need to do this. Our finances, the business. All these have to be safeguarded to make sure that we go on."

Belle stepped closer. "I understand." She drew in Silvija's scent, brushed her hand along the beast's neck, and kissed the strong throat.

Before she could move away, Silvija captured her and pulled her closer still. Their lips met in practiced liquid precision. Desire swam to the surface and Belle opened her mouth greedily. Her tongue glided against Silvija's and the beast's hand tightened on her nape. Breath came and went between them. Silvija pulled away first.

"Go," she said. "Or neither of us will get food tonight."

Belle smiled weakly and left to join the other beasts for the hunt. They would have to be quick. Sunrise was less than two hours away. Ivy and Julia were waiting for her when she left Silvija. They stood as one from the sofa where they had been talking quietly, and left the house. Food and the bright lights of the tourist town were barely a mile away.

It wasn't long before the paved streets of the neighborhood gave way to the hard concrete of the main part of town. The smells of people, of food, and fruit, and thievery and desperation rose up around them. The foot traffic on the street was light, with only a few humans meandering in the early morning darkness in groups, or couples, or alone.

By tacit agreement, the three beasts split up. Belle waited until the others were far away, until their scents blended with everything else in the air, before she went for what she wanted. Belle didn't want to feed on a lone human. She wanted someone who had a friend, maybe two. She wanted to fight. She didn't want to feel helpless anymore.

*   *   *

"Hey, princess."

She only half turned around at the greeting. From the corner of her eye, she saw a group of men walking slowly up behind her. In her tank top and long skirt, she knew that she looked soft. Pretty. Especially from behind.

"Can we get a little bit of your time?"

"Certainly."

She turned around so they could see her face. The years in Alaska had been good to her. Satisfaction in Silvija's arms had made her even lovelier, softened her features, made her lips full and inviting, plumped her breasts, and made a beguiling cup of her pelvis. She didn't consciously show this new loveliness to the men who approached her like pigs to the feeding trough but she was very aware of it. Belle smiled. There were five of them, and harmless. She almost felt bad for what she would do to them, but she needed something to push the sense of helplessness away. Besides, she was hungry.

As they came closer, one of them whistled. "You're a tall one."

"I like them tall and queenly," his friend said, moving respectfully toward her.

"The pussy still sweet," another said with a not-quite-nice smile.

"You're right about that," Belle said. "The taller the woman, the sweeter the pussy. Must be something about the altitude."

"What you know about pussy? Your mouth have personal experience with it?"

"Yes. My hands too."

The men paused. "You a dyke?" one asked.

Belle tilted her head, as if thinking about it. "I guess I am. Yes."

" 'Round here woman who lay with woman end up dead."

"Of pleasure, surely." She kept her tone purposefully light

and playful. They followed her as she walked backward, her flowered skirt fluttering in the light breeze as she guided them away from the main street.

One of them noticed what she was doing and smiled. "Maybe it's not pussy alone you have appetite for."

"Tonight, no." She caught her lower lip with a sharp canine. "Tonight, I have other pressing needs."

"You must want some dick in your life."

The other men laughed at the American saying and Belle watched them with amused eyes. They were such children, making jokes, not really sure what women wanted. What if she had been one of those naive ones walking on the streets with her breasts out and mother's milk still on her breath? Would the men simply take what they wanted and leave her bleeding in the alley?

"Not exactly."

It was after four in the morning and the crowds were dwindling on the streets. The few raucous voices raised in greeting, celebration of a well-needed vacation, or joy washed over Belle in the narrow street. The smells from the gutters— spoiled fruit, piss, and spent money—mingled with that of fresh fruits, good times, and a forever sense of time. It was an alley like this one that Julia had left her in to die or to kill. That time was barely a breath ago. Belle still very much remembered the woman she had been and the dyke she wanted to become.

If she *had* been that dyke, a human, these men would have had no compunction against killing her with rape and with fists before leaving her for the maggots to find. The wind brushed against her face.

"You're right, though. I do need something you can give me."

She beckoned to the first man. The one who had called her "princess" in that sweet way. Would she have been tempted by him as a human? His body was slim and leanly muscled, the nipples flat and hard against his chest beneath the dark green mesh T-shirt he wore. Up close he smelled like guavas, Red Stripe beer, and sweat.

"Baby, I'm going to make you feel so good."

He brought her close to him, pulling at her hips so she could feel the bulge of his dick.

She grasped his shoulders and brought him closer. "Isn't that what your kind always says?"

He bent to kiss her mouth and she moved her head to press her lips and teeth into his throat. From experience she knew there was pain. But there was pleasure too, in that first bite. Then she began to suck. His fingers sank deeply into her hips with surprise.

"What the fu—"

He began to struggle but she held him still. Her hand slid up to cover his mouth and quiet his cries. His blood was intoxicating. He'd eaten a good meal not long ago, and the beer only added a more robust flavor to him. Mango sweet, he was. Belle moaned softly.

"It must be good to her if she making noise already."

His friends watched her with their hungry eyes. Noticing only that his hips bucked against her and she was in her own heaven.

"Me want mine now." Another one stepped forward and around Belle. His hands fumbled with her skirt as his breath came fast from excitement. She wasn't ready for him yet. Belle kicked back and snarled into the dying man's throat, not releasing her hold on him. The man behind her went down with a bone-snapping crunch and cried out.

"A eat she a eat 'im!" he shouted, clutching his leg. "She feedin' on 'im!"

His friends suddenly perked up, their minds on something besides their dicks. One man's eyes went wide. His Adam's apple bobbed up and down in his throat before he just turned and ran.

"Duppy!" he choked out as he disappeared out of their hidden street.

Belle watched them as she sucked the sweetness from their friend, eyes opened to see what they would do.

A gunshot sounded the same instant she felt an acid sting in her belly. The bullet passed through her. Belle's meal bucked in her arms and sagged against her. The triggerman fired again and she spun his friend, using the body as a shield to take the second shot and then the third. She didn't give him a chance to fire a fourth. With a low growl, she threw the empty carcass and it dropped the three men like bowling pins. In the same motion, she struck out with a savage kick and smashed her foot into the fool who fired at her. His neck snapped and his head did a complete 180. Blood flew from his mouth, splashing the light post and garbage cans with red.

His two shell-shocked friends scrambled to their knees and tried to reach for the gun. Belle swept it up in one hand and squeezed the trigger twice. The first one clutched his throat and went down gurgling. The second folded to the ground without a sound, the bright red dot in his forehead the only indication why. Belle's eyes swept around the bloodied alley and her brow wrinkled at the thought of the one who had escaped. But she didn't have time for regrets. People were coming. Hasty footsteps made their way to the formerly quiet alley. The raised voices talked of police, and that wasn't something that she needed right now.

At the first gunshot, she knew people had started running. People in the area were too used to gunmen making a mess of the streets over something or another. It often didn't pay to linger on the scene with shots being fired. And Belle had counted on that. But now it was the police.

Belle lifted the crippled one who shot her into her arms and ran quickly down the opposite end of the alley. Except for his awkwardly turned head and broken legs, he didn't have a mark on him. His heart was still sluggishly beating. She carried him through the empty street, then when she saw signs of life, leaned him against the wall, keeping him lifted while she pressed in, loverlike, and nibbled on his throat. A few men walked past, chuckling at her enthusiasm for her lover in the darkened street. In the alley she'd just left, she heard the police and voices. Soon, they would come looking.

She finished him quickly, glutting herself on his blood until her veins and belly were thick with him. When no one else walked by, Belle slit his throat deeply with the knife she'd taken from the house and left him slumped against an empty jerk chicken stand, nearly bloodless.

Sunlight licked roughly at her heels by the time Belle made it back to the borrowed house. She had almost missed the signs—the steadily pinkening of the horizon, the rasp of unpleasant awareness like sandpaper on her skin—having gotten used to the freedom of twenty-hour-long winter nights in Alaska. Ivy and Julia lay in the bed, already naked and curled together ready for sleep, but Silvija was still awake and at the computer.

"I brought you something," Belle said to her, slipping up behind Silvija in the darkened study.

The giant slowly turned in her chair. When Belle had her lover's full attention she took off her clothes, baring her body to Silvija's slowly interested gaze. Her nipples were puckered and hard in the cool room.

"What's that?" her beast asked with a slightly raised eyebrow. But she was already standing up, and coming closer.

Silvija's lashes flickered as she watched Belle, licking her gaze up the smaller beast's body, over her swelling pussy lips, her breasts, and the fat nipples that looked even fuller with her body full to bursting with blood.

Belle tilted her head to one side and watched her lover. Still watching, she touched a finger to her nipple and winced as a fingernail emerged, pulling tautly at the skin and bringing blood with it as it slowly burst from beneath her skin. She cupped a breast and cut into the skin above her nipple with the lengthened fingernail. A semicircle of blood flooded to the skin's surface.

"For you."

The blood ran red and fresh over her dark skin. She felt Silvija flush cold at the sight of the hot blood.

"How come you always seem to know just what I need?" Silvija asked.

"I just know what I want."

Silvija bent closer and burrowed into Belle's throat before retreating to walk slowly around her, smelling her hair, the delicate line at the back of her neck. Silvija's hands brushed Belle's buttocks as she passed. "You've fed well."

"Very."

When Silvija faced her again she was completely naked. Belle caught her breath. Every time she saw the beast naked she was overcome. The stolen blood rushed beneath her skin, galloped in her veins.

"So." Silvija lightly stroked Belle's lower lip. "What do you have for me?"

Belle flicked out her tongue to lash Silvija's finger. "Anything you want."

She cut her breast again, squeezing the soft flesh until the blood rushed up, overflowing even more on her skin. Silvija licked her lips and stepped closer. She dropped her head and licked at the shallow cut, catlike and careful.

"You don't have to be gentle," Belle said.

Silvija's tongue rasped against her nipple and Belle gasped and pushed the flesh even more toward her lover's mouth. The cool breath in Silvija's mouth pulled the flesh tighter, made it harder until the nipple ached. The ache traveled down her body, shimmering under the muscles of her belly to settle into her pussy.

Silvija's mouth tugged at the nipple, tugged at the cut, and her gentleness was not so much anymore. Her hand cupped the neglected breast, stroking and pulling at its nipple until Belle was going mad.

They hadn't touched since that time in the snow. Then all she had of Silvija were her hands and mouth. Now Belle wanted it all. She pulled her lover up and backward until they tumbled back on the sofa, her body beneath the beast's. Silvija laughed, a rusty sound that squeezed Belle's chest. She skimmed her hands over the beast's back, into her hair and over her face.

"Let me take your pain away," Belle said.

"It's not that simple."

"I know. But let's pretend."

Their kiss bruised. Silvija opened her mouth instantly, hungry for her. The long tongue snaked out and she met it with her own, dancing delightfully in each other's mouths until they both groaned. That was all it took. Her legs widened and Silvija's naturally fell in between them, naturally slipped against her swollen clit and wet pussy until she was rising up to thrust against that thigh, her mouth open, her pussy wet. She kissed her lover fiercely, dragging at her hair, pulling her closer and closer until both their mouths bled from the pleasure. Silvija lapped up the nourishment, sighing at even that small bit of food.

Belle clung to her, wanting that contact as much as the other beast wanted it. More. But there was a reason she made herself so full. She pushed her lover away, no small task since the beast was intent on tasting every centimeter of her mouth, licking up any drop of blood in the process. As a last resort, she pinched Silvija's nipple, hard, and the beast flinched back, but not before savagely biting into Belle's lower lip.

"You can never just take the pain, can you?" Belle growled, licking the new blood from her mouth.

"Tell me the rules and I will."

"The rule for today," Belle said without hesitation, "is do what I say."

Silvija acquiesced, moving back as Belle indicated until she was kneeling on the floor. Belle moved to the edge of the sofa, spreading her legs for her lover. The other beast smiled.

"I like this position." She bent her head and inhaled the cool scent between Belle's thighs. "A lot."

Her smelling soon became tasting. Belle gasped at the rough contact. The single, cool lick had her bent back in the wide sofa, the heat cradled in her hips offered up to the loving worship of the beast. Silvija's mouth moved avidly on her pussy. Desire tumbled inside Belle, somersaulting over her belly and into the nipples pointing skyward and trembling. Silvija lapped hungrily at her pussy, sucking on the fat, blood-flushed clit, sliding her tongue deep inside Belle, fucking her until she gasped and blinked mindlessly at the ceiling. Her hips thrust against Silvija's face, fucking, taking all it could of the pleasure the beast so selflessly gave.

Silvija sucked her, fucked her deep and hard until the shudders flew into her thighs. Her hips vibrated against the couch, her fingers dug into the upholstery until she felt it give under her piercing claws.

"Yes . . ." Belle hissed, drowning in sensation.

Belle felt Silvija move away, she felt her mouth slip from her pussy, and she sighed. But fingers returned instead, gliding lightly over her still trembling flesh. She shoved them away. "I'm finished—" The fingers thrust deeply into her and she groaned. The fire abruptly started again from the not quite old sparks and she moved on her lover's fingers, sighing. Cool breath brushed against her thigh and then a soft tongue licked her.

The velvet upholstery caressed Belle's bottom as she moved to the rhythm set by her lover's fingers. The hot, slow slide became something more when the thumb brushed her clit, then stroked it, working her until she didn't know what brought the most pleasure. The fingers, the thumb, the velvet rubbing against her ass, or knowing that any moment now Silvija was going to give her what they both wanted so badly.

With a hoarse groan, Silvija sank her teeth deeply into

Belle's thigh. The femoral artery burst like a ripe tomato, offering up its juices to the beast's mouth. She didn't waste a
single drop. She gobbled it up like a good girl while still feeding Belle her bliss, stroking her deeply with curled fingers.
Delight shuddered through Belle's body, tingling through her
arms and toes and fingers until her entire body was sensation
and dark meaning and nourishment and love. All of it for
Silvija. She called out hoarsely, jerking in the sofa, ripping the
arm of the thing to shreds. The spring dug into her hands,
and still she held on to it as if it was the only thing anchoring
her to this reality. Belle panted as Silvija's teeth released their
hungry grip on her skin. The fingers slipped free of Belle's
seeping pussy. Her tongue gently licked the puncture wounds
and already Belle could feel herself healing. She sagged in the
sofa.

"Thank you," Silvija murmured, kissing her thigh.

The beast tugged her to the floor with her and they curled
up on the surprisingly soft rug. Their bodies fit neatly together as Belle rubbed against Silvija, taking advantage of the
residual electricity shimmering between them. Her breasts
scraped against the beast's and her thigh moved, languid and
heavy, up and over Silvija's hip.

"Anytime," Belle murmured.

Chapter 29

"We won't be here long," Silvija reassured her the next night before she disappeared into the study to work.

But what will we do while we are? Belle kept the question behind her teeth and went to find Julia and Ivy. They were both restless, playing a barely attended to game of chess on the living room floor.

She dropped moodily into a chair and plucked at the knee of the too-short jeans she'd found in the closet. Julia tossed a box of matches back and forth in her hands. It made a musical sound that seemed to please her, so she did it again and again. Belle glared at her. The little beast ignored her look and only tossed the box a little higher, entranced at the heft and noise of the matches. Belle sucked her teeth and looked away.

There was a plan taking shape somewhere in the house, but Belle wasn't privy to it. She was irritated about being kept in the dark but was content to wait until information came.

Even though Ivy knew as much about what was going on as Silvija did, she wasn't so complacent. "This waiting is driving me crazy." She jumped up from the chess game to twitch aside the curtains and peer outside.

Belle looked at her and shrugged. She hadn't lost a brother

in this, only her home and a few beasts she had considered her family. Silvija was all she had. She knew that at some point the beasts who had run them out of Alaska would come hunting for them, but as long as she had Silvija, none of that really mattered. She could fight and take care of herself, and Silvija, if need be.

Earlier that night, they had all gone on a raiding party, returning with motorcycles, weapons, and food. New blood from the drained bodies that lay stuffed in a deep freeze at the back of the house pulsed through their veins. But even with weapons, strength, and transportation, they were still waiting.

"You should go, then, if the waiting is not for you," Belle said, just for something to say.

Ivy looked at her. Before Belle or Julia could say another word she took up her bag from the corner and left.

"Why did you say that to her?" Julia looked annoyed. "She's only going to go off and get herself killed."

"But at least she's doing something about these killers. That has to feel better than waiting around here like lapdogs."

Julia was silent for a moment. "Then we should go too."

Belle rolled her eyes, but stood up. Impotence was not her style anyway and waiting had done nothing to make her feel any less so. "Okay."

The night was still. Not even the dogs in the neighborhood that usually traveled in packs, nightly terrorizing anything in their path, were out now. All was sleep and silence. The two vampires walked together, if not companionably, then side by side in silence into town. The tourist area had already recovered from the shootings a few days ago, quickly bouncing back from that incident of violence that was like so many others before it. When droves of people, especially those attracted by the money brought onto the island by tourists, congregated in one place, there was bound to be death. Unfortunately, it was something most people in Montego Bay knew and had come to live with. And with so many unsolved crimes in the area, the police often moved quickly on to the next criminal incident or easy money.

Back to normal, all was paradise again. At barely nine o'clock, unlike last time, there were more women in the crowded streets, holding hands with their lovers, in packs and laughing, or by themselves out for a good time.

"Oh, that's a nice one." Julia pointed to a girl with a graceful back who was wearing jeans.

"Didn't we come out here to find food?" Belle asked. "Besides, aren't we supposed to leave conspicuous ones alone?"

"Don't get on that high horse, Belle," Julia said, still looking at the girl. "One human is the same as any other. As long as we do it right and they don't trace it back to us."

But the girl with the coltish gait reminded Belle of someone, and she didn't want that hint of memory, that tenuous link to a long-gone humanity, to die. "Maybe. But I still say no."

"You're not Silvija. You can't tell me what to do. You only fuck her and that's only when she lets you." Julia started off toward the child.

The familiar scent of lavender perfume, slightly diluted by age and earth and the sea, reached Belle before they reached the girl. Her footsteps slowed, then stopped altogether. Julia easily left her behind. *It can't be her. Not here.*

The girl stood at a fruit vendor's stand buying a fresh green coconut. The man with his Rastafarian hat and strong teeth flirted with the girl, reluctantly giving her change as she juggled her green coconut with its clear straw. The vendor's eyes flickered in instinctive alarm as Julia came up behind Kylie. He didn't know what he was afraid of, but Belle did. Still, she couldn't move.

This was her child. Kylie had grown up well. After all these years her body had fulfilled the promise in her mother's height, her skin had darkened from its watered-down caramel to a robust milk chocolate, and she was beautiful. Big eyes, blade cheekbones, full mouth with a teasing hint of red. At eighteen she dressed in the typical teenage girl's uniform— jeans, high-end tennis shoes, and a slim-fitting blouse that showed off her breasts and collarbone.

"Hi there," Julia said to Kylie. "Do you need help with that?"

Belle finally stepped forward. It took her an eternity to reach the other side of the street and to Julia's side. By the time her shoulder brushed Julia's, the fiend had lowered her head next to Kylie's and was speaking in that deliberately seductive voice that had lured Belle to her own undoing over a decade ago.

"I'm okay," Kylie said with a polite smile as she fumbled with her change purse. She didn't see Belle.

The girl probably thought of Julia as a determined dyke with nothing more on her mind than a midnight romp in the nearby bushes. But Julia touched Kylie's hand and lowered her voice even more. "I'm new to the island and am having some trouble understanding some of the people around here. Can you help me?"

Her daughter was as naive as Belle had been. "Sure," Kylie said, stepping away from the vendor with the green coconut, aromatic with its sweet water, in her hands. "Just let me tell my auntie that I'm going."

Julia's soft spoken beauty had disarmed the vendor and he walked her and Kylie with an envious smile. Two beautiful girls to approach his stall on such a lovely night. Nice. His thoughts weren't hard to read.

"This won't take long," Julia said, gently guiding Kylie away from the main stream of traffic.

Thoughts of *Will Kylie recognize me?* warred with *It doesn't matter as long as Julia doesn't get her filthy hands on her.* Before Belle could think of the consequences, she was at Julia's side again and lightly touching the beast.

Belle dropped her learned American accent. "Me know 'ow fi get roun' dis ya place."

"But I don't want *your* help," Julia said. "I asked this lovely young lady and she already said she would escort me."

Kylie's gaze flashed to Belle, bounced off, then returned. Her mouth opened once, then closed. Belle's hand grasped Julia, digging into the flesh.

"Leave the child to her business," she grated. "We have other things to deal with tonight."

But Julia was leading them quickly away from the crowds and toward a secluded park. Whatever Kylie had glimpsed in Belle's face disoriented her. She wasn't paying proper attention to what was going on and to where they were going. As soon as they stepped away from the busy street Belle pried Julia's fingers away from her daughter. "This is enough."

"She looks so much like you," Julia said in wonder. She allowed her hands to be pulled away from her human treat, but she stayed close. "Would she be as tasty as you were? I wonder."

"You're not getting the chance to find out," Belle said. "Let her go."

Julia's words shook Kylie out of her trance. "Mommy?" Her voice rose, unsure and childlike, into the glowing darkness around them.

Belle growled, "Get out of here, Kylie."

"Oh, this is too sweet. So, she really is yours?" Before Kylie could step away, Julia grabbed her and pulled her closer. "This would be too delicious." The coconut fell from Kylie's trembling hand. Its water splashed over her sneakered feet and rolled away into darkness.

Belle growled again and slapped Julia once—hard—across the mouth. The shock of the blow loosened Julia's hold on Kylie and the teenager staggered back, still staring at Belle.

"That was the last time, Julia. I don't like repeating myself."

And Julia made the second mistake of her long existence. She hissed, baring her long curving teeth, and slapped Belle back. Belle's next hit came with claws. The frustration of waiting in their gilded prison for someone to tell her what was happening came abruptly to the fore. It barely mattered that her daughter was standing there with her mouth dropped open, her skin smelling like the lavender perfume that Belle had left on her dresser all those years ago.

Julia's cheek opened up in four jagged claw marks. Blood flew from the cuts, lighting up the ground and nearby leaves with its faint phosphorescence. The little beast gasped and came for Belle, but she backhanded Julia and sent the smaller body sailing through the air, slamming heavily into a tree trunk. Julia grunted. Before she could stand up, Belle kicked her in the stomach, once, twice, then again and again as the motion became a rhythm she didn't want to control. The beast whimpered on the ground, curling up to protect her belly and face from the blows.

Kylie's cries sounded out behind her, but they were nothing. How dare Julia challenge her? If anything she owed Belle respect. She owed her life.

"Do you understand? You owe me, you little bitch." Belle grasped her by the front of her shirt and lifted her high against the tree. "You *owe* me." She slammed her against the tree until the beast's body echoed hollowly, sounding heavy and wet with each slam, until ribs snapped, organs ruptured, her nose bled, and Julia couldn't even reach out her spindly arms any more to try and push Belle away.

"Stop it!" Kylie screamed. "You're killing her."

Belle ignored her daughter, slamming Julia's body against the tree again. She resisted the urge to drink the beast dry, leaving her desiccated body to fall apart under the morning sun. But only barely. Blood poured from Julia's bruised and battered body, flooding over Belle's arms and clothes. She was sticky with it and the scent rose up, rich and ripe in the air, making her shudder with pleasure.

"What are you!"

Kylie's ragged shout shook Belle from her fever. She let

Julia go and turned to her daughter, not bothering to look as the body slid down the tree trunk to pool at her feet.

"I am nobody you know," Belle said.

Her bloody hands hung down her sides. She looked at her daughter, at the trembling mouth and confused eyes; eyes that saw her as a beast, something much worse than the pathetic and bleeding Julia. The sound of frantic scurrying coming from the nearby area—people scuttling away and minding their own business—distracted Belle. Then she looked back on her daughter. The image of the girl, lovely, sweet, and forever lost to her, fixed on her brain. She nodded once at the child. Then walked away.

Powdery sand sifted through her bare toes as Belle walked on the beach. A fishing boat bobbed lightly in the surf, half stuck in the sand, but more solidly tied to a tree with its branches tipped in respect toward the sea. Water lapped gently on land, peaceful and powerful, so unlike how she felt now. Belle walked into the water, heedless of her clothes, to wash the blood and dirt from her hands. The stinging salt water took most of the blood smell, stripping it from Belle's skin in thin snaking ribbons that disappeared into deeper water. Years ago, Silvija had passed on the lesson of wearing dark colors. Before, she'd thought of it as an affectation, something Silvija did because she knew how irresistible she looked in black. But now Belle knew it was for the blood. Blood never showed up in black.

The moon was a miraculous sparkle on the water and everywhere that her eyes touched, but her awareness of it was distance, like the faint echo of a pleasant but long-gone conversation. She stepped out of the water, walking slowly with the heaviness of waterlogged jeans, bloodstained shirt, and her heavier thoughts weighing her down.

Her daughter was here in Mo Bay. And she had seen what her mother had become. The wind brushed against Belle's face, easing its cool fingers across her cheeks, lips, and over the thin blouse plastered to her unbound breasts. As a human she would have shivered; now she just waited for the cotton to dry.

Enough self-pity. It was time to gather her things and head back. With her shoes in hand, Belle went to the park where she left Julia. The only sign that Julia had been there were splashes of red against the tree trunk and a bloody trail leading out of the park. Belle put on her shoes and followed the trail back to the house. The closer she got to the house, the fainter the blood trail became, until it disappeared altogether. Belle could see where Julia had healed as she walked toward their temporary shelter, the organs settling back inside her body, the bones knitting back, the flesh sealing itself, claw marks disappearing from her face, the purple bruises giving way to clear brown skin, teeth anchoring firmly once again in Julia's jaw. She was as good as new.

But the house wasn't. Belle stared at the trampled garden and mangled decorative bars that had once protected the door. The front door had been ripped off its hinges and pitched halfway into the house as if someone had broken it down and walked over it to get inside. Bloody handprints smeared the doorway and the wood grain surface of the door.

"Julia."

Her voice echoed hollowly in the house. With quiet footsteps she walked through every room. They were all empty. Familiar scents lingered in the house—Julia's, Ivy's, and Silvija's—but there was another. Something vaguely familiar, yet not. Other vampires. And humans. The blood started to pound in Belle's veins. Ivy and Silvija were gone. Sunrise was far away, but that didn't make her feel any better.

Goose bumps of fear rose up in a wave on her skin. What could have done this? Was this Julia's way of getting back at her for the beating? But Belle knew that wasn't the case. It was the foreign smells, smells that screamed "danger!" as much as Silvija's voice had over a week ago in Alaska.

"If something comes for us here, we need to be ready," Silvija had said earlier that night to her, Ivy, and Julia.

The black Kawasaki Ninja wasn't Belle's favorite. The bike was too loud. It hurt her ears. There was no subtlety with the machine. Anyone would be able to hear her coming. But at this point, Belle thought, subtlety wasn't called for anymore.

Belle quickly changed into a dry pair of jeans and T-shirt, grabbed her guns, and jumped on the bike. The motorcycle screamed to life between her legs and she revved the engine. If whoever took her family wanted to be found, there was only one place they could be. Belle threw the bike into gear and took off.

Chapter 30

Belle rode the barely accessible but faster back way over dirt roads and through a shadowy cane field to the cottage. She parked the bike at the base of the steep, moss-covered cliffs with the sea a rumbling presence below them and clambered up to the cottage with a rifle slung across her back and two .45s strapped in holsters at her sides. The cottage looked much the same as it did thirteen years before. Whoever Silvija had taking care of it was doing a good job. The grounds were well tended, the structure of the house unmolested by weeds and decay. Long before Belle was able to see into the house she could hear voices inside. Her sneakered feet were silent as they moved over the grass and twigs. The only thing she could not disguise was her scent.

Only one car sat silent and dark near the entrance to the cottage. A big Lincoln that looked more suited for city cruising than kidnapping vampires in the bush. Moonlight gilded everything in silver, showed the liquid dew shimmering on the leaves, a family of cockroaches scuttling across the dirt, and the signs of betrayal that had been too blatant to see.

Different scents swirled in the air, lavender, a familiar basil and rosemary blend, distressed clove, and lime. Belle swallowed. This was not what she expected. Not at all. With quiet steps, she moved to the back window, being careful to keep her scent downwind from the occupants of the house.

Still, the smell of fear permeated the very woodwork of the cottage, spilling out of the windows into the cool February evening.

Belle peered into the house. Nothing. No humans. No vampires. No Silvija. From the looks of it, the house was empty. But the smells didn't lie. They must be in the basement. She remembered the place where Silvija had chained her the first time the beast ever touched her in lust, that place where she had begun to hate the beast and love her at the same time. And now here she was again.

There was only one tiny window to the basement, barely big enough for an enterprising rat to crawl through. She'd have to do it the direct way. Although she had a pretty good idea, there was actually no telling exactly how many creatures were in the basement. It was better that she walk in there and find out.

Belle quietly dropped her rifle at the tiny porthole to the basement and walked back around to the front of the house. Tucking her pistols out of sight, she went up the front steps calling out.

"Julia." She knocked on the door briefly before walking inside. "Julia, sorry about what happened earlier. I don't know what I was thinking."

No one came to the door to meet her. No gun sprayed bullets as she walked into the cool room with its padded window seats, stained glass windows, and comforting darkness. Chains rattled below her. One set of human lungs drew in harsh irregular breaths. Scents sorted themselves out and settled into the fighting, conscious part of her brain. There were three scents that she did not recognize. Two humans, one vampire. There was another beast down there, one whose skin held the essence of pears, summer ripe and sickly sweet, that brought Belle instantly back to Wildbrook and the day that she and Shaye were attacked. The other familiar scent made her throat clutch in grief.

She cleared her throat. "Julia, are you in there?"

Belle heard the small vampire try to call out and get abruptly cut off. So, they were tied up. A few steps closer to the basement door and a familiar scent rose up from the darkness. The girl emerged, smiling and lovely in dark jeans and a pink shirt that brought out the splash of natural color in her lips. Her hands were clasped behind her back. Clasped around the deadly shape of an automatic rifle.

"Belle," Shaye said. "I didn't know you were here too."

She stared at Shaye's bloodied hands and coy smile.

"What have you done with Silvija?" The question tore its way past Belle's throat. "Where is she?"

"Why are you so concerned about her when your duty lies in protecting your child?" Shaye tilted her head, as if truly puzzled.

Belle's insides froze. "Kylie? You have my daughter?"

"And you thought you only had Julia to worry about." Shaye smiled.

For a moment, the smile seemed as innocent as it had always been. Helpful, with only a hint of mischief. She was nothing more than a slightly naughty teenager, but at heart, a good one. Then Belle blinked, and the illusion disappeared.

"But what am I talking about? You didn't care about her when you went off to fuck Julia in that tourist trap." Shaye took the gun from behind her back, hefting it in competent-looking hands.

Belle growled low in her throat. "Where is she?"

"Who? Your lover or your child?" Shaye grinned again at Belle's look. "Oh, she's downstairs. With the other prisoners."

If she shot Shaye, the others would hear the sound and come running. Belle's eyes roamed over the space behind the girl she once considered her friend. The doorway to the basement remained dark, but she sensed a motion just beyond her vision, a presence waiting to leap up if something unexpected happened.

"You want to see?" Shaye asked.

Three automatic rifles followed Belle's progress down the steep steps. She quickly scanned the room. Her face went hot, a bubbling heat that was both the remnants of her late evening snack and pure unadulterated rage. Kylie's face was bruised, her lip split and bleeding sluggishly over her chin and down her neck. The impact of one slap. Belle could almost see the imprint of the inhuman strength wielded against her child. Kylie sat bowed and chained on the floor, her arms shackled above her head, and her eyes closed and seeping silent tears. Belle clenched her teeth.

"What's this?" she hissed.

"A reunion, of course." Shaye smiled again.

Julia lay on the cold floor, her face a barely recognizable mess and her body limp and weak in its double coil of shackles. She was healing, but not fast enough. Or at least that's what Belle saw at first glance. Another quick scan told a different story. Most of it was just blood. Old blood from her earlier rendezvous with Belle. Her eyes peered out from between matted and bloody lashes. They were alert. And waiting.

Belle's eyes flinched from Silvija before coming back to rest on the bound beast. Barbed wire wrapped around her in sharp, vicious spikes from head to ankle like a cocoon, bleeding her in a thousand places. The wire had taken out one of her beautiful eyes. A piece of the curled barb lay flush against her eyeball, the sharp point disappearing into the cornea where it had ripped a jagged, weeping hole. Silvija's eye was trying, impossibly, to heal itself with the barb stuck inside it. She bled where she lay in the center of the room, eyes flashing defiance even though she looked like defeat itself.

Ivy was nowhere in sight. Belle knew better than to ask about her. She smelled the amazon. She was somewhere nearby, somewhere close.

"I thought we were family," Belle said.

"I thought so too." Shaye followed her down the long stairs. "Then you came along."

As Belle walked deeper into the room, the two human men
with guns trained on her backed up slowly, fingers resting
lightly on the triggers. Two vampires put their hands on her.
The unfamiliar one smelled like fresh milk, was thickly muscled and female. She didn't meet Belle's eyes. But the other, he
watched Belle with amusement. This one was from Wildbrook,
she was sure. This was the one who had toyed with her that
sunless day. The one she had cut open but not killed. The
beasts dug sharp fingers into her skin and dragged her toward another set of shackles dangling from the ceiling. With
quick economy, they fastened her in them, with the humans
still keeping guns aimed at her.

"Don't tell me you've had a grudge against me all this
time," Belle said, striving for bravado. But her voice cracked.

Kylie's eyes were open and watching her.

"Fine, I won't." Shaye's smile was sharp and cruel.

"Tell me why you're doing this. I thought everything was
fine between us." Belle gestured with her bound hands to
Silvija lying half blind and bleeding on the floor. "I thought
you loved her." Her voice rose on a disbelieving wail.

Shaye looked down at Silvija with soft eyes. "I do love her.
She is my everything."

The years came back at Belle in a rush, the nights she'd
spent confiding in Shaye, the evenings, the days she thought
she was sleeping with someone she could trust. It came at her
in a moment of crippling clarity. "The human on the glass.
The police who came searching." Belle's voice trembled.
"The attack in Wildbrook. You caused all that?"

Shaye smiled. "You're not as stupid as I thought."

Belle staggered at the nausea that rocked her. The chains
scraped at her wrists. "Why?"

"Do you remember how she loved me again after I took
the human body away? Answer that question and ask me
again why I did it."

"And this? Why are you doing *this*?" Belle's voice broke
again. Nothing should hurt like this after death.

"Because, you naive bitch, Silvija is not mine anymore."

"She was never yours." Belle's eyes flickered to Silvija. "If you love her, why are you doing this?"

"Ask me that foolish question again," Shaye growled and her small teeth flashed bone white against her skin. "She was mine. She paid more attention to me. She loved me. And then you came along."

"This is stupid." The scent of limes teased Belle's nostrils. "If this is all about Silvija, then why did you take Kylie?"

Shaye smiled. "Your precious child. You know that I almost had her? Years ago when I first learned who she was, I almost brought her down like a deer in the woods. She looked at Belle's face. But Silvija stopped me."

That photograph that Shaye had given her years ago. It wasn't out of love, it was to tease. It was to be her last glimpse of her child before Kylie was made into Shaye's evening meal. A growl rose from Belle's throat.

"And to think that you never knew." Shaye's eyes flashed to Silvija. "She must have loved you even then when you two were just playing those stupid sex games."

Kylie's mouth was bleeding sluggishly and Belle unconsciously licked her lips. The lime scent drew closer, its acid tint in the air a welcome change from Shaye's false innocent smell that was churning Belle's stomach.

"That's why you destroyed us? Because you couldn't share? That's bullshit." The chains rattled gently when Belle grasped the length of them above her wrists.

"It may be bullshit, but that's what has to happen. You took everything from me. Now I'm going to take everything away from you."

"I wish you wouldn't do that," Belle said.

She ripped her hands free of the shackles and shot Shaye before anyone else could move. The first bullet hit her in the right eye, the second in the left. Shaye's head flung back twice with the force of the bullets. She screamed in rage and pain, whirling with the rifle in her hand and squeezing the trigger.

Three bullets later, Belle rolled out of the way of answering shots. She heard Ivy tumble down the stairs, guns blazing the same moment Belle ran toward Kylie, wrenching loose the iron shackles and dragging her across the floor to a smaller room where her daughter would be safe from gunfire.

"Don't move," Belle hissed.

Ivy's bullets mowed ruthlessly through the two humans with Shaye. Their bodies bucked backward with the spray of gunfire and their blood gushed beautifully, flying against the walls like syrup.

Silvija was badly bloodied, but already healing. As Belle reached her, the giant hissed, "I want Shaye."

Turning over the mess of barbed wire and gnarled flesh, Belle could see that Silvija had already been working at freeing herself, but the severity of her wounds had slowed her down. Her hands were gouged, ripped, and torn, but she had managed to claw a hole in the wire.

Belle flinched at the stinging bullet from Shaye's gun, but kept silent, not wanting to give the blind beast a sound to more accurately focus her rage on. Belle stared desperately at the wire holding Silvija captive. There was no way to tell where the wire began and ended. She grabbed and ripped at it in frustration, gritting her teeth against the pain. *Hurry. Hurry.* Shaye would begin to heal soon if Ivy hadn't done her any more damage.

Belle risked a quick glance behind her and almost regretted it. The amazon took on two of the beasts at the same time, drumming into their flesh with an empty rifle, flashing her deadly legs through the air to bring them to their knees. The female vampire's head exploded from a close-range spray of bullets, splattering both her and the remaining assassin with blood and gore. Ivy already bled from several bullet holes, but they didn't slow her down.

What worried Belle was Shaye's near recovery. The girl was already healing, stumbling less and getting more accurate with her shots.

"Give me your knife."

Belle startled at Julia's sudden appearance by her side. The little beast looked remarkably healthy except for the smears of blood on her face, throat, and arms. "Give it to me," Julia growled.

Belle reached down to surrender the knife from its sheath on her leg. She handed it to Julia blade-first, and then the beast was gone in an instant without a thank-you.

"Hurry," Silvija said.

She squirmed, aggravating her wounds as Belle freed her. When the barbs were no more than discarded pieces of wire around her, the beast leapt up, stronger than she looked. Belle's hands stung. She lay them palm up across her thighs, tears of anger and pain stinging at her eyes.

Nearby, she could hear sniffling, smell the pungent aroma of fear rising up from Kylie in the hidden room. But Belle didn't go to her. The adrenaline bled slowly from her as she sat simmering in the aftermath of her fear. Julia whipped around the half-blind Shaye with Belle's knife, cutting at the girl's legs, thighs, and back through the denim. Shaye screamed in rage and irritation as blood leaked from her small wounds, then closed an instant later. Julia leapt up and slashed her cheeks, then her throat, then the thinner skin across her chest. Silvija roughly pulled the little beast away and flung her across the stone floor. Julia crashed against the wall with a dull thud.

"Stay," Silvija said softly.

Belle watched Shaye reel one last time from Julia's teasing cuts. Her eye was clearing, becoming useful again. Her small teenager's body was slight next to Silvija's furious height. Belle almost felt sorry for her. Almost.

"Why did you destroy our family, Shaye?" Silvija's voice trembled with anger, with sadness. "I've done everything for you. Everything."

Shaye stood before Silvija, her body weaving in the air as if tossed by a silent wind. "You didn't treat me like an adult.

Why couldn't I have been your lover? I've been waiting so long for you."

"And because of that you killed Stephen? Liam? Eliza?" Her voice rose in a roar. "Everyone in the house?"

"Yes," Shaye hissed. "Because of that, because you didn't give me what I really wanted, I took them away from you."

Silvija groaned, a jagged sound of pain and regret and sorrow. "Shaye." The child's name rumbled from deep in her throat. "You had everything." She shook her head. "Everything."

"You're wrong."

Silvija snapped her neck. The sound echoed hollowly in the room as Shaye collapsed beneath Silvija like a forgotten marionette, her eyes wide open. In a few seconds she would revive, and then what? Julia rushed from her corner and, quick as a cobra, buried the twelve-inch knife in Shaye's throat, pinning her to the floor. Silvija didn't try to stop her, not even when the little fiend pulled a matchbook from her torn pocket and touched the flame to Shaye's hair.

Fire caught and held, hissing over the coiled hair, swallowing Shaye's face, then flashed down her body, swallowing her as if she were a dried and hollow tree. A gasp choked from the smoldering body, then a ragged, gurgling scream. The charred and weeping hands grabbed at the knife but only succeeded at breaking off more flesh with the immovable weapon. Belle tried to close her senses to it, but couldn't. Shaye's taint, her screams, slid into her nose, her hair, and her clothes. She jumped back as Shaye's body jerked against the floor, bringing the wave of flames closer. The scream died away.

Silvija turned away from the fire, tears splashing down her face. Belle wanted to go to her, but stayed still. She wanted to go to her daughter, but couldn't move in that direction either. Ivy's vampire was still alive, but he was more a lump of meat than anything vaguely resembling a man. Ragged whimpers left what remained of his throat. Blood and flesh were smeared all over the angry and grieving Ivy.

"Mommy?"

The remnants of Belle's family looked up as Kylie emerged from the tiny closet. Her tear-streaked face and trembling mouth would have stoked pity in the coldest of human hearts, but because of what they were, each beast became instantly aware of its own hunger. Of the human blood simmering in Kylie's veins. Belle went to her child.

"I don't understand," the teenager whimpered softly against her chest. "I want my granny."

"I'll take you to her soon, sweetheart." How, exactly, she had no idea. Belle didn't even know what her child was doing by herself in Montego Bay.

Ivy slapped the remaining vampire down one last time, knelt on his chest, and neatly cut off his head with a knife. Kylie gagged and turned away. Belle awkwardly hugged the girl to her, steeling herself against her delicious blood and fear scent.

"We have to get her out of here." Silvija scrubbed her hands across her face and sighed.

When she spoke all action in the room began again in earnest. They were used to this, taking orders from Silvija, and cleaning up. Julia snapped out of her basilisk's stare at Shaye's burning body and moved smoothly to her feet. She went to the small closet and returned with a shovel and thick garbage bags. Together, she and Ivy put what was left of the bodies—Shaye, the two vampires, and the two humans—into them.

"Come on," Belle said.

She swept Kylie's light weight up in her arms. As she passed Silvija with her precious bundle, her eyes briefly met her lover's. She shook her head but said nothing. *Later*, her gaze promised. Mercifully, sunrise was still a couple of hours away. Belle settled her child into the passenger seat of Shaye's car; then after making sure there were no surprises lingering in the backseat or the trunk, she started the car and drove them away from the cottage.

The years hadn't dulled her susceptibility to temptation. The scent of her child's very human blood made Belle aware once again of her unsatisfied hunger, but she forced back the tingle in her teeth and made herself give comfort.

"I'm sorry about this," she said inadequately.

Shivering in the seat beside her, Kylie shook her head. "I don't understand."

"I know. I'm sorry."

All the apologies in the world wouldn't change anything. They wouldn't return Naomi to her family, they wouldn't erase tonight's terrors. But Belle wanted to give them anyway. She wanted to repeat her "I'm sorry" until someone forgave her.

Kylie shook her head again. "They told me you were dead. You *are* dead."

"Yes, that's true." There was nothing to pretty the facts. Naomi didn't exist anymore. Over years, the pain of her death had dulled. Silvija's love and Julia's distractions had replaced what she had with her human family. For years that had been enough. Now with her child close, the yearnings rose again.

Belle cleared her throat. "Years ago—" She paused. Was the truth the best course of action now? "Years ago when I visited Negril, I got sick." She met Kylie's wide and frightened eyes. The girl huddled against the door, watching her mother with terror, listening. "I was bitten, and everything changed."

The dark landscape glided past the windows as the car purred smoothly over less than smooth roads. It would have been nothing to kill Kylie here. No human would ever know what she did. And her family would understand. They had smelled the girl in the confines of that dungeon. They knew what temptation was like. Belle gripped the steering wheel.

"Why didn't you come home and tell Granny? She would have understood."

"I did try to come home, but I couldn't tell Mama anything. I couldn't even see her."

Belle licked her lips, remembering her desperate hunger all those years ago. "My illness wouldn't have been able to fit into the life that you have now. Understand?"

Kylie nodded. Her head bobbed desperately on top of her neck. Belle knew that the girl remembered vividly what had just happened in the cottage, and would never forget those terror-filled moments as long as she lived. She also had to know that those creatures—the creature her mother had become—had no place in her small-town life with its church days, community outings, lazy seaside trips, and innocence.

"I'm sorry," Belle said again.

The car rumbled forward as each woman trembled in her own silence. There was no way that Kylie really understood what all this meant. It all boiled down to the fact that she lost her mother and now a stranger who wore Naomi's face was telling her some awful, impossible things. That her life could have been different. That she could have grown up with a mother who loved her and who wanted nothing more than the best for her.

"Sometimes things happen," her child said, "that you can't control." She looked at Belle. "Because I went with that lady, I could have become like you today." Belle didn't bother to deny it. "I could have been dead. But you came. And then the other ones came too. That wasn't something that I could have said no to. When you were younger, I think it was hard for you to say no as well."

Belle's eyes burned with the sudden onset of tears. The world beyond the windshield grew blurry, but she blinked it to rights. "Thank you."

She couldn't take the child back to Montego Bay. It was too far to reach there and back before sunrise. But she could take her back to the house that Belle had known as Naomi.

She could deliver Kylie safely back into her grandmother's arms. When they reached the familiar hills and houses of Friendship, Kylie looked around with a question in her eyes.

"I can't take you back to Mo Bay, Kylie. Unfortunately, it's too far for me to drive right now. I can send you some money in a few days for fare back to your aunt Claudine if you'd like."

"No. No, it's okay. I'll just phone her and tell her that I'm safe here."

Belle nodded. Shadows of trees and old ghosts greeted her as she drove slowly down the winding lane. There were only a few people walking around at this time of night, but Belle left the big car's tinted windows up anyway. She pulled up to the gate.

"Be safe, Kylie," she said impulsively. "Don't go off with strangers, no matter how harmless they seem."

Her daughter nodded and offered a tremulous smile. Her eyes drank Belle in, lingering on her face. Then she leaned quickly across the seat to give the beast a quick hug. "I'm sorry too, Mommy."

Belle sat, frozen, in her seat as Kylie quickly got out of the car and walked behind the gate. She blinked and waited until Kylie's grandmother opened the door and closed it behind them before she drove away. By the time she walked back through the door of the cottage, her tears had long since dried.

The scent of Shaye's death still lingered in the air, but the other vampires were gone. To feed, no doubt. Belle tore off her clothes and got in the shower. The hot, needling spray sank much-needed heat into her body. She felt that she should leave the cottage and do something, but her body didn't have the energy. Belle leaned back against the cool tiles and let the hot spray spill over her face, throat, and breasts. The tears started again, but she did nothing to stop them.

Desire. Her life had changed so much because of it. She felt torn apart, set adrift, flayed by it. Belle clenched her teeth against a sob that rose up in her throat. Shaye had almost killed them all because of it. If she had lost Kylie too . . . A flicker of a sound interrupted her orgy of self-pity. Her eyelashes fluttered against the hot spray, but before her vision cleared, a cool body pressed against hers from behind. It smelled of fresh blood and cloves and sadness.

"Belle."

Water cascaded over their heads, washing through their eyelashes and their open mouths. Belle released the cry she had been holding. The sound expanded in the tiled bathroom and she leaned back against her lover, shuddering helplessly. Silvija's hand brushed over her throat and shoulders, before settling on her belly. She pulled Belle even closer. Tears, Belle's and Silvija's, spilled between them, running red through the otherwise clear water.

The water grew cold and for once Belle felt it. Silvija led her out of the shower and pressed a towel into Belle's hands before quickly drying her own body. She watched Belle the entire time, as if worried that she would turn to ashes and blow away at any moment.

"Come," Silvija said when she was finished.

Silvija took her to the bedroom that already had its shutters closed and curtains drawn against the approaching sun. The room smelled clean, of a recent airing and only a little of the dust from being closed up and empty for the better part of two decades.

Belle's eyes quickly scanned the room. "Where are the others?"

Her voice sounded small and wounded, but she couldn't help it. She didn't want to go through the effort of changing how she sounded, of protecting herself.

"It will only be the two of us today."

Silvija sat on the bed and pulled an unresisting Belle into the V of her thighs. And started to dry her body. Her touch was gentle, taking away the moisture in Belle's hair, face and body, lingering on the sensitive expanse of her back, pressing delicately into her skin until Belle was a little more relaxed, a little farther from the edge of tears. When her lover sank to her knees to dry the backs of her thigh and her feet, tears threatened to come back, but she blinked at the ceiling and they receded.

Silvija drew down the covers and urged Belle into bed. The sheets were cool against her slightly damp skin and, reflexively, she shivered. From the rest of the house, she heard the rustle of bedclothes and soft words between Julia and Ivy that she deliberately turned her ears from. How could they go back to fucking as if nothing had happened today? As if Shaye—the one person she'd considered her friend on this entire horrific journey into her own inner beast—hadn't betrayed them all and killed most of their family?

"It's not easy," Silvija said. "I know that, but we should take comfort where we can. Her betrayal doesn't mean the end of us, Belle."

The beast's skin slid against her back as she pulled the covers up and over them. Her scent lay close to her too, saturating her with comfort. Belle took that comfort, snuggling against the beast just as Kylie used to snuggle to her a lifetime ago.

"Thank you for keeping Kylie safe," Belle said.

"You have nothing to thank me for."

"Yes. Yes, I do." Belle breathed in Silvija's scent and expelled it in a cool breath. "When did you know that Kylie was in danger?"

"When you told me about the photograph. Although you didn't tell me who gave it to you, I knew that person didn't mean your child any good. We tease and kill for sport. Out of boredom. That could be the only reason one of us would get a photo like that."

Belle shook her head. And she had been so naive then. Even when she knew later that beings like her did very few things out of altruism, she had let herself forget that day when Shaye had given her the photograph and the child's eyes had shone with such genuine pleasure that she didn't even think twice about motive. She'd trusted that her friend was just that.

"It's finished," Silvija said.

She brushed her fingers over Belle's hip and up to her belly. The sound of lovemaking from down the hall slipped under the door, lapping over them with those particular noises and that particular scent of Julia and Ivy together, of passion and the burial of pain and starting over.

"We've survived worse and we'll survive this."

But what had been worse than this? Silvija's hand caressed her belly in a languid rhythm until Belle's eyes fluttered, then fell, reluctantly, closed. The beloved's skin against hers was a small heaven. She relaxed against it, savored their mingled scents in the small bedroom. Kylie was safe. Her lover was safe. And tomorrow, they would rebuild and go on. They had no choice.

Chapter 31

The previous night had exhausted them all. Even rambunctious Julia was subdued as she came downstairs from the bedroom she had shared with Ivy. She immediately went to a seated Silvija, draping her slight weight across the giant's back. Belle looked up from her position in Silvija's lap.

"Go find your own pillow," she said.

Julia didn't move. "You've always been a selfish one."

"I learned that particularly nasty trait from you." Belle rolled her eyes but didn't bother to press the issue. It wasn't worth it.

"We should pack and go," Silvija suggested gently.

Belle smiled. It was not like her beast to be gentle. They had all been traumatized, indeed. Silvija touched her hair.

"Yes," Belle said. "We should go."

She reluctantly eased out of her lover's lap and sat up in the sofa. There was nothing to pack, nothing to do but go. The thought brought a melancholy droop to her mouth. At the same time, she knew that they couldn't stay here; not with Shaye's desecration as vivid as the bloodstains on the basement floor.

"I'm going down to the cliffs for the bike I left there last night." One last excuse to say good-bye to this place. "Give me a few minutes."

With Julia's solemn eyes on her, she left them. Belle slipped quietly into the dark, around to the back of the house, and down the rocky cliffs to the beach. The bike was right where she left it, almost thrown against the rocks with its wheels turned haphazardly in the sand. Tiny rippling waves rushed up and over the tires, leaving behind their dark, salty stains.

There was no real reason to get the bike. Anyone walking on the beach was welcome to it. Only it was something to do. One last good-bye. Belle grabbed the handlebars. Then smelled something on the breeze that didn't belong. A lavender scent flowed to her on the brisk wind. Fear made her swallow and she straightened quickly, almost dropping the bike on her foot.

A lithe figure skated gracefully down the steep slope of the cliff, sending a cloud of rock dust in its wake. Her feet hit the sand with a soft, wet sound and she straightened. Kylie.

But it was wrong. Even as her child came closer, she could smell how wrong she was. Belle could see the blood smeared at the corners of her mouth, remnants of a meal rather than an injury. The bike fell away from her, hitting the jagged cliffs with the sound of breaking glass, the crash of steel against the rocks, the sound of Belle's world shattering.

"Mommy." Kylie's voice floated to Belle. "I couldn't stay away."